Radigan & North to the Rails

Louis L'Amour

BANTAM BOOKS

RADIGAN / NORTH TO THE RAILS
A Bantam Book / March 2008

Published by Bantam Dell
A Division of Random House, Inc.
New York, New York

These are works of fiction. Names, characters, places, and incidents either are the product of the author's imagination or are used fictitiously. Any resemblance to actual persons, living or dead, events, or locales is entirely coincidental.

Photograph of Louis L'Amour by John Hamilton—Globe Photos, Inc.

Cover image by Fred Pfeiffer
Cover design by Yook Louie

ISBN 978-0-553-59179-8

Printed in the United States of America
Published simultaneously in Canada

www.bantamdell.com

OPM 10 9 8 7 6 5 4 3 2 1

Radigan

Loma Coyote
San
Pedro
Mountain
Coyote Creek
Cerro Jarocito
Nacimiento Peak
Rio Peñas Negras
Blue
Bird
Mesa
Valle de San Antonio
San Antonio Creek
AREA OF
DETAIL
MAP
Rio Cebolla
VOLCANIC CRATER
NACIMIENTO MOUNTAINS
Guadalupe Canyon
Horseshoe
Springs
Cebolla
Valle
Grand
Redondo
Peak
Rio Puerco
Guadalupe River
Jemez River
Jemez
Springs
Pajarito Peak
Ojo del Oso
HONDO CANYON
Jemez
Red Mesa
San Ysidro
N E W

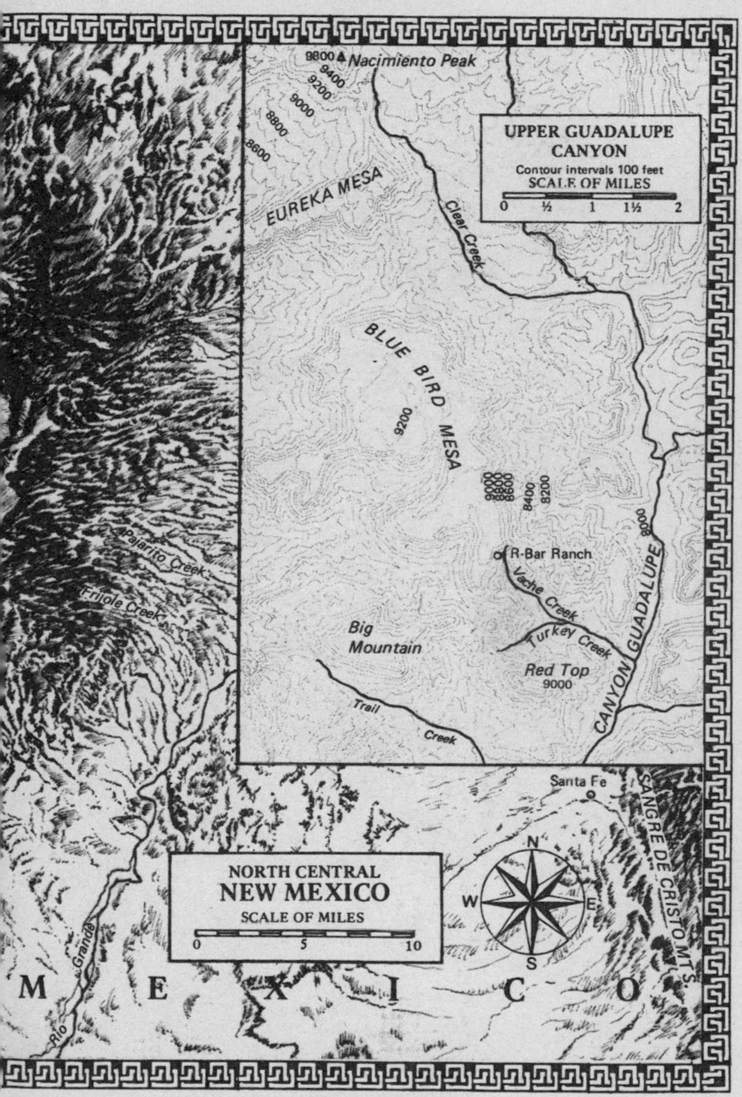

Map by William and Alan McKnight

CHAPTER 1

THE DRIVING RAIN drew a sullen, metallic curtain across the fading afternoon, and beneath his horse's hoofs the earth was soggy with this rain and that of the rains that had gone before. Hunching his big shoulders under the slicker, Tom Radigan was thinking of the warm cabin and the hot coffee that awaited him when he glimpsed the trail across the meadow.

A walking man will kick the grass down in the direction of travel, but a horse with the swinging movements of its hoofs will knock the grass down so it points in the direction from which it has come. What Tom Radigan saw was the trail of a ridden horse that had come down from the lonely hills to the southwest and headed into even lonelier hills beyond his ranch house.

Squinting from under his dripping hat brim in the direction the trail pointed he saw nothing—only a trail that crossed the knee-high grass of the meadow and disappeared into the hills beyond.

"Now what in thunderation," he said aloud, "would anybody want back in there on a day like this?"

Or on any other day, for that matter.

In a world in which most things have a reason, Radigan was disturbed. Northern New Mexico in the

1870s was not a place where men rode for pleasure, and especially not in a driving rain on the heels of several days of driving rain; nor was there anywhere to go in that direction other than the bluff back of the ranch.

Nor was it a riderless horse, for a wandering horse does not move in a straight line nor at the pace this horse had traveled.

Ordinarily, Radigan would not have seen the trail for this was not a route he usually chose, but for the past months he had been moving stock into a remote area known locally as the Valle de San Antonio, a well-watered valley nearly twenty miles from his home ranch.

Three days ago he had driven a dozen head of cattle to augment the herd already there, and had remained long enough to trap and kill two mountain lions who had begun poaching on his herd—and he had also killed a cinnamon bear. There were now three hundred and some head of cattle in the upper valley.

Returning, he found this trail, which could scarcely be more than an hour old.

Whoever had made the trail had chosen a route that could not have been accidental; no casual rider would have come that way, but only someone who did not wish to be seen. There were easier ways and more direct routes.

Tom Radigan's R-Bar outfit was remote, hidden back in the hills far from any accepted route of travel. He worked his range alone but for one hand, a half-breed Delaware who had once scouted for the Army and was known as John Child.

Nothing about that trail or the direction of travel made sense, and Tom Radigan was a man who was disturbed by the illogical.

Coming out of the draw where the meadow lay he looked across the fairly wide sweep of Canyon Guadalupe and over the gradually rising bench beyond it toward the ranch. During a momentary lull in the rain the ranch buildings and the trees around them were plainly visible, for the ranch was almost three miles away but a thousand feet higher than his present position.

Uneasily, he studied the ranch, and then bit by bit he surveyed the intervening country. The route of the strange rider led across the hills to the north and west, but mostly to the west.

Nothing in his life gave him reason for a sense of security, nor had he ever been a reckless man, nor one given to taking unnecessary chances. He had, even as a boy, often been accused by the more foolhardy of being afraid to take chances, and the very idea of taking a risk that was not demanded by circumstances was repugnant to him. Yet much of his life had been lived where caution was the price of survival, and being the man he was, he had survived. He did not take chances, but had helped to bury men who did.

So now he took none. He rode slowly, utilizing every bit of terrain that offered cover or concealment, and avoiding his usual route by swinging south of a rocky promontory by a way that ran parallel to the trail.

The problem of the strange rider was disturbing, yet approaching the ranch with care he saw no one. A thin trail of smoke lifted from the chimney, but there was no other movement, and there should have been. Riding in from behind the stables and corrals, Radigan drew up and surveyed the situation with care.

Behind the ranch house which faced him across the clearing, the mesa towered five hundred feet above the low buildings and their surrounding trees. At the base of the mesa Tom Radigan had found that most precious of ranching commodities—water. And he had found plenty of it.

A dozen springs flowed from cracks and caves in the lower wall of the mesa to gather in a pool at its base, and from the pool a small stream trickled off down the mountain to lose itself in Vache Creek some distance from the ranch. Before the water left his own immediate ranch yard Radigan turned it aside to irrigate a small home garden as well as several acres of alfalfa, the first planted anywhere around of which he knew. Leaving the garden and the alfalfa the remaining water trickled into a series of small pools where his stock came to water.

A wanderer and a prowler of the back country, Radigan had come upon an ancient Indian trail that led him to this place. There were no signs of life but wild animals, and a few arrowheads of a kind used by no Indians of the time. There had been no tracks, no evidence of any human visit, so here Tom Radigan built his cabin and corrals. Later, he drove in a small herd of cattle, forty head of cows and two good bulls. He brought with him four mules and three saddle ponies, a small remuda which he augmented by capturing wild horses in the breaks of the mountains to the north where all was utter wilderness for many miles.

It was knowledge of that wilderness which now made him cautious. A man on the dodge running to one of the three or four outlaw settlements reported to exist up there would not have chosen this route, either. Nothing about that rider made any kind of sense—unless he had an enemy of whom he was not aware.

Tom Radigan was a tall, quiet man who rarely smiled except around the eyes, and who talked little but listened well. His was a disconcertingly direct gaze in times of trouble, and men who faced him at such times found that gaze unnerving and upsetting to sudden action. At least such reports had come from three men . . . two others had been in no condition to volunteer any information.

Under the slicker he wore a blue Army shirt faded from many washings and wool pants tucked into Spanish boots. Belted low he wore a Colt six-shooter, and there was enough ammunition in his belt.

Out of Illinois by way of Texas, Tom Radigan was one with those others from Illinois who were to make their mark in the Western country such as Wild Bill Hickok and Long-Hair Jim Courtright. A man with a liking for solitude and a desire to build something stronger than a stack of chips, Radigan had looked for just such a place as he had found here, and he had been careful to choose an area where he was not likely to be disturbed by neighbors.

In the four years at the ranch under the mesa his herds had increased by breeding and purchase. He sold none of his original stock but managed a living and some buying money by trapping and washing gold. The trapping was good in the winters, and the deposits of gold were thin, but the gold was nearly all pure profit for a man with a rifle and a steady hand could live well on the upper range of the Nacimientos and Sangre de Cristo Mountains.

Tom Radigan was a considering man. He took his time to study things out, and he was never one to come to quick decisions or solutions. He took his time now.

Four years of comparative quiet had not lulled his sharpness of sense—his hunting alone would have kept that alive—nor had it made him less wary. There were many reasons why a strange rider might come up the Canyon Guadalupe, but none of which he could think for coming over the rugged mountains to the east of it . . . unless he wanted to approach without being seen. And if he wanted not to be seen he wanted not to be seen by Tom Radigan or his one ranch hand.

A welcoming man, Tom Radigan could think of no reason why anybody should avoid him unless it was an enemy or someone who planned to do him harm.

He sat his saddle for fifteen minutes in partial concealment, his every sense warning him of trouble.

The rain had begun again, but a slower rain now, blotting out the landscape and bringing a chill to the evening. The altitude was 8,700 feet and winter was closing in.

The rain could turn to snow at any time, and the forest to the north would be closed to any traveler. His route to the settlements below was only occasionally closed, and it was downhill all the way, yet most travel would be ended with the first good fall of snow.

He scowled, watching the house, the hills, the forest and the mesa rim.

If an enemy or some chance thief who needed supplies and a fresh horse wanted to kill him that thief would be watching the trail up which he had not come. The yard before the barn was visible only from the rim of the mesa and the talus slope behind the house. But his approach was safe until within a step or two of the barn door, and if he moved with care...

The gelding stamped impatiently and Tom Radigan swung down and opened his slicker, moving his Colt into an easier position. Then, remaining on the side of the gelding that kept the horse between himself and any marksman on the talus slope, he went around and into the stable.

His first thought was for the horse. Stripping off the saddle and bridle, he rubbed the animal down with a piece of sacking, his mind turning over all the possible facets of the situation. He was probably being a fool; the rider might have been someone lost and searching for shelter.

Yet there was no sound from the house, and John Child did not appear, as he usually did. It was the half-breed's custom to stroll out from the house, help him with the horse and exchange gossip about the activities of the day.

Through the partly opened door he studied the house. By this time it would be dark inside and John would have lighted a lamp... you'd never catch John Child moving around in a dark house of his own free will.

Yet John's horse was in his stall, and his saddle in its proper place. So why had not John come to greet him, and why wasn't the light lit?

He might have walked away afoot, but that was unlike John who never walked farther than from the house to the corral or stable. He might be inside the house and sick or injured . . . the only alternative was that John was trying to warn him of something.

A warning of what?

The situation at the ranch now seemed part of the sequence of affairs begun with the strange trail across the meadow. Never a trusting man, Tom Radigan had lived by taking care, and if someone were in the house waiting for him they would be apt to have the light going to make the situation as normal as possible. And the mud around the door had few tracks . . . he studied those tracks again.

Somebody had come out and gone back. The steps from the house were even and regular until the fourth step which was skidded sharply in the slippery mud, and the returning steps were longer. Whoever had come out of the door had started toward the barn, had wheeled and sprang back for the house.

It was very quiet. There was no sound but the falling rain.

Nothing in the house could have made John Child turn and rush back so suddenly so it had to be something outside.

So then: there was nothing in the barn to frighten John, nor was there cover for an enemy to the east and northeast. There was cover from the southwest, the way Radigan had come, but Radigan had seen no tracks there.

That left two possible places and one so remote as to be out of the question, but the second place tied in with that unknown rider.

Nobody could have shot at John from the rim of the mesa because nobody knew the way up there but John and himself, but a shot fired from the talus slope back of the house would have found a target at just about the point where John had wheeled and dashed back into the house.

All right, that was it, then. Somebody was or had been on that talus slope behind the house, and that somebody might still be there waiting for a shot at John or himself the instant one of them appeared in the open yard. Approaching from the southwest as he had, Radigan would not have been visible from the slope, not until he had been right by the barn door. Nor would he be visible again until his second or third step out of the barn.

Radigan could wait where he was until it was full dark, which might be no more than a half hour, or he could go now and risk a shot.

Whoever had fired that shot—if there had been a shot—undoubtedly wanted to kill him and not John Child, or he wanted both of them.

Yet this was purely supposition. Nothing at all might be wrong.

Nothing in his life had given him reason to take chances. From Illinois he had gone to Kansas where he served his apprenticeship as a military man with General Lane during the bloody fighting in that border state, and from there he had gone to Sante Fe as a freighter, surviving two savage Indian attacks. For two bloody years he had fought Comanches in Texas. It was the sort of conditioning to make a man careful.

He was reasonably sure there had been trouble, and even at this moment John might be lying inside the house badly hurt. It would do Radigan no good to get himself killed trying to help him, and the surest way to help John was to eliminate the danger.

Drawing back inside the barn he squatted on his heels and lighted a cigarette. If a man were to hide on that slope there were a dozen possible places, but none of them would conceal a horse.

So the sniper's horse would be hidden down in the trees on the lower hill, and somewhere east of the ranch. There was no cover directly east of the ranch yard, but around the corner of the hill there were scattered clumps of trees and brush, and then lower down, thick forest. The rifleman had hidden his horse somewhere down the slope and then had crawled up in the talus where he could cover the ranch yard.

Within the hour it would be completely dark.

After dark there would be no reason for anyone to wait up on that slope for there would be nothing to see. Therefore the hidden man would return to his horse and ride off somewhere to give up or await a better chance the following day.

Not even a mouse trusts himself to one hole only, and Radigan was no mouse. In the side of the barn that formed one wall of the corral there was another door made of sawed logs that was perfectly fitted and left for emergencies. He had never used that door since it had been built, but now he did.

Easing himself out that door, which was invisible from any place the watcher could be, he went down the slope behind the barn and into the trees. On a run, he began to circle the ranch area to get where a horse might be concealed. Pausing for breath in a clump of trees he told himself he was a fool—the half-breed had probably gone off somewhere.

But where? His horse was in the barn, it was raining, there was no reason of which he could think for Child to leave the house...and where had that strange rider disappeared to?

A watcher on that slope, if he wished to kill from ambush, must have his horse close in case something went wrong, which left four possible places of concealment. One was a wash where the runoff from the slope had cut a deep gash in the earth, another was a nest of boulders, the third a patch of brush, and the fourth a notch in the rocky face a hundred feet down from the bench on which the ranch stood. That notch could give easy access to the talus slope, and a horse waiting below it would provide a fast escape.

Rain fell steadily, and a slight wind stirred the leaves, whipping cold rain down his neck. He held his rifle muzzle down beneath his slicker, from which he had slipped an arm to hold the Winchester, as he worked his way to a new vantage point.

It was almost dark and at any moment the man might be returning to his horse. Every step Radigan took was now a danger, and he made no move without checking the terrain before it.

Far up the slope, a stone rattled.

Darting across a small open space he reached the nest of boulders, but there was no horse, no tracks. There was little time, and as the crack in the rock seemed the most likely place, he tried it next.

Rain whispered on the leaves, the world was gray and black now, shaded by rain and the coming of night.

He paused in the shadow of a boulder, his feet on the sand of a gradual slope. He worked his way through the trees, and the ground was soggy beneath his boots. Raindrops felt his cheeks with blind, questing fingers . . . the black trunks of the trees were like iron bars against the gray of gathering pools.

Alert, nostrils distended, every sense reaching into the night, testing the air for what it held, he waited, and there was no sound. Walking on, he rounded the corner of a rocky promontory and saw the horse.

Standing head down, partly sheltered by the overhang, it waited.

He had been right, then.

He stood close beside a sentinel pine, holding his body to merge with the blackness of the trunk. It was dark now.

Rain talked to the leaves. No bird moved—birds and rabbits were wise enough to take shelter when it rained. The horse stood disconsolate in the rain, and the rocks were black and wet.

It was cold . . . he relaxed his grip on the gun action and shifted his hold. The crack in the rock merged its blackness with the surrounding dark so he could scarcely distinguish the opening, but the horse shifted its feet and the saddle glistened wetly.

A boot scraped on stone, a pebble cascaded among the rocks.

Delicately, Radigan tilted the Winchester barrel up to meet his left hand. He held the gun at hip level, ready to lift it for a quick shot.

There was a moment of silence, then a boot crunched on sand. A dark figure moved the shadows in the mouth of the rock, and in the moment before the man reached the horse, Radigan said, "You looking for somebody?"

The man twisted and the flat stab of fire thrust toward him from the darkness and the rain, crossing the heavier sound of his Winchester, firing almost of its own volition, an instant late. He felt the shock of the bullet as it hit the tree beside him and spattered his face with tiny fragments of bark.

He fired a second time, realizing as he did so that the other man was fast, and a dead shot. Without warning more than his words the man had wheeled and fired . . . he saw the man's body crumpling to the sand and the horse shy back, snorting. Tom Radigan moved a bit more behind the tree and waited.

He was not about to run up to a man shot down, or seemingly shot down. He waited without movement, listening to the slow whisper of falling rain: there was no other sound.

The horse blew through his nostrils, not liking the smell of gun smoke. A wind stirred the corner of Radigan's slicker.

The shot was a dart of red flame and a smashing concussion. A finger tugged at the slicker and Radigan fired, levered the Winchester and fired again into the dark bulk of the body.

Silence again, and rain. It was dark, but his eyes were accustomed and he could make out the body against the gray sand.

He waited, feeling sure the man was dead . . . this time he was dead.

Who had he killed? What was the man doing here, far from any other ranch or town? How had he even known about this place? In the four years since Radigan came to the bench above the Vache there had been no more than a half-dozen visitors.

The man had come to kill, or else he would not have fired so suddenly at a strange voice speaking from the darkness. And he had been a man skilled in the use of arms, arriving by a route he must have known or to which he must have been well guided.

The minutes dragged, and Radigan waited. Many times the first man to move was the first to die, and he had learned patience. After a while there was a short, convulsive sigh and a boot toe scraping in the sand. The man was dead.

Radigan moved to another tree, his rifle held ready for another shot.

Near the white palm of an outflung hand Radigan saw the wet shine of a pistol barrel. He came from behind the tree and walked toward the body. The tied horse, not liking the mingled smell of powder smoke and blood, backed off, snorting softly.

"Easy, boy. Easy now."

The horse quieted, reassured by the calm voice. Radigan had a way with animals—they trusted him. Even the bad ones seemed to buck under him merely to uphold their reputations, but with no heart in it.

Radigan prodded the body with his toe, rifle held for a shot, and when there was no move he turned the body so the face lay white under the dripping sky.

Squatting near the body, Radigan felt for a pulse and found none. Spreading his slicker, he struck a match under its shelter, and looked at the dead face, mouth slightly open, eyes wide to the rain.

Young—not more than twenty-one or -two. A narrow face with a hard mouth and thin lips, a forehead too high. The holster was slung low and tied fast.

Lifting the body, Radigan draped him over his saddle, then retrieved the rifle and pistol and leading the horse he walked back to the barn.

As he entered the yard the door opened and John Child stepped out with a lantern.

Child took the dead man's head in his grip and turned the face to the light. "Know him?"

"No . . . do you?"

"No, I don't. Something familiar there, though."

Radigan noticed a small patch of bandage on Child's skull and indicated it with his eyes. "He hit you?"

"Burned me. I had your coat on." He looked at Radigan across the darkness. "What's the matter, Tom? What's wrong?"

"Damned if I know." He explained about the tracks that came over the hills far from any trail, indicating the man had come with purpose in mind, using a way that would avoid the chance of being seen. "Somebody hunting me, John. Or you."

Child considered that. "You," he said finally. "My enemies are dead." He looked at the body. "Bury him in the morning?"

"No. I'm a curious man, John. A wanting-to-know sort of man. I'm going to leave him tied across that saddle and turn the horse loose."

There was a moment of silence while the rain fell,

and then Child muttered, "Damn!" There was wonder and satisfaction in his tone. "I'd not have thought of that."

"Maybe, just maybe it'll work. The horse might be borrowed or rented, but it might be his own. In any case, that horse is likely to go home. Or maybe to where it was fed and stabled last."

"You'll do," Child said. "You'd have made a fine Indian, Tom."

He studied the body, noting the four bullet holes. "He was a tough man."

"And fast," Radigan said. "He was fast and he was good. He was awful good. Two shots in the dark, one hit the tree I stood against, the other nicked my raincoat. This was a man knew his business, John. He was a man hired for the job. I'm guessing."

"Who?"

That was the question, of course. From time to time a wandering man made enemies, but none that mattered and none who would come this far off their trail to hunt him down. It made no kind of sense, just none at all.

He swore suddenly. "John, we're a couple of children. Give me that lantern."

He held the light up to the brand. It was a Half-Circle T—no brand he had ever head of. Then he pulled the dead man's coat loose and searched the pockets, but there was only a little money, no wallet, no letters. Yet the man had come from somewhere and behind his coming there was a reason.

"Tom." Child waited a moment while the time ran and the rain fell. His voice was very serious. "Tom, you be careful. Whoever wants you took no chances on leaving evidence. He's clean. No identification. They took no chances of him being caught or killed."

"They didn't think about the horse."

"No, but the horse is strange around here. That's no brand we know."

"No, but this horse was fed somewhere, watered somewhere. This here is a grain-kept horse, and I'm gambling this man has been around a day or two, studying the lay of the land, and his horse might go back to where he was fed."

"In the morning?"

"Now. We'll let him start now, and in the morning I'll trail him down." Radigan indicated the sky. "Look—the rain is breaking. The tracks will still be there."

Leading the horse to the trail south he slapped him hard across the rump, and stood while the horse jumped away and then trotted off down the trail, the dark bulk of the dead man in the saddle. They watched him and listened until they could no longer hear the slowing *clop-clop* of the horse's hoofs. Without words they turned and went into the house and Tom Radigan suddenly realized he was tired, dead tired.

"Coffee's on. It'll be stronger than hell."

"What else?"

"Beans, beef... what d'you expect?"

Child put down the lantern and lighted a coal-oil lamp. Radigan hung his hat and slicker on wooden pegs driven into the wall and glanced toward the fire. He had been thinking about that fire for a long time.

The room was long with a huge fireplace on one side, and a beamed, low ceiling that cleared Tom

Radigan's head by no more than a few inches. It was a frontier room, but somehow more pleasant.

There had been a lot of years when he had thought of a place like this. It lacked a woman's touch, but it was strongly built and comfortable, built to last as Radigan had planned it during the long nights on night herd. It had a view down the valley, and was built for strength and a good defense, for there was always a chance of needing that in a strong new country where men did not readily settle into the ways of law. But there were windows with wide, deep sills, windows that would someday carry plants . . . geraniums, maybe. And there was an inside pump, good for defense, of course, but good also for a woman. It would save her steps and time. It was a rare thing in this country to have an inside pump.

"Got myself a couple of cats," Radigan commented.

"Lose any stock?"

"Over a time, maybe four or five head. These lions were latecomers, I figure. But no lion ever had any sense. Got them both in the same trap, just reset it. Caught them in the same place on successive nights. Never do that to a wolf."

John Child was a square-shouldered man, dark and strong-boned, a man who looked as if he were hewn from oak. The Indian in him was strong, but the white man in him had made him painstaking in his work. He dished up the food, steaming from the fire, and then poured coffee. "You set up to the table, Tom. You're about done in."

Radigan rolled up his sleeves revealing the white skin of powerful forearms, the brown of his hands resembling gloves by comparison. He bathed carefully, working up a good lather with the homemade soap. He washed his face, digging his soapy finger into his ears, then dampened a towel and went behind his ears and finally combed out his stiff brown-red hair. And all the while he was thinking, backtracking himself across the days to find some clue to the unknown dead man and the why of his coming to the ranch on the Vache.

He dropped into a chair almost too tired to eat. In the past few days he had ridden more than a hundred miles, rounding up cattle, moving them to new range, cleaning water holes, branding a few late calves, then trapping lions and killing a cinnamon bear.

"Forgot," he said, "there's bear meat on the saddle."

"It'll keep in this weather."

"Ever eat lion?"

"Sure, many a time. Best meat there is. First time I heard that from a white man was from Kit Carson, down to Lucien Maxwell's place, but the mountain men favored it above anything else."

Child filled his own cup and sat down. "Don't you gorge yourself. There's more."

"You make a pie?"

"No."

Radigan lifted his head and scented the air. "Bear sign?"

"Figured you'd smell 'em first off. When you didn't I knew you were tired. Ma used to make doughnuts when I was a youngster and when I'd come from school I'd catch that smell, even if it had been hours old."

"You get me some, John. You ain't much for work, but I'd keep you on just for making bear sign. I never saw your beat."

"Time was I've been kept making bear sign for three days without letup, make 'em by the dishpan full, and none left at the end. Men ride miles to get a handful of bear sign."

They were silent, busy with their food and thoughts. Only Radigan was eating, however. After a few minutes he asked, "You eat?"

"Sure. I'd started out to feed the stock when that feller nicked me. First off I was of a mind to go scalp huntin', but he had me nailed down so I ate . . . first thing I was taught was to sleep whenever there was time and to eat when there was food."

John Child went to the deep cupboard and brought back a plate of doughnuts. "Dig in boy. There's a plenty."

"John . . . who d'you reckon he was?"

"Gunman, that's for sure. Trigger tied back on his gun. And a mighty fine rifle. He's got to be a hired killer."

Tom Radigan took down his rifle and went to work cleaning it. As he worked he occasionally ate bear sign and drank coffee.

It had been too good to last. He owned seven hundred head of cattle, and a nice bunch of mustangs. He had spread his cattle around through the mountain meadows where there was good water and good grass, and from time to time he shifted his small herds to new areas where the grass was still long. The winters were vicious, and the snow drifted deep in most of the canyons. It was a brutal struggle to keep the herds alive but there were areas where the wind swept the grass free of snow, and there were protected valleys where little snow gathered. There had been natural increase, and several times he bought cattle from movers. As there were no other ranches close by and the remote valleys restricted the wandering, the task of handling the cattle was a small one.

Radigan's progress had been steady, and in another year he would make his first drive to market. His income from trapping was sufficient to pay Child his wages and to put by a little, and from the first he had taken time out occasionally to wash out a little gold from the streams. None of them carried much, but to a man whose wants were simple it was enough.

The ranch on the Vache had been no sudden thing. From the first he had made up his mind to look for just the place he wanted, and when he found it his plans were well made and he was ready for the hard work they demanded. Every step he must take had been carefully planned, and he believed he had covered all the possible risks and chances to be expected. From the beginning he had been aware that the days of free range could not last, and he had never planned on the vast operations of the bigger ranchers. He was content with a small outfit but one that paid well, and he had solved the problem of making it pay.

At daybreak he was out of bed and into his socks and shirt. Then he stirred the coals and laid on a few chunks of pitch pine to get a hot fire going, then he put on the water for coffee.

When he had bathed and dressed he took time out

to shave, the wiry stubble on his jaws yielding reluctantly to the razor. He was usually clean-shaven except for his mustache—his one vanity.

John Child came in. "Saddled that blaze-face sorrel for you. It's clearing up nicely."

"Thanks."

"Want I should ride along?"

"Stick around. There's enough to do and I don't want the place left alone now. You keep your guns close and don't get far from the place."

Child grinned at him. "I'm a Delaware . . . you forgettin' that?"

"It's the English in you worries me. The Delaware can take care of itself."

"I've put up a lunch . . . and some of them bear sign."

Radigan shouldered into a buckskin coat and went down to the corral. The sorrel was a good trail horse, half-Morgan and half-mustang, with lots of bottom and enough speed.

He stepped into the leather and Child put a hand on the saddle. "You watch yourself. That dead man's face is something I remember and I remember it with trouble."

No need to worry, Child told himself. Radigan was a good man in woods or mountains, and like an Apache on a trail. He had been a Texas Ranger for two years and built a solid reputation, but he was not a man to shoot unless pushed into it.

The trail was plain enough, for there had been a hard rain that wiped out tracks before the shooting and wind enough to dry the mud and set the tracks since the rain stopped. The horse had galloped a short distance, settled to a canter and then to a walk. Several times it had hesitated as if uncertain, then had set out down the trail. The trail led right to the bottom of Canyon Guadalupe and after that there was small chance to wander.

San Ysidro was nothing much as a town. Three stores, two saloons and a third saloon that was called a hotel because they occasionally rented rooms, and a scattering of houses, most of them adobe. It was just short of noon when Tom Radigan rode into town.

There were four horses at the hitching rack and a buckboard, but nobody on the street.

Three of the horses were branded with a Running M-on-a-Rail, a brand strange to him. He tied his horse at the hitching rack and went into the saloon. Two of the men at the bar were strangers, the third was Deputy Sheriff Jim Flynn and the fourth a man in buckskins who trapped over in the Nacimientos. His name was Hickman.

They nodded to each other and Flynn asked, "Travelin', Tom? Didn't figure to see you around here this late in the year."

"Man has to get out, time to time." He glanced briefly at the two strange riders. They looked to be tough, competent men. But why here? There was no Running M-on-a-Rail in this part of the country and no open range. There should be a third rider... where?

Deputy Sheriff Flynn was doing some thinking of his own. He had been marshal of two cow towns, sheriff and deputy sheriff elsewhere, and as far as he was concerned San Ysidro was the end of the line. He was married now and the father of two children, and he wanted no trouble here.

A handy man with a gun who knew his job thoroughly, he had always been worried by Tom Radigan.

He had known such men before. Hickok and Courtright, of course, but Radigan was more like Tilghman, Gillette or John Hughes. He was a dangerous man, but a man with quality, tempered in harsher fires than San Ysidro could offer.

A quiet man, Radigan minded his own business and rarely drank, but Flynn understood the potential. Knowing his business as he did he also knew there was no logical reason for Radigan's presence in town today. Radigan had bought supplies only two weeks ago and they usually lasted him all of two months, but this had been an order for the winter and unusually heavy. Nor did Radigan come to town for company or to get drunk. The deputy sheriff took another look at Radigan's face and decided this was a war party.

Toying with his glass, he estimated the situation. What had happened that was different than usual? What could have happened to bring Tom Radigan into town right now?

The answer was obvious. The strange cowhands and the stranger with the buckboard. All were armed, all looked to be tough, capable men; and more than that, they were better dressed, hence better paid. These were not simply cowpunchers but fighting punchers. And fighting men are not hired unless to fight.

"Stage is about due," Flynn commented.

"No rush this time of year," Downey the barman

said as he leaned his thick elbows on the mahogany. "Folks just naturally start avoiding this country just shy of first snowfall, and they're smart."

One of the strange riders looked around. "Does it get cold here?"

Flynn nodded, looking into his glass. "You're up high, man. You're right near a mile above sea level here, and anyplace out of town it's higher." He indicated Radigan with a jerk of his head. "Up at Tom's place it's a half-mile higher. And *cold*? Seen it forty below up there, many a time."

The door opened then and a big man came in. As tall as Radigan's six feet and two inches, he was thirty pounds heavier than Radigan's one hundred and eighty-five. His square, powerful head sat on a wide thick neck and powerful shoulders, yet for all his beef he moved easily, and he glanced sharply at Radigan, then again.

"I know you from somewhere," he said.

"Maybe."

"You live around here?"

The cowhands had straightened up at the bar and so had Flynn. "Could be."

The newcomer hesitated as if to say something further but a shrill yell from down the street and the rattle of hoofs and harness brought the stage up to the door.

Flynn, Radigan thought, was relieved, but he made no move toward the door until the three cowhands had gone out. The big man stood in frowning concentration, then called after the last man through the door. "Coker," he said, "shake the snow off those robes in the buckboard."

Radigan glanced out the window. It was snowing, not very seriously, but snowing nonetheless. He felt relieved. A good snow now might close the country for all winter. His first glance registered the snow, but the second caught the horse tied behind the stage.

Hickman stepped in the door. "Sheriff," he said, "we've a dead man out here."

Downey came from behind the bar. All of them went out but Tom Radigan. He refilled his glass.

Hickman glanced at him curiously. "Ain't you curious?"

"Me?" Radigan glanced at him. "I've seen a dead man."

He tossed off his drink and stared at his glass, wondering why he ever touched the stuff. He didn't really like it and he had discovered long ago that it took a lot to have any effect on him and when he got the effect he didn't like it.

The door pushed open and men came in carrying a body which they stretched on the pool table. The big man followed them in, his features a study in puzzled anger. A man obviously the stage driver entered with Downey and Flynn.

"About ten mile out," the driver was saying, "we come around a bend and there was this horse, walkin' toward us. We figured it was somethin' for you."

The deputy sheriff stared sourly at the dead man. Why didn't they let the horse keep going? Clean out of the county? "Anybody know him?" he asked.

Nobody spoke up. In the silence Hickman glanced quizzically at Radigan. Flynn noted the glance.

"He's some shot up," Downey commented, "and I'd say early last night." At Flynn's questioning glance

Downey flushed. "Worked with doctors durin' the war," he said. "I know something about wounds."

"He could have come quite a ways," Flynn commented, "since early last night."

Tom Radigan was sure he knew what Flynn was thinking, that the unknown dead man could have come from the ranch under the mesa. There were not too many places he could have come from except maybe Jemez or Jemez Springs. Deputy Sheriff Flynn, Radigan decided, was no fool.

"All the wounds are in front," Radigan commented.

"That's where you'd expect 'em to be," Hickman said. "That's Vin Cable."

Flynn turned sharply around. "Damn it, Hickman!" he demanded irritably. "What would Vin Cable be doing up here? He's a warrior, a dollar-on-the-barrelhead fighting man."

Hickman shrugged. "How should I know what he was doin' here? Maybe somebody is startin' a war?"

"Cable must've killed five or six men," Downey said.

"That folks can testify to," Hickman added. "No tellin' how many he dry gulched."

The big man turned sharply on Hickman. "You talk a lot," he said.

"You don't like it?" Hickman's voice was mild. He was idly whittling with a bowie knife.

"Stop it," Flynn said, glaring at him. The deputy looked as sore as a hound dog with a bad tooth. He smelled trouble, Radigan surmised and, good officer that he was, wanted to avoid it.

Coker came to the door and called to the big man, "Ross, Miss Foley is ready to go."

Radigan followed them to the street, and Flynn trailed after.

A tall young man was helping a girl in a gray traveling dress from the stage. She had dark-brown hair and, as Radigan saw when she glanced up at him, green eyes. He escorted the girl to the buckboard and paused there as Ross joined them. Whatever he said caused the young man to turn on him, startled and angry. The girl waited, listening.

Flynn seemed to make up his mind. "You folks planning to settle around here?"

Ross turned squarely around to face him. "We do. We've rented the Hansen place until our cattle come in, and then we're moving up on Vache Creek."

Flynn started to speak but Radigan interrupted. "I wouldn't count on it," he said.

All eyes were on Radigan.

"And why not?" Ross demanded.

"Because he missed," Radigan said quietly.

CHAPTER 2

THE WIND SKITTERED a dry leaf along the boardwalk and one of the stage mules, shifting his weight, jangled the harness. Radigan's three words hung in the still, cold air, a challenge issued and a line drawn.

The man who was helping the girl into the buckboard turned his face toward them. "What's that mean?" he demanded.

His was a lean, handsome face with a hint of repressed savagery behind it that Tom Radigan had seen in faces before. There was impatience in such men, impatience that could lead to trouble, impatience that might get them killed or lead to the killing of others.

"My name is Radigan. The R-Bar is my outfit and the R-Bar is Vache Creek."

"I'm afraid you don't understand." It was the girl speaking, and her cool, cultured voice seemed to be merely tolerating stupidity in one who knew no better. "We own twenty-two sections along Vache Creek."

"Along Vache Creek," there was no yielding in his tone, "there is but one ranch and room for but one. I own it."

She arranged her skirt with one casual hand, and the smile went no farther than her lips, lips that were a shade too thin, eyes that were too cool and measuring. "You are mistaken, sir. I am sorry for you, of course, but men who squat on land that does not belong to them must expect to be moved off. That land has been in my family since 1844."

"And you were so sure of your title that you sent your insurance on ahead?"

Ross Wall took a quick, belligerent step forward. "What's that mean?"

"Read it any way you like." Ross was the dangerous one at the moment and Radigan's eyes held on him. The foreman was a fighting man, and he looked a hardheaded man who would take some convincing. "An outfit that sends a gunman ahead of them can't have too much confidence in their title."

"You accusing us?"

"Vin Cable didn't come here for fun. He didn't take a shot at my *segundo* for fun and, from all I hear, he was a man who commanded a high price. I think he was paid insurance that there'd be no argument about titles."

Flynn interposed. "Tom, we'd better look into this. After all, if they have a title—"

"Any title they have isn't worth the paper it's written on." Radigan was brusque. "Moreover, there isn't range enough in Canyon Guadalupe to winter a jackrabbit, and the only range on Vache Creek is my range. There will be no cattle along that creek whose brand does not read R-Bar."

Hickman stood with one foot against the wall, a lean man in soiled buckskins who listened with cynical amusement.

The girl spoke again. "I am Angelina Foley. The

land along Vache Creek is part of my father's estate, and the terms of Governor Armijo's grant are clear. No doubt you have made improvements on the land." She opened her purse. "I am prepared to pay for those improvements, and to buy what stock you have."

"That's fair," Flynn said quickly. "How about that, Tom?"

"The land is mine. It will remain mine. If you had taken the trouble to inquire in Santa Fe you would know the status of any grants by Armijo."

For the first time Ross Wall looked uncertain. He glanced at Angelina Foley, awaiting her lead, for obviously this was something for which he had no reply.

"Would you fight a woman, Mr. Radigan? I thought Western men more gallant."

There was no yielding in Radigan. "When you opened the ball," he replied, "you called the tune. Anybody, man or woman, who comes hunting a bullet title to my land is going to have to prove title with more than conversation. And a woman who takes cards in a man's game holds the status of a man and is entitled to no more respect."

"Now, see here!" Flynn said angrily. "You've no proof of connection between Vin Cable and this lady! None at all! You just back up on that! Back up, d' you hear?"

Abruptly, Radigan turned and walked back into the saloon. The body of Cable had been removed from the billiard table to a back room where it was partly visible lying on another table.

Jim Flynn followed Radigan into the saloon and

leaned on the bar beside him. "Have a drink, Tom?" Flynn tried to speak casually.

"I have one. Thanks."

"Too bad . . . tough time to lose a place, winter coming like this."

Radigan shot Flynn a hard glance, but made no reply.

"If I were you I'd talk to these people, and try to work out a deal. Their herd is already on its way here."

"What's got into you, Jim? Are you deputy sheriff of the county or their lawyer? That land is mine. I've lived on it and worked it and have an airtight title. You don't suppose I'm going to be pushed off my land with a bluff like that, do you? You'd better decide where you stand, Jim."

Flynn's face flushed with dark blood. "I stand for the law, and I'll enforce the law! You put that in your pipe and smoke it!"

"Seems to me," Hickman commented mildly, "that Radigan's case is the best one, Jim. He's been in possession four years we know of. He says he's got an airtight title. Was I you, Jim, I'd give that some thought."

Hickman's interference angered him, yet there was sense in what he said. Still, Flynn told himself, it was unreasonable that such people could be bluffing, or that such a girl could be dishonest. These were quality . . . he had seen it at first glance, and he was a man who had been taught respect for decent women. The idea that an educated, intelligent lady would have a hand in anything shady was beyond consideration. Nor would an outfit of this size have come here without having a clear title. Like many another man he had respect for money and power, and these newcomers showed every indication of both.

"A girl like that wouldn't lie," Flynn said.

Radigan had no humor in his smile. "If you can say that, Jim, you've been lucky in the women you've known."

The door opened and Angelina Foley came in with Ross and the younger man.

"I am asking you again, Mr. Radigan, to vacate the premises on Vache Creek."

He turned to face her. "Somebody's misled you, ma'am. Have you ever seen this land you claim? Have you any idea what you're getting into? Canyon Guadalupe runs north of here, and rim to rim it'll vary from maybe a half-mile to a mile. In the bottom it isn't anywhere more than a few hundred yards wide, and nowhere along that canyon is there graze for a herd.

"North of there it narrows down and sometimes in the winter we're snowed in for a month at a time, one time it was three months. In the summer that country will carry quite a few cows in the high meadows, but to winter cattle up there calls for a special brand of know-how that no Plains country puncher will learn in a season. Most places folks will tell you a man who tries to winter cattle a mile and a half above sea level is crazy.

"I'd say, ma'am, that you've been poorly advised to bring a herd up here at this season. My advice would be to head out of here for the nearest fort or reservation where they're buying cattle for the Indians and sell out. After you've spent a winter here, if you still want a piece of this country, you can find a piece that's not already taken."

"My land is on Vache Creek, Mr. Radigan," she replied coolly. "I am asking you to vacate in the presence of witnesses. If you do not, well, I'm afraid my men won't take kindly to your being in the way of ranch operations."

"Seems odd," Radigan said quietly, "that you'd come into a cold country in the late fall knowing you'd built no buildings on the land. Looks like you knew about mine and figured to have me out of them. Seems you should know you have to feed stock part of the winter, and yet you bring a herd up here. Figuring to use my feed, too? Was that why Vin Cable came first?"

Jim Flynn's brow puckered and he glanced at Angelina Foley, his eyes registering doubt for the first time. It was a telling point, and any man who had grown up around cattle would recognize the logic of it.

She turned toward the door, then glanced back. "You have heard what I said. You have been notified to vacate. When my herd arrives, we will move onto the land."

The bat wings swung to behind them, and there was silence in the saloon and stage station.

"There's six men here," Hickman advised, "and there must be a dozen or more with the herd. I'd say you'd chosen yourself a fight."

"I've one man worth a dozen of these, plenty of grub and more than a thousand rounds of ammunition. If it's war they want they've come to the right place."

He downed his drink and turned to the door. It was time he started back. The few flakes of falling snow had disappeared, but the suggestion remained in the air, and the sky above was flat and cold.

At the door Hickman's voice stopped him. "Jim," the trapper suggested mildly, "there's a thought behind this. Now these folks have a right smart outfit. Good horses, good clothes, good rigs. Wonder why they left wherever they were? Folks that prosperous don't usually pick up and move. Mostly, movers are poor folks."

Flynn turned around, ignoring Hickman. "Cable was shot in front," he said, "and any man who can get lead into Vin Cable in front is entitled to it, but I'm a curious man."

Briefly, Radigan explained, telling the story simply and without embellishment from the moment he saw the trail across the meadow. Despite himself, Flynn was fascinated. A fighting man himself he read between the lines. Most men would have gotten themselves killed in such a situation, but Radigan had out-thought, out-tricked and outshot his man.

"He have a grudge against you?"

"I never knew who he was until Hickman put a name to him." Radigan paused. "Jim, I'd suggest you examine their papers before there's any trouble. They'll have some sort of a trumped-up claim, I'm sure of that. But look them over."

"Papers?"

"They'll have a deed or something. They wouldn't just come in here and demand a ranch without something to show."

Jim Flynn felt like a fool. He had been ready to order a man off his ranch on the mere say-so of a bunch of strangers. He must see those papers... worst of it was, he had a time with reading. He felt irritated and trapped. When he had taken this job it had promised peace and quiet with only an occasional drunken Indian to make trouble—and now this.

When Radigan rode his horse into the ranch yard John Child came out of the house with a lantern. He watched Radigan dismount stiffly and within the warm stable he listened while Radigan stripped bridle and saddle and related the events of the afternoon.

"It's a hard-case outfit," he said finally, "and my hunch is the man behind it is that Harvey Thorpe, the girl's foster brother. He did little talking, but he did a lot of looking and listening."

"And they're bringing cattle? If they get caught in the canyon by a heavy fall of snow they won't have any more cattle than a jaybird."

"That's working for us... they don't know this country. I started small and built carefully and most of the stock we have now was born right here, and they've learned to rustle for their grass in rough country."

The R-Bar was almost twenty-eight miles north of San Ysidro. There were two Indian villages closer, and a few white men in each, but none that concerned him. In the time he had lived on Vache Creek there had been few visitors, and most of them riders passing through, and not one that he could place as a possible scout for the Foley outfit. Most of the riders, and he could count them on the fingers of his hands, had been drifters heading for the breaks to the north to hide out from the law, heading for Loma Coyote.

Did Angelina Foley know of what this range consisted? The rugged mountains, high mesas, hidden valleys and hanging meadows? His cattle were scattered because of the grass, and now were mostly held in proximity to stacks of cut hay, yet here and there he had built fences, utilizing natural features of the terrain wherever possible. During that first winter he had been constantly in the saddle, scouting the places where the wind left grass exposed and where snow did not drift. Coming from Illinois he had known something of cold weather before he came west, and during the drifting years he learned more both from his own experiences and from ranchers he talked to in Montana and Nebraska. It would require such knowledge for these newcomers to survive.

Child shivered. The wind off the mesa was cold, this time of night. "If you need hands," he suggested, "there's some you could have."

"Look, John," Radigan said, "if this comes to a shooting fight, you don't have to stay. It's my fight, and—"

"Oh, shut up! You can't hold this down alone and you damn' well know it. Nor would I let you if you could."

He led the way to the house. "How much do they claim?"

"Twenty-two sections. Take 'em four or five years to find it all."

"How much do you claim? I don't recall you ever told me."

"Don't recall you asking. I claim about twice that

much, and I need every bit of it. I was figuring on selling out next year and keeping only the young stuff. I want to build to five or six thousand head."

"You'll need grass."

"I know where it is, lots of it."

Inside the house, Radigan glanced around with surprise. The place had been cleaned thoroughly, the floors scrubbed, the windows washed, and all the pots were shining. "You expecting visitors, John?"

Child shrugged, his face bland. "No tellin' when a bachelor goes to town. Time you were married, anyway."

"Me?" Radigan was astonished. "Now where would you get an idea like that? And where would I find a girl who would have me? I wouldn't know how to treat her unless she had horns."

Radigan went prowling for bear sign and found a dishpan piled high with them. "You stay out of them," Child admonished. "Spoil your supper."

"Seems to me," Radigan said, "you're the one who should get married. You're getting fussier all the time. Should have married years ago."

Child surprised him. "I was married, one time. Married a Cheyenne girl I stole from the Utes who'd taken her prisoner one day. She was right pretty, and mighty scared of those Utes, so I spoke her language and it was a comfort to her. Nighttime I cut loose a couple of horses and the girl and took out. They chased me more'n a hundred miles."

"What happened?"

"We lived north of here. Had one boy, but he was killed in a fall from a horse. Utes again. We were travelin' when they came up on us. They got my wife, shot her through the head first off. I made a run for it with the boy, and he was killed, too."

"Tough."

"We had some good years . . . raised a girl, too. She lived with us four, five years and then we put her in a convent in Mexico. She was thirteen then."

"She wasn't your daughter?"

"No. Comanches took her from a wagon train where they'd killed her family. I traded four horses for her. She stayed at that convent a couple of years, then she lived with some high-class Mexican woman and her husband until they decided to go to Spain. She didn't want to go."

Radigan filled his plate and sat down at the table. He had not realized he was so tired. Part of it was the warm room after the long, cold ride—he felt sleepy.

"Whatever happened to her?"

Child cleared his throat and Radigan glanced at him. "What's the matter?" Radigan demanded. "Are you sick?"

"No. Well—she's coming here."

"*What?*" Radigan was wide awake. "Are you crazy? What would we do with a girl here in the middle of a fight?"

"Where else can she go? And when I told her to come on, well, this here fight wasn't heard of. She's eighteen now and she figures I'm the only person she can come to."

Radigan got to his feet, exasperated and worried. "Damn it, John! What's got into you? This is no place for a girl. Why, she's not even a blood relative!"

"Seems like she is. Wrote to me all the time. She always wanted to come back to the mountains. I guess

I was the only father she ever had, although I ain't fixed to be much of a father. She always wanted to come back here, but I talked her into staying on. Those were mighty fine folks she was with and I figured a girl should learn about things like keepin' a fine house and such."

Radigan was exasperated. There was no use blaming John Child, but to have a girl coming here at this time . . . if one thing was needed to make matters worse, this was it. Two men can go on the dodge in the hills no matter what the weather, but they'd have trouble enough caring for themselves without carting a female along.

"Seems I might take her to Santa Fe," Child admitted reluctantly, "but she wanted to be with me, and well, she never really had a father."

Radigan looked at him, then his good humor got the better of him and he laughed. "This is worse than the fight. That we could get out of. What do we know about women?"

When supper was over he went outside, first lowering the light, to make a final round of the ranch. The news meant that John Child must go and he would have to stay on alone. With only two men it would be bad enough, but one man alone?

Not for an instant did he consider allowing the girl to remain. It was no place for even an Indian girl to be, let alone a girl who had grown up in a convent. The house was a position that could not be held throughout a long fight. If they could make a brief stand there it would be fortunate, but they must plan to get away, to move, to keep themselves alive.

The object of battle was the destruction of the enemy's capacity to resist. And as long as they were mobile they were free and able to fight back. If they were tied down they would be destroyed.

The principle of warfare, so far as Tom Radigan was concerned, was attack, always attack. It did not matter that he would be alone, or outnumbered at best, he must attack. Even a stronger enemy could be put on the defensive and kept there.

This was the reason behind the secret caches of food and ammunition, and every move was being made with the idea of retreat to the forest and mountains. And tomorrow they would begin pushing stock back farther into the remote valleys.

Two days they worked, and it was hard, driving work from morning until night, with the late hours before bedtime devoted to planning. And then Jim Flynn showed up.

"They've got the papers," he said. "They've got a deed. It was a grant from Governor Armijo giving them title to the old Villasur grant."

"He didn't have it to give. That grant isn't worth the paper it's written on, Jim."

"I don't know about that, but you've got to get off."

"No court has ordered me off. My title hasn't been disputed in court. These people are trying to run a bluff. Armijo didn't own that land, the state didn't own it. He had no title to give anyone, and believe me it will take a lot more than they have to get me off."

"We've got to settle this thing," Flynn protested irritably. "I won't have a cattle war."

"Then please remember I'm in possession. Let them go to court. That's the proper way to advance a claim, not by hiring a gunman and trying to kill the man in possession."

"You don't know they did that."

"Who else?" Radigan turned toward the door. "Come on in, Jim. Let's talk about this. Anyway," he added, "what are they going to do if I don't move? Use force? You talk to them, Jim. Believe me, they haven't a leg to stand on."

Flynn sat his saddle stubbornly. He could not believe that such people as Angelina Foley and Harvey Thorpe would try to push a claim to which they had no legal right. He was sure that Radigan was wrong and his persistence was irritating. Never had he had any business with land titles or courts. His experience with the law was simply the enforcement of it against toughs and gunmen.

Radigan turned around. "Jim, tell them to take their claim to court. I'm staying on."

"You're almighty sure," Flynn said angrily. "What are you—a lawyer?"

Radigan walked back to the horse. "Jim, between 1825 and 1828 there were three temporary governors here in New Mexico, and one of them was Armijo. In 1837 there was a rebellion at Taos and a mob of rebels killed Governor Perez. Armijo managed to become commander of the counterattack and when it was successful had himself proclaimed governor.

"There's a lot of stories and at this late date a man can't get at the truth of it all, but there's folks that say he murdered a lot of people including the rebel governor as well as some of his own supporters and friends. He managed to bribe himself into favor with the government of Mexico and his appointment was confirmed.

"He was replaced in 1844 by Lejana, but after a year he was back in office, and making a mint of money by holding up traders on the Sante Fe Trail for a heavy tax on each wagon.

"Moreover, he finagled around with some of the old land grants and rewarded friends with grants of land to which he had no legal title. My guess is that this Foley girl got hold of one of those old grants and she's trying to make it work for her."

Flynn was out of his depth and knew it. He could handle a drunk or a lynch mob, and on two occasions had shot it out with gunmen who wanted to prove themselves. The only legal paper he knew anything about was a warrant.

"You got as much?" Flynn demanded belligerently. "What's your claim? Squatter's rights?"

Radigan shook his head patiently. "Jim, I have legal title to all the land I need, including water rights, and more than that, I'm in possession. My title will stand investigation. These people are deliberately trying to put me off land that I own."

"Don't blame me!" Flynn said angrily. "Don't blame me if the lid blows off!"

Tom Radigan put his big hands on his hips. "I won't blame you, Jim, but I suggest you go to them and order them to stay out of this part of the country. You're the deputy sheriff, and these people will be breaking the law."

Flynn's face darkened. "You don't tell me my job! I know my job, and I'll do it!"

"You seem ready to enforce the law against me,"

Radigan replied. "And I'm the only one who is in the clear."

"I ain't so sure about that!" Flynn swung his horse. Without a backward glance he started down the trail toward town. It was going to be a long, dark ride.

Two miles below the ranch and overlooking the canyon of Vache Creek was a huge promontory that thrust itself out from the canyon wall like a great watchtower, and there Tom Radigan took up his post. By day a man could see for miles down the canyon, and by night he could hear. The still, cold air let sound travel for miles.

Leaving his horse picketed near a clump of aspen he walked out on the broad brow of the promontory and seated himself beside a rough wall of stone that gave partial shelter from the cold wind.

There were other trails. One led over the Nacimientos behind him from the Rio Puerco, but it was a dim trail known to few besides the Indians and difficult to follow. There was another from the east that led from the Springs to Cebolla and then the mesa to a point just opposite his present position. The chance that they would know of either of the trails was slight.

At midnight he turned over the watch to John Child and at daybreak, after a quick breakfast, he was in the saddle. "She should be there," Child told him. "The way I figure she should be coming in on today's stage, but you'd be better off to let me go. I d'clare, Tom, sometimes I don't figure you're in your right mind . . . they don't even know me."

"They'd know. They'd have you spotted in no

time. The risk is mine, so you just sit tight and be sure nobody moves in while I'm gone."

"Tom," Child hesitated, "want I should ride up to Loma Coyote? Or I could send up a smoke? There's some good men up there, fighting men."

"Forget it." Radigan started his horse and then looked back. "If you see any of them, find out who's around."

"Stark is there." Child walked after the horse. "You remember Adam Stark. He was a Ranger the same time you were, killed a man in El Paso and went up the trail. Best rifle shot I ever saw."

"Good man."

San Ysidro was quiet under the late autumn sun. It was just short of noon when he rode the buckskin down the street and almost the first man he saw was Sam Coker. They tied up at the rail only a few feet apart, but Radigan was not worried. Coker was a trouble hunter, but it was rare that a trouble hunter would start something without an audience.

Hickman was seated at a table in his soiled buckskins, his feet on the table and a bottle at hand. Hickman, Radigan had noticed, always had a bottle but the level of it rarely diminished.

The room was long and low, the building was adobe. The bar was half its length, and there were only a few tables, it was a shabby, down-at-heel room bare of any decoration aside from the fly-specked mirror behind the bar. Downey was at once the stage agent and saloon-keeper, a lonely, hard-faced man who had tended bar in a dozen boom mining towns and who retained few illusions.

"Stage be in about one o'clock?" Radigan asked.

"Should be." Downey pushed a bottle at him. Downey liked him, Radigan believed, as much as he liked any man, but he must be getting a lot of business from the newcomers.

"Join me?" Hickman suggested, pulling his feet off the table. He glanced past Radigan at Sam Coker who had come up to the bar.

Radigan carried his own bottle to the table. "The sign doesn't read for peace," he commented.

Hickman grinned. "I can read the smoke." The door had opened and two other men came in. "The big one is Barbeau. He fancies himself in a brawl. He picked a fight with a drifter the other night and gave him a wicked beatin'. The other one is Bitner."

Downey brought them a tray of food and Barbeau turned to watch. "And the condemned man ate a hearty meal," he said.

"And Balaam's ass spoke," Radigan said.

Barbeau turned sharply around and stared at him, while Downey chuckled and Hickman grinned widely. Two other men at another table were both grinning.

"What was that?" Barbeau asked.

But the moment had passed, and Radigan was eating, ignoring him. Barbeau stared at him, then looked around truculently, hoping for some false move. He was ignored and after a minute he turned his attention again to Radigan. "I wonder if he can fight like he can eat," he asked.

"Maybe somebody should find out," Coker suggested.

Radigan was enjoying the meal, as he had not realized how hungry he was. "Hadn't figured I was this hungry," he said, "but John made some bear sign the other day and I've eaten nothing else for the last two days."

"You want warriors," Hickman said. "You let that get out. You could get more fighting men with bear sign than you could with money, grub being what it is in this country." He filled his glass. "I've seen cowhands ride sixty, seventy mile for chance at bear sign."

Barbeau took another drink and then turned with his back to the bar. He was spoiling for a fight and did not like being ignored, and the drinks had fired his blood and convinced him he was ready.

At the table Radigan had missed nothing. An old campaigner when it came to brawls, he knew every move that was being made. He glimpsed Coker moving a little toward the door to cut off any retreat, and Bitner had moved toward the rear. Barbeau was a broad, thick man with a coarse beard and the thick hands of a really powerful man. He had heavy features and a hard jaw set above a short, thick neck.

Low-voiced, Radigan told Hickman, "Stay out of it. This is my fight."

Hickman studied him quizzically. "Three's quite a handful," he commented. Then he added, "He comes right in, slamming with both hands. And he's hard to stop."

Barbeau was getting set. Radigan needed no map to see how the trail lay, and he sat very still, looking into his cup and mentally cataloguing the room around him and its tactical possibilities. And then the door opened and Angelina Foley came in.

She came directly to Radigan's table and he got to his feet politely.

"Now look at that!" Barbeau sneered. "A real gent!"

"Mr. Radigan?" Her eyes were even greener than he had remembered. "I heard you were in town and hoped to see you before you left. I wanted to tell you how sorry I was that we are putting you off the land. If we could pay you for your trouble . . . ? The offer is still open."

"You're mistaken, Miss Foley. Someone has given you some wrong information again. I'm not moving."

"Please!" Her finger touched his sleeve and her eyes were very large. "We own the land, and you must go. I am afraid that if you do not go some of my men will want to force you to move. I thought . . . well, when I heard you were in town I hoped we might reach an agreement."

"Will you sit down?"

She hesitated an instant, then seated herself. Radigan sat down and as he did so he heard Coker say, "Any minute now, they'll serve tea."

Radigan turned to Downey. "Do you have any tea?"

"Tea? *Tea!* . . . Well . . . sure, but—"

"Make some, and serve it to us here, will you? But make a lot . . . make a gallon of it."

"A *gallon? Of tea?*"

"That's right."

Hickman leaned back in his chair studying Radigan with a curious glint in his eyes, but Radigan turned to Angelina. "You were about to say—?"

"I wish you'd reconsider . . . I mean, about moving. And I meant what I said about paying for your improvements. Naturally, we are as sorry about this as you."

"But I'm not sorry." Radigan smiled at her. "I'm not sorry at all. I do regret that you have come so far without checking, without knowing what you were getting into. If you really wish to see how little you have in your favor, just take it to court."

"But the courts are so far away, Mr. Radigan!" Her eyes opened wide. "And they take far too much time! I am sorry, indeed, but Mr. Thorpe and I have more than three thousand head of cattle coming up, and if you won't move, we'll have to move you."

"Know anything about that land, ma'am?"

"I haven't seen it, of course, but Mr. Thorpe has. Why do you ask?"

"Simply this. If I were to move off that ranch and let you have it, you couldn't winter three thousand head of cows up there . . . if you had a free hand and no trouble at all, you still couldn't do it. There isn't range enough, there isn't feed enough. If a man had a good winter he might get through with a thousand head."

She stared at him, taken by his obvious sincerity, but not wanting to believe him. "But I heard it was the finest grass in the world, and that there was plenty of water."

"It is all of that, but there isn't enough of it. I've hoped to open trails to other valleys where cattle could be kept, but as it is, that's mostly timber country, over half of it stands on edge, and probably the easiest way to be rid of you would be to step out and let you try it. You'd lose cattle, men and horses."

"You seem to have done all right. I can scarcely believe you, Mr. Radigan."

He nodded to indicate the men at the bar, aware they were listening. "Above all, what will you do with your hands?" It was a chance to inject some doubt into their minds. "There isn't work up there for more than two or three men on the few acres you'll have."

"Acres?" she protested. "There are miles, twenty-two square miles, to be exact."

Downey came in with the tea. "Had to use two pots," he explained. "Never had such a big order before."

Radigan took the smallest pot and filled their two cups and then he quietly drew his gun. "Serve the rest of it to them." Radigan indicated the three men at the bar with his gun barrel. "I'll see that they drink it."

Coker's features stiffened and his hand started for his gun but stopped as Radigan's gun muzzle swung to cover him. "Start drinking. You, too, Barbeau."

"I'll be damned if I do!"

Radigan's gun tilted a little. "You asked for a tea party and now you've got it. Start drinking or I start shooting."

Hickman was grinning widely. Startled, Angelina Foley could only stare from Radigan to her men, astonished and unbelieving.

"If you aren't drinking by the time I count three," Radigan said casually, "I'll break an arm for each of you."

He came easily to his feet and moved across the

floor toward them, keeping Angelina and the door in his line of vision.

"I'll kill you for this!" Barbeau shouted.

"Maybe—but I can start shortening the odds right here. You wanted tea, now get on with it."

Coker slammed down his cup. "I'll be damned if I will!" he shouted and grabbed at his gun butt.

Radigan's gun barrel slashed right and left and Coker hit the floor as if dropped from a roof. "Get on with the tea drinking," Radigan said calmly, "or I'll pile you three deep."

Angelina Foley was white with anger. "See here!" she protested. "You can't do that!"

"I'd hate to hit a woman," he said.

Involuntarily, she sat down. "You . . . you wouldn't dare!"

"If you play games with men," he replied, "you'll play by men's rules."

He handed his six-gun to Hickman. "Barbeau was hunting a fight," he said. "You just keep them off my back."

Barbeau slammed down his cup and turned sharply around. "Fight?" he yelled. "You'd fight *me*?"

Radigan hit him.

Barbeau staggered and Radigan stepped in, watching Barbeau's fists, and whipped a wicked left into Barbeau's belly. Barbeau was a talker as well as a fighter—he had expected to do some talking about what he was going to do, and he had been startled by Radigan's willingness to fight, and the savagery of Radigan's attack confused him. He backed away, but Radigan gave him no chance to get set. A left and right to the face shook him up, and desperately he put his head down and charged, swinging.

A wild right staggered Radigan, but the rancher stepped outside of a left and brought his fist down on Barbeau's kidney. The heavier man gasped and plunged in, grabbing for a clinch. Radigan hit him flush on the chin with a short right that stopped him in his tracks.

Barbeau stared through his raised fists at Radigan. This fight was not going as his fights usually went. The right he had taken was a stunning blow, and Radigan looked cool and easy, not even breathing hard. For the first time Barbeau realized he might be whipped and the thought was maddening. Recklessly he charged, swinging powerful blows with both hands. For a few minutes they fought hard, and Barbeau drove Radigan back across the room. Bitner was cheering, and Barbeau was sure he had Radigan going. He felt his right land solidly, and automatically he slowed to let Radigan fall.

In the instant he slowed, Radigan struck him in the mouth, splitting his lip and spilling blood over his shirtfront. Astonished, Barbeau saw Radigan standing before him...the rancher had taken his best punch and had struck back at almost the same instant.

Barbeau rushed, but the heart was out of him. Wildly, he knew he was not going to win. Never before had he hit a man solidly with his right hand when that man had not fallen, but the punch apparently had left Radigan undisturbed. Radigan had grown up around the camps of Michigan loggers before coming west to Texas, and he had served a postgraduate course in fistfighting among the freighters and the riverboatmen. Few cowhands of the seventies knew anything about fistfighting. Arguments were settled with guns and fists rarely used, hence Barbeau's victories had been won over men to whom fistfighting was completely foreign. To Radigan fist and skull fighting had been a way of life from boyhood into young manhood. He had lost fights, but he had won many more, and Barbeau had none of the rough skill to which he was accustomed.

Barbeau rushed again, trying to grapple with Radigan, but the rancher gave ground suddenly and the overbalanced Barbeau fell forward. Grabbing Barbeau by the collar, Radigan jerked him forward over his own extended leg and hurled him to the floor.

Barbeau lay on his back, staring up at Radigan from dull eyes.

Then slowly he started to get up, and Radigan backed off to give him room. When Barbeau was on his feet, Radigan walked in, feinted, and hit the heavier man in the belly. Filled with tea, Barbeau backed up, gasping and gulping, overcome with nausea. He backed away, lifting a hand to ward Radigan off. He was battered, bloody and beaten, and he knew it.

Radigan picked up his gun and dropped it into his holster. Coker was sitting on the floor holding his head in both hands.

"I don't want trouble," Radigan said, "but I won't run from it."

He turned to face Angelina Foley. Her face was white, her eyes hard with anger.

"I doubt if you realize what that Vache Creek country is like," he said, "but if you want to come up with one man, and I'd suggest Ross Wall, who is a cowman, I'll show it to you. Most of it is over seventy-five hundred feet above sea level, and it is the most beautiful mountain country in the world. It is also one of the roughest, coldest and has the most snow."

Downey was standing near the window. "Stage coming," he said.

Radigan put on his hat and walked outside. His knuckles were split and sore but he felt good. It had been his first fistfight in a long time, and he was suddenly glad he had put in much of the summer splitting rails for fences and cutting wood for winter. Nothing like an axe or a crosscut saw to put a man in shape.

He remembered Thorpe. With him such a fight might be different, for Thorpe was no Barbeau, and despite the fact that he looked the fashionable young man there were shoulders on him, and there was something about the lean savagery of his face that was a warning. Also, when they had first met he had noticed scars on the man's knuckles.

The door closed behind him and he turned to see Angelina Foley looking at him. Her gaze was cool, curious, and, for the first time, almost respectful. "Would you have struck me?" she asked curiously.

He had never struck a woman in his life, but he looked at her as if surprised by the question. "Why, of course," he said. "I meant what I said."

"You're no gentleman, Mr. Radigan!"

He grinned at her. "No gentleman would have a chance, dealing with you. You'd tease, flatter, maybe cry. You'd pet him, lie to him, cheat him. Well, you can cry for me or pet me, but you'll never do the rest. Try cheating me and I'll spank your little bustle."

Her eyes held a challenge. "We may be on opposite sides, but you're a man, and I like you. You may call me Gelina."

"You're a beautiful, desirable woman," he said, "but I wouldn't trust you across the street. Before this is over you'll hate me more than you ever hated any man, but seriously, take my advice and leave now. This fight will exhaust everything you've got and leave you nothing."

She smiled. "You have one man working for you, Mr. Radigan. I have thirty. I think I'll win."

He nodded seriously. "But I have something else working for me. The most dangerous ally a man could have—the weather. What will you do with your cattle when the ground is three to six feet deep in snow and no feed anywhere?"

The stage rolled to a stop and the cloud of dust that had pursued it now caught up and drifted over it, settling on the horses and around them.

Radigan watched the driver climb stiffly down from the box, his face red from the chill wind. Hickman had followed him out, and Downey was opening the door to help the passengers down. Radigan shifted his weight and a board creaked under his feet. Looking across the stage he gazed toward the distant mountains, and then a girl got out of the stage and the easy banter stopped as if cut with a knife. Whatever Tom Radigan had expected it was not this.

Under a perky little bonnet her eyes were guileless and blue, her face was that of an innocent child but her body was such that no clothing could conceal the lines of her figure. He caught his breath, half-hypnotized as she came up the steps. He was aware that everyone on the walk was staring, and aware she was thoroughly enjoying it.

She turned to Downey and said, "I am looking for Mr. Child or Mr. Radigan, of the R-Bar."

Downey started to speak but his lips found no words. In this land of few women there was nothing in his experience that prepared him to cope with this emergency. He stared and his lips parted and then he dumbly indicated Radigan.

She turned to him and surveyed him gravely out of large blue eyes. "You're not my father," she said, "so you must be Mr. Radigan."

Her eyes went past him to Gelina Foley. "Is this your wife?"

Radigan chuckled. "No, ma'am, this is my enemy, Miss Gelina Foley."

She looked at Gelina with a thoughtful expression. "I think she's my enemy," she said. "She likes you."

Hastily, Radigan said, "Gretchen—that is your name isn't it?—can you ride?"

"I can ride anything that wears hair," she said, "but I'll have to change my dress." She glanced quickly at Gelina. "Do you like her?" she whispered audibly.

Gelina's face flushed and deliberately she gathered her skirt and descended to her buckboard where Bitner was waiting to help her in. Without a backward glance, they drove away. Inwardly she was fuming. Why! That . . . that baggage!

Angrily, Gelina flounced in her seat. The very idea! Why, that girl was no more than a child! And with a body like that! Accustomed to the attention of men, she realized jealously that from the moment that girl had gotten out of the stage nobody had so much as looked at her.

Her anger, she realized, was unreasonable. She sat back in the buckboard and began to plan. They must move at once, and she would run them out of the country. They would not wait any longer. After all, there were but two men there, and they could not be on watch all the time and still do the things that had to be done.

Her brows gathered. He had spoken of snow. Involuntarily she glanced at the dull sky. But that was nonsense. It never grew very cold here, this was New Mexico. Nonetheless the leaden sky depressed her, and without knowing why she was increasingly worried. Remembering what Radigan had said, she began to wonder just what it was Harvey Thorpe had in mind—it was he who had insisted they come here. But leaving Texas was imperative, and this was the only property to which they had claim. And it should take only a few days to be rid of Radigan.

Yet even as she thought that she remembered the cool, masterful, almost easy way in which he had beaten Barbeau. She had rarely seen a man whipped more thoroughly. And Vin Cable was dead—there had been four bullet holes in his body.

It was not going to be as easy as Harvey believed. Suddenly, she was glad Ross was along.

GRETCHEN CHILD RETURNED from Downey's home where she had met Mrs. Downey, a buxom, motherly Irish woman, and where she changed her clothes. She now wore a neat gray riding habit and whatever the dress had left to imagination the habit revealed. Uncomfortably, Radigan was aware that she would be unlikely to find anything that would make her look less exciting than she was.

As if, he reflected grimly, the Thorpe-Foley trouble was not enough!

He helped her into the saddle but she really needed no help. He saw at a glance that whatever else she might be she was at home in a saddle.

"You'll not be able to stay at the ranch," he warned. "It won't be safe."

"I trust you," she said.

Hastily, he explained. "I didn't mean that. We've a range war on with those people back there. A shooting war, I think."

"I saw your knuckles. Has the war started?" She looked at him seriously. "I'm strong. I can work, and I can use a gun. I'm really strong." She held out her arm, doubled to make a muscle. "Just feel of that."

CHAPTER 3

THE CATTLE CAME first. They came up the canyon on the third day after Radigan's return with Gretchen Child, and they came in a solid mass, hurried on by a dozen cowhands. Obviously they had been driven up the canyon earlier and held at the *cienaga* during the night.

The cattle came first and they came fast. Radigan was putting a little feed in the makeshift corral hidden among the fallen rocks from the weathering of the mesa when he heard Child yell.

He heard him yell, heard a shot, and he dropped the pitchfork and came running. He shot the first steer into the yard, but a glance told him there was no stemming that tide of beef and he ducked into the house after John and slammed the door, dropping the bar into place. Almost before he could reach the window the yard was crowded with cattle.

Child rested the muzzle of his Winchester on the sill of the window beyond the door and glanced over at Radigan. "Smart," he said, "mighty smart. We're not supposed to get out."

A big steer was pressed tight against the door, and others were so close to the windows that Radigan could have reached out and scratched their backs. The ranch yard was jammed full of steers pressed in a compact mass. Beyond them, to left and right, the herd was spreading out in loose formation, but those in the yard were held tight by a circle of cowhands and tight-drawn ropes. The cowhands were out of sight behind the barn or in other concealment.

"Hi, the house!" The voice was the booming one of Ross Wall. "You want to get out, toss your guns out the window!"

Child glanced at Radigan but he motioned for silence. Several minutes passed. After the first few minutes of realization Gretchen had calmly returned to her housework, putting a meal on the table as though there was no enemy within miles. Yet Radigan noted she wore riding boots and a rough skirt—she was ready to go.

Wall did not know about the tunnel, and that was what would save them. Nobody knew about that but John Child, and obviously somebody in town had told Wall or Thorpe or both of the fact that the ranch house had but one entrance.

And without the tunnel they would have been helpless, for there was no escape from the house except by the tunnel, for driving the beef into the yard had imprisoned them just as surely as if walled with stone. They could kill the beef, but if they did they would then be killed themselves and no one would say they were killed without cause.

"If you want to eat," Gretchen said, "it's ready."

"Go ahead, John. You sit down. I'll take mine here at the window."

"Hello, the house!" It was Wall again. "Radigan, I know you're in there, and you haven't a prayer! Throw us your guns and we'll let you out!"

They would get the house, but at this time of year,

hoping to move in themselves, they would not burn it. Living in the hills would be rough but they could stand it for a short time, at least. Keeping well back away from the window, Radigan considered the situation.

Long ago he had planned for just such an emergency, but he had expected the trouble from the Utes. He had built for defense, but had planned for abandoning the place if it became necessary. Here, as at the barn, there was another way out, but the way out of the house was through a tunnel that opened in thick brush at the foot of the mesa near where the horses were picketed. It was not far behind the house, and it was unlikely anyone would examine the talus slope at the mesa's foot. To the casual eye it looked like a thousand other such slopes at the base of a thousand such mesas.

There was no way they could get at the house from the rear so it was unlikely anyone would find reason for checking that slope.

He could hear the murmur of voices from beyond the cattle. Obviously, the fact that no reply came from the house was disturbing to them, for there is no bargaining with a man who won't talk.

Gretchen brought coffee to the window, keeping well out of line. Radigan smiled at her. "You walked right into trouble. I'm sorry."

"Will we have to leave here?"

"Yes."

"We will need blankets and warm clothes," she said. "I'll get them ready."

He watched her as she walked away, amazed anew at the calm with which she accepted the situation. He glanced out the window again . . . they had to stall until after dark, for the chance of escape in daylight was less . . . all was quiet. The cattle were jammed tight and held there, pressing against the door.

Ross Wall hunkered down beside the fire, spreading his cold hands to the flames. "He's there, all right. No way he could get out. I talked to a man down to San Ysidro, man helped build this place and he swears there was only one door. Small house like that, there's no need for another."

Thorpe squatted beside the fire and rolled a cigarette. "We've got to get him out of there. If he's got grub he could spend the winter there."

Wall looked around gloomily. "He sure didn't tell no lies about grass. If this is all there is we can't hold the herd on it for a week."

"There's more."

Wall hunched his heavy shoulders under his coat. The more he saw of the situation the less he liked it, and from all he could see the ranch looked like a two-man operation, and if it started to snow. . . .

"I better start some of the men scouting for grass. If we don't find some we'll have to drive out of here."

"Are you questioning my judgment?"

Ross Wall rolled his quid in his big jaws. "You said the grass was here, an' Miss Foley took your word for it. I hope you're right."

"It's here."

Harvey Thorpe looked around slowly. The open space before the mesa did not look as large now as it had when empty of cattle, and despite himself he was worried. There was other grass back in the hills, but where was it? He had expected to find well-marked trails and he could find no trails at all. From the appearance of things this was all there was to the R-Bar, yet people at San Ysidro and others at Santa Fe had said Radigan ran several hundred head on land that would support several thousand.

"All right," Thorpe said finally, "send out a couple of men." He studied the house. "There's smoke from the chimney, but it looks like a dying fire."

"Well-built house. They would need little fire."

It was growing colder. Ross Wall looked at the sky. He was a tough, hardheaded man who rode for the brand; an order from Angelina Foley was all he asked from anyone. He was the perfect feudal henchman, and as he had served her father so he now served her, and she was, he thought with satisfaction, a whole lot smarter than her father. Her father would have stayed in Texas and fought it out when there wasn't a chance of winning, but Angelina knew when to cut and run, and what to take with her when she did. They had rustled her herds so when she left she simply drove off everything in sight.

Personally, he thought Radigan correct in his suggestion to sell off the cattle, especially the doctored brands, of which there were too many for comfort. Holding the herd was probably Thorpe's idea, but a man did not always know where the ideas originated for Angelina had a way of attributing ideas that were actually hers to someone else.

He poked a stick into the fire. There was not much time. They had to get Radigan out of there, but without a killing if possible. Ross Wall held no objections to killing when every other way had been tried, or when necessity demanded, but killings had a way of stirring things up, and a man like Radigan might have many friends.

He had not seen the beating Radigan had given Barbeau, but he had seen Barbeau afterward and from all accounts it had been a thorough and artistic job, and it had left Barbeau a silent, hardworking man with all the bully knocked out of him for the time. Nothing he had seen of Radigan allowed him to believe that moving the man would be a simple task. He did not believe with Coker that one fast, hard-shooting rush would do it—the man inside that house was intelligent and a fighter.

Wall had been impressed with Radigan's manner—he did not seem to believe himself outnumbered, nor did he hesitate to handle a fight when it came to him. A hard man and a fighter himself, Wall recognized the same traits in his antagonist and respected them. Nonetheless, he had a job to do and the look of the sky bothered him.

Born in Vermont he had come west as a child, but there lingered a memory of mornings at home when his father would come in from the barn coated with snow, and when long icicles hung from the eaves. Those winters had been cold, with a deep, penetrating cold, and men had been frozen to death in some of those winters. This was New Mexico, and he had always thought of it as a warm and pleasant place, which it was, but they were high now and the chill in the air worried him.

Everything either Thorpe or Angelina had was tied up in that herd. Behind there was nothing but enmity and shambles, and the rustled cattle forbade their ever returning to Texas. Their only chance for survival lay right there, digging in fast. Yet he wished they would sell the herd and not gamble.

He looked down at the thick, hard-knuckled hands he held over the fire. He was forty now, no youngster by Plains standards, and he had worked twenty years for the Foley outfit. The Old Man had been a pirate, but a genial one, and in a period of ranching and free branding he had become rich, but he made enemies along the way, and tried to take in more territory than he'd a right to.

Angelina was smarter than her father, and cooler. When he thought about Angelina, Ross Wall worried. She was too cold, too shrewd, and she used her beauty as some men use a gun. Harvey Thorpe now... Ross had never made up his mind about Harvey. The Old Man married Harvey's aunt and Harvey had always lived with her, and for a few years Harvey had been the Old Man's shadow. Then he drifted away, and not much was known about those years, but when he returned he played a smart hand of poker, and he could use a gun, and once, when Ross happened on Harvey when he was changing his shirt, Ross saw bullet scars on his side—but Harvey had said nothing about them.

The feud broke and the Old Man was killed. Harvey had acted fast. Ross never knew exactly what happened but the man that killed the Old Man was shot to death at close range in his own doorway, and when his son ran around the house, Harvey had killed him, too.

The fighting had been sporadic for several years, but the men Harvey gathered around him were fighters rather than punchers and the ranch deteriorated while attention was given to fighting a feud they could not win, and along with it came lawless acts perpetrated by some of the men Harvey brought in. There came a time when it had ceased to be a feud with other families and had become a community matter, and word came to the ranch that vigilantes were being organized by the solid people of the community to act if the Rangers failed—and they had been sent for.

Flight followed, and a wholesale sweep of all the cattle they encountered in moving. Ross liked none of it, but about some of those cattle there was a question of title so he had gone along. And now they were here, and inside that house was a tough man who had to be dislodged and they could not burn him out.

He drew back his warmed hands and rolled a smoke. All through the Texas trouble he had left the fighting to Thorpe and had worked to preserve the ranch, without hands enough and without money enough. While gunhands loitered about the ranch or swaggered it in saloons, the water holes were trampled into mud, cattle died bogged down in swamps and fences torn down that allowed cattle to stray into the breaks when not actually rustled.

Of the hands he now had only six or seven were good punchers. The others were fighting men, gunhands like Barbeau and Coker or men he suspected of cold-blooded murder like Leach.

One thing Radigan said had stuck in his mind. The remark had been passed on to him by one of the hands. By Bitner, in fact. Radigan had said cattle could be handled on this range with few men: if that were so he might get rid of this lot they now had. Huddled near the fire, he considered that, and wondered how far he might go without trouble with Thorpe, for it was he who wanted such men about. He wanted to be rid of Coker, most of all. And after him, that troublemaker Barbeau who had driven two of his best hands to quit.

Ross Wall got to his feet. "Going to look around," he said, to no one in particular.

Thorpe did not even look up as Wall walked away, but in his mind Wall was thinking of something that had just come to him. He could be rid of Coker, and be rid of him without trouble with Thorpe. The men inside that house were good men with guns, and if Coker happened to get into an exposed position when the shooting started....

Angelina Foley came up the canyon at daybreak in the buckboard and left her rig at the foot of the promontory. From there she rode on up the trail on a horse provided by Wall. The cattle were still jammed tight against the door and the chimney trailed a smoke into the still morning sky. Both Wall and Thorpe sat beside her and looked at the bunched cattle. Few of them had been able to reach water or grass and they were bawling and restless.

She shivered in the early morning air and looked enviously at the trail of smoke coming from the warm, well-built house. Then she turned her eyes from the house and surveyed the area with puzzled eyes. "Harvey," she said, "you told me there was grass here, grass for thousands of cattle."

"He's got several hundred head somewhere," Thorpe replied. "There are valleys around. We'll find them."

"Have you looked?"

"No luck so far," Wall told her. "I've had two men scouting the country but so far not even a trail has turned up."

She looked at the house. "Can't we get them out of there?"

"We can," Wall said reluctantly, "but we'd have to kill Radigan. Might stir up more trouble than we want."

"Those cattle need water," she told them. "Drive them off. I'm going up to the house."

From inside the house Radigan watched the riders come down and watched them move the cattle away. When they were gone, Angelina Foley started for the house. Cautiously, Radigan opened the door. "Always nice to have guests," he said, "get down and come in."

As she entered the door Ross Wall and Thorpe started forward, and Radigan put a bullet into the dirt at their horses' feet. "You stay back," he said, loud enough for them to hear, "we don't want to hurt anybody."

He glanced at John Child who moved to the window with his Winchester.

She stopped inside the doorway and glanced around, surprised at the neatness of the small but compact house, the shining copper kettles, the swept floor, and the inside pump, a rarity anywhere in the West of the period. It was a warm, friendly, comfortable house, and for an instant her eyes met those of Gretchen.

This was the girl she had seen arrive on the stage, the one who had so angered her. She looked like a lovely young girl now in her simple cotton dress, standing beside the wide fireplace.

"Will you sit down?" Gretchen suggested. "The coffee is hot."

Radigan seated her with all the formality of a gentleman at a fashionable dinner, and Gretchen brought a steaming cup of coffee to the table and a plate of doughnuts.

"You live well here," she said to Radigan. "I'm sorry you have to move."

"We like it here," he commented, ignoring her remark, "and we've learned how to live with the country."

"I don't see much grass," she said. "I confess I believed it to be range country."

"You'll find much that you don't expect," he assured her. "I've seen snow to the eaves of this house. Sometimes in the winter we have to open a tunnel to the barn so we can feed the stock."

She was frankly incredulous, but he continued. "It makes me wonder who could convince you that you wanted to live here, or that you could ranch here. I think there is more behind this than appears on the surface."

"The land is mine," she said, "and that is the only reason we came."

"About that," he tried his coffee and put it down hurriedly. It was much too hot. "Your claim is based on an Armijo grant, and he had no authority to grant land to anyone, nor did he ever have title to this land. This was part of an original grant by the King of Spain, ratified later by the government of Mexico, and still later by the government of the United States.

"It was for years considered useless land, too far from anything and of no immediate use, so I moved in, looked it over, and bought out the original grant. You could have learned in Santa Fe that I have legal title to thirty-six sections in this area. Your grant is not and never was worth anything at all, and whatever your father gave for it it has been lost. I am sorry, but those are the facts. In court you would never have a chance."

She was coldly furious but her expression did not change, yet within her there was a sudden emptiness. Had her father never managed one successful thing? And why had Harvey not discovered this? Why had he not known about the scarcity of grazing land? Yet there was no turning back. There was no way back at all. She could sell her herd—yes. But the cattle were a strong argument in her favor, and an outfit moving into a country with a herd automatically garnered some degree of respect. There was no turning back.

She looked up at him and smiled. "I wish we could settle this peacefully, Mr. Radigan, but you may be sure the case will never go to court. It will be settled right here—now."

She had finished her coffee. Abruptly, he got to his feet. "If that is the case, we're wasting time," he replied brusquely. "We've nothing further to discuss. I am giving you one hour to get your cattle and outfit off my land."

Angelina did not move. She put down her cup and smiled at him, a radiant smile. "I am sorry we are enemies," she said. "I'd hoped we could be friends."

"We can still be friends," Gretchen suggested.

"Move your cattle away and find a ranch of your own and then come back and see us."

" 'Us'?" she quoted. "Well!" Angelina got to her feet. "I was not aware that you had become a partner in Mr. Radigan's ranch. Or," she glanced meaningly from one to the other, "have you already established a claim?"

Gretchen's face grew pale, then flooded with color. "I have no claim," she replied, "only my father is loyal to Tom Radigan and I hope I shall be."

Angelina walked to the door. "You will be," she said. "I have no doubt of it."

She went outside into the cold air and for a minute she stood still, fuming inwardly. That—that little! Then she swung into the saddle. All right then, Harvey knew how to do it. Yet even as her decision was made she kept seeing the way Radigan's dark hair curled around his ears, and the grave thoughtful expression of his eyes.

And soon he would be dead . . . killed.

No matter. He had had his chance. And there was no other way. She kept telling herself that.

Harvey Thorpe hunched his shoulders against the cold, and glanced irritably at the gray sky. "You're sure there isn't another door?"

"I looked. There was only the one."

"What do you think, Ross?"

Wall shifted his weight in the saddle. "We can do it, but we're going to lose men. No use trying it from behind. A man coming off that rock slope would get himself shot to doll rags."

Thorpe looked at the house. They could move into

the barn and shoot into the house through the windows, but it wasn't going to be easy. Radigan was apparently set for a siege. "We've got to do it," he said.

"Coker's a good man with a gun," Wall suggested. "If we could get Coker and Barbeau where they could cover the windows, we might make it too hot for them to stay in there."

"All right," Thorpe swung his horse, "let's take it."

Ross Wall moved swiftly. The cattle were driven into the bottoms and held in a loose herd by four men, and the others climbed into position where they could fire upon the house. Three men occupied the barn and two moved into the corrals, and there was no firing. Coker he placed among the trees to the right of the house, Barbeau to the left.

Angelina rode back down the hill and dismounted near the fire. She extended her hands toward the flames, watching Bitner, who had remained by the fire for the time being. "You've seen him. What do you think about him?" she asked.

Bitner glanced at her out of his tough, cynical eyes. "You never seen a cattle war, ma'am," he said. "This here shapes up like a first-rate one. Man never knows when one starts as to how it will end, or where. Yes, I've seen him close up, and he ain't no bargain. That there Radigan is a grizzly bear from way back up in the hills. He'll take some killin' an' when he dies he won't go by himself. I hired on for fightin' wages. Ma'am, I reckon we'll earn 'em."

"There's only two men."

"Two. Ain't many, is it? But they're forted up, an' they know how to fight." He stirred the fire and piled on some dried wood. "Two men can make a fight of it, and that Radigan's a fighter from who flung the chunk."

A rifle shot came to them. It was Coker who had fired, and they could see the smoke from his position, although they could not see the house. "Coker," Bitner said. "He's quick on the shoot."

There was no other sound for several minutes and Angelina listened the echo away, thinking of what it might mean. Men might die—but men had died before. A dozen had died in the feud from which they had just come, and several more disappeared or were wounded.

The shot fired by Coker struck the windowsill and ripped a gash. It was a wooden sill laid on the rock of the house. Radigan glanced at it and waited. He was in no hurry. There was no sense shooting until somebody gave him something to shoot at.

Gretchen, under his orders, was making up three packs of food. Blankets had already been cached, but each would take one along and a groundsheet. No telling where all they would camp.

A bullet shattered glass and imbedded itself in the ceiling. John Child shifted a little, then fired suddenly. Barbeau jerked back, swearing. There was a burn across his shoulder that stung like fire and he felt a trickle of blood down his back. It was only a break in the skin, but he felt a sudden chill. These men could shoot.

All afternoon there was sporadic fire with no harm on either side. Harvey Thorpe, nested down among some boulders, studied the house irritably. Not more than four shots had come from the house . . . either they had little ammunition or they were careful.

Barbeau had been scratched, and Coker had a boot heel shot off. Twice shots had come dangerously close to Wall.

The packs were completed and placed near the tunnel door. Child had been out through the tunnel and had fed corn to the hidden horses. He was worried, and stayed with them for some time. Sooner or later somebody was going to try circling behind the house and if they did they would be sure to find the horses. There was little concealment back there, and on much of the talus slope a man would be exposed to fire from below with no cover at all.

When darkness came Radigan slipped outside and waited against the wall of the house with a six-gun. He was sure an attempt would be made to creep under the windows and lie against the wall for quick shots through the windows. He wanted to be ready. Seated with his back against the wall, Radigan waited.

The air was cool, not as cold as it had been, and the dryness seemed gone from the night. A faint wind stirred the pines and out in the stable a horse stomped.

He saw a faint movement near the wall of the barn and the corral corner. And then the man came, bent low and running in his sock feet. Radigan stood up, the darkness of his body merging with the darkness under the wide eaves of the house. The man came up, running quietly, and failed to see Radigan until too late. The gun barrel swept down in an arc and caught the man behind the ear. He slumped, tried to straighten, and Radigan hit him again. He went down then, and lay still. Using some rawhide piggin strings, carried by every cowhand for the purpose of tying a calf's hoofs together after it had been roped and thrown, Radigan tied the man up nicely, and then gagged him with a chunk of old sacking.

The man on the ground groaned, and tried to move. "You take it easy," Radigan advised in a whisper. "It won't do you any good to wear yourself out. You lie still and maybe I won't slug you again."

A slow hour passed, and nothing happened. Then a second man started from the barn, and Radigan saw him coming. He came with a rush, and evidently the prisoner heard him for he grunted loudly and tried to call out. The oncoming man slid to a halt and his gun came up. Radigan dropped to one knee and when the man fired, he replied instantly, and just as quickly, hit the ground and rolled. Over his head bullets thudded and smacked into the house and the bench at the door.

"You try that again," Radigan said to the prisoner, "and you'll get yourself killed by your own outfit."

An hour went slowly by, and Radigan crawled to the door and scratched his signal to come in.

Gretchen was beside him instantly. "Tom, Tom, are you hurt?"

"Just hungry."

"You got one," Child said. "I saw him get it."

"And a prisoner."

Radigan sat at the table and drank coffee in the dark. There was food on the table, and when he had eaten he carried a cup of coffee to the window and drank it while eating a doughnut.

"All right," he said finally. "It's time."

The stars were out when they reached the horses. It

took them only a minute or two to saddle up. Child strapped on the packs and they led the horses off the slope into the trees. In the next few minutes they would know if they were going to make it without being discovered.

The trail led close along the mesa and with Child in the lead and Radigan as rear guard, they worked their way along under the trees and away from the house. When they had gone a quarter of a mile they got into their saddles and rode away.

Nobody talked, nor felt like talking. Behind them was the warm comfort of the ranch house and before them lay the forest, the night and the cold. No telling how long it would be before any of them slept under a roof again—if they ever did.

They rode west . . . and there was no trail. They rode west into the somber darkness of the forest, and only occasionally could they see the stars. It was cold . . . a wind from off the high peaks whispered the pines, moved restlessly, making violins of the pine needles, moaning low among the rocks and across the waste spaces above the timberline.

Tom Radigan moved into the lead, for only he knew where they now went, and in the darkness where there was no trail, and where all landmarks had mysteriously disappeared into a common darkness, he led on, knowing his way along the slope of the mountain and finding the openings among the trees as if guided by some mysterious thread.

From behind there came no sound as the besiegers waited for daylight. Two men had advanced to attack, and two men had disappeared, one surely dead and the other vanished. In silence they would be watching the dark house, worried, uncertain, angry.

How long would it be before they knew the house to be empty? Hours, perhaps. And every minute a minute of advantage. In these hills Tom Radigan knew it would take a lot of searching to find him—or an accident. It was like him that he did not discount the possibility of accident.

They might have held out at the house, yet if their horses were discovered there would be no escape at all, and it was always better to be mobile than to be pinned down by the enemy. Yet he did not retreat to escape, he retreated to be able to choose his own time for attack. The battle had been joined now and the time for negotiation was past. Whatever might have been done to avert the fight was now in the past. A man was dead....

An hour they rode, and then they emerged from the trees on a vast slope, dotted here and there with the night black clumps of aspen, and they still rode west with the vast black bulk of the mesa on their right, towering five hundred feet into the sky above them. They rode in silence with only the wind for company and the ragged shadows of sentinel pines for lookouts. Radigan paused once and let the other two ride up beside him.

"How're you coming?" he asked Gretchen.

"All right, Tom. I can ride all night and all day if you like."

"Good girl."

John Child was silent. The moon was up now and the stars faded into its greater light. Only on the horizon were there clouds.

"We're turning north." Radigan pointed west and south with a sweep of his hand. "See that line of mesas? They look like a fleet in battle formation. Well, they point our way north. I think we'll bed down somewhere in the breaks south of Nacimiento Peak."

As the crow flies they had covered no more than three or four miles, although the ground distance was twice that. Now, turning north with the distant, towering peak as guide, they rode again without a trail, riding in single file. Occasionally they were in forest, but much of the distance on long slopes with clumps of aspen and brush.

They traveled slowly for the terrain was unfamiliar even to Child and Radigan. Both men had ridden over it by day, but at night nothing looks the same, and there were no landmarks they remembered. Moreover, their activities had largely centered on the other side of the mountain, east of the ranch. On their left the land fell away in a long slope toward the valley of the Rio Puerco, but this was off the R-Bar range, and out of the territory where their cattle usually strayed.

The night was still. Several times Radigan drew up and listened for any sound of pursuit, but there was no sound but the sound of the wind, always the wind.

Riding along the slope the ground suddenly fell away into a small basin almost filled with a grove of aspen. In the midst of a horseshoe formation of aspen and boulders there was a hollow away from the wind and a faint sound of trickling water. Radigan pulled up. "We'll take a break. Have some coffee."

Child's saddle creaked as he swung down, and

Radigan dismounted, reaching a hand up for Gretchen. Her hand was surprisingly strong as she swung down.

"Tired?"

"We've only started."

Despite the rain they found bark from the underside of a deadfall, and leaves in the same place. There were dry branches under the trees, and in a minute or two a small blaze was going. It was very small—a man could cover that fire with his hat—but it was enough for coffee, and small enough to be unseen, sheltered as it was by the low ground and the aspen.

Radigan went back into the darkness and located the spring. An owl went up out of the brush with a *whoosh* of sound and he dropped his hand to his gun, then grinned into the dark. He squatted on his haunches and filled the coffeepot after tasting the water. It was cold and fresh.

Only a trickle, it came out of some rocks and fell into a small basin before trickling off down the slope.

Firelight flickered on the flanks of the horses and reflected from polished saddle leather. Overhead a few stars sparkled, and Tom Radigan squatted on his heels and looked across the fire at Gretchen. There was no sign of weariness in her, and she looked excited and alive. Child caught his eye and grinned. "On the trail again," he said, "I wonder if a man ever gets away from it."

It was cool and damp in the hollow, but the coffee was hot and tasted good. Suddenly he felt exhilarated. All right, so they were in a fight, that Foley outfit weren't getting any virgins if it was fight they wanted. He'd been through the mill and, as for Child, that breed was as tough as they came. He'd been around and over the country, and he'd be in there fighting when that bunch of flatland punchers were hunting themselves a hole.

Firelight danced with the shadows among the slender trunks of aspen. The leaves pattered daintily in the brief wind, and Radigan huddled his second cup of coffee in his hands and thought about what was coming, but when he thought of that he thought of Angelina Foley. What was the relationship there? Foster brother? Or something more? And why had they come here?

True, she had a claim on this land, even if one that would hold water in no court, anywhere. But people who are doing well do not often leave the place where they are. She had an outfit of fighting men, and a foreman who was by all the signs a competent man, if a hard one. So then, why would they leave? An outfit with as many cattle as they had was in no trouble... unless they themselves had been driven off their range, or had other trouble.

That might stand some looking into. But none of this need have happened if Deputy Sheriff Flynn had taken a strong stand at the beginning, but now that it had begun there was no telling when it would end. Many such a fight went on for years: like that Sutton-Taylor fight, in Texas; it was not over even now.

When he had carefully put out their fire and smothered any coals remaining he did what could be done to wipe out any evidence of it, placing an old branch over the spot and holding up a handful of leaves to let them fall as they would over the ground below. It would stand no careful check by a tracker, but to the casual eye, if they came this way, it would offer nothing. Mounting up they rode on, pointing toward the dark bulk of Nacimiento Peak. They made camp just after daylight at the fork of Clear Creek back of Eureka Mesa.

They had ridden nearly twenty miles describing a rough half-circle around the ranch area. At their camp they were a mere eight miles from the R-Bar ranch, but the trail they had left would be difficult to follow. For several miles they had ridden across bare rock, and Radigan had used several tricks, such as doubling back on their own trail, following creek beds and the like, and twice he had them separate and make separate trails, later meeting at a chosen rendezvous up ahead.

Their camp was in a rocky gorge where water had hollowed caves from the canyon walls and then had cut lower into the rock leaving the cave levels well above any possible water. In one of these caves, screened by bushes and trees, they made their camp.

"You think they'll trail us? Or just settle down and enjoy themselves?"

"They won't enjoy themselves because we're going back. We're going to see what we can do to make them want to be someplace else."

Radigan got up and took his rifle. "I'll take first watch, John. And I'm going to scout around a mite."

It was growing light. Radigan took his Winchester and walked down through the rocks to the mouth of the gorge. Ordinarily he would not have stopped in such a place, but the canyon looked like a good hideout, and there was a chance that before the night was over they would need the shelter the cave afforded.

There was also an abundance of driftwood for fuel. And small chance of the place being found. The brush growing before the water-hollowed cave screened it so there could be no reflection on the opposite wall of the canyon. Once away from the cave, it could scarcely be seen. What about up the canyon? He glanced up thoughtfully, but took a way down the canyon to see how much of the country could be seen.

The ranch was about eight miles due south and some of his cattle were not far from here on the Penas Negras. In this area he knew every bit of the country south, and much of it to the east. He remembered again some of the stories he had heard of those canyons to the north. There were outlaws there, and renegade Indians, bronco Utes mostly.

How long would they be stalled before they realized the house was empty? Had they discovered it yet?

He walked down to the mouth of the canyon which ended in a great jumble of boulders, many of them bigger than houses, solid chunks of rock tumbled together in grotesque shapes. And there were cliffs and a thick pine forest.

With his field glass he searched the terrain to the south, studying it with extreme care from the greatest distance to the closest. He picked up several deer, and once a black bear, but nothing human. The view to the west was good, but there, too, he could see nothing.

They would rest for a few hours, and he would make some plans. Despite their long ride they were again within striking distance of the ranch, and he had no intention of allowing the Foley outfit to get settled on the place. Fortunately, the horses he had on pasture were not far from here, held in a small valley that served as a corral with its sheer walls, plentiful grass and water. There were twenty-two head of horses there, most of them wild horses Radigan had himself broken to the saddle. Throughout the early part of the day they loafed and slept, and meanwhile Radigan did some serious thinking. He was a tenacious thinker, who wrestled with an idea until every detail was worked out, and now he realized that with the winter staring them in the face the first thing they needed was a base of operations that was warm, comfortable, and hidden from discovery.

Moreover, he had a few moves to make to render his own position secure. He anticipated no assistance from Flynn, nor would there be any forthcoming from the authorities in Santa Fe, although they would appreciate that right was on his side. But he intended to appeal to both, and to get his case on record. These steps were merely to secure his own position from attack by the law; the counterattacks he would make on his own. He neither expected nor wanted the help of the law.

He finally dropped off to sleep and awakened suddenly to find the canyon filling with shadows. The fire crackled and there was a pleasant aroma of coffee. Gretchen sat by the fire watching him. John Child was still asleep.

Radigan sat up and scratched his head. "Have you slept at all?"

"I'll sleep later. Everything is all right. I took a walk around down the canyon, but there was nothing in sight."

"You'll do to ride the river with," he said. "Did you learn that in a convent?"

"I learned that from Uncle John," she said, indicating Child. "He's as careful as you."

"It's a way of life. And there's times when it is the only way if you want to live." He rolled a smoke and lighted it with a twig from the fire. It was going to be a cold night. "John told me the Indians wiped out your family."

"I remember so little . . . we seemed forever coming west that we lost track of time. At least I did. Sometimes I thought the rumble of wagon wheels was the only sound in the world, that and the wind; there was always the wind in the grass.

"There was my father and mother, and I believe there was an uncle . . . it's so hard to remember. I had gone to the creek after some water with my father, and suddenly we heard shooting and yelling. Oh, I was frightened! Father made me hide in some willows and then he went to see what was happening, and I waited a long time and then went to find him and the Indians saw me."

"They treat you all right?"

"Oh, yes! They were excited about my yellow hair, and they were kind. But they smelled so funny, and I tried not to cry. After that they made me work but they were nice to me and the Indian who found me treated me like his own child."

Radigan walked out into the canyon and, catching a deadfall, dragged it to within easy reach of the cave mouth. It would provide fuel for the night. He walked up the canyon and gathered several large chunks and brought them back to the fire. The rim of

San Pedro Mountain was crested with gold from the setting sun, and a deep rose lay along the flank of Nacimiento Peak. The sky was clear.

When he had saddled up he returned to the cave and accepted a cup of coffee. "No time to waste," he said. "I want to get started before the light gocs."

"Be careful."

"That I'll be."

He went out to his horse and slid his rifle into the saddle scabbard. Gretchen had followed him out. "Tom—be careful."

A lost ray of sunshine caught her golden hair in a web of gold light.

"Sure," he said, and reining the horse around he cantered down the canyon.

An hour later he was seated on the side of a rugged peak something over a mile from the ranch, studying it with his field glasses. The cattle were standing about, and a horse was tied at the corral. After a moment he saw a man come from the house with a rifle. There was no other movement.

Then when some of the cattle moved he saw the faint flicker of a campfire at the base of the promontory. Several dark figures moved about. Some of the cattle had strayed up almost as far as his own position and he studied them thoughtfully. If a stampede started . . . it was just a thought.

Darkness came suddenly and he came down off the slope and rode down among the cattle. Drifting back and forth across the valley, which was narrow, he started the cattle moving south. He worked slowly and with care, and a cold north wind helped. The cattle turned their tails to the wind and drifted. By the time he was a quarter of a mile from the fire he had at least two hundred head moving south. Suddenly he drew his pistol. For an instant it lay across the pommel of his saddle as he watched the dark figures of the plodding cattle, and then he fired and at the same time let go with a wild Texas yell and spurred his horse into the cattle. They broke and ran with two more shots and his wild yells to urge them on.

More than four hundred head were between his own group and the fire, and they started with a lunge.

There was a wild yell and a shot from the fire and then it was blotted out by a surge of bodies. The stampeding cattle swept over and beyond the fire and went charging off down the canyon. From the house there was a shout and the slam of a door, and then a pound of hoofs. Tom Radigan turned his gelding and walked it across the valley and lost himself against the blackness of the trees.

Skirting the marsh, Radigan found the Cebolla Trail and followed it over the mesa to the cluster of houses that marked the village.

At a house on the edge of town he drew up amid the yapping of dogs and when the house door opened he said, "Pedro, it is Radigan."

The door closed and he heard the pad of bare feet coming toward him. "What is it I can do, señor?"

"That black horse! I'll leave mine here."

"Come!"

Pedro led the way to the corral and roped the black. When the saddle was shifted, Radigan said, "Better hide my horse. These are not good men."

"Do you need help, Señor Tom?"

"No, no help."

"There are men. At Loma Coyote there are men. Good men for the fight. If you wish it I will ride there and they will come to you."

"No, not yet."

He rode south and camped that morning at a spot above San Ysidro. When he had slept an hour the sun was up and he saddled up again and rode down into the town.

Downey was sweeping off the boardwalk in front of the stage station. Slowly, he straightened up. "You're in trouble, Tom," he said. "I heard they ran you off."

"Did you?" Radigan tied the black to the hitching rail and straightened. He needed a bath and a shave, and a good meal. Suddenly he realized how hungry he was. "I left because I didn't want to be pinned down."

Flynn came around the building and stopped when he saw Radigan. The deputy sheriff measured him carefully, and then said, "You leavin' the country?"

"This is my home."

"I'd advise you to leave. You've lost your place, which means there's nothing to keep you here."

"You've made up your mind then?"

"What d' you mean?"

"You've chosen your side, is that it?"

Flynn's face seemed to flatten out and grow hard. "I've told you. You start anything and I'll take you in."

Radigan measured Flynn carefully. "Don't try it, Jim. You've a wife and family. You don't want trouble because you're afraid you'll lose all that. The day you try to take me in, you've lost it."

Jim Flynn's jaw set, and slowly his feet shifted. And then he looked into Radigan's eyes and suddenly everything within him seemed to go still and cold.

Radigan was not bluffing.

"Don't push me, Tom," he said, but even as he spoke there was certainty in him that if he attempted to arrest Radigan he would be killed.

"The day you try to arrest me without cause, Jim," Radigan replied shortly, "that day you'll die. I am in the right here, and it is you who've followed off a pretty red wagon because it's new. I'm going over your head, Jim."

"What's that mean?"

"I've written to the governor, and to the sheriff. I have notified them of the situation here. My certificates of title are registered in Santa Fe, and if you interfere in this, except to run that Foley outfit off, you are an accessory after the fact of a crime."

Jim Flynn suddenly found himself with nothing to say. If Radigan had written to the sheriff and the governor, and if Radigan was in the right, then his own job was not worth a tinker's damn. At the same time he suddenly realized he had a strong distaste for a gun battle with the man who had killed Vin Cable.

At the same time the letter gave him an out and he was quick to accept it. "All right, I'll wait. I'll wait until I hear from the sheriff, and then I'll act, and if it's you I come after, I'll take you."

Tom Radigan made no reply. He knew what had happened to Flynn and he sympathized with him. What was it Sir Francis Bacon had said, "He who hath wife and children hath given hostages to fortune, for they are impediments to great enterprise."

Well, at least they made a man think.

Radigan went inside and accepted the drink that Downey poured for him.

"Breakfast?"

"Sure."

"You killed one of them?"

"I think so."

"You did. They'll be in this morning, Tom. Some of them will be in."

"I'll think of that after breakfast."

He had written no letters, but now he did. He wrote the letters of which he had told Flynn and he wrote one other. To a Ranger captain in Tascosa, and it was an inquiry about the Foley-Thorpe outfit and their cattle.

He was on his second cup of coffee when Flynn pushed through the door. He walked immediately to Radigan's table. "You want to fight the Foley outfit?"

"Are they coming?"

"They sure are, four or five of them."

He nodded briefly. "Thanks, Jim." He had started to get up and then heard the pound of horses' hoofs and looking out the window saw the riders pulled up at the rail—five of them.

"Too late!" Flynn said angrily. "Damn it, you're too late!"

"I wanted some more coffee, anyway," he said, and sat back down.

Flynn turned sharply around. "You can get out the back door! *Quick!*"

"I like it here."

Flynn stared at him, then started to speak. His

mouth opened and then snapped shut and he walked to the bar. "Give me a drink," he said hoarsely.

Radigan picked up the pot and filled his cup. Then he leaned back in his chair and relaxed, watching the door.

Boots sounded on the boardwalk and somebody laughed.

Then the door swung wide.

CHAPTER 4

THE THREE COWHANDS who entered first were strangers to him, but the last two were Barbeau and Bitner.

They bellied up to the bar laughing and talking loudly, and obviously unaware of his presence. Whatever else the death of one of their number had done, it had not depressed them to any appreciable extent. Radigan made no move, remaining at the table, and watching them.

His trip into San Ysidro had been necessary. He wanted a final understanding with Flynn, and that unavailing, to write letters to the governor and to the county sheriff. Whatever was to come his own position must be legally secure. He anticipated no help as a result of the letters, but they did officially notify the authorities of what was transpiring and that no help was forthcoming from Flynn. After that it would be up to him, but they would have been notified of the situation and that he must take steps to preserve his property.

Flynn remained at the bar, but the cowhands appeared not to notice him. Barbeau was regaining some of his old truculence, and Bitner was, as always, a silent, morose man; but, Radigan guessed, far more dangerous than Barbeau.

Where Radigan sat the room was in partial

shadow, and from the bar his face would not be readily visible. Even as he considered that, one of the cowhands glanced his way, looked off, then taken by something threatening in the silent figure at the table, he looked back. After a moment he whispered to the man next to him, and they all looked around. The cheerful conversation at the bar was suddenly stilled. Flynn straightened up and turned slightly toward them, and Bitner's attention was suddenly on Flynn.

"Where d' you stand?" Bitner's tone was casual.

"I'm the law. There'll be no trouble here."

Barbeau laughed.

Tom Radigan had not moved. Now he slowly took up the makings that lay on the table near his coffee cup and began to roll a smoke. He was waiting to see what Flynn was going to do, but if trouble came, he knew he was going to kill Bitner first... Bitner was the most dangerous of the lot, but the three strange punchers all looked to be tough, confident men.

Flynn persisted. "You boys have your drinks, then move along. You start any trouble in town and I'll come for you."

"He killed a man of ours."

"Maybe, but you heard what I said."

"And it don't make a bit of difference," Barbeau declared. "You can walk out of here, Sheriff, or you can keep out of it. Don't make us no difference."

"I'm staying. You start trouble and you'll go to jail."

"You'll take us?" Barbeau scoffed.

"I'll take you," Flynn replied. "Now you, Barbeau, you want to make a fight of it?"

Barbeau hesitated. He was a fair hand with a gun,

but Flynn had not become a deputy sheriff for nothing, and he was not at all sure he wanted to gamble. Moreover, they had orders to stay out of trouble in town.

Flynn walked in on Barbeau. "I've told you, Barbeau. Have a drink if you want it and get out of town, but you'll start nothing here."

Barbeau hesitated and Bitner spoke up. "Let it go, Barb. Our time will come."

Shrugging, Barbeau turned toward the bar and Downey filled his glass. Radigan had been watching Downey with interest. His right hand had remained below the edge of the bar, and it was Radigan's hunch the shotgun was there. Radigan picked up the pot and filled his cup.

He was in a dangerous position. Outside of town he would be fair game. Flynn, despite the fact that he was deputy sheriff of the county, had practically said as much. He would keep the peace here, but outside of town a man would have to fight his own battles.

Yet the black horse bore no brand they knew, and they might suspect his horse was stabled elsewhere. Radigan had a hunch they would go outside, check both ways out of town, and wait for him, and common sense told him he had no reason to buck the kind of a deck they would stack against him. He pondered the question while he waited.

Downey came around the bar. "More coffee, Tom?"

"Please."

They would be expecting him north of town, on the route back toward the ranch, yet they would have a man or men at the trail that ran southwest out of town, too. There was a point of rocks that came down to the trail a bit over a mile out of town, but just this side of that point a dim trail, scarcely visible anymore, left the main road and went up through the rocks and cut back, climbing higher and higher toward Pajarito Peak, but well this side of the peak there was a break in the long ridge that divided that trail from the valley where San Ysidro lay.

If he could get out of town—if he could get to that trail—and if they let him leave town, he'd have a chance, because the logical waiting point was at the point of rocks.

He finished his cigarette and drank the remaining coffee, and then the men walked out of the saloon, and he was alone. "Thanks, Jim," he said.

"Don't thank me. I just don't want any trouble."

"All right."

Radigan got up and walked to the bar and paid Downey, who dropped the money into the cash drawer without glancing at it. "Watch yourself, Tom. They'll be waiting."

Radigan glanced out the window. Their horses were gone, but there was a man loitering across the street and up a short distance.

Radigan grinned. "God have pity on the poor sailors on such a night as this!"

Downey said, "You'll do, Tom—only those boys want you."

"Pack me a bait of grub, will you? I may be in the hills a couple of days."

"That girl didn't get hurt, did she?" Downey asked.

"No. Lot of iron in that girl, Pat. She'll be around when the chips are cashed in."

He shrugged into his coat while Downey put the last of the bundle together. Radigan was thinking of all the buildings down the street. There were three on the right side of the road, three on the left, and scattered houses back of that, lanes, barnyards, stables. The Hansen house was on the left but back from the road, and the idea came to him suddenly.

"See you," he walked out the door and closed it carefully behind him. He crossed the walk as if going away from the saloon, then turned and stepped quickly into the saddle on the black horse, swung abruptly around the saloon and behind it.

The action was swift and unexpected. The watcher across the street was caught flat-footed, but instantly he dashed across the street. Before he could round the saloon, Radigan rode from behind it and was across the street and behind a building there. He rode down into the wash, came up through the trees, walking the black in soft sand to make no noise. And then he rode directly for the Hansen place.

It was a big, old adobe with an upstairs gallery and it stood among some cottonwoods with corrals and a barn behind it. The sun was high, and Radigan walked the black along the trail, knowing the horse was unfamiliar and gambling nobody was apt to be there who would know him. He walked the horse past the house and tied in among some brush under the cottonwoods beyond the house.

From inside the house he heard a pleasant soprano voice singing an old love song. He listened for a moment, then rapped on the door. A breeze stirred the cottonwoods and they chafed their leaves with soft whispering. The singing stopped and he heard footsteps within. He shifted his weight and the floorboards creaked slightly, and the door swung open.

Angelina Foley was quite obviously astonished. He removed his hat. "How do you do, Miss Gelina? Are you receiving callers?"

Momentarily she hesitated, then she stepped back. "Come in. You startled me."

"Some of your men seemed to be in a fighting mood," he commented casually, "and I thought I'd let them cool off a bit." He smiled. "And I thought it might be a good time to get better acquainted."

"You're assuming that I wish to know you better?"

"Don't you?"

"I'm not sure." She motioned to a divan. "You have your nerve, coming here."

"Can you think of a better place?" He relaxed on the divan. From where he sat he could see the trail leading up to the ranch. "If one has to wait, why not where a man can talk to a beautiful girl?"

She waited, and he looked around the house. It was a roomy old place, cool, comfortable and quiet, yet much had been done to change it. There were curtains in the windows today, and a piano—how long since he had seen a piano outside of a barroom?

"You sing very well. Do you play?"

"Of course."

"Will you?"

"Mr. Radigan, if you have any business with me, please state it. I have no intention of playing for you, and I think it impudent of you to suggest it."

"It is all too rare when we hear music out here,"

he replied, his manner reflecting no reaction to her evident impatience. "Especially old Italian folk songs."

"You know that song?" Her surprise was evident.

"We come from many places," he replied. "You'll find among Western men some who know many things beside cows and range conditions." He paused. "Miss Gelina, I'm curious. Why did you come here?"

"Because of the land I own," she replied coldly. "What other reason could there be?"

He shrugged, turning his hat in his hand. "I was wondering. Usually folks who have a good working ranch and a herd the size of yours don't leave the place where they are. I'm wondering why you left, and why you work a bunch of hands who handle guns better than they do cows."

Angelina Foley glanced toward the door. She was alone here, with only the Mexican woman cook for company, but she was thinking rapidly, trying to discover some method of attracting some of her hands back to this ranch. Radigan had guessed shrewdly that this would be the last place they would think of looking, and moreover, every remark he made gave greater reason for worry. This was no ordinary cowhand or cattleman.

"I wrote to the governor," he said.

She stiffened. "You *what*?"

"I wrote to the governor," he repeated. "They know me in Santa Fe, and I wanted them to know what was happening here."

She was frightened, but she knew at once that they were in real trouble. This was the last thing they had expected. When they prepared to drive west out of

Texas, Harvey had assured her there would be no trouble as they not only had claim to the land to which they were going but the man squatted on it would be eliminated before they arrived. She had suspected for some time that Harvey had some further idea in the back of his head, some idea for going to the New Mexico ranch. She had not inquired too much about that.

The move was essential. Her father had managed the ranch poorly, had spent too much money, and had become involved in hopeless quarrels. It was due to her own quick action and positive thinking as much as to Harvey that they had abandoned the hopeless fight and moved to New Mexico. The trail they had left behind them was not a pretty one, but due to Ross Wall they had brought the herd safely across the long, dry drive and had left behind all pursuers—left them dead.

Now, if an inquiry began there would be immediate repercussions from Texas.

Instantly she knew he must not guess her panic, and she saw that somehow she must win him over or he must be killed. Or better yet, made to disappear. If he merely disappeared there would be a period of waiting to see if he reappeared, and by that time they would be settled on the ranch with friends of their own.

"It's too bad there is trouble between us." She got up and walked to the window, and as she spoke her thoughts raced swiftly ahead, searching out a way through all the nooks and crannies of possible solutions. "You're a strong man, Tom."

"Just a cattleman," Tom said as he rose from the divan.

"No, far more than that. I wish we could have met under other circumstances. A girl in my position, who has to run a ranch like a man, doesn't meet many men who are of interest to her."

She was not, she reflected, just talking. Every word was the truth. She turned suddenly and looked at him, seeing for the first time through the implication of her own words, and realizing it was true: this was the man she should have met before this.

He was a handsome man. And without doubt a courageous one. There was nothing of Harvey in him, Harvey who had an ulterior motive for everything, and who was always searching for some way to make money without work.

She crossed the room to him. Over her shoulder he saw that the road was still empty. "Tom, what do you want out of life? I mean, what are you working for?"

"I want to make that ranch pay. You have no idea what a job that is. I mean, you've come here from a Plains state where the problems are tough enough, but you know the answers to them, as I did. Up here one has to learn new answers, new ways. I'm cautious, so I came with few cattle, and I worked particularly hard to keep them alive. By the time I found the answers I'd managed to wet-nurse a small herd through two winters, and by then I could branch out a little."

"Is it that hard?"

"Worse! You're welcome to come and see for yourself if you like." He gestured with a quick dismissing wave of his hand. "Your folks probably think they've won, but we left the ranch because we didn't want to be pinned down, and we aren't worried because we know what will happen this winter. You'll lose that herd, lose everything you've got. Your hands will quit because you have easy money hands, except for Wall, and maybe a few others. Of course," he added, "you might be lucky. We might have a good winter."

His words had the ring of truth and she was worried. The herd was all she had, and if they lost it they would have nothing.

Sensing her doubt, he said, "Have you looked at that valley lately? You've had the cattle on it for several days, and the grass is about gone. You've too many cows for the range you can get."

He was the one they must be rid of, for once he was gone there would be no trouble from John Child or that girl. The girl they could destroy by implication, and Child would probably go down with her, or he could be tracked down and killed.

How to get Radigan? His appeal to the authorities frightened her, for it was the one thing they had never expected and the one thing that could destroy them. Yet if he disappeared, seemed to ride away on his own, then it would be a simple thing. The whole affair would die down and their seizure of the ranch would be an accomplished fact which a visit to Santa Fe by Harvey and herself would cement into finality. Harvey could be polished and ingratiating, and she knew what a beautiful woman could do to most men. With Radigan out of the way.

"Do we have to fight?" she protested. "I mean, do we have to be enemies?"

She came close to him. "Tom, I am sorry, I really am. Can't we end all this? You must understand how

I feel? After all, my father left the land to me, and it is all I have of his."

"I'm sorry."

She looked up at him, making her eyes wide, her lips parted a little. "Tom, please! We mustn't be enemies!"

He looked down at her and suddenly she felt he was laughing at her. He made no move to take her into his arms, although the invitation was there, nor did he move away. He just looked down into her eyes and said quietly, "We need not be enemies. I wish it wasn't that way, so why don't you give up this notion and move away?"

She was furious. Her anger flashed wickedly for an instant, and then she drew back, and smiled quickly, almost sharply at him. "No! I couldn't do that. It—it would be almost a betrayal. Of my father, I mean."

She turned away from him and walked to the window. Glancing past her he saw the road was still empty. Suddenly he was aware that she, too, was watching that road, which meant she was either expecting or hoping for someone.

She knew she must stall, she must find some way to keep him from leaving until someone came. She knew now there was no other way: he must be killed. Either killed here or trailed until he could be killed elsewhere.

There was no doubt in her now, no hesitation. She was startled at that. It had been one thing to agree to the killing of an unknown squatter, quite another to order the slaying of a man she knew and with whom she had talked. Yet there was no desire to wait, to think it out. If she was to own that ranch, Tom Radigan must be killed. It was simple as that.

Her father had been the weak one. He got them into fights but always hesitated, moved too slow, or talked too much. Those were mistakes she did not intend to make. This was her land, and without it she was no one, and she had nothing. With it she could hide the stolen cattle far back in those hard-to-find valleys where Harvey Thorpe said Radigan's cattle were, and if they were trailed here, they could assume utter innocence and there would be no evidence.

Radigan picked up his hat. "I'll be going now." He was growing increasingly nervous. There was no telling what a woman would do, and her men might be coming at any time, and by now they would have given up the search close to town. He might make it to the trail he wanted without being seen.

Desperately she tried to think of something to keep him, but he moved to the door and stepped out onto the porch. As he did so she saw Barbeau, gun in hand, standing by the porch, and she reached out quickly and grabbed Radigan's gun arm with both hands, just as Barbeau's pistol came to bear on him. She grasped his arm with desperate energy and fearful that he would draw a gun, she jerked him off balance just as Barbeau fired.

The bullet smashed into the doorjamb, missing Radigan by inches, and he reached across with his left hand and drew the Colt, flipping it around and firing just as Barbeau got off his second shot.

Barbeau, worried for fear of hitting Angelina, and frightened because of his miss, missed again by an even wider margin. And then Radigan's bullet slammed into him, knocking him sidewise. Jerking free, Radigan sent Angelina staggering and sprang off the porch.

Barbeau, shot through the shoulder, had dropped his gun. He was reaching for it with his left hand when Radigan fired again. He had fired into Barbeau's body, but the bullet hit the heavy buckle at an angle and glanced off, knocking the wind out of Barbeau and tearing a wicked gash in his forearm, and then Radigan was around the house and running for his horse.

A rifle fired from the house and he dove for the brush, falling on his hands as a second bullet clipped brush ahead of him. He rolled over, catching a quick glimpse of Angelina herself standing near the porch working the lever on the Winchester. His roll had put him on hands and feet and he dove forward in a plunging run that crashed him into the brush. Dodging quickly to change his line of travel he reached the black. The horse was frightened and it was a wild minute before he could get a foot into stirrup and swing to the saddle. Behind him another rifle shot cut the brush and he heard running feet. Then the black was running, heading toward the San Ysidro Trail, yet an instant later, when the horse swung up on a slight rise he saw a dozen horsemen fanned out between him and the trail, coming fast.

There was no hope for it. He swung the black on his hind feet and headed east at a dead run.

There was another rifle shot as he swung past the ranch. And dead ahead of him, barring his escape to the northeast, was the gigantic wall of rock that towered up in cliffs fifteen hundred feet high: the cliffs themselves, he knew, were not that high, but it was a climb up to them and hopeless when he got there. There were many convolutions in those cliffs, but he knew there was no way up or through them.

The black was a fast horse and was running all out, but the black was not grain-fed like his own horses and how much it could take he could not begin to guess. Behind him the fanned-out riders were bunching except for a couple who had continued to ride due east, evidently to prevent any attempt at escape to the south, and to eventually cut him off in the east.

Ahead of him a great promontory of the escarpment reached out into the flatlands as if to cut off his escape. If those riders who continued to ride east encountered no ravines they would be riding a trail that would meet that promontory and so cut him off, completely. Past it he seemed to remember the mouth of Hondo Canyon opened wide, offering access to the hills to the north. If he reached that point of rocks first, he might escape, and if he did not, then it was a back-to-the-wall fight until his ammunition gave out and they closed in on him. All he could then hope for was to take some of them with him.

Using his spurs, he raced the black for the point. The wind whipped his face, and his hat blew off and hung to the back of his neck by the chin strap. The black was lathering, but running freely and with no break in its stride. Behind him there were occasional shots, but it would be merest chance if one hit him at this pace.

He did not look back, but his glance went again and again to the riders who were running only a little behind him and on his right. On his left the wall of the mountain closed in nearer and nearer. The black horse ran like a frightened rabbit, ducking and dodging or jumping mesquite clumps, running as if it knew that death ran close behind.

A bullet whipped by so close it frightened him and he jerked his head as if from an angry bee. The point of rock loomed up ahead of him, the black's feet spurned the sand beneath and the cold wind cut through his shirt. Now the riders on his right were angling toward him: within the next few minutes he would know.

And then he did know. They were going to meet him right there. They had to.

It was then he drew his gun. He palmed the Colt and tried a fast shot at the nearest man's horse. He fired three times as rapidly as he could trigger the Colt, and suddenly the horse shied, slowed an instant. It was not a hit, just a disconcertingly close bullet, but the startled horse slowed and the rider following plunged into him, and in that instant of confusion and plunging horses, Radigan went around the point on a dead run.

Hondo Canyon opened wide before him, a mile wide at the mouth but rapidly narrowing into a mere cleft in the rocks. The only trails he knew ended in dead ends at the head of the canyons, but there might be a chance on the left, or western canyon. He ran the black up the canyon, then sighting a split in the wall on his right he put the horse up the steep slope. It plunged desperately and then, nearly to the top, staggered and almost fell. Radigan swung from the saddle and holding the reins scrambled toward the top. Behind him a shot exploded and a bullet clipped a fragment of rock within inches of him. Stung by fragments, the black lunged ahead and they were over the rim.

Sliding his Winchester from the scabbard, Radigan dropped near a fallen log and snapped a quick shot into the plunging horses below. A man screamed and he levered shots into the group as swiftly as he could get off the shots.

A horse went down, kicking and fighting, and the riders scattered for shelter. A bullet from his Winchester kicked sand at the heels of one, knocked another loose from his saddle. The man fell, his boot caught in the stirrup and the horse ran with him, dragging the fallen man by his caught foot.

Crawling back, Radigan got slowly to his feet. Despite the chill he was bathed in sweat and the black was streaked with lather and trembling. Catching up the reins, Radigan walked slowly away under the trees. It was just past noon.

He walked steadily, leading the horse, knowing they would first catch the horse that was dragging the rider, and then they would try to find another way up. They would suspect him of having left, but they would not be sure, and they would be delayed. They might, although he scarcely hoped it would be so, break off the chase for the time. He had hit a man and a horse, perhaps two men. And the dragged man, if still alive, would be in no condition to fight.

It was a good day's work. Three to four of them out of action at least, and a lot of luck.

On his right there was a great ridge of rock shaped like a great ship. Keeping to shelving sheets of rock he left no trail to speak of, and moved steadily along. After a while he mounted up.

This was wild, relatively unknown country to him, although John Child had told him there was a spring up in these mountains called Ojo del Oso. With luck he would find it.

Scarcely a half hour later he did find it. He refilled his canteen there, and watered the black, rubbing him down with a handful of mesquite. He could not see his back trail, and in these rocks there would be no dust plume to indicate pursuit, nonetheless he must act as if there was pursuit. To the north the mountains towered high, and west of him there were steep cliffs and canyons to cut him off. His only route lay to the east or northeast, but by riding northeast he might swing around to the hideout where John Child and Gretchen waited.

Far off, perhaps twenty to twenty-five miles east, was the canyon of the Rio Grande, and the finger canyons of Frijole and Pajarito Creeks pointed the way to the mother river.

North he rode, ever higher and ever rougher the country, and colder the wind. It was a wild and lonely land. Several times he startled deer, and once saw a grizzly. It stood on its hind legs for a better view of him, and watched him from a hundred yards away as he rode by.

He reloaded his six-gun—the first time since he could remember that he had waited so long to load up after firing. It had become an almost automatic reaction, yet back there he had had no time. The afternoon lost itself against the mountains and inquiring shadows crept down from the hidden canyons, and peered at him from under the towering trees. A searching wind found him with its cold fingers, and he patted the black and talked softly to it, and the black twitched a responsive ear to his words.

It was cold, so very cold, and the only way lay up into the still colder regions among the high peaks and across the lonely, wind-swept plateaus where no man rode willingly. He sagged in the saddle, and the black plodded on, all the splendid fire gone from its muscles.

Under a ghostly, lightning-struck pine, he swung down. But he did not stop, walking on, responding to the resentful tug on the bridle by a harder tug. He followed the contour of the hills, working steadily north. A few flakes of snow fell.

Before him the view opened out showing a mighty panorama of rugged mountains and canyons lost in darkness, of forests blasted by lightning and the gray, bleached bones of long dead trees. Under the low gray clouds the scene was weirdly somber and majestic. The higher ridges and peaks vanished in the low clouds and before him the wide shelf upon which he rode stretched out, bare and unpromising.

From behind his saddle he took his sheepskin coat and shrugged into it. Fortunately it was split high in the back so he could wear it while riding: only he did not ride now, but strode out at a fast pace, heading along the vast shoulder of the mountain. On his right a canyon dropped away, probably hundreds of feet to a stream at the bottom, but he walked on, looking ahead for some place that promised a camp for the night.

Darkness crept out from the icy peaks and night

fell. Still he stumbled on, the horse plodding along behind him, and when he came at last to a place for camping, it was only a corner among the rocks and trees but it offered shelter from the wind.

In a V where two huge boulders came together he built his fire, and facing it he built a lean-to of evergreen boughs where the faces of the rocks would reflect the heat of the fire into the shelter. By weaving boughs among the living boughs of the trees he made a crude shelter for the black horse, and some of the heat would reach it there. Of deadwood there was more than sufficient, and he made a good fire to warm the rocks, then carried his saddle and gear into the lean-to.

With a handful of evergreen needles he rubbed down the black horse and gathered snow to melt for coffee, preferring to keep what water he had in the canteen. It was very cold. He unwrapped the food packed for him by Downey at the saloon, and then hung a feedbag on the black with a little corn he had carried behind the saddle.

He had a groundsheet and two blankets which he unrolled on a bed made of boughs. He sat within the lean-to and ate, drinking his coffee and wondering about John Child and Gretchen. Had they been discovered? It was unlikely.

Snow began to fall. Not the intermittent flakes but fine, icy particles, and it did not stop but continued. A wolf howled somewhere out in the forest and the black horse shifted his feet uneasily. Radigan spoke to the horse and stretched his hands toward the eager flames. From time to time he added a stick, and it was very cold, the wind coming around the boulders and plucking at the fire, stirring it with irritable fingers.

The icy snow rattled on the rocks and the dried branches or fell whispering into the evergreens. He was high on the mountainside, perhaps 8,500 feet. Finally he drank another cup of coffee laced with whisky and then crawled into the bed.

Twice during the night he crawled out, shivering with cold, to replenish the fire, and the last time it was so cold and so near to dawn that he stayed up, huddling over the fire. He brought the black in closer and built up the fire. Outside a heavy blanket of snow lay over everything, and it would have covered any trail he might have left. Up to this point, anyway. If they came this far they were going to have a cinch following him.

Day came reluctantly, and Radigan tugged on his boots again and stirred about, making coffee and warming water for the horse. He ate some cold beef and drank scalding coffee, and finally, after warming the blanket over the fire, he saddled up and packed his bed.

In the cold, white light of early dawn he moved out into a world where everything had changed during the night. The black was a good mountain horse and he walked delicately, not trusting the snow. He rode what he estimated to be six miles, riding north but pushed farther east by the terrain, and suddenly he came out of the trees and drew up looking over a magnificent bowl among the hills.

It was obviously what remained of a magnificent and gigantic volcanic crater. The floor of the valley was at least five hundred feet below the point where he sat his horse, and was surrounded by clumps of spruce and aspen that gave way to a thick growth of these trees mingled with stands of pine. In the summer this would be an enormous meadow, and looking away into the distance he could see it was at least twenty miles in length, or close to it. Within the crater there must be more than one hundred and fifty square miles of territory.

The black horse seemed as surprised as he himself, pricking its ears at the vast valley that lay before them. This was without doubt the same valley of which the Indians had told stories long ago.

Skirting the valley he found a way down to the bottom, and when he reached it he moved out across the snow. Near the cliffs the snow had drifted in spots, but for the most part the vast plain was but thinly covered. He scuffed the snow away and found the grass below was thick, cured on the stem, and good hay. While he looked around the black began to crop the brown grass.

Suddenly he realized this was the place he had been seeking. Here he could graze a lot of cattle, and this rich grass would provide better feed than any of the lower prairies. Undoubtedly his own ranch lay only a few miles to the westward, and within an easy drive of this place. There was a small stream that ran through the bottom of the valley, so water was no problem. He knew suddenly that this was where he would drift his own cattle if the fight became worse.

At the valley where their remuda was corralled he roped a fresh horse. John Child had been there since the snow, and Radigan trailed him back to their hideout through the darkening hours of the third day. He was within a short distance of the place when he heard a shell jacked into a chamber and he froze in place. "It's all right!" he called. "It's me!"

"I see you." It was Coker. He stepped down into the trail, a wide grin on his face. "Come on up. You got comp'ny."

For an instant he felt like reining around and running for it, but there wasn't a chance. He was fairly caught between the walls of the canyon, plain to see against the new-fallen snow, and he knew that Coker would like nothing better than an excuse to kill him.

His hands were numb with cold or he might have tried for a gun. He put his right hand under his armpit to warm the fingers. There was yet time. And there was a chance. As long as he had a gun, there was a chance.

They were at the cave. He recognized the bulky body of Ross Wall, and a squat puncher named Gorman who had been in the saloon at San Ysidro when Flynn had backed them down. He was fairly caught.

John Child was there, seated against a wall, his hands tied behind him. And Gretchen was there, but her hands were untied and she was cooking.

"I was hopin' you wouldn't come back," Child commented.

"Cold out there." He swung down stiffly. "We've had a snow."

"Radigan," Ross Wall was brusque. "You've got feed stacked somewhere. We want to know where."

"Sorry."

Coker grinned at him. "Ross, let me have him. I can get it from him."

Radigan merely glanced at him. "You couldn't get

anything from me," he said. "I wouldn't give you the time of day."

Wall interrupted Coker's reply with an impatient gesture. "You've had it, Radigan. I can't do a thing for you. Maybe if you talk I can get these others off, but I'll tell you right now that we have orders to lose your body in one of those canyons north of here where nobody will find it."

"We had a visitor," Child commented.

"Shut up!" Coker turned sharply around.

Gretchen sensed it was something Radigan should know. She looked up from the fire. "He said he'd be back," she said.

Coker turned on her angrily. "You, too! Shut your mouth!"

Ross Wall glanced at Coker. "That'll do," he said. "You'll not talk to a lady that way."

"She's no lady," Coker retorted. "She's—!"

Gretchen grabbed a stick from the fire and swung the burning end at Coker's face. He sprang back, but not fast enough and the stick caught him across the mouth. He staggered off balance and fell, crying out with pain and grasping his burned lips.

Gretchen stood up. "I'll cook for you," she said to Wall, "because you're hungry men, but I won't take any slander from such as he is."

Coker was moaning and holding his mouth. Wall merely glanced at him. "Go back to your cooking," he said.

She went back to the fire, and moved a pot more firmly into position on some stones in the fire. Then she said, "The man was Loren Pike. He said he and Charlie Cade were at Loma Coyote."

Wall's eyes showed his sudden attention. "Did you say Loren Pike? The Ranger?"

"He was a Ranger," Radigan explained. "About the time I was. He left the outfit to settle a personal quarrel."

"What are they doing here?"

"Friends of mine. I told you I was a Ranger, too. Fact is, I wrote to the Rangers in Tascosa just the other day."

Radigan could see the idea did not please Ross Wall. The foreman walked to the mouth of the cave where Radigan's horse still stood. For several minutes he stood there, staring down the darkening canyon, and Radigan watched him while Coker moaned and swore in a corner of the cave, holding his mouth with both hands.

Wall knew very well that many of the Rangers stuck together through thick and thin, and often after they had left the service they returned to help one another, and the thought gave him no pleasure. More than that, Loren Pike was a known man, a good man with a gun who had been active in running down cattle thieves. Moreover, he had been cousin to the Bannings with whom the Foley outfit had been feuding. Had he followed them?

"Who's Cade?" he asked.

"Friend of mine. We rode together, a year or two. If he don't find me here he's going to be mighty unhappy."

"What are two men?" It was the stocky puncher who spoke.

"Either one of them would take your pelt and tack

it on the barn door without raising a sweat," Radigan told him.

The more Ross Wall considered the situation the less he liked it. Handling Angelina Foley was bad enough, but after that slick-talking Harvey Thorpe came home there was no holding her, and the outfit had gone from one trouble to another. He knew little about her claim to the present land except that her father had always talked of a ranch he owned in New Mexico.

The snow would make feed a real problem, and unless they found the feed that Radigan had stacked against the bad months they were going to lose a lot of cattle. Matter of fact, they were going to lose some anyway. Now this.

If those men were coming back they would have to be killed too, for they would ask questions that must not be asked. And they would know too much. Maybe they already knew.

"They know about this fight?" he asked Child.

"What d' you suppose we talked about?"

He might have guessed it. Still, it might be some time before they came back, and he had heard of Loma Coyote. Suppose he detached four or five men to ride up there and ambush the two? But where would it end? When a man tried to solve his problems with a killing it always led to still another. He swore softly, looking out at the gathering night, knowing there would have to be a showdown with Thorpe, and not relishing the thought.

Wall had his orders. Find Tom Radigan and get rid of him. Get rid of him so he could never be found again. And that was all very well, but with such men as Pike and Cade involved, the disappearance of Radigan might easily begin another blood feud. How could a man make a ranch pay under such circumstances? He stared downcanyon gloomily. For that matter, how could anyone make a ranch pay in this country? Radigan said he knew how, but Ross Wall had heard men talk big before.

Gretchen took the first plate of food to Radigan, and the second to John Child, placing it on the ground and then coolly untying his hands.

Child chafed his hands and wrists, glancing over at Radigan who sat quietly. The squat puncher was watching them with a rifle across his knees. Ross Wall turned and walked back into the cave, accepting his food with a quiet thanks, and staring at it somberly before he started to eat.

Radigan had been disarmed, but his weapons lay across from him within easy reach, almost as if he were being tempted to try for them. From Coker's earlier attitude and the manner of the others now, Radigan was sure he was marked for death and, in fact, could see no other alternative for the Foley outfit. He moved with great care, always keeping his hands in view, and while he ate he was thinking, working around the herd of his thoughts trying to get a rope on the one he needed . . . a way out.

So far they had come off second best in the fighting, but that was pure unadulterated luck, as he would have been the first to admit. He had thrown his shots at the horses with only hope that they would land and that they had done what he hoped had been the purest chance.

Flynn had kept him out of a bad spot in San

Ysidro, and his flight into the mountains and the subsequent snow had helped to get him away from the fight scot-free. He was under no illusions as to the outcome of such a fight if everything else went as it usually did.

A cold wind was blowing from the north. "This wind holds, you'll have a drift, your cattle will drift clean out of the country."

Wall shot him a sullen glance and made no reply. Trust a cattleman to be thinking of that.

Radigan finished his meal, accepted more coffee, and began to roll a smoke. He wanted to keep his hands free, and wanted Child's free, so he tried to keep Wall thinking, worrying. "Look, Ross," he said conversationally, "why not let the herd drift? Why don't you boys follow it out of the country? This is a fight you can't win, and if you kill us, how will you find the feed? Believe me, you can look for a long time, and unless you're mighty lucky, you'd not find it, and you know as well as I do that you're working on a mighty slim margin."

He paused and, lifting the cigarette to his lips, shot a glance at the nearest gun, and knew it was too far. But the cowhand named Coker was close. He was not eating, but had rubbed some grease on his burned and swollen lips. If he could drop on his side and grab Coker, reaching around him for his gun, he might manage it. But the chance was too great.

"Take it from me, Loren Pike and Charlie Cade will be back, and Cade owes a lot to me. So does Pike. They won't come riding into a trap, either. They'll come riding down here expecting a full-scale war, and they'll be loaded for bear.

"Why, Ross, up there at Loma Coyote there's eight or ten of the toughest fighting men in the country, and all they need to know is there's some cattle down here they can have for the taking, and they'll trail along with Loren Pike.

"You ever hear of Adam Stark? He's the best rifle shot in this part of the country. Out of Tennessee by way of Texas, and a good man anywhere. Well, Adam is up there at Loma Coyote, and he's been itching to get into this fight. Ask John Child there—he's a close friend of John's—and he's been wanting to come down. Figure it out for yourself. These boys know the terrain, they know cattle, and you can just bet that whatever cattle get through the winter will be driven off.

"You know something, Ross? All those brands don't look so good, and I've been wondering how they'd look if a man skinned one of those steers and checked that brand from the back of the hide. I'm wondering what brand would show up."

"Shut up!" Ross Wall turned angrily. "You talk too damn' much!"

"I'll shut him up," Coker said. "You just give me the word, and I'll shut him up!" He mumbled the words through puffed lips. "I'll kill him!"

The fire crackled, and outside the snow fell steadily. No use trying a break now, for a man could be tracked easily unless he had a good enough start for the snow to fill his tracks. There was nothing to do but to wait, and Radigan settled back. He was good at waiting, better than any Indian, as John Child had often said. Well, this was a time to see just how good he was. Moreover, he was beginning to get an idea of how he could handle the situation, just a glimmer of an idea.

Firelight flickered on their faces, gleamed on gun barrels and buckles, and outside the snow fell softly into the cushiony silence. The opening of the overhang was a black wall streaked with the slow fall of snow. Ross Wall stared gloomily into the fire and Radigan had noted the habit before and filed it for future reference. A man who stares into a fire is blind when he looks into the darkness, for a moment at least. And who needed more?

If they hadn't found his feed by now there was small chance they would find it with this snow in the passes. He knew where the snow drifted, and the few routes there were that might be used. During the four years of residence on the ranch he had learned to plan his campaigns against the elements as a good general plans his strategy during a war. It was the price of survival.

Yet sometimes these first falls of snow did not last, but were swept away by the first change in the weather, and such might be the case with this one, and even a brief thaw might open up the passes, even if not for long.

The squat cowpuncher had leaned back against the wall, partly pillowed on his own saddle, and was snoring gently. Coker stared sullenly at Gretchen, and said nothing at all, and there was no light anywhere but the light from the flickering fire. Radigan poked a stick into the coals and watched it ignite, and he had a hunch that Wall had been told to find him and finish him off, and that Wall had no stomach for it. The big foreman was a cattleman, and in fighting he might kill a man, but he was no murderer.

Under the circumstances to attempt an escape could result only in death, and in the close quarters of the cave, a wild bullet might kill anyone. So could a ricochet. Gretchen would be in as great danger as any of them, perhaps more so, considering the cold hatred obvious in Coker.

The snow fell steadily, and Radigan knew if it continued through the night it would be extremely difficult if not impossible to get out of the canyon. And three additional mouths would make great inroads on their food supply.

A flurry of wind blew into the cave mouth and danced the flames. A spark flew near the sack of corn for the horses, and Child reached over and put it out. It was very late.

Ross Wall got up and walked to the cave mouth and looked out, and when he came back his face was lined with worry. "How deep can it get in these canyons?"

"Here?" Radigan shrugged. "In a snow like this, counting for snow drifted by the wind, it might get eight to ten feet deep, and probably much less. But it often gets twenty feet deep in these canyons in the winter. Always danger of slides off the peaks, too."

His body was tired and he leaned back against the wall, yet the fatigue had not spread to his mind and he knew, whatever happened, he must remain alert. Yet if John Child was awake . . . He glanced over at the Indian and indicated by sign language that he must rest. Child nodded and Radigan settled himself more carefully, and as he did so he marked in his mind the position of the guns.

Despite the fire it was cold in the cave for there was no great depth to the overhang, and although the space was partly shielded by trees and undergrowth these were scant protection from the wind. Huddled under his blanket, Radigan slept fitfully, awakening at times to listen to the rising wind, the crackle of the fire, or the breaking of sticks as John Child replenished the flames. Without the necessity for conversation they had accepted the task of keeping the fire going, and nobody had offered any argument against their doing it, yet each understood the reason was not one of being helpful, but merely to offer them a little freedom of movement that might, in time, be utilized.

Ross Wall did not sleep. He sat staring at the flames or got to his feet and paced back and forth. Radigan could appreciate his concern, for downcountry there were nearly three thousand cattle, poorly fed these last few days, and only too ready to drift. Moreover, nobody was with those cattle who felt sufficient responsibility. They might, if sheltered from the wind, remain close against the canyon walls throughout the storm, and they might again begin to drift.

Radigan glanced nearby at the huddled, sleeping form of Gretchen. Only she was not sleeping. She was looking at him from wide blue eyes and, as she looked, she moved something under the covers and he saw the butt of a pistol, momentarily revealed, then hidden away beneath the blanket.

A pistol.

He considered it with care. How Gretchen had

managed to secure it, he could not guess, but it was further evidence that she was thinking all the time. He had to have that gun, but he had to have it only at the right time and the right place. For the time being it was safer with Gretchen, who was less likely to be searched.

Attempting to return to sleep he found it impossible, for now that he was fully awake the cold of the rock floor of the cave was such as to permit no sleep. He threw off the blanket and shrugged into his sheepskin coat. "Get some sleep, John," he advised. "I'll tend the fire."

Coker watched him from under heavy lids. The gunman's lips were in frightful condition, swollen and inflamed with great blisters where the burn had left its mark. He dared not change expression, and occasionally when some involuntary movement caused his face to twitch he gasped with pain.

The fuel supply was growing small, so drawing on his gloves, Radigan walked to the edge of the overhang and stepped out into the snow. He heard sharp movement behind him, and the click of a back-drawn gun hammer but he coolly began breaking branches from one of the deadfalls he had brought near for fuel.

This, he reflected, was one way it might be done. If one man was asleep and he could get the other to turn his back on the cave—it was a chance. Also, he thought, he might make a break for it in the snow, even without a gun. There was a rifle and three pistols at the cache on the mesa back of the ranch, and there was another rifle and a shotgun in the cache near San Antonio Valley. There was food in both places.

That was one way it could be done, but he could not go alone. He trusted Wall to prevent any attack upon Gretchen, but suppose Ross Wall had to leave her alone with Coker and the other man? Coker was filled with a hatred only held in check by Wall's presence.

For the first time he began to think seriously of the problem of escape. Until now he had needed rest, until now he had wanted to learn more of their position, but now he knew the time was drawing near when they must escape. Wall, he was sure, had been told to kill them, and while he might delay, he might just ride off and leave them to Coker. He brought an armful of wood close to the fire, but he did not bring in too much.

It would soon be day, and the snow was still falling. There would be no chance to get the horses, no chance to get food. They must rely upon their chance of getting to the nearest cache, but in this snow a man on snowshoes could move faster than a horse.

Snowshoes.

A man could contrive snowshoes. Long ago, he had been shown how to do it by an Indian. Not snowshoes for fast going, but shoes that would at least keep a man on the surface.

At first they would have to move fast, and that meant they must get out of the canyon they were in. Glancing downcanyon he studied the walls and the trees. The snow here must be at least four feet deep, and in places deeper. Wind flurries whipped snow into the canyon that drifted there and remained.

When the time came to move, it would have to be a quick move. Quick and decisive.

Radigan walked in and seated himself close to the fire. He held his hands out to the fire, but as he moved them out he moved his left hand, palm down, in a slight downward movement, then did the same, only farther out, with his right and repeated with his left. To a casual observer he might only be stretching his arms in a way to draw his sleeves back, but Radigan knew that John Child had caught the Indian sign language for "walk."

A moment later he turned his hand up and drew the sleeve back a little, and managed to hold three fingers alone as he did so.

Child, sitting across the fire, appeared half-asleep. Radigan glanced at Gretchen who was watching him, and as shc caught his eye she nodded slightly, indicating she understood. He had not expected her to know sign language but it was the sort of thing John Child would be apt to teach a youngster, and which a youngster would want to know.

Suddenly Ross Wall got up and walked to the mouth of the overhang. "This ain't going to ease up," he said, "and there's not enough grub to last out a bad storm."

He turned to Radigan. "How far is it to the ranch from here?"

"Might be eight miles, almost due south."

"It's colder, and we've not grub enough to last out the day. We could all die here."

"That's right. And you wait much longer and that snow will be so deep you can't get out. Fact is, you may not make it now."

"Eight miles ain't far," Coker scoffed. "I could walk it on my hands."

Radigan ignored him and addressed his remarks to Wall. "In places this snow will be drifted up to the lower limbs of the trees, sometimes eight feet deep. Believe me, it doesn't take long in this country with no wind to sweep much of it clear."

Not long, he told himself, but still there are places. He was thinking of them now, and knew that if the right break came they would take one of them for the first brief distance, then right into the deep woods and make some snowshoes.

"I'll go," Wall said suddenly. "Mine's the best horse, and I've got a chance to get through."

Coker was staring at Gretchen, a hard satisfaction in his eyes. He would be left in charge. Or he could take charge. After that he would kill Child and Radigan. Radigan could almost see his mind working, and he could tell from the way Wall averted his eyes from them that he was thinking the same thing.

"Something else you boys didn't know about this country that you're going to find out mighty fast," Radigan commented. "Those light cow ponies you use in Texas are no good in heavy snow. It takes a horse with muscle and bone to handle it, the Montana kind of horses."

"We'll make out." Wall gathered his gear, then plunged out into the snow.

When he came back he was leading his horse, and he stood it inside the overhang while he brushed off the snow and put a blanket on, then he saddled up. Radigan watched him critically. Wall did not think of warming the bit, and the horse fought it until Wall finally bridled the horse with the help of Coker.

"You should have warmed that bit," Radigan told them, and Wall turned angrily.

"You talk too damn' much!" he flared. "There's other men handled stock besides you."

"Some people never learn," Radigan replied, grinning.

For a moment he thought Wall would strike him. The big foreman took an angry step forward, and Radigan merely looked up at him, smiling. Wall stared at him for a moment, then turned sharply away.

"You know, Ross," Radigan said, "if we'd worked for the same outfit we'd have gotten along all right."

Wall said nothing nor did he face around, and Radigan said quietly, "I wonder how you'll face yourself after this? I wonder how you'll sleep at night?"

For an instant Wall stopped gathering his gear, standing absolutely still. When Radigan next saw his face it was white, but he did not look at any of them. Merely stepping into the saddle, and then he said, "Coker, you and Gorman stay here. I'll send some grub back up right away, and some of the boys will break trail for you to come out. You take care of the prisoners."

"Sure." Coker was grinning. "I'll take care of them. Harvey told me just how to take care of them."

Without a word Ross Wall rode out into the snow. There was a narrow ledge along the wall that he could ride downcanyon for a short distance, and below the canyon there was some flat ground where the snow would not be so deep. Yet he had gone no more than a hundred yards before he knew he was in trouble.

The horse stepped off the ledge and went belly-deep in the snow, then deeper. Floundering desperately, the gelding fought his way down the canyon to the open ground, jumping and plunging. Ross Wall reined in and looked south, scowling at the rough, broken country, much of it heavily forested, and for the first time he was afraid.

It was cold. In the cave he had not realized how cold. It was very still, yet there was already frost on the horse, and he realized anew that Radigan had been right. His horse was light and fast, an excellent cow horse, but lacked the sheer power for bucking heavy drifts. It was bitterly cold, and the snow still fell. A man could die in this country.

He was not going back. He had no desire to face what was to happen in that cave. Thorpe wanted it to happen, and maybe even Angelina Foley wanted it, but he was no killer, no murderer. As for Coker, he would be in no hurry to send men back. Let the man live with himself a little. It would do him good, and there was food enough for another couple of days for two men, if they were careful.

Suddenly, from behind him he heard a shot. It was faint. It was far away, but it was a gunshot. Coker had wasted no time.

CHAPTER 5

COKER SIMPLY TURNED and fired. But he turned too fast and shot too quick, and his bullet went where Radigan had just been.

For Radigan had been completely fooled. He expected Coker to talk because Coker was that sort of man. It was his pattern to play the big man for a few minutes before he killed, but Coker simply spun around and fired, throwing his bullet fast and considering the turn, with amazing accuracy.

Only the fire was sinking and Radigan had dropped to a squatting position to add fuel, and the bullet cut the air right over his head.

Yet as he spun and fired, Radigan threw himself forward and grabbing the gun that Gretchen thrust at him he rolled completely over and fired.

And missed.

It was point-blank range but he was moving and made the same mistake Coker had made by firing too quickly. But his second shot was faster, and it ripped upward into Coker's throat, ranging upward and outward to emerge just above the gunman's ear.

Coker had been so sure—and he was eager to make Gretchen suffer for his swollen and burned lips—he had turned and fired and then he was dying on his feet with blood gushing from his mouth and a puzzled expression as if he could not comprehend what had happened.

He had automatically fired a second time and the bullet had smashed into the fire, scattering sparks, but then the gun slid from his fingers and he tried to speak, staring at Radigan with dawning horror in his eyes, realizing in that last awful moment that he was dying.

His knees sagged then and he fell face forward with his feet in the snow at the entrance and his head toward the fire, and Radigan turned with his gun ready and saw Gorman stretched out on the floor with blood trickling from a split scalp where Child had clubbed him with a chunk of firewood.

Gretchen was a sickly pale, and she turned quickly from the dead man at the cave mouth and said, "We'll need a hot meal." She paused then and seemed to stiffen herself. "I've got to—"

Radigan caught her as she started to faint and she clung to him an instant, fighting it off. "I'm sorry," she said. "I'll be all right."

Child had picked up a Winchester. "D' you suppose Wall heard those shots?"

"He heard them. But he won't be back."

Child walked to the opening and caught Coker by the foot, dragging him out into the snow where he lay facedown. Then he walked back and began methodically to sort the gear in the cave and pack for a leave-taking.

Radigan indicated Gorman. "Leave him some grub. We'll soon be at the cache, and he's done us no harm."

Radigan went to Coker's body and pulled off the

cartridge belt and shucked the shells from the loops. The gun Gretchen had tossed him had been his own, and now he retrieved his belt and holstered the gun after reloading. He found his Winchester, checked the barrel and the loads, and then took his bowie knife and went to the trees to cut some branches.

He cut four of them, then went to another tree for two more. Each of these was about seven feet long and slender, whiplike. Over the fire he warmed them after stripping away the shorter branches that held the needles. When he had warmed them carefully he took one and working with it carefully he bent the whiplike end around and lashed it to its own base in a rough oval.

With strips of rawhide he made a web back and forth across the oval, and John Child began working on a second shoe. When Gretchen had their food ready, they ate in silence, then returned to their work. It was at this point that Gorman came to.

He opened his eyes and stared up at the hanging roof, then sat up abruptly, catching his head in both hands from a sudden throb of pain. Stupidly, he looked around.

His eyes found the body of Coker, then looked quickly around for Wall, who had left when he was half-asleep. Finally they came to rest on Radigan.

"You start anything and you join your friend out there. Sit tight and we'll leave you grub enough to last a couple of days. There's fuel enough for weeks, and if you leave here, you're crazy."

Gorman nodded to indicate Coker. "I had no use for the man."

"All right." Radigan was brusque. "You stay out

of this and we've no quarrel with you, get into it and you can follow Coker."

Gorman made no reply, but lay down and turned his face to the wall.

It was afternoon before they got away. Radigan took the lead and headed south at a good clip. All he asked the snowshoes was that they see them through to the food cache on the mesa near the ranch.

He set an easy pace. There are things a man learns about the cold, and the first one is never to work up a sweat, for when a sweating man slows down or stops the sweat freezes inside his clothing, forming a thin coating of ice near the skin. After that, unless one finds shelter quickly, it is only a matter of time.

He had also learned not to dress too heavily, but to wear the garments loose so they form a cushion of warm air next to the body. The Eskimos knew these things long ago, and so did the northern Indians, and a man can live long in any kind of country if he will use his common sense and learn what he can.

It was very cold but the air was clear. They were above eight thousand feet, and at this low temperature and in the clear air sounds could be heard for miles. But Radigan knew the time had now come to push the fight if ever they were to push it. The cold was their greatest asset for they understood cold and he doubted if any of the Foley-Thorpe outfit did.

Somewhere below them and to the east Ross Wall would be working his way through the deep snow to the ranch, and by this time he would begin to realize some of the things Radigan had told him. That light horse would not be able to carry a heavy man far in this deep snow, and Wall would be lucky if he was not afoot by another hour, or even by now.

In good weather he could have covered that eight to ten miles in a couple of hours, but now he would have to seek out places where the earth had blown clear of snow, and he might be miles out of his way. If he made it by dark he would be lucky. Radigan said as much.

"If he makes it at all, he'll be lucky," Child said grimly.

They walked on. The going was slow, but after their muscles warmed up they moved more easily, and Radigan paused often to conserve their strength. He knew the country well and kept to high ridges where the travel was easier, always pointing toward the mesa back of the ranch.

The wind picked up and blew cold, whining among the tall pines like lost banshees, or moaning low among the icy brush and around the strange rock formations. The sky became a flat gray, unbroken expanse that told them nothing, and they came down off the ridge into the lower country, into the thick forest, and the wind began to blow harder.

How far had they come? Five, six miles? The days were short and darkness was not far off, and they had been traveling at least three hours.

"We're in for trouble, Tom." John Child was breaking trail and he had stopped abruptly and turned. "She's picking up to blow."

"No use to wear ourselves out," Radigan said. "We'll find a place to dig in."

They started on.

The wind was raw against their faces which grew

stiff from cold, so numb it was difficult to speak, and the wind prevented hearing.

Suddenly John Child turned into the woods again and he stopped at the base of a huge deadfall. Here some great wind or other cause had uprooted a giant spruce and thrown it down with a mass of earth clinging to the root pattern. The roots and earth stood up in a solid wall seven or eight feet in diameter.

Without words, Radigan and Child moved into the forest and were busy with their knives, building a lean-to with the open face toward the root mass. The lean-to was covered with a thick thatching of spruce boughs, and inside a bed was made thick with other boughs. On the snow close to the root mass Radigan laid several heavy chunks of wood side by side to make a bed for the fire, then built a fire whose heat could be reflected by the root mass into the lean-to.

"Couldn't we have gone on?" Gretchen asked. "I mean, it's only a few miles farther."

"We'd still be sleeping in the cold, and by then we'd be more tired. When you travel in the cold, never exhaust yourself. Only exhausted people need freeze, believe me. If all travelers in the snow and cold would think of that, few of them would freeze. Just find some shelter or build some and curl up and sleep it out."

"But if you sleep, won't you freeze?"

"Not unless you're already exhausted. If all the heat inside your body is gone, used up in struggling, then you'll freeze, so just stop in plenty of time. I've slept out many a time when it was forty, fifty below."

The shelter was in a little hollow, and the still-falling snow added to the warmth by covering the spruce boughs with a thick cushion of snow. Wind whipped around the corner of the shelter into the space, so they built an added windbreak of spruce boughs.

They huddled over the fire and drank scalding coffee and chewed on jerked meat. Nobody felt like talking. Outside their shelter the wind whipped snow into the air and by the time they had finished their coffee it was blowing a gale. They had gone into camp none too soon.

ANGELINA FOLEY STOOD by the window of Radigan's ranch house and looked down the trail. She was frightened, and she was cold. But the cold was inside, not outside, for the room was warm and comfortable. The cold inside was the cold of fear, and of a kind of hatred such as she had never dreamed possible of herself.

Harvey Thorpe was at the table behind her, and across from him was Ross Wall. The big foreman had come in only minutes ago, and was sagging over the table, his face drawn with exhaustion. He had been lost most of the night, and his horse was dead—it had collapsed from exhaustion after bucking the deep snow for hours—and it was pure luck that Wall had found a cluster of trees and brush that offered partial shelter where he could build a fire. He had come into the ranch, staggering and falling. How he had lived through the blizzard of the night before he would never know, nor how he had gotten here. Fortunately, he could have been scarcely two miles from the ranch when he found his shelter, but he must have traveled twice the distance from the cave to the ranch to get here.

"He's dead then." Gelina heard the satisfaction in Harvey's voice and for some reason it angered her.

She turned on them. "I'll believe him dead when I see him dead."

"Don't be foolish." Harvey looked up at her, his pale blue eyes almost white in the reflection from the window. "Coker wanted to kill him, and he had his chance."

He got to his feet and crossed to the window. "All you have to do, Ross, is ranch—run the cattle and do the best you can. You'll have four men."

He looked up.

"And the rest?"

"I'll take care of them. You don't see anything. You don't know anything."

Ross turned the idea over in his mind, studying it reluctantly. He needed no blueprints, and he should have guessed, knowing Thorpe as he did, and the crew he had around him.

"It's the wrong time," he said patiently. "It won't work, Harvey."

Thorpe smiled. He was feeling expansive. He tucked his thumbs in his vest pockets. "Ross, you've no imagination. This is one of the most remote ranches in the country, but a ranch where dozens of trails come down from the north, old Indian trails, no longer traveled, trails that can take a man quickly to Denver, Leadville, or a dozen other places.

"I tell you it's perfect! A quick move into one of those towns, or to a mining camp where they're shipping gold, then back here by a roundabout route, using the trails we know. I knew when I saw it this was the place, a legitimate ranch with no close neighbors, easy access to the places where gold is, and easy escape."

"It won't work," Ross insisted. "If what Miss Foley says is true, there's liable to be an investigation, anyway."

Thorpe shrugged. "Believe me, it's a *fait accompli* now, and nobody will be anxious to cause trouble for us. Radigan will have disappeared, and we are quiet, honest ranchers who pay our bills and preserve the peace. We'll keep ourselves clean around here, you see, and nobody will ever be the wiser."

"No."

They both turned at the sound of Angelina's voice, and Thorpe started to speak, but she interrupted.

"No, Harvey, we won't do it."

"You want to go to work in a saloon?" he asked mildly. "Or start a restaurant? That's all that's left."

She was silent. During the days of snow the herd had scattered and drifted, and without doubt many of them were dead, just as Radigan had warned her—he had been so right, and she hated him for it.

She hated him and now she hated Harvey, for now she saw how she had been duped, not that she hadn't agreed to much that had been done, including the theft of cattle and the arrangements for the killing of the supposed squatter on the ranch they believed belonged to them, but it was obvious now that from the first Harvey had had his own plans and had acquiesced in hers only to forward his own, and he had maneuvered her into a position from which no escape seemed possible.

More than once she had suspected Harvey Thorpe's activities during those absent years, and now she was sure. But had she a choice? And after all, might it not work? It was true there was money in the mining camps of Colorado and Nevada, and it was true this was a relatively foolproof hideaway. Anybody approaching could be seen for some distance before arriving at the ranch. Yes, it might work.

And mining the stages and the gold shipments was quicker, easier, and scarcely more risky than ranching.

Radigan was dead. She had hated and feared him but he was dead, and now she felt a curious emptiness, a sense of loss.

It was an unfamiliar feeling, and it disturbed her, for never before had she given much thought to anyone, and in the case of Radigan, she herself had been first to order his death. Yet now that he was dead she felt uncertain and lost, as if something she valued had gone out of her life.

Standing by the window, listening to the talk behind her, she sensed Wall's reluctance, and remembered what she had often said to Harvey, that they must be careful with Ross, for there was a point beyond which he would not go. Now she was aware of that more keenly than ever, yet he said nothing, and if left to handle only the honest work of handling cattle, he might stand aside and remain quiet.

What about her? Somehow in the last few days control had slipped from her fingers, leaving Harvey in command. He had taken the reins so quietly and skillfully that she was confused, for until now she had despised him and been sure he would run her errands for her, and listen to her. Now she knew she was mistaken, and she knew she did not like the thought. Something had to be done!

Yet, why do anything?

Why not sit back and let him engineer the robberies, and when there was enough to warrant it, find one man who would use a gun for her. And then San Francisco, New York, Paris, Vienna—and lots of money.

This way she was free. If they were caught, it was all his action. She had no idea . . . why, she was just ranching . . . Wall was her foreman, and see what they had done. Naturally, she could not control Harvey Thorpe. Yes, it would work, and just that way.

"Ross," she would begin now, "as soon as the storm is over, take two men and try to find an estimate of what we have left. Then we'll start building back."

When Ross Wall had gone she walked to the table and sat down. Harvey rolled his cigar in his teeth and smiled at her. He was feeling good, for now, after a long wait and a lot of submission to her will, he had won. From here on he was in the driver's seat, and he liked the feeling. Moreover, he could see that Angelina was aware of the shift of leadership. "On the fifth of next month," he said, "there is a shipment of gold leaving Leadville for Denver. It will never arrive."

The bullet smashed into the table between them and she heard the tinkle of glass. She stared at the deep furrow plowed into the wood of the table, shocked by its suddenness.

The second bullet shattered the lamp and spilled flame over the room, but Thorpe, acting swiftly, beat out the flames with a blanket before they had time to take hold.

They crouched near the floor in the darkness, frightened and breathing heavily, smelling the smoke, the spilled oil, and the singed wool of the blanket.

"You're so clever," Angelina said wickedly, "so very clever! He's still alive, Harvey, and you've failed again. *Radigan is alive!*"

Harvey Thorpe made no reply. Crouching in the darkness he was suddenly swept by a wave of blind, unreasoning fury. He wanted to leap out into the open, to kill, to cripple, to beat down. But the enemy was beyond him, somewhere out there, elusive in the dark.

"It can't be!" he protested. "It's somebody else! It simply can't be!"

"Your plans, they're so complete, Harvey. So thorough. I don't know how you do it."

"Shut up!" His tone was low and vicious, never before had she heard him sound so murderous. "He's dead, I tell you. It's that breed, or somebody."

Crouched in the darkness, waiting for further shots, she tried to examine her own position clearly. For the first time she realized that she felt active dislike for Harvey Thorpe. That she had not realized this before was due in part to their respective positions, for the ranch had been left to her, the cattle were in her name, everything was hers and she felt in no way obligated to him, while hers was definitely the superior position. Yet this move had been advised and instigated by him. It had seemed a good move, and she had been prepared for it, yet now she could see where she had played into his hands, and with the herd gone, or at least badly hurt by the storm, their positions were reversed. All this she had thought of earlier, but now she was wondering what her next move would be. That Ross Wall was loyal to her and to her alone, she knew. Also that their economic position was very bad: perhaps it would be better, if they eliminated the present danger, to go along with Harvey until he had acquired the gold, then take it for herself. She was sure she would never be suspected of conspiring with him to rob stages, and even if they suspected her, she naturally would have had no demonstrable hand in the robberies.

They waited in the darkness. Harvey sat with his back against the strong wall of the house in the direction from which the fire had come, and now he rolled a smoke in the dark, and lighted up.

"There's nothing he can do," Harvey said, finally. "He can't live out there in the cold forever—look what shape Ross was in—and we can bottle him up and keep him in this country until we can hunt him down."

"What if he knows of those Indian trails you talk of?"

"Mostly, they're snowed in now."

"Won't that affect your plans to get away after the holdups?"

He was silent for several minutes and then he said irritably, "No—we'll make provision for that."

Harvey Thorpe, she recalled, was a man who planned carefully, but did not like objections to his plans. He did not like to admit that he might be in error, and he was also an optimistic planner: he expected the breaks to go his way. This, she remembered having heard, was true of the criminal mind; few of them were ever willing to assess the full weight of the forces against them.

Yet he might win, for a time, at least. Getting to her feet she went into the other room and brought back a blanket which she hung over the window, and after that she lighted a candle taken from a box in the kitchen. With a broom she swept up the broken glass and threw it out, along with the ruined lamp.

When she returned to the living room Harvey had gone. Her thoughts returned to Tom Radigan.

Was he actually dead? The more she thought of that, the less she believed it. He was a shrewd fighter, one who missed few chances, and no matter how strongly Wall might believe him dead, she was unconvinced. Coker was not the man to kill Tom Radigan.

For several days nothing happened. The sun came out and melted the snow in exposed places, and Ross Wall, working tirelessly, checked their losses, and the reports he brought to her were not as bad as she had first expected. True, they had lost several hundred head, but it was mostly the weakest stock that would scarcely last out such a winter in any event. If the bad weather had remained they could have lost the entire herd, but now they had a respite.

The activities of the few riders Harvey had left her were limited by the snow-filled passes and trails blocked with snow. As most of her life had been spent in Western country she knew how difficult it was to search every corner of any range. And in this broken, tumbled and forested country it was virtually impossible. She had known of cowhands who had worked a range for years, and then discovered canyons they had never known to exist. Yet somewhere near Radigan had his own cattle and where they were there was feed.

Harvey was busy with his plans. He had divided the remaining force into three groups of six men each, and each had been given a project. Each group was to strike at the same time and then each was to get out of the country, fast. The country they were to cover was far to the north, but there were at least two ranches where they could get fresh horses, ranches owned by men who were themselves outlaws. Scouting north, they found the trails open as far as they rode, and there was a good chance they could make their strikes and escape before another snow fell.

Wall had been working with only four cowhands, and he came to Gelina as she was saddling for a ride. "I declare, Miss Gelina," he said, "we've covered a sight of country, but not one brand of his stock have we found, nor a single stack of hay."

"Maybe you've worked too close to the place," she suggested. "It must be a valley, or a plateau."

"We've been working west and south," he said, "but we'll try east and north, across the river."

She drew the girth tighter. "Ross, are there any tracks? Of people, I mean."

He hesitated. "I know what you mean," he said, after a moment, "but I've hesitated to say. Bitner found the tracks of the man who shot into the cabin."

She turned to face him, waiting. Yet even before he told her, she knew what was coming.

"It was Radigan, all right. He was on that pinnacle south of the place, although how he got there without being seen beats me. We found his tracks, and I know his tracks, and we backtrailed him to a camp in the hills a couple of miles over west. Mighty nice place, and they had a-plenty to eat."

"They?"

"Yes, ma'am. There was three of them. Radigan, John Child and the girl."

So Coker had failed after all? And what of Gorman?

Suddenly, she realized she was glad. She wanted Radigan alive. Yet was it that? Or was she pleased that Harvey had failed?

"Ross," she said, "you told me you'd found some grazing on a mesa over that way. I want you to cull what is left of the herd, and pick out about five hundred head of the best stock, and I want you to scout around and find the best grass you can, and get them on it."

He looked up at her, and she knew he understood exactly what she was thinking. "We may not be able to save them all," she said, "but I want to save enough to start again—elsewhere."

"All right." He shifted his feet and got out the

makings, beginning to build a smoke. "I take it we're to make no talk about this?"

"No, no talk. Just do it."

"That Flynn," Wall said. "Harvey shouldn't think too little of him. He's no fool."

"Harvey's the fool." It was the first time she had let her feelings be known. "Radigan will beat him. Harvey's too reckless."

"I'll start working those cattle," Wall said. "You can depend on me."

That she could. She watched his broad back as he rode away and wondered who, if anyone else, she could depend on. Yet as he disappeared she was wondering if she would not do best to depend only on herself, and to keep her thoughts to herself. There might be a way to win out of this yet. If Radigan and Harvey destroyed each other, then she would remain in command of the situation.

And then Gorman showed up. He rode in on a gaunted horse, his face drawn and pale, his eyes fever-bright. She was alone on the ranch when he came in and she got the story first. It was brief and to the point, the story of Coker's death, and he added, "I found a deer in the deep snow and killed it. I've been eating meat without salt for the past three or four days, and not much of that."

After he had eaten and drunk coffee he rolled a smoke. "Ma'am, one thing I got to tell you. That Radigan! He wasn't worried. I mean not even a little. I never saw a man take things so easy-like, and I think there is reason for it. I think they knew exactly where they were going, and I think they went to Loma Coyote for help."

Gorman told her then what she had already heard from Ross, about the men at Loma Coyote, about Loren Pike, Charlie Cade and Adam Stark.

TOM RADIGAN ROLLED out of his blankets and stirred the few coals that remained from the night's fire. To these he added some fragments of bark and pitch pine he had split the previous evening. Shivering with cold, he moved swiftly to get the fire going, then dived back under his blankets. Glancing across, he saw Gretchen laughing at him from her bed.

"It's cold!" he said defensively.

"Naturally! But you should have seen yourself, jumping around like a cricket on a hot skillet."

"Tomorrow morning," he said grimly, "you build the fire!"

"All right! But I'll put the materials close by my bed so all I have to do is reach out with one hand and get the fire going."

"Anybody who'd make a fire like that," he said, "would steal sheep."

They waited, watching the hungry flames reach out with red tongues and caress the cold sticks. The fire grew and crackled, warming the cave on the mesa.

Actually, as to distance they were not more than a mile from the ranch itself, and the cave they occupied was one of a series atop the mesa that backed up the ranch, but they were on the northwest side of the mesa and the cave could only be entered from the top, so far as anyone knew. The room they occupied was a small one that was an offshoot of a much larger room, and one that Radigan had prepared long ago.

His own preparations had only followed those of some other man who had preceded him by many years, for he had found an artificially hollowed basin there in the outer cave into which water flowed, and he had found a rusted halberd and part of a breastplate.

Here, sometime in the bygone years, some lost adventurer, perhaps from the army of Coronado, had taken a last refuge from the Indians. And from all the signs here he had lived for some time, years, perhaps. Cut off by the Indians, he must have fled ever farther into the wilds until finally at a last extremity he had found this place, and remained here. Gradually, over the years, he had fitted it out as a combination fortress and home.

Into the rock walls he had cut shelves, and in the outer wall he had cut two windows, or portholes, perhaps, that allowed him a means of covering the approach to the cave. And here he had lived.

Coming upon the place quite by accident, Radigan had immediately seen its value as a haven of refuge if the Utes caused trouble, and had supplied it with utensils, stored food and ammunition, and had, over the years, brought in a plentiful supply of firewood. The smoke hole used by the previous occupant he had improved by a chimney from the crude fireplace, and the smoke issued from the top of the mesa through the roots and then the branches of a gnarled and ancient cedar. These served to dispel the smoke until it was scarcely visible a few yards away.

This was the first and best of the caches of supplies he had planted.

As the fire grew, the cave warmed up and Radigan rolled out of bed and dressed swiftly. Child followed.

"How about that trail north?" Radigan asked suddenly. "Figure a man could get through to Loma Coyote?"

"When do you want me to start?"

"Not you—me." Radigan walked to the deep-seat window and peered out. The approach to the cave was up a winding slide that was just short of being too steep for a horse to make it, and from below gave no hint of a means of access to the mesa's top. The window allowed a view down the slide for much of the distance. "You stay here, and I'll go," Radigan said.

"Those boys know me," Child protested.

"Pike knows me. So does Cade. The others can get acquainted. Anyway, it wouldn't do for me to stay here with Gretchen."

"Afraid?"

"Me?" Radigan stared at her, then grinned. "No, I'm not afraid, but you ought to be. There's no telling what might happen if we were left here alone."

"Nothing would happen," she replied, "unless I wanted it to."

Radigan measured her with cool eyes. "Now maybe that's so, and again maybe it isn't. Don't offer me any challenges."

He went into the outer cave where the horses were and fed them. He glanced at the hay—not much left, but there was a good bait of corn left, and there was a chance they could ride it out on what they had. There was food enough, that was sure. And ammunition enough to wage the Battle of Gettysburg all over again.

He saddled up, and went back for his blanket roll and saddlebags. Gretchen was up and had coffee on, and they sat down around the fire.

"About time somebody had a look at those cattle for San Antonio way," Child suggested. "I could do that."

Radigan looked over at Gretchen. "That means you'd be here alone. Could you make out?"

"I could." She added a slice of beef to his plate. "I would be all right, and if anybody found the place, I'd be able to stand them off."

"The snow's gone from the slide," Child said, "and we can get out without leaving any trail, so you'll be all right. I can't figure any way they could find you up here."

When he had led the horse to the opening of the cave, Radigan walked back to meet Gretchen. He took the last packet of food she gave him and thrust it down in his saddlebags. "You be careful," she warned.

He turned and looked down at her. Somehow, despite the cold and discomfort of their days, she had continued to keep herself attractive, and now looking down into her eyes, he felt her concern. "You do the same," he said, "and don't you go out of the cave unless you go on top of the mesa, and if you do that, keep well back from the sides. And whatever you do, don't cook at night."

"You told me that. At night you can smell the food cooking."

"That's right. A wood fire don't matter so much because it could come from their own fireplace, but the smell of food is going to make them mighty curious."

"I won't."

He stepped into the saddle. Her fingers lingered on his sleeve. "You be careful," she repeated.

He glanced at her again, and was startled to see tears in her eyes. He looked hastily away. Now why would she be crying? There was no accounting for women, and it wasn't as if he was a relative or anything. He walked the horse the last few steps out of the cave and then started down the slide. It was steep, but a horse could make it. At the end he drew up and listened, but there was no sound.

He reached the bottom, glanced each way, then put his horse across the open and into the trees. He was visible for no more than two minutes and, once under cover of the pines, he turned in his saddle and watched John Child across the open. Then they both waited, unmoving, watching all around them for several minutes. Finally, Child said, "I guess we made it."

Radigan nodded. Reluctantly, he turned his horse and headed down through the trees. It was not right to leave a girl alone like that, alone for days on end, and probably scared. Although Gretchen was less afraid than any woman he had ever known . . . not one word of complaint through all of this, and never once when she shirked her work. In cold and snow, everywhere, she had held up her end of the work and the riding.

Where the Vache Creek trail met with the easy way to Valle San Antonio, they parted.

John Child looked twice his size in the heavy buffalo coat. He drew up, the steam from his breath making a plume in the still, cold air. "You be careful, Tom," Child said. "All those boys up there aren't friendly."

"All right."

"You watch especial for Swiss Jack Burns. He's a gunman from over Kansas way. Fancies himself."

"Yeah?" Radigan grinned. "With Loren Pike over there he's probably dead by now." He gathered his reins. "Loren, he never was much given to let be. Fact is, he's a right impatient man, sometimes."

Radigan picked out the broad shoulder of Cerro Jarocito to the north. East of there was a spring and it was only about six miles to that spring. Call it seven to be sure. Then three or four miles over to Coyote Creek and about six or seven miles north to Loma Coyote. It was a good eighteen miles, anyway you looked at it, and cold riding. Five or six hours if he was lucky, and no telling how much if he was not lucky.

He was riding a dapple gray, a good horse that would weigh all of twelve hundred pounds and one who knew how to travel in snow and over icy trails.

The wind was from the north, the sky was slate gray and promising snow, a promise Radigan did not want fulfilled. The trail had not been traveled since the storm, and at places the snow had crusted hard. By noon, when he should have had ten miles behind him he doubted if he had come more than six, for several times he had gone out of his way to skirt drifts of snow, and once had gotten himself tangled in a thick growth of lodgepole, and had to ride more than a mile to get out of it, and two more miles before he found his way back to the trail. He was swearing when he found it and the dapple was agreeing with him, shaking its head with disgust.

He had watered the horse at the spring, and when they reached Coyote Creek the water was frozen over at several places, which made crossing difficult, for the ice was not strong enough to bear the weight. The wind blew cold down the canyon from the north, stiffening Radigan's face and making his hands numb.

It was late dusk when he came down out of the canyon and rode across the bench and into the town.

The narrow street was as still as the day the earth was born, still and cold in the last light of day, with lights showing in the Ramble House, and across the street at the Utah Saloon. The only other light showed at an eating place, a light that showed from beyond a fly-specked window.

Loma Coyote was not much as towns went, and as towns went, Loma Coyote would someday go. It was a stopping place for drifters, a cooling-off place for men wanted by the law and who had found other places too hot for comfort. There was nothing going on at Loma Coyote that anybody could mention, a couple of miners who worked dismal prospect holes in the nearby mountains but did most of their drilling without a single-jack at the walnut bar of the Utah Saloon.

The population rarely exceeded thirty persons, all but three or four of them male. Once the population had leaped overnight to a surprising fifty-six, but that was during a Ute war when prospectors and trappers fled the hills for the doubtful security of Loma Coyote.

They were silent men, accustomed to loneliness, and the combination of too much company and too much of Loma Coyote's own brand of whisky had led to results somewhat less than surprising. By daybreak of the second day the population had decreased to fifty-three, and there were three bodies lying in an empty shed awaiting a spring thaw for burial.

By the sixth morning the population was almost back to normal, for one by one the newcomers decided the Utes were less to be feared than the population and whisky of Loma Coyote.

At the far end of the street was a huge, drafty old structure that could only be a barn, and a lantern hung outside over a scarcely legible sign that indicated the premises were a livery stable.

In the front of the building was a dark little room in which a stove glowed cherry-red but there was no other light.

Out of the gloom a voice called. "Hay a-plenty, an' he'p yourself. Corn if you're a might to, but that'll be four-bits extry."

"That's a lot of money."

"Take it or leave it, but you stick your lunch-hooks into my corn bin without I say and you'll catch yourself a death of cold, because I'll open your belly with a shotgun."

The old man came out of the "office" carrying a sawed-off shotgun, and he held up a lantern, peering at Radigan. "Man can't be too careful, that's what I always say. You're *un*-titled to feed your hoss here, but them as wants corn I figure can pay for corn, because most likely they're running from something."

"I'm not running, old man. I'm looking for a friend of mine. His name is Loren Pike."

"Never heard of him. No memory for names. I figger names don't cut much ice, this here country. Man changes his name 'bout as often as he changes his address, and with most folks hereabout, that's mighty often."

"I own a ranch south of here. The name's Radigan."

He peered at Radigan again. "Maybe you own a ranch, maybe you don't, an' iffen you do, maybe you won't own it long. Not what I hear folks say."

"I own it, and a year from now, ten years from now I'll still own it." Radigan stripped the saddle from the dapple. "And if I have any trouble from you I'll ride back up here and burn this flea cage around your dirty ears."

The old man drew back. "Now what kind of talk is that? Ain't I puttin' your hoss up for you? Didn't I say he'p yourself to corn? Didn't I?" The old man looked at him shrewdly. "Why, you might be the man John Child works for?"

"Child works for me."

"All right. I'll rub your horse down, and I'll give him a bait of corn. And if you're lookin' for any newcomer you might try the Utah or the Ramble. Most folks favor one or the other. On'y my advice to you is to get out of town. Sleep in the haymow if you're a might to, but stay shut of those places. Swiss Jack is full of trouble tonight."

Tom Radigan walked to the door, ducked his head

against the cold wind and walked down to the eating house. He opened the door and stepped in, accompanied by a few blown flakes. A big, hard-faced woman stood behind the counter and shoved coffee over to him. "You can eat," she said, "but if you're lookin' for anything else, it ain't to be had. Not tonight, anyway."

"I want to eat."

She looked at him. "Yes, I reckon you would. Be an hour 'fore you get any notions, I'd say, get the cold out of you then, and you'll be looking for something else. Takes a while for the cold to get out of a man's muscles. I've got three girls here, one sixteen and two nineteen, and I can handle more business than the three of them—and better."

"I'll settle for a thick steak."

"You'll take b'ar meat, an' like it. We ain't had any cow meat around here since the storm. Fellers drive it up from the south of here, but the trails are closed."

Radigan ate in silence while the big woman talked on, apparently neither listening to his occasional comments or caring if he listened to her stream of conversation.

When he had eaten he tossed a dollar on the counter and she handed him three quarters in change. He took a last gulp of scalding coffee and got up, shoving out into the cold. "Don't you come the high and mighty on me!" she called after him. "You'll be back!"

He crossed the street, following a beaten path, to the Utah Saloon.

It was a bar no more than ten feet long and of

hand-hewn planks, and the man behind it was nearly as tall as the bar was long. Two men leaned on the bar and several others sat around at tables. They all looked up when he came in, and, seeing he was a stranger, looked again.

"Whisky," he said, "or whatever you serve by that name."

The big man leaned over the bar. "You don't like our drinkin'? Then you can do without."

"Give it to me. I don't know whether I like it or not."

"You'll decide or you won't get it."

"All right! I like it." Radigan glanced around at the others. They returned his gaze solemnly, and he said, "If these gentlemen like the whisky, I'll buy."

The big bartender turned again. "Now see here, stranger. That's again you've throwed a doubt on my liquor. I don't like it."

"See?" Radigan grinned at the others. "He admits he doesn't like it himself."

The big man interrupted angrily. "I said no such thing. I meant—"

"Trying to weasel out of it," Radigan said. "Well, fill a glass and I'll see if I like it."

The big man stared at him for an instant, then went behind the bar and poured a drink. Nobody else moved. "The offer stands," Radigan invited.

Nobody moved.

"See? Nobody likes it."

He tasted it. For an instant he thought his throat was on fire, then he backed off and looked at the glass. "A barrel of branch water, two plugs of tobacco, a bar of soap to give it a bead, and a couple of ounces of strychnine, and maybe three gallons of alcohol. Color the whole thing with greasewood, and that's about the formula. No wonder nobody drinks it."

He tasted it again. "Started by selling to the Utes, I'll bet. No wonder they went on the warpath so much."

"You're breedin' trouble," the big man warned.

"No I'm not, and I don't want trouble. Now you haul out that jug from under the bar and I'll have a decent drink."

The bartender muttered gloomily and reached under the bar. Immediately the others got up and walked over to join Radigan.

When the glasses were set up and the drinks poured, Radigan said, "I'm Radigan of the R-Bar outfit. You should know the brand. You've eaten R-Bar beef, time to time."

A round-faced man with a sour face looked at the whisky in his glass, then tossed off half of it. "You accusin' us of rustlin'?"

"Stating a fact," Radigan said. "And I'm not the man to begrudge a beef now and again, although why you waste time on my little herd when there's nearly three thousand head in the country that don't belong there."

"You invitin' us?"

"Telling you. What you do is your own affair, only they're no friends of mine. Fact is, I'm right in the middle of a first-class cow war."

The door opened behind them in a gust of cold wind and a slender blond man came in. He was tall, wiry, and his face was narrow with straight brows above long, deep-set eyes. He wore a short sheepskin coat that gave his gun hand plenty of room and a round beaver cap that fitted his narrow skull tightly.

At the same moment there was a clatter of horses' hoofs in the outer street, and Radigan glanced out the window. In the narrow shaft of light he saw Harvey Thorpe, and the men around him were Thorpe's men.

Radigan tossed off his drink and shrugged into his coat. The newcomer was watching him. "I don't know you," he was saying. "I'm Swiss Jack."

Radigan grinned at him. "My name is Will Haftowate. And that's what you'll have to do."

"What?" Swiss Jack looked inquiringly.

"You'll have to wait," Radigan said. "I spoke of a cattle war: that's it, out front."

Swiss Jack glanced over his shoulder. The group of riders were dismounting outside. "That's no cattle war. That's Bob Harvey, and if he wants to see you, I'm going to keep you for him."

"Let him alone." The big bartender had leaned across the bar. "We don't hold anybody for anybody here."

"Now, see here—"

The back door closed softly, and Swiss Jack turned sharply around. Radigan was gone.

CHAPTER 6

THE WIND BLEW cold off the mountain as Radigan paused on the icy back step, listening for sounds within. He could hear the murmur of voices but could distinguish no words, and he waited only until he heard the front door open and then he walked swiftly along the well-beaten path to the outhouse and went past it to the barn.

He paused there, his shadow merging with the heavier shadow alongside the barn wall, and he calculated swiftly. There were only a few buildings in town and all would be searched at once, therefore shelter within any of them was out of the question.

The arrival of Thorpe and his riders was a puzzle, for it was impossible they could have known of his coming here. They might be looking for Pike and Cade, but that was doubtful as thus far they had no argument with them. Hence it was logical to assume they had come here for some other reason and their arrival at this time was purely coincidental. But why would they come here?

And Thorpe had at least a dozen riders with him, and perhaps even more.

Swiss Jack had called him Bob Harvey. Was that a mistake? Or another name Thorpe had used? Radigan recalled his own first impression, that Thorpe was a tough man, one who had been known somewhere before this. But Bob Harvey? He turned the name over in his mind, but it meant nothing to him.

No use standing where he was. He went around the corner of the barn, his feet crunching on the frozen snow under the eaves. Back of the barn, and perhaps thirty yards off was the creek bed. He started for it, moving swiftly, not wanting to be caught outlined against the snow, and when he reached the blackness he stopped to catch his breath and to listen.

The back door had slammed. Was the search starting? If there was a search he was sure it would be Swiss Jack who started it: the others, whatever else they might be were men who kept their own counsel.

He moved back into the brush along the creek, then went down along the icy rocks. His Winchester was with his saddle and gear back in the livery stable, but to go for it now was fatal.

He saw men fanning out from the barn, going from building to building. Obviously, the idea that he might have remained outside on such a cold night had not occurred to them, but it would soon come to mind. Yet only a few minutes had passed when he heard a call. It was Thorpe's voice. "All right! No time for that! Come on in! We'll take care of him on the way back!"

The way back from where?

He saw them straggle back and mount up, and then they rode out of town in a tight cavalcade as if bunching against the cold.

If men traveled on such a night there, haste was imperative and they must have far to go.

Nobody commented when he came back into the saloon and this time the bartender reached under the bar for the good jug and poured a drink. "On the house," he said.

"Cold out there," Radigan commented.

"Especially," it was Swiss Jack, "if you have cold feet to begin."

Radigan took his drink and his time. Then he turned slowly around and looked at Swiss Jack. He looked at him for a full minute while the room was silent. The fire crackled and inside the potbellied stove a stick fell. A man shifted his feet and poured a glass full and the trickling of the whisky could be heard plainly in the room.

"Yes," Radigan said quietly, "I had cold feet from a long ride, and cold hands, and there were a few more outside than I was in any mood to tackle. There must have been a dozen of them."

"So?" Swiss Jack was sitting back in his chair, smiling.

"There's only one of you."

Swiss Jack was surprised. He had expected everything but that and for an instant it caught him unawares, and also, he instantly realized, he was in no position to draw a gun and any slightest move on his part could be construed as a move to draw. If the big man at the bar was any hand at all with a gun, then Swiss Jack himself was as good as dead. And he was not ready to die.

For a long moment he sat very still, wondering if he dared move from his slouched position without feeling the tear of hot lead in his guts.

Radigan knew exactly how Swiss Jack was feeling and he was in no hurry to let him off the hook. "I said just anytime," he said, "but if you reach for a gun, I'll kill you."

Swiss Jack's mouth was dry and he could feel his pulse throbbing heavily. He dearly wanted to move, his position had become cramped, but he was quite sure now that the big man was not fooling.

Radigan watched him, his eyes cold but his lips smiling slightly. He did not want to kill this man, yet he knew that if it became necessary he was not going to lose any time doing it or any sleep afterward. He did not want to brag but he knew that sometimes even a dangerous man will hesitate before tackling an equally dangerous one.

"You called that man Bob Harvey. I don't know the name."

"Your hard luck."

"Not mine. He's yellow enough to hire his killing."

Swiss Jack laughed. "Bob *Harvey*? You've the wrong man. Bob can kill his own cats."

"He hired Vin Cable to kill me."

He saw the sudden awareness in Swiss Jack's eyes and knew now that whatever else Swiss Jack might do he was not going to begin a fight under any misapprehensions.

"You're Radigan?" There was a slight note of incredulity.

"I'm Radigan."

By now he knew the story of the killing of Vin Cable would be known wherever Western men gathered, for such stories were quickly passed on from campfire to card table across the country. And especially were such stories the gossip of such places as this, where they were meat and drink to the lonely men who lived by the gun.

The door opened then and three men came into the room. The first was a tall, square-shouldered man with auburn mustaches and auburn hair that touched his shoulders. The second was shorter, a man with a square face and a square build who carried himself very erect, a man whose features were swarthy and handsome in a hard-bitten way. The third was even taller, very narrow across his rounded shoulders and with a small head atop a long neck, and a great beak of a nose.

Radigan said, "Howdy, boys." He did not remove his eyes from Swiss Jack. "I'm selling tickets for a ball. You boys want to choose your partners?"

"If it's your fight, Tom." Loren Pike had grasped the situation at once. "We're already tuning our fiddles."

Charlie Cade and Adam Stark walked around Radigan to the bar and leaned their backs against it, looking at Swiss Jack.

"You really call this a fight?" Pike asked gently, indicating Swiss Jack.

"This is the soup. The main course is being served when Harvey Thorpe or Bob Harvey or whatever he calls himself comes back down the trail."

Swiss Jack was getting stiff. He knew he was going to try moving soon, and he was glad there was only one man to reckon with for the men who stood before him were all very tough men.

Radigan walked slowly over to the table. "Your hands aren't tied, Jack," he said conversationally, "and I think you said something about holding me for Harvey. You want to make a start?"

Swiss Jack was looking up, his eyes on Radigan's chest. If he did draw, would his gun clear the table? Could he jerk free of the table and get his gun up before he died?

"Seems to me you're in a bind," Radigan said. "Just get up out of the chair. You'll get an even break. Just get up mighty easy and don't make any sudden moves."

Swiss Jack could not make himself believe it. He was going to have his chance. Slowly, he eased sideways out of his chair and straightened up and his eyes lifted to Radigan's and Radigan hit him.

Swiss Jack never saw the blow coming. He was not set to take a punch and he was not yet on balance. The blow caught him alongside the jaw and lights exploded in his skull and the next instant he was seated on the floor and his skull was ringing. There was a smoky taste in his mouth and he started to get up but a big hand caught him by the scuff of the neck and slammed him back into the wall with such violence that a bottle on the bar tipped over. His skull hit the wall with a vicious rap and his eyes tried to focus and he tried to reach for a gun.

He had never been in a fistfight in his life. Guns were a gentleman's weapon, and he had always relied on a gun. A hard fist caught him in the mouth and he tasted blood. He came off the wall swinging, but a wicked blow in his belly took his wind and doubled him up for the lifting knee that broke his nose.

"Swiss Jack," Radigan spoke without anger, "I

came in here a stranger, minding my own affairs, and you decided to take a hand.

"Now," Radigan continued, "I'd suggest you settle down for the winter here, or you ride out to the north. But don't come south of here because if I see you south of Loma Coyote and west of Santa Fe I'll take it to mean you're looking for me."

He turned and walked to the bar. "I need some top hands," he said to Loren, "who aren't gun-shy."

GRETCHEN SPENT THE first day cleaning up the cave, checking the trail regularly, and during that first day she cooked not at all, only making coffee to go with the jerked beef and the cans of tomatoes she opened. She was, she admitted to herself, frightened.

On the second day the wind was blowing hard into the west, and so away from the ranch, and on that day she got out some dried apples and baked three apple pies. She had already decided on a party for them when they returned, and she had begun preparing.

What she did not know was that Bitner, scouting wide for the R-Bar cows, had swung even farther west than usual on what was to be the last venture in that direction before they started sweeping the mountains to the east of Vache Creek. And returning from that ride he caught a whiff of fresh baking.

It was impossible, he knew it was impossible, yet he knew that smell, and his stomach growled in response. He drew up and sat his horse in the face of the wind, trying to get another whiff of it, but none came. Just as he was deciding it was all imagination and wishful thinking, it came again.

For an hour he cut back and forth across the wind, trying to trace that vagrant aroma, but without success, although he did catch the scent several times, and by that time he was closer to the ranch by several miles.

When it was almost dusk he gave it up. It was nonsense. Probably they were baking at the ranch, and even if Radigan was holed up out here somewhere, they would hardly be baking pies or cake. Although, come to think of it, there had been some doughnuts left in a pan when they took over the ranch.

They had turned the barn into a bunkhouse and there were several men there when he rode in. After a few minutes he went up to the house to report to Ross Wall, who was talking to Angelina Foley.

When he opened the door he expected the odor of fresh baking to hit him with a wave, but it did not. His nostrils found no expected odors there, nothing but that of a wood fire and fresh coffee.

Bitner was a cautious man, and after a moment he merely reported what he had seen and found, which was nothing but empty country. He kept the smell of baking to himself. After all, it was probably his imagination.

The cattle were in bad shape. The grass they had found was eaten down to the grass roots and the cattle were not used to pawing snow away from grass to eat it and were poor rustlers. That Wall was worried, he could plainly see, and Miss Foley's face looked drawn and worried.

And then a man rode in from Loma Coyote with

the news that Radigan had been seen there, and Gorman told him while they were having a smoke, "I saw tracks over east of here, I'd swear they were the tracks of that big roan that the half-breed rides."

"Fresh?"

"Yesterday or the day before. And if he went he's still out there. I cut for sign all the way back and up and down along the creek. He hasn't crossed back."

Suppose, Bitner told himself, they have a hideout near the ranch? And suppose both men are gone? Then that girl will be there alone.

The girl alone.

She was a lot of woman, that one. Bitner's narrow eyes closed over his thoughts. He was no chaser, but when a man was away from women for months he got to feeling it.

Bitner was out at daybreak and he rode west along a faint trail with the mesa towering over him on his right, and he had no idea in mind except to find where that smell of baking had come from. Not that the girl was not in the back of his mind, clinging there like some noxious vine, working its feelers into his thoughts with memories of the girl, her high-breasted figure and the way she walked.

Damn! That was a woman! And living with two men like that! No decent girl would think of it. Claimed Child was her father! Why, that breed couldn't father a blonde like that out of—anything. Bitner knew what trouble could come to a man from fooling around with a woman in the West. He knew it, but he was not thinking about it. He knew a man could steal cows, commit a murder and even steal a horse and get away with it, but to fool around with a woman, especially a decent woman. The least he could get was a hanging.

He knew all that but he could not get the girl out of his thoughts. She was there, like a cocklebur in a horse's tail, and nothing was going to get it out in any easy way.

He walked his horse along the slope, working his way west, and thinking it out. If they had a hideout close to the ranch the chances were it was somewhere around that mesa. It loomed up there, hundreds of feet above them, and no man could see what was on top, and so obvious nobody would ever think of looking there.

Radigan, he was a cagey one. Thorpe should have measured his man more carefully before trying to move in as he had, but Bitner, being no fool, could see a lot of things Thorpe had not considered. There was a good chance he would never get back from this trip, and as far as that went, that Foley girl was mighty handsome... do her good, too. She was too high and mighty and too free with the orders to suit him. Bitner took a hefty bite from his chewing tobacco and rolled it into a corner of his jaws. Do her good, that's what it would, but alongside this Child woman she was nothing. No wonder Radigan wouldn't fall for the Foley girl. Bitner knew about that, for he had seen the gleam in her eye when she went after him. She made like she was an enemy, but if Radigan so much as showed a sign of interest she was ready.

The dim trail, ancient as time itself, played out somewhere near the mesa, but trending away from the wall. Bitner drew up and spat a blob of brown juice into the remains of a snowdrift. He tested the air for the smell of cooking but found nothing but good, clean pine forest. He sat his horse, waiting patiently, for Bitner was a man who knew patience.

He worked at it the rest of the day and came in at night without saying anything except that he had been hunting. He was tired and so was his horse, and knowing the man for a top hand, Wall asked no questions.

Half the night Bitner lay awake thinking of Gretchen Child, and turning over in his mind every possible approach with the slow patience of the confirmed hunter. Nobody, he remembered, had examined that mesa, and certainly nobody had ridden around it, and it was a good long ride and one he decided to make. After all, he might be in this country a good while and he might as well get acquainted. He settled down into his worn blankets and slept, and far to the north a small column of riders was filing into place beside the road where they would camp, and their goal was not far off.

Harvey Thorpe was feeling good. Suppose they had missed Radigan. The man was on the dodge now and eventually they would kill him or run him out. A few more miles of riding and they would be in position to make their strike: the word he had from Leadville was that the stage might carry seventy thousand in gold. It was better than the cattle business.

Sure, he would come out of it with a third, but it was enough for now. And he might do a lot of things with a fast count; he had handled a lot of money and knew how to make a count look better than it was.

Radigan was beat. The long ride atop the other rides and he was tired. He holed up at Loma Coyote to wait out the weather a little, and to recuperate. John Child would be back at the hideout on the mesa by this night, and he was not worried.

The trouble was, John Child was lying unconscious beside the trail twelve miles east of the ranch where he had been thrown when his horse was startled by a sudden flushing of birds from the brush. Child had been tired, too, riding half-asleep in the saddle, and now he was out cold and had been for an hour. And his horse was just slowing to a walk, a couple of miles farther on.

Gretchen awakened on her third morning alone with a distinct feeling of uneasiness. She dressed hurriedly and went to the window and peered out. She could see nothing. Her range of vision was better from one of the inner windows, which was, like the first, concealed by a break in the rock, so she went back into the cave and looked out. And she saw a rider.

He was not passing by, he was cutting for sign, and he was working the ground as carefully as an Apache. Gretchen had not grown up with Indians not to know when a man was hunting a trail and close to what he wanted to find. She watched him, frightened and fascinated. Yet her first thought was for John Child and Radigan. What if they returned and he saw them first?

She went back into the cave and fed the horses. She got a pistol and belted it on, then picked up a rifle. She was a good shot, and if she got the chance: she had no occasion to kill any man, but this one was a danger to those she loved. When everything was arranged she went to the entrance and looked down. No sign of him there.

Radigan had showed her a rock she could push down. It might not kill a man but it could give him some uncomfortable moments and might make him think again before he tried to come up the slide a second time. She tested that and it moved under her hand. Yes, she could roll it. She checked the windows, and the man was no longer in sight. That frightened her more than ever, because not being able to see where he was she could imagine all sorts of things. And the worst of it was, Radigan and her father were due back at any moment.

She looked out again, and saw the man farther down the slope, working through the trees. Had he failed to find any tracks? Or was he aware he was being watched? Suppose he waited until dark and then came up?

The day wore on slowly, and she went ahead with her plans for the party she had promised herself she would provide for their homecoming. Into her small pack she had hidden one very nice dress. It was right for a party, and she got it out hoping some of the wrinkles would hang out. She hung it up and looked at it, then went back to the window. There was no sign of the man.

Taking the rifle she went up to the top of the mesa and worked her way close to the edge, keeping off the skyline. He was there, riding back toward the ranch and some distance off. That did not mean he could not come back.

Gretchen had never thought of herself as brave or lacking in bravery. As a child she knew the Indians had thought her courageous. But bravery, she realized, was not a simple thing. Anyone could be brave under familiar circumstances, but put that same person in a strange place, among strange people and subjected to a different brand of fear and he might not be so brave. Many a man who was afraid of high places could walk into gunfire without hesitation, and a man who might ride any dangerous, man-killing horse might hesitate to rush into a fire to save someone. Usually a man was brave in a situation where he understood the risks, and what she thought of now was not in her estimation a matter of bravery or lack of it. She had a job to do and she decided she would do it.

If that man returned she must stalk and kill him. She could not run the risk of him lying in wait for Radigan and her father.

She covered several miles along the other side of the mesa, staring off into the gathering dusk, looking into the trees and over the bare hillsides, hoping they would return. She returned to the cave and built a small fire to make coffee, and she knew she was afraid.

It was very dark in the cave. The only comfortable feeling was the sound of the horses chomping on their grain in the stalls in the main cave.

She took straw from the pile near the horses and scattered some of it in the opening, hoping the rustle of it would arouse her if anyone walked over it. Farther inside she placed several little rows of stones that a man might kick in walking, and these would rattle on the bare floor of the cave. Yet she was frightened, and she lay awake for long hours, listening into the dark.

At daybreak she awakened suddenly, conscious

that she had overslept. For a long time she lay absolutely still, listening, straining her ears for the slightest sound, and heard nothing. She got quickly to her feet and, taking the rifle, went to the windows, then the cave opening. There was nothing, no one in sight anywhere. Perhaps she was being foolish, the man might have lost something or—But she knew she was not. She knew the man had been looking for her, for them.

She made coffee and ate more of the jerked beef and some cold corn bread, and at intervals she went to look and saw nothing. She fed the horses only a little for the hay was all but gone and the corn was precious.

Her dress was hanging out surprisingly well and she longed to put it on. She had planned to wear it when they arrived and she was sure that would be soon. Again she checked the openings, but nothing was in sight. Taking her rifle she went to the top of the mesa and worked close to the edge, but there, too, she saw nothing.

From the other side of the mesa she studied the country to the north from which either Radigan or her father must come, but she saw nothing. She was sure once, that she did, but then there was no further movement so she gave up and went back.

Suppose they never came back? Suppose both of them had been ambushed and killed? Suppose once more she was to be an orphan with no one to turn to, no place to go, and no money?

She shook her head, refusing to accept the idea, and then she went back to the cave, and suddenly determined, she changed into her dress. Excitedly, she looked in the small mirror she had but could see only a little of herself at a time. She had put her hair up the night before, but now she let it down and combed it out. When her hair was put up properly she looked at herself in the mirror and knew she was beautiful, and it was the way she wished to look when Tom Radigan returned home. The dress was white, with only a little color.

"I . . . I look like a bride!" she said aloud.

The voice came from behind her. "You sure do, lady!"

Suddenly she was cold, utterly cold. For a long moment she did not move, her mind working swiftly and with astonishing clarity. She knew she was in dire trouble and there was no help to be expected unless—unless—but their coming now was too much to hope for.

She turned slowly to see Bitner standing in the opening from the larger cave, and she recognized him at once. His face and name were familiar for when she arrived on the stage she had seen him and heard him called by name.

He was a lean, tall, sour-smelling man, unshaven and dirty, the juice from his tobacco staining the whiskers about his mouth.

"I was wondering when you'd get here," she said. "You certainly took long enough."

Bitner blinked. He had expected fear, screams, protests, anything but her present calm. And her appearance. Her very beauty left him awkward and uncertain as to his next move, for he was unused to women of such beauty and they robbed him of self-possession. But her shoulders were very white, and he stared at her, his mouth growing dry with eagerness. At the same time her attitude and appearance confused him and the fact left him angry. She was only a girl, and she was alone.

"I'm here now," he said crossly, "and I guess you know what I've come for."

"I saw you searching for the trail," she said. "I've watched you for several days. I could," she looked at him steadily, "have killed you."

He looked at her, disturbed by her coolness and the uncomfortable feeling that he might have been, for days, right under her rifle.

"Won't do you no good," he said. "You missed your chance."

"I was making some coffee," Gretchen replied. "Would you like some?"

Every delay was a victory, every moment she could keep him talking increased her chances of something happening, of some opportunity, some chance to do something, anything. But whatever she did must be right the first time: there would be no second.

"Well . . . I could do with some coffee," he agreed.

Why not? Warm him up. It was mighty cold out there. He glanced around with new respect for Radigan. Had it mighty nice up here. Plenty of grub, warm shelter, feed for the horses and firewood; why, he could last out the winter here.

She walked right by him. She would never have believed, a moment before, that she could walk so close to him, but although her flesh crawled with fear, she did it.

"Pretty fancy," Bitner said, indicating the dress. "You wear that in some dance hall?"

"It is a party dress, Mr. Bitner," she said. "I wore it at parties in Mexico. I attended a convent there."

"You," he was incredulous, "in a convent?"

"Why not?" she looked around at him. "I am seventeen, Mr. Bitner, and although you seem to doubt it, I am a lady."

He sneered, yet he felt a rising doubt. "Likely story! Livin' with two men!"

"John Child is my foster father. He and his wife were the only parents I ever had." She had located the bowie knife they used to slice meat. "He is a very good man, and Mr. Radigan has been nothing but a gentleman."

Bitner stared at her sourly. This was not going as he had planned, but somehow the right moment had not come. Meanwhile a cup of coffee would taste mighty good. He peered at her, trying to make out whether she was like she said, or like he had suspected. His opinion of her was convinced, however, and he decided she must be lying.

She stirred the coals under the coffee and got out two cups. The knife was just visible under the edge of an old coat she had used when she first got up in the morning, and she purposely avoided the area, not wishing to attract attention to it that might lead him to discover the knife. Bitner had seated himself close to her guns, which were useless under the circumstances.

When she handed him the cup he touched her hand with his and grinned at her meaningly. Gretchen seemed not to notice but inwardly she cringed.

"Ain't nobody comin' back here," Bitner said suddenly. "If you're expectin' it, you're wrong. We ain't seen nothing of Radigan since he rode north."

They knew that, then?

"He won't live long up there. Not with Swiss Jack Burns around. And if he does the boss will take care of him on the way back."

"He's been away?"

"He's away all right." Bitner gulped the hot coffee and muttered a little, looking around the cave at the few sparse articles of clothing and the beds. "That breed is good as dead, too." He puckered his brow. "We don't know what happened to him, but he's afoot out there in the cold, and he's hurt. We found blood on the snow and his horse came in to the ranch, so we backtrailed the horse. No sign of Child, but blood on the snow."

Sardonic humor glinted in his hard eyes. "No use gettin' your hopes up. Nobody ain't going to come to help you out." He crossed one leg over the other. "Best thing you can do is make up to me. A woman can't live in this country without a man."

She dropped her hand to the haft of the bowie knife and swung it in a wide arc. It was her chance and he was warm, relaxed, momentarily off guard. She swung the wide blade and turned with it, swinging it almost at arm's length, and she was just short. The tip of the blade slashed across his biceps and he dropped the cup and toppled over backward as the blade slit his shirt and left a long, red scratch across his abdomen. Instantly, Gretchen knew she had failed, and that now there would be no respite, no further chance at delay, and she had no doubt that after he had stayed with her as much as he wanted that he would kill her: he must kill her.

Gretchen did not think, she ran. But as she ran she caught up her rifle and ran into the outer cave, then scrambled on up the slide to the top of the mesa. The wind was piercing, but she ran. She ran wildly, desperately, conscious of the clambering, stumbling footsteps of the man behind her.

Yet almost at once she was out of sight among the scattered piñons.

She had not lived among Indians for nothing, and quickly she fell to the ground among some scattered rocks and low brush, and she lay still, the rifle forgotten in one hand, the knife in the other.

She had failed, and now he would hunt her down. She had drawn blood, and the cut across his biceps might be deep, and if it was he would not devote much time to a search until he had done something to treat the wound. And after that he would come for her.

She checked the rifle. There was a shell in the chamber and three more in the magazine: four shots.

It was not enough.

She was not that good a shot, and unless she let him come close she would probably miss, and she could not afford to miss often.

Yet, a moment later when she saw him moving some distance off, she tried her first shot. It was a warning, to remind him she had the rifle, and he dropped from sight among some rocks, and being Indian in that part of her thinking at least, she moved at once. She retreated to a safer shelter, farther back on the mesa, and settled down there to wait for whatever move Bitner might make, and for a time he made none at all.

The day was drawing on and the air was cold. With night it would be piercing cold and windy atop the mesa and she dared not have a fire, nor was there any shelter she could find, nor a blanket anywhere.

She knew then it was well she had been an Indian, if only for a few years, for an Indian knows how to endure without crying to the sky, he knows how to withstand cold, hunger and the wind, and she would withstand them.

She knew then the dress she had on was the last thing she should be wearing; it was white, and too easy to see on the mesa's top, or anywhere. But it was a woman's dress, a dress for a woman to wear to meet her man, the last feminine thing she owned, and she was going to live with it or die with it, but dressed as a woman should be.

Gretchen remembered the cabin under the mesa and the warm fire, she remembered listening for Tom Radigan's step, and knew she was in love with him, knew it deep in every throbbing corpuscle, knew it in her muscles and bones and in the crying need of her body, her loins yearning for the man he was. And she knew then she was not going to die alone on the mesa top, she was not going to be killed and raped by such as Bitner. She belonged in her heart to Radigan, and she would belong to him in the flesh or to no man. She was not going to save that last bullet for herself, she was going to save it for him, for Bitner, and she was going to give it to him, right in the belly at point-blank range.

She had never felt like this before, but right now she was backed up against death with all the nonsense and the fancy words trimmed away. The hide of truth was peeled back to expose the bare, quivering raw flesh of itself, and there was no nonsense about it. She had been taught the way a lady should live, and how a lady should act, and it was all good and right and true and the way a pretty girl should be taught, but out here on the mesa top with a man hunting her to put her back on the grass it was no longer the same. Save the manners for the parlor and the ballroom, and save the womanly tricks for courting, but this was something else and there was no fooling about it. She was going to kill a man and when he died she was not going to be sorry.

There are times in life when the fancy words and pretty actions don't count for much, when it's blood and dust and death and a cold wind blowing and a gun in the hand and you know suddenly you're just an animal with guts and blood that wants to live, love and mate, and die in your own good time.

Gretchen Child had the feel of the Indian in her, and she settled down behind the rocks and brush partly sheltered from the raw cold wind off the snow peaks, and she waited there, as ready to kill as any trapped lioness, and almost eager for it.

She was only a few months from a convent and a graceful house where ladies were gentle, fragile and delicate, but there was none of that here. She only knew in her guts that she wanted to live and that out there over those snow-dressed mountains her man was coming nearer, and she wanted to be waiting for him as a woman should.

Suddenly something fierce and wild came up in her and she jacked a shell into the chamber and made the sound ring, and then she called out, hoarse and wild, "Come on, Bitner! You want a woman, so come and get me, and if I don't kill you, Radigan will!"

Bitner, two hundred yards off, caught her voice coming downwind, and settled down behind his rocks, not liking the sound of it. He heard the sound of the Winchester, too, and said to himself, "Why, she's crazy! She's gone loco!"

But the need for her was in him and he settled down to see what a cold night on the mesa could do.

She was dressed flimsy, with shoulders bare to the wind, and not much body to the cloth in her dress. Right now she was full of beans, but a cold night might do a lot to her, and he could wait. He had waited this long.

TOM RADIGAN HAD come out of the trees to the north of the mesa, riding with the wind at his back and his eyes busy, sure he had heard a shot, although the wind was away from him.

To the east a few miles Charlie Cade, Loren Pike and Adam Stark were flanking it down through the trees in a thin skirmish line, hunting for Foley riders and studying out the country. Come hell or snow blowing there was going to be a fight before the sun lifted to noon tomorrow, and Radigan had an idea there'd be blood on the mountains before Pike, Cade and Stark turned tail.

He circled warily to the west, not liking the faint sound that had seemed to be a shot. The day was far along, but light enough for clear seeing, and once he thought he'd glimpsed something white on the rim. Two hours later he had circled and was coming up on the south side, and there he found tracks in the snow, searching tracks of a horseman cutting for sign.

There was a cold feeling in him then, and he turned the black horse he was now riding and started up the slope toward the mesa, and he rode right out in the open. He rode up to the steep rock slide and drew up, not liking the thought of bracing that slide with God knows what at the top.

Once he thought he heard a voice cry out in the late afternoon, but the sound whipped away and he knew he must be mistaken. Everything seemed all right. He could see the edge of the boulder placed for rolling down, sitting right where he'd left it. He stepped back and sat down to pull off his boots, and then slipped his feet into the Blackfoot moccasins he always carried for woods work, and then he took his rifle and started up the slide.

He had taken only one step when he heard the shot. It came clear on the wind, but caught by echoes and slapped around among the rocks. A shot right enough, and from somewhere above, but somewhere. There was no pinning down the sound.

He put out a moccasined foot and tested the rock, then swung his weight up. He wanted no rattling stones to warn of his coming, no sound, anywhere.

On top of the mesa Bitner chewed at the ends of his mustache and grinned into the wind. The little fool had grabbed a rifle and it was his she had taken, not her own, and he knew how many cartridges were left. It was a thing a man always knew, if he wanted to stay alive.

That last shot was number three. One bullet left. She had tried to get him, and once she had been close. He had taken a chance this last time, allowing her to see him plain enough to make her eager. He knew she was not too good with a rifle, although she could shoot. And she shot a split second too late and missed by a narrow margin, but enough. He milked the rifle down to one shot, and he had an idea he was going to have to gamble on that one if he wanted the woman, and he did, more than ever now.

It would be a fight, but he liked his women full of fight. He bit off another chew and thought about it, taking his time. And she was a lot to think about. The wind blew cold, moaning around the evergreens and stirring icy snow around the rock where he sat.

Bitner rolled the tobacco in his jaws and decided she was a pretty canny woman. Small chance of her trying her last shot at a distance, so he could get close without too much risk. And when he got close he'd have to get hold of that rifle or chance a shot of his own to get the rifle away from her.

He moved out from the rocks and ran twenty feet to a tree. Nothing happened. He dashed thirty feet farther to a slab of rock, and waited an instant. Anytime now, she was only over there a little way.

He Indianed it around the rock, and caught a glimpse of white at the edge of a rock. If she was there, he had her. He stepped out quickly, watching that edge of cloth, and just as he stepped into the open a rifle blasted.

He felt the hot burn of the bullet and sprang back,

to see the girl standing there, fifty feet off in another direction.

Why, the dirty little—! Fooled him, fooled him like he was a youngster with an edge torn from her skirt.

And then he lowered his rifle.

She'd fooled him, all right, but she had missed, missed a clean shot. Sure, he'd burned his neck with the bullet and it would be raw and sore, but he'd have a woman to. . . .

"Bitner!"

It was a man's voice, conversational in tone, and it was behind him. He sprang like a cat, turning as he leaped, and when he hit the ground, his rifle—hers actually—was hosing flame. He staggered and something hit his wind a wicked blow, and he settled on his feet, flat on the rocks, and saw Radigan standing there, standing straight, his right side toward him like a blasted soldier at attention on the parade ground; like a man in a duel.

Bitner got his Winchester up and squeezed shut on the trigger and felt the rifle jump in his hand, but the recoil or something staggered him and, puzzled, he saw his bullet kick dust from the rocks between them. Well, by God, he'd . . . he was lying on his face on the cold rock, and the snow was blowing away from his face because he was breathing hard. He heard the dying echo of his shot. It sounded like two shots, and he got his knees under him and started to get up.

It was the blood on the mesa top that bothered him. Somebody was shot almighty bad, somebody was really bleeding like a stuck hog, somebody—the blood was there, around his knees and on the rock where he had been lying. His eyes had refused to focus but now they did and he saw it was his blood and he had been gutshot.

He had gutshot a man once and it had taken the fellow a long time to die.

Bitner used the rifle for a crutch and got to his feet. He could see the girl, looking like an angel in her white gown, walking from behind the rocks toward Radigan. It was that dress that had thrown him, right there at the beginning; in a place like that he had not expected to see anybody in a white dress, and before he got himself adjusted to it she had taken a cut at him and gotten away.

It was a hell of a way to die, over a woman he had only seen a time or two and who didn't want any part of him, anyway.

He was swaying on his feet, and wanting a shot at Radigan, but more than anything he wanted a bullet through the skull. He had always had guts enough, but did he have guts enough to die from a belly shot without crying like a baby? That man he had shot, he'd cried and screamed.

Something raw and horrible tore from his own throat, and he lifted the rifle and felt the slam of the bullet and knew he had won. He had won because he was dying, going, dead.

The last thing he remembered was lying with his cheek against the rock and remembering how he had helped his ma shave his pa after he had been killed. "A man shouldn't be buried like that," his ma had said. "He should face up to the Gates like a man, with his beard trimmed."

He had no son, so who was going to shave him? Who would fix his body for burial?

A man should have a son.

He saw his bloody hand lying inches before his eyes, the cold wind drying the blood on it, and he tried to open his mouth to tell Radigan that a man should have a son, and beyond that there was nothing further.

Gretchen had come to Radigan quickly. "You all right?" he asked. He asked it without looking at her, for he was watching Bitner. She knew the man was dying and Radigan knew it but he did not move his eyes from Bitner for even an instant.

"I'm all right," she said, "I was hoping you'd come."

"Sorry I was late."

"You weren't late. You were right on time."

ROSS WALL CAME up to the house from the barn in the first bleak morning light. He stamped the snow from his boots and came in at Angelina's call. He held his hat in his hand, his blocky head looking like the head of a big grizzly in the shadow cast by the lamp.

"Ma'am, I want we should saddle up and ride out of here, right away this morning."

Angelina Foley felt something seem to turn over inside her. "What's happened?"

"Nothing yet. Nothing I know of, only Bitner didn't come back, and if Bitner doesn't come back, he's dead. It's another man gone, and one of the best."

"Is that all?"

"No," he said bluntly, "it ain't all. Not by a damn' sight."

If his other words had not impressed her, these did. It was the first time Ross Wall had ever sworn in her presence.

"It ain't all. There's strangers around, three or four of them. Mighty salty looking men, Gorman says. He came on three of them up in the trees last night; they just sat their saddles with Winchesters in their hands and looked at him. They didn't say I, yes or no, they just looked, and he looked back. Then Gorman rode back here and asked for his time."

"Is there more?"

"Yes. I never did cotton to what Harvey wanted to do. I never liked him nor trusted him, nor saw what you and your Pa saw in him. He's brought you to trouble, and I'd like to see you out of it.

"Those men out there." He pointed. "I think they're waiting for him. I think he'll come back through the snow and he'll ride right up to here and they'll shoot him right out of his saddle.

"And that isn't all. The sheriff is down at San Ysidro. I don't mean Flynn, but Flynn's boss. Name is Enright, or something. He rode in yesterday with three deputies and he has been asking questions around, and one of those deputies has a horse with a Texas brand."

Angelina Foley walked to the fire and picked up the coffeepot. It was always a woman's way to turn to food in an emergency. Fix a hot meal, make coffee; it was a sensible way. And that was what she should be doing, making a hot meal for some man rather than trying to prove how smart she was and how she could run a cow outfit as well as any man. She had not even managed to run a home, not anywhere.

So all their fancy dreams of wealth were empty. All Harvey's confident talk, his striding up and down, his gestures—they were as empty as he was—all those big ideas from men who would rather steal than do an honest day's work with their fine contempt for men who did work. Fools, Harvey called them, hayshakers, so now where was he?

"Can we get out of here?"

For the first time she saw hope in Wall's eyes. "I think so. I think they'd be glad to be shut of us. We couldn't take anything, of course. Just personal stuff. But we could ride out, ma'am . . ."

"Don't call me ma'am," she said irritably. "My name is Gelina."

THEY WERE COMING down Vache Creek now, six of them, one with his skull tied in a bloody bandage, one with a broken arm, now in a sling. Their horses' hoofs dragged and the men slumped wearily in the saddle.

Harvey Thorpe was numb as well as exhausted. They were all numb.

The ride had been cold and they had been anxious to get on with the holdup. The stage showed up on time and they had ridden out and stopped it, confident of their numbers, confident of their guns.

Only the man on the box had a shotgun and he didn't drop it, he didn't hold up his hands. His first charge of buckshot had torn a man's face off and the second dropped a man, screaming. Amid plunging horses and wild shots he had coolly picked up a Winchester and opened fire. Other men were shooting from the stage itself and horses were down, men screaming, and Harvey Thorpe had been among the first to break into flight. A few miles away they had come together, and they had kept on going. And nobody had anything at all to say.

The thing none of them wanted to say was that the men they had called hayshakers, the men who worked for their money, had been ready for them.

What happened to the others Harvey never was to know. All he did know was that one man sitting up on the box of that stage had not thrown up his hands: he had simply opened fire. From then on it had been nightmare, pure nightmare.

It was not supposed to happen. Their guns were supposed to frighten the stage driver and express messenger into immobility while they were robbed. That was the way it was supposed to happen.

Harvey knew but one thing, and he knew deep within himself that when he heard that shotgun blast and saw that man's face vanish in a mask of blood, his own guts had turned to water.

They rode into the ranch yard and somebody said, "Harvey!" And it wasn't one of his own men.

The exclamation made him look up and he saw Radigan standing there in the middle of the ranch yard.

He was standing there with his hands empty, just waiting. And then Harvey saw Loren Pike in the barn door, and Charlie Cade at the corner of the corral, and lean, round-shouldered Adam Stark leaning against the doorpost of the house. And beside the corral and still farther away was John Child. And even a less wary man than himself would have read the story in their presence here, in their manner.

A man behind him said, "Count me out, Harvey," and Harvey Thorpe heard a gun drop into the dust. And behind him other guns dropped.

Harvey looked at Radigan and felt the hatred inside himself like something raw and sore. Radigan had been nowhere near that stage, but suddenly it seemed as if Radigan had been the man on the box who lifted that shotgun. Without him everything would have been all right.

Out of the welter of thoughts left in his brain came a slow, cool knowledge that he could not win but he could still defeat Radigan. Alive, Radigan was the victor, but dead he was nothing at all, simply nothing.

"Gelina let you come here?"

"She's gone," Radigan said. "She rode out with Wall and a pack horse. Heading for California, I think."

So that was over, too.

Behind him he heard horses walking away, getting clear of him, and Radigan stood there, waiting. Nobody had asked him to drop his gun, nobody suggested he surrender.

Of course, within a few days they would know all about what happened in Colorado, and he would be a wanted man. It was strange he had not considered that, but all his plans had been predicated on success.

Why, they could hang him! And they might.

And Radigan, standing there with his feet apart, just waiting for him to draw and die.

"I'll be damned if I will!" Harvey said angrily. "You're all just waiting for me to make a move so you can kill me! I'll surrender! You think I'll hang, but I won't! I'll beat it! I can still win! I tell you—!"

He meant every word of it, believed it all. Why, so many things could happen in a trial, and he still had friends, he could still dig up some money, he'd show them, he'd . . .

Harvey Thorpe had no intention of drawing, but he did. He felt his hand dropping for the gun and something in his brain screamed that it was madness, he could not win, but he could kill Radigan, he could. . . .

"I didn't think he was going to, there at the end," Pike said. "I thought he was throwing in his hand."

"Even a coyote in a trap," somebody else said, "he'll snap at anything, just to hurt, to kill."

"How'd you guess, Tom?" Cade said. "Because you had to guess, it was that fast."

"Can we do anything for him?" That was John Child. "I mean, is it too late?"

"Sure," Pike replied, "the man's dead."

And he was.

North to the Rails

To all the pioneers whose
journals and letters have done
so much to provide me with material

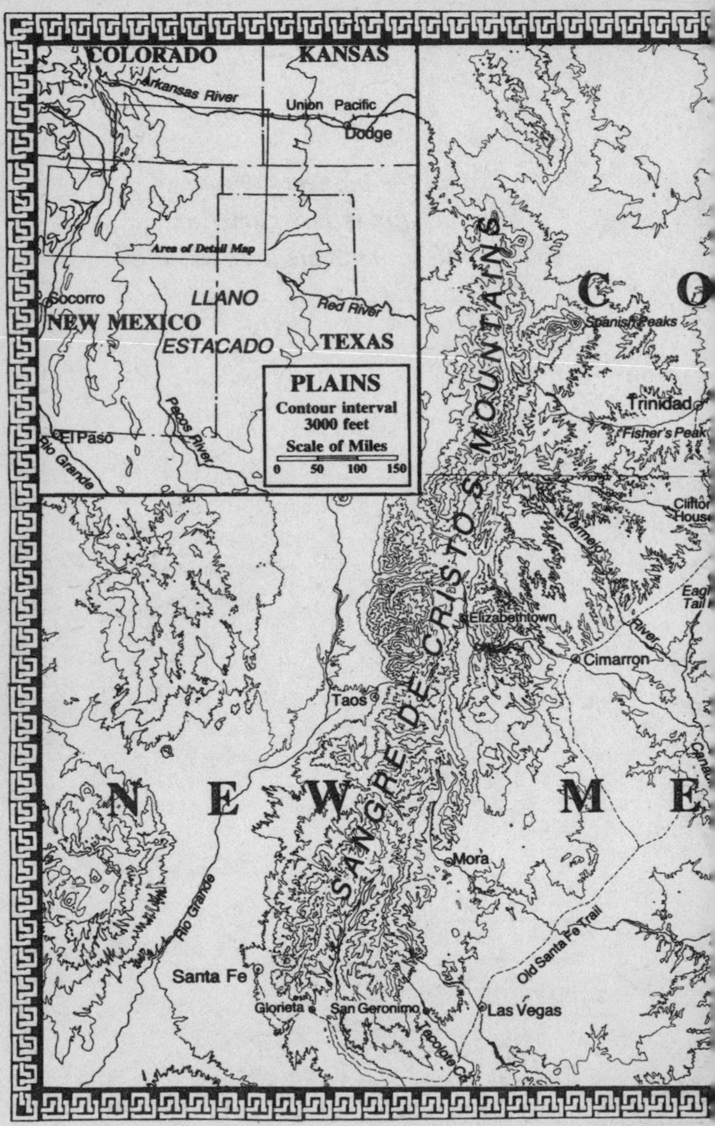
COLORADO
KANSAS
Arkansas River
Union Pacific
Dodge
Area of Detail Map
Socorro
LLANO
Red River
NEW MEXICO
ESTACADO
TEXAS
PLAINS
Contour interval
3000 feet
Scale of Miles
0 50 100 150
El Paso
Rio Grande
Pecos River
SANGRE DE CRISTO MOUNTAINS
CO
Spanish Peaks
Trinidad
Fisher's Peak
Vermejo
Elizabethtown
River
Cimarron
Taos
N E W M E
Mora
Rio Grande
Old Santa Fe Trail
Santa Fe
Glorieta
San Geronimo
Las Vegas
Tecolote Cr.

Map by Alan McKnight

CHAPTER 1

THEY COULD CALL it running away if they wanted to, but it made no sense to kill a man, or risk being killed over something so trivial. He had never used a gun against a man, and did not intend to begin now.

He glanced back, but the town lay far behind him, and there seemed to be no reason for pursuit.

Dawn would be breaking soon, and they would be expecting him on the street to face Dutch Akin, and Dutch would certainly be there, right in the middle of that Las Vegas street, a gun ready to his hand.

It was a savage custom, a ridiculous custom. His mother had been right to take him away from it, back to the eastern city where her family lived. She had never loved the West . . . not really.

He had been a fool to come west, even on business. But how could he have imagined he would run into trouble? Though he rarely took a drink, and was not inclined to argue, he had taken a drink while waiting for either Pearsall or Sparrow, and he had gotten into an argument. All right . . . he *had* made a mistake, but how was he to know they would make so much out of so little?

To hell with Dutch Akin, and with Las Vegas! He would be damned if he'd get himself killed over a few careless words in a saloon. It made no sense—no sense at all.

What would they say when they realized he was gone? When he failed to appear? At the thought, his ears reddened and he felt uncomfortable.

To hell with them! It was better to be a live coward than a dead hero.

Coward . . . the word rankled. Was he a coward? Had he been afraid? He searched himself for an answer, and found none. He did not believe he was a coward. He had come away to avoid a ridiculous situation . . . or was he just telling himself that? Was he not actually afraid?

He seemed to feel his father's eyes upon him—those cool, thoughtful eyes that knew so well how to measure a man and judge what he had in him.

He remembered his father, the day they brought him home on a shutter, still alive, but badly shot up. There had been three men. One of them had taken a drink, waved a bottle, and staggered, but when Borden Chantry had come to arrest him the man suddenly dropped his bottle and two other men stepped from ambush, and his father had gone down in a wicked crossfire. He got off one shot, that was all. The three men had then fled the town.

His father had lived for two days in considerable pain before the doctor arrived from the fort; by the time he got there his father was dead.

It was as his mother had told him: if you lived by the gun you died by the gun.

But he remembered overhearing someone say as they left the cemetery, "I'd hate to be in their boots when Tom Chantry grows up!"

His father had been a cattleman, reasonably successful by any man's standards, but then had come the great freeze-up, and when the snow melted his father was a poor man, and so were a lot of others. Cattlemen could always get credit, and when they sold their herds they paid up; only Pa had no herd to sell.

The men of the town respected him, knew he had a family to feed, and they also knew that he was a man good with a gun, so they offered him the job of town marshal.

For six years he ran the town, and kept it free of serious trouble. He rarely had to draw his gun, and several times he held his fire to give the other man a chance to drop his, and they usually did—all but one.

That man elected to fire . . . and missed. Borden Chantry did not miss.

That was the shooting that led to his death, for the men who came up the trail to kill him were friends of the dead man, and they staged the ambush that wiped out Borden Chantry.

It did no good to remember all that. Tom Chantry touched his horse with a spur. It would soon be light and he wanted to be far away before they discovered he was gone. He had been a fool to come west in the first place. Both Ma and Doris had tried to talk him out of it, but there was a shortage of beef in the East and he had argued with Earnshaw that they could buy it on the plains. No use dealing with a middleman.

Doris' father was Robert Earnshaw, a dealer in livestock in New York City. Lately he had branched out into real estate and banking, although livestock was still the backbone of his business. He had been quick to recognize the profit to be had if Tom Chantry could go west, buy cattle on the plains, and ship them east, and Tom had come west with his blessing.

Beef had been scarce in Kansas, but a cattleman told him of a herd that was being held outside of Las Vegas, New Mexico that still might be had. The owners, Pearsall and Sparrow, had been holding the cattle to speculate, but now were in a bind for money. Tom Chantry had immediately left for Las Vegas, sending a message ahead to make the appointment with the prospective sellers.

He had registered at the hotel and gone at once to the saloon where cattlemen were known to gather, and where Sparrow had said they would meet. While he waited, he had a drink.

Dutch Akin had come in, bumping him hard as he lurched up to the bar, then turning to glare at him with a muttered reference to a "dude."

Tom Chantry ignored the rudeness, although he felt irritation mounting within him. He edged over a little without seeming to do so, giving Akin more room. He knew he should go, but he had come all this way to see Sparrow, and the man was expected. It was simple courtesy for him to wait . . . so he waited.

Chantry had finished his drink, hesitated, then ordered another. He had not eaten since early that morning and knew that he should not have that second drink, but he was embarrassed to stay at the bar without ordering.

By the time he had finished his drink Sparrow had

not come, so he started to turn away from the bar. Without warning a rough hand grasped his shoulder.

Suddenly furious, Chantry turned around sharply. Akin was grinning at him. "Dude, diden you hyar me? I invited you to drink wi'me."

"Sorry, I didn't hear, but I've had enough, thank you."

" 'I've had enough, thank you.' " Akin put his hand on his hip and aped the words in a falsetto; then his voice changed. "I'll tell you when you've had enough! Now belly up to the bar an' drink!"

"No."

The room was quiet. Every eye was on them. The drunken man suddenly seemed to be no longer drunk. "When Dutch Akin invites a man to drink, he damn well better drink," Akin said evenly. "You drink, mister."

"No."

It was foolish. A ridiculous situation. Tom Chantry was irritated with himself for remaining long enough to get involved, but there was no help for it now.

"I am sorry, my friend, but I have no wish for another drink. I was just leaving."

"You'll leave when I get damn good an' ready for you to leave. Now belly up to the bar."

Chantry merely glanced at him, then turned to leave the room. Again he felt the hand touch his shoulder, and this time his reaction was swift. He swung around quickly and, throwing his left hand back, took hold of the grasping arm and jerked hard.

Dutch Akin hit the floor with a crash, and as he realized what had been done to him his hand swept back for his gun.

"*Dutch!*" The sharp voice cut through the haze of anger in Dutch Akin's brain.

A short, slender man in a business suit and a white hat was holding a gun in his hand. "The gentleman isn't armed, Dutch. If you haven't noticed that, you'd better. You draw that gun and I'll put a hole into you."

"This ain't none of your affair, Sparrow. This is just me and him."

Sparrow? Chantry turned his head to look. A man of about forty-five, well-dressed, cool, competent-looking. This was the man he had come to see.

"It is any man's affair as long as this gentleman is not wearing a gun. If you shoot an unarmed man you'll hang for it, Dutch. I'll see that you do."

Dutch got up slowly, holstering his pistol. "All right," he said calmly. "All right, Sparrow. But I'll be on the street at daybreak wearin' this gun, and he better be armed, because if he ain't I'll break both his legs."

Dutch turned sharply and walked from the room.

Chantry held out his hand. "Tom Chantry here, Mr. Sparrow. Thank you—thank you very much."

They walked back to the hotel together. "Bad case, that Akin," Sparrow commented, "a real troublemaker. But he's good with a gun, so be careful."

Chantry shrugged. "I doubt if I ever see him again. Actually, *you* are the man I came to see. I understand you have a herd of beef outside of town that you might sell."

"I might." They had reached the deserted porch of the hotel. Sparrow bit the end from a cigar. "But you are mistaken if you think Akin won't show. The man may be a trouble-maker and a loud-mouth, but he's got sand, and he's killed a man or two. You can expect him."

"It's absurd, Mr. Sparrow. The whole affair was uncalled for. He will have forgotten all about it in the morning."

Sparrow lighted his cigar, threw the match into the dust, and then spoke around the cigar. "No, Mr. Chantry, he will not have forgotten it. Nor will anyone else. Come hell or high water, Dutch Akin will be in the street tomorrow, and if you don't own a pistol you had better buy or borrow one. You'll need it."

"Are you seriously suggesting that I be out there in the street? That I engage in a duel with this—this ape?"

Sparrow glanced at him. "Are you by any chance related to Borden Chantry?"

"I am his son."

"Then I would think—"

Suddenly, Tom Chantry was impatient. "Mr. Sparrow, I came to Las Vegas to see you, to make you an offer for your cattle. The firm I represent, Earnshaw and Company, is an eastern firm, and until now we have done our business through others. We've hoped to set up some business connections out here and buy cattle at the source. We had hoped to buy your herd. I did not come out here to be involved in brawls or shootings, or anything of that sort. I dislike violence, and will have nothing to do with this affair."

"I see."

Sparrow's manner had grown cool. "I knew your father," he said after a minute, "and I respected him.

I was not interested in selling cattle at this time, and we're holding them on good grass so there is no need. However, I thought that the son of Borden Chantry and I might strike a bargain."

"And we are ready, sir."

"You went east soon after your father's death, didn't you?"

"Yes, sir."

"The situation back east is very different from out here, Mr. Chantry. Money is not always the only consideration. Out here we place emphasis upon the basic virtues, and I have noticed that the more organized our lives become the less attention we pay to such things as courage and loyalty. Organization seems to eliminate the necessity for such things, but out here they are the very stuff of life."

"And what does that mean?"

"Simply this: that a man's courage or lack of it is a matter of economic importance in the West. There are few ventures that can be attempted out here where courage is not a necessity, and anyone engaged in such a venture has a right to know the courage of those who are to share the risk."

"What you are saying is that if I do not meet Dutch Akin tomorrow I had better go back east?"

"Exactly that. We will agree the circumstances are disagreeable, but such things cannot be avoided, and you have no choice."

"I don't believe that."

Sparrow shrugged. "It does not matter what you believe. Your father understood, and he lived by the code."

"And died by it."

"That sometimes happens."

"Then," Tom Chantry replied quietly, "I am in the wrong country. I have no desire to kill...or to be killed. I shall go to Dutch Akin and apologize."

"He will despise you."

"Very well, but that will be the end of it."

Sparrow drew on his cigar, then took it from his mouth as though it suddenly had a bad taste. "No, Mr. Chantry, that will not be the end. It will be only the beginning. The bullies will know you are fair game, that you will not fight, and therefore are to be bullied with impunity. The decent people will simply ignore you, the bullies will hunt you down, and some of them will keep on pushing just to see how much you can take before you do fight.

"Understand this, Mr. Chantry, the love of peace and the unwillingness to fight never kept anyonc out of trouble."

They left it at that, but during the night Tom Chantry made his decision.

Turning now in the saddle, he looked back again. There was nothing—nothing at all.

All around were the vast sky and the open prairie. To the north there were mountains, ahead was a broken, rugged country. It was not until then that he realized what he had done.

He had ridden west, not east.

CHAPTER 2

TO THE EAST lay home, friends, security from all this. His mother and Doris were in the East, his job and his future were there. Yet he had ridden west. Why?

What impulse had caused him to turn west when east was the logical direction? Was there some urge within him to avoid security? To avoid escape?

His choice back there had been simple. To use a gun, or not to use it.

He did not think he had actually been afraid, but how was he to know? Sparrow's attitude could be that of everyone west of the Mississippi, and of many of those east of it. Such a story would get around, of course, and even those who commended him for good judgment would suspect his courage.

By turning west he had escaped nothing but the immediate meeting with Dutch Akin, for the situation might arise again. If so, would he run again? How often could he run?

But that was not the important thing now. He had come west to buy cattle that could be shipped east. If he could not get them in Las Vegas he must find them elsewhere, and that meant he might ride north to the Wyoming country and ship over the Union Pacific.

Earnshaw had advanced the money for his trip west, and he carried a draft against Earnshaw's bank with which to pay for the cattle. It was his duty to complete the business that had brought him here; Earnshaw was depending on him.

Tom Chantry considered the situation. Santa Fe lay to the west, not over three days' ride, he believed. It was doubtful if the required cattle could be found there; and if found they must be driven to the railhead, which meant a drive through Las Vegas—something he could not consider at this time.

His logical course was to strike north, but first he must have bedding, supplies, and a pack horse.

The horse he had purchased at the livery stable seemed a good one, and Tom Chantry was an experienced judge of horseflesh. He had bought and sold stock for Earnshaw long enough to be.

Ahead of him lay the stage station at Kearney's Gap; lights showed in the windows, although the sky was gray with dawn's first light. He turned his mount and rode up to the hitch rack.

Behind the house he heard the squeak and complaint of a windlass. He walked to the edge of the porch and looked past the corner. A man with rumpled hair, his suspenders hanging loose, had just drawn a bucket of water.

"Howdy!" he said cheerfully. "Coffee's on. Be fryin' eggs. Come in an' set."

How much time did he have? Traveling would begin at daybreak, and the stage would be coming from Las Vegas shortly after. He did not want to be here when it arrived.

Over coffee he spoke of Santa Fe and Socorro.

"If'n you're headin' for Socorro now," the stage tender said, "you're headin' right. But a man who wanted to get to Santa Fe a-horseback is a plumb fool to ride the trail. Right yonder"—he pointed—"is a good horseback or pack trail across the mountains. Rougher, but a whole sight shorter. Thisaway you swing south and take a big bend. No need. You headin' for Santa Fe?"

"Socorro," Chantry said, "but I'm traveling light. You haven't got any trade goods, have you?"

"A mite. Sell some of the Injuns once in a while. What was you needin'?"

Less than half an hour later, with two blankets, a sack of grub, and a bowie knife to cut firewood, Chantry headed west. When out of sight of the station he turned abruptly from the road and cut back into the brush to find the other trail.

He found it at Agua Zarca and followed it toward the crossing of the Tecolote at San Geronimo. Without leaving the saddle, he removed his coat, stripped off his white shirt, and donned a dark red shirt bought at the stage station. Then he tied his coat behind his saddle.

At noon, well back in the scattered piñons, he unsaddled, watered his horse at a seep, made coffee, and ate a couple of dry biscuits.

Slowly, the tension left him. The smell of the piñons and juniper, the coolness and quiet of the day, the slow circling of far-off buzzards, the cloud shadows on the hills began to soak into his being and left him rested and at peace. When he mounted up and started on once more, he was at one with the land.

His first desire had been to get away from Las Vegas, but now that he was away he knew his best bet would have been to ride north toward Mora and thence to Cimarron, where there would be a lot of cattle.

He reached the Santa Fe Trail again near Glorieta, skirted Santa Fe, and took the trail for Taos. The way he had left Las Vegas rankled. He did not like being considered a coward, and he did not believe he was one, but a good many people would believe so.

But that was behind him. Once in Cimarron, he would buy the cattle, drive them to the railhead, and within a few hours after that he would be on his way back to Doris.

Doris . . .

He took his time. He camped when the mood was on him, and rode on again when he grew restless; when possible, he avoided the main trail.

He was somewhere south of E-Town when he heard the horse. It was coming fast, and he pulled over to be out of the way.

The horse was a blaze-faced roan, and it was carrying double. The riders pulled up when they saw him.

"Howdy there, stranger! Comin' fer?"

"Santa Fe," he replied.

They were young, rough-looking, and one man had a bandaged arm.

"See many folks on the trail?"

"Nobody."

"You'll likely see some. By this time there's a-plenty of folks headin' our way. We was in a shootin' back yonder in Elizabethtown. Hank got himself winged and got his hoss kilt right under him. Good hoss, too."

"Bud," Hank said, "you notice somethin' peculiar? This gent ain't wearin' no gun."

"Rough country," Bud commented. "If'n I was you, mister, I'd wear a gun. You never know who you'll meet up with."

Chantry shrugged. "I don't wear a gun. If you'll pardon my saying so, I think guns lead to trouble."

"You hear that, Bud? He ain't wearin' no gun."

"Maybe guns do lead to trouble," Bud said seriously, "but they's times when not wearin' one will." Suddenly he held a pistol. "Git down off that hoss, mister."

"Now see here! I—"

"You git down off that hoss or I'll shoot you off, an' I ain't goin' to tell you again."

Hank was grinning at him, his lean, unshaven face taunting. "He'll do it, too, stranger. Bud here's kilt four men. He's one up on me."

"There's no need for this," Chantry said. "I've done you no harm."

He felt the sting of the nicked ear and then heard the blast of the pistol, although probably everything happened at once—the stab of flame, the report, the flash of pain from his ear.

"Mister, I ain't a-talkin' just to hear the wind blow. You git down."

Slowly, carefully, Tom Chantry swung down from his horse. Inwardly he was seething, but he was frightened, too. The man had meant to kill him.

Hank quickly dropped from his seat in back of Bud and swung up on Chantry's horse. With a wild, derisive yell they rode off, and he stood in the trail staring after them.

The place where they had come upon him was among scattered trees, but before him the country opened wide. It was high, lonely country, and ice still lay in the lake beside the trail. As far as he could see there was nothing—no house, no animal, no man. But he was alive. Had he been wearing a gun they might have killed him . . . or he might have killed one of them.

An hour later he was still alone, still in wide, open country, but he seemed to be a little nearer the mountains that rimmed the high basin.

That man had not missed by intention. He had wanted to kill. He had meant to kill. It was a shocking thing, an unreal thing. Chantry had held no weapon, had made no threatening gesture, and yet the men who had stolen his horse and his outfit would have killed him . . . and could have.

Would they have robbed him had he been armed? His mind refused to acknowledge the thought, but there was that doubt, that uncertainty. Had he been armed they might have tried to get the drop on him, to take his gun, and then rob him.

Suddenly he saw a thin, distant spiral of dust. It drew nearer and nearer, dissolved into a dozen hard-riding men. They drew up, the dust swirling around them.

"Did you see two men?" one of them asked. "Two men on one horse?"

"They are on two horses now. They stole mine at gun point."

"You mean you let 'em have it? Those were the Talrim boys . . . they murdered a man back yonder, and it ain't the first."

"I had no choice. I wasn't armed."

They stared at him. The bearded man shrugged. "This here's no country to travel without a weapon." He turned in his saddle. "Tell you what you do." He pointed. "Over the hill yonder—maybe three miles—there's a shack and a corral. You'll find a couple of horses there.

"You take one of them and ride on to Cimarron. Leave a note on the table in there . . . that's the Andress cabin and the old man will understand. You can leave the horse for him in Cimarron, or just turn him loose. He'll go home."

And then they were gone, and he was alone on the road, with the dust of the posse drifting around him.

It was coming on to sundown when he reached the Andress cabin and caught up one of the horses he found there. There was no saddle, but he had ridden bareback before this. He twisted a hackamore from some rope and mounted up.

Then, remembering the note, he swung down, tied the horse, and went inside the cabin. It was still and bare—a table, two chairs, a bunk in a corner, a few dog-eared magazines, and some old books. It was neat, everything was in its place.

He sat down and, searching in vain for paper, finally took an envelope from his pocket and scratched a brief note on the back with a pencil he carried. He weighted the note down with a silver dollar to pay for the use of the horse, pulled the door shut after him, mounted again, and rode out on the trail to Cimarron.

His face itched and, putting up a hand, he found there was dried blood from the nicked ear. He rubbed it away, then felt gingerly of the ear. The bleeding had stopped, but the ear was very tender. Moistening his handkerchief at his lips, he carefully wiped the dried blood away from the ear.

That had been a narrow escape. It was pure luck that the shot had not killed him, and pure whim on the part of Bud Talrim that he had not fired a second shot to better effect.

Tom Chantry shuddered... it was the same sudden reaction one has that usually draws the remark, "Somebody just stepped on your grave."

He might have been dead, and he might have been robbed, leaving no identification, with nothing to tell who he was or why he was here. It was appalling to consider how close he had come to an utterly useless death and a nameless grave. Back home nobody would ever have known what happened to him.

He made his decision then. He was going to get out of this country, and he was going to get out by the first stage, the very first train. He was going back east and he was going to stay there and live in a civilized community.

Since the shocking death of his father there had been no violence in his life. He had grown up first in a small New England village, going to school, fishing along the streams, hunting rabbits, squirrels, and then deer. He had gone to church, and had taken for granted the well-dressed, quiet-talking people, the neat streets, the well-ordered little town.

He had been aware of the town officials, the local constable, and the talk of courts and trials. He knew the town had a jail, although it was rarely occupied by more than an occasional drunk. Later, in New

York, the police had been more obvious. There were fire companies, and workmen to repair damage to the streets.

With these memories in his mind, he had also been conscious now for several minutes of the drum of a horse's hoofs on the trail behind him. He turned to see a rider on a bay horse—the very bay he had seen in the Andress corral when he caught up the horse he was riding. The rider was a tall, straight old man with a white mustache and clear blue eyes.

"Howdy, Chantry!" he called. "I'm Luke Andress. No need to leave that dollar. In this country if a man needs a horse all he needs to do is let a body know."

"Thank you." Briefly, Tom Chantry explained.

"Murderers," Andress said; "savages. But you ought to carry a gun. If you'd had a gun they'd never have tried it...not to your face, anyway. Those Talrims are back-shootin' murderers. At least, those two are."

"Do you think the posse will catch them?"

"Them? No, they won't—not by a durned sight. Those Talrims are a bad lot, but they're mountain men. With two horses under them and what grub you had they'll lose themselves in the mountains west of here. They're better than Injuns when it comes to runnin' an' hidin'."

Andress glanced at him. "You figuring on ranchin' it?"

"No, I came out to buy cattle, and after what's happened in the last few days I can't get out of here fast enough."

Andress was silent as they rode on for a short distance, and then he said, "It's a good country, Chantry.

It's like any country when it's young and growin'. It attracts the wild spirits, the loose-footed. Some of them settle down and become mighty good citizens, but there's always the savages. You have 'em back east, too."

"Not like here."

"Just like here . . . only you've got an organized society, a police department, and law courts. The bad actor there knows he ain't goin' to get far if he starts cuttin' up. Folks won't stand for it. But you walk down the street back there and you can figure maybe two out of every five folks you pass are savages. They may not even know it themselves, but once the law breaks down you'd find out fast enough. First they'd prey on the peaceful ones, then on each other . . . it's jungle law, boy, and don't you forget it.

"Out here there's nothin' but local law, and a man can be as mean as he wants to until folks catch up with him, or until he meets some bigger, tougher man. This is raw country; the good folks are good because it's their nature, and the bad can run to meanness until somebody fetches them up the short. That's why you'd better arm yourself. If you're goin' to be in this country you'll need a gun."

"Guns lead to trouble."

"Well," Andress said dryly, "I can see where not havin' a gun led you to trouble." He paused a moment. "The thieves and the killers are goin' to have guns, so if the honest men don't have 'em they just make it easier for the vicious. But you hold to your way of thinkin', boy, if you've a mind to. It's your way, and you got a right to it."

Cimarron showed up ahead, lights appearing, although it was not yet dark.

"Go to the St. James," Andress said. "There are some cattlemen there almost every night. They come in to play cards, or to set around and talk. You'll find some cattle, but if you're not goin' to carry a gun you'd better talk soft and stay clear of whiskey."

A room, a bath, and a good dinner made a lot of difference. Tom Chantry stood before the mirror and combed his dark hair, then he straightened his tie and shrugged his coat into a neater set on his shoulders.

Now for business . . . a thousand head of steers and the crew to drive them to the railhead. With any kind of luck he could be on the train for New York within a matter of a few days.

The saloon at the St. James was not crowded, for the hour was early, but it was at this hour that most of the business was conducted by the clientele. The western saloon, Tom Chantry knew, was more than merely a drinking room; it was a clearing house for information as to trails, grazing conditions, Indian attitudes, and business and political considerations generally.

At the bar Tom introduced himself to Henry Lambert, who owned the St. James. Lambert had once been chef at the White House, brought there originally by Grant, for he had cooked for Grant during part of the war.

"I am interested in buying cattle, Mr. Lambert. My name is Tom Chantry. If you know of anyone—"

"Mr. Chantry"—Lambert's face had stiffened slightly at the name—"I do know of cattle that might be for sale, but I would not advise you to buy them."

Surprised, Tom turned toward him. "Would you mind telling me why? Buying cattle is why I came to Cimarron."

"Mr. Chantry, I am a Frenchman, but I have become acquainted with the customs here. To buy the cattle would be easy, but you must get them to the railroad. I do not believe you could hire the men to do it."

"You mean there aren't any? At this time of year?"

"There are men, but they would not work for you, Mr. Chantry. I hope you will not take offense, for I am only telling you what is true. You see, there are no secrets in the West, and there has been talk, here in this bar, about how you failed to meet Dutch Akin."

"But what has that to do with hiring a crew?"

"Mr. Chantry, it is a long, hard drive from here to the end of the track. Much of it is through country where roving bands of Cheyenne, Comanche, and Kiowa may be found, and the Arapahoes too, I think. It is a hard country, without much water, with danger of sandstorms, stampedes, and other troubles. Men do not want to trust themselves to the leadership of a man whose courage is in question."

Tom Chantry felt himself turn cold. He stared at the cup of coffee before him for several minutes before he spoke. "Mr. Lambert," he said finally, "I am not a coward. I simply do not believe in carrying guns, and I do not believe in killing."

Lambert shrugged. "I do not believe in killing either, and yet a dozen men have died in this very room, died with guns in their hands.*

---

*Actually twenty-six men were said to have been killed in that room during the wild days.

"There is too much killing, yet the fact remains, that we live in a wild country, and one relatively lawless; and no man is willing to attempt a cattle drive that may demand the utmost in courage, with a man whose courage is suspect."

When Chantry spoke his voice was hoarse. "Thank you, Mr. Lambert," he said.

He sat alone, staring at the coffee as it grew cold in the cup.

CHAPTER 3

AFTER A SHORT time the depression left him. He would not be defeated. If there were cattle for sale he meant to buy them and, somehow or other, get them to market.

Luckily the Talrim boys had not thought to rob him of anything but his horse and his outfit. That was what they needed, and the thought of going through his pockets had not occurred to them. He still had his letter of credit and the money he had been carrying.

He was considering his next move when Luke Andress came over to the table, carrying a beer. "Mind if I sit down?"

"Please do."

"Had any luck?"

"No. And from what Lambert tells me I couldn't get the hands to drive a herd if I bought one."

"So what are you goin' to do?"

He considered that for a moment, and then said, "Mr. Andress, I am going to buy cattle, and I am going to drive them through if I have to do it myself... alone."

Andress chuckled. "You may have to, but I'll tell you what. See that big gent over there at the bar? The one with the elk's tooth on his watch chain? He's got maybe five or six hundred head you could buy. Lee

Dauber has eight or nine hundred head. I think you can dicker for 'em."

"Thanks."

"Now here's another thing. See that tall, good-lookin' fellow at the table yonder? That's French Williams. He'd sell you beef...he'll have seven or eight hundred head, but you'd better leave 'em alone."

"Why?"

"French is a mighty peculiar man. He's a smilin', easy-talkin', friendly man...almighty friendly. He sells a lot of beef, one time or another. He must have some uncommonly good bulls, because judgin' by the amount of beef he sells each cow must be havin' three calves."

"I don't want any brands that could be questioned."

"Nobody will question French's brand. Anyway, he never puts a brand on anything that's ever been branded before."

Andress turned his beer stein on the table and said, "Boy, I don't know why, but I like you. What I've told you about French could get me killed."

"I won't repeat it."

They sat silent for several minutes and then Tom Chantry said, "I know what I am going to do."

"What?"

"I'm going to buy cattle from those men if they will sell, and then I am going to hire French Williams to take them through for me."

Luke Andress stared at him, then began to chuckle. "Boy, you've got nerve, I'll say that for you! But you be careful of French! He won't go into any deal unless he figures to come out ahead."

There was no use wasting time. If the word had gotten around, they all knew he had backed out of a fight with Dutch Akin, and the only thing left for him was either to skip the country or take the bull by the horns. He got up, excused himself to Andress, and walked across the room.

Two men sat with French Williams, and they all looked up when he stopped at their table.

"French Williams? I am Tom Chantry."

French looked up lazily. "I've heard of you."

"Then they have told you that I backed down for Dutch Akin. The simple facts of the case are that I haven't time to go around shooting every Tom, Dick, and Harry who wants to get drunk and start a fight. I came here to buy cattle. I hear that you and some of these other gentlemen have cattle for sale. I've also been told that I'll never be able to hire a crew to take my herd to the railhead. But I don't believe it.

"I want to buy what cattle you have for sale, and I'll pay cash for them. I will also buy whatever cattle are for sale by any of the other gentlemen in this room on the same terms."

"And how do you figure to get them to market?" French had scarcely moved. He was sitting back in his chair, staring up at Chantry, cool and calculating, almost insolent.

"I have been told by various people that you are a shrewd dealer, and that you are not to be trusted." His voice was loud enough for others to hear, and they were all listening. "I have heard that anybody who gets into a cattle deal with you will lose his eye-teeth. I don't believe it."

French Williams' expression had tightened a little as Chantry talked, but his eyes had never left Tom's face.

"You don't?"

"No, I do not. That is why I am offering you one-third of the sale price of the herd if you will drive my cattle to the railhead."

For a moment there was silence in the saloon, and then French Williams chuckled. "Sit down," he said. "I want to buy you a drink."

"All right, and I'll buy you one."

Chantry sat down, and Williams' black eyes glinted with amusement.

"You don't think I'll rook you?"

"No. I think you're a man of your word."

French eyed him curiously. "You're either a damn fool or you're pretty smart. Well, we'll see who's smart and who isn't. You think I'm honest and I think you've got sand, so I'll tell you what I'll do.

"I will take your herd to the railhead for expenses... if you will come with us and stay all the way through. If you don't stay with it, I take it all... every last steer."

French was smiling, his black eyes taunting.

"That's the deal. Take it or leave it."

Chantry pushed the bottle toward him. "Pour your drink, French. We're in business."

"You'll take it?"

"Of course."

Chantry turned toward the bar. "Mr. Dauber? Let's talk about cattle."

Lee Dauber walked over to the table, a glass in his hand. "I can deliver. How do I know you can pay?"

Tom Chantry placed his letter of credit on the table. "There it is."

Dauber dismissed it with a gesture. "A piece of paper. I go by a man's word. You backed down for Dutch Akin. How do I know your word is good?"

French Williams looked up. "Lee? *I* say his word is good. Any argument?"

Lee Dauber shrugged. "Your funeral, French. All right, we'll dicker. I've got a thousand head, give or take a few."

For an hour the talk went on, and at the end of it Tom Chantry held title to twenty-two hundred head of cattle, stock for which he had paid with sums drawn from his letter of credit. Of the money behind that letter of credit only a little of it was his own; the remainder belonged to Earnshaw and Company.

With luck the drive would take them thirty days, perhaps a bit more or less; and if he made it through, he would have a herd whose price would not be less than fifty thousand dollars, of which two-thirds would be sheer profit. On the other hand, if he failed he would lose everything, and Earnshaw would take a heavy loss.

He was guessing on the time it would take to get the herd to the railhead, for he had never made a drive with cattle, although he knew something of the problems involved. Moreover, the railroad was moving west... he was not sure French Williams knew that, and he did not intend to tell him.

The railroad had been stalled at Dodge City for several years because of the financial depression and the inability to raise money for the investment. Now the rails had started moving again, and when he left the railroad he had been assured they could hold to a speed of about a mile a day, laying track. That might be optimistic . . . what he was going to need was information, information for himself alone.

There was always the chance of some casual traveler relaying the knowledge, for it was certainly no secret, but rumors had been flying during all the time since construction stopped, and many western men had simply given up believing anything until they saw it.

Alone that night in his room, Tom Chantry stretched out on his bed, hands clasped behind his head, and thought the thing through.

He was under no illusions about French Williams. The man was hard as nails and dangerous as a rattler, but he was a man of fierce pride, and Chantry knew he had touched it when he called him a man of his word.

Obviously French was a gambler. It was a game of winner-take-all, and French was not the kind of man to enjoy losing. What he was gambling on was, in essence, Chantry's staying quality. Tom Chantry was no fool, and he knew that French Williams would make it very rough.

Did Williams believe him a coward? That remained to be seen. More likely than not he had no thoughts on the matter, and cared less. He would test Chantry's nerve with sadistic pleasure . . . and would be an interested observer of Chantry's reactions.

Actually, French Williams was risking only his time. And he might like a ride to Dodge anyway. The risk was all for Tom Chantry; the gain, if he won, would be great. But had he any right to take such a risk with another man's money?

They needed beef badly if they were to continue operations as planned. Tom Chantry considered the gamble he had taken and admitted, reluctantly, that he had been foolish. He had been challenged, and like any green kid he had accepted the challenge.

Now he must plan. He must try to foresee what French would do. The most obvious thing was the old western trick of giving him a bad horse to ride, and this he had every right to expect. It was usual for any tenderfoot on a cow ranch or a cattle drive to be given a bad horse just as a joke.

Well, let them try. He had been riding horses since he was a child, and even back east he had never quit riding. He had handled some pretty bad ones, but he doubted that he had tangled with anything like what they could give him out here, and he was sure they were even now planning on that.

He knew it was going to be rough, especially as he had taken water for Dutch Akin. No cowhand would consider that anything but cowardice, and they would have nothing but contempt for him.

At daybreak he was up, and after a quick breakfast he went to the livery stable and bought two horses. Both were tough and well-seasoned, and he paid premium prices for them. He bargained, but the horse dealer knew he wanted horses and knew what he wanted them for. He got good horses, and the price he finally paid was not as bad as he had expected. One was a line-back dun, the other a blue roan, both bigger than the usual cow horse, but agile enough.

The dun was an excellent cutting horse, the blue roan was fair; both had the look of possessing staying quality. "Which I'd better have myself," he said to himself.

He bought a used saddle, a blanket, and all the essential gear. At the general store he bought a slicker, a bedroll, and a little other equipment.

"You better have yourself a gun," the storekeeper suggested.

Chantry shook his head, smiling. "I doubt if I'll need it. I will have a Winchester, though. I've never killed a buffalo, and we might need the meat."

He bought a Winchester '73 and four hundred rounds of ammunition. "If I am going to use this," he commented, "I'd better have some practice."

"Better not try it near a cattle herd," the storekeeper said dryly, "or you'll have a stampede."

They all thought him a tenderfoot, he reflected, and in one sense it was true, but he was western-born and a lot had soaked in that stayed with him. One did not live in the environment during the impressionable years and not retain something from it.

His father had been a man who talked of his work and his life, and he was a man who had known men and stock, who had pioneered in wild country. Had he been trying, even then, to instruct his son? After all, what did a father have to pass on to his children but his own personal reaction to the world? Of what use was experience if one could not pass on at least a little of what one had learned?

For the first time Tom Chantry thought of that, and suddenly he was seeing his father in a new light. Like many another son, he had failed to understand the true nature of the man who was his father until he himself began to cope with the problems of which life is made up.

THEY WERE TO make their gather and pool the cattle on the Vermejo River, east and a bit north of Cimarron, and their drive would begin from there.

He would go there and join them. He would ride his own horses, but if they suggested a bad one, he would try it. He could be thrown, but he could also get back on. Tom Chantry decided he knew what to expect, and he was prepared for it. The trouble was, he did not know French Williams.

He knew little enough about the Vermejo River. Only that it began somewhere in the Sangre de Cristos and flowed down from the mountains, across the old Santa Fe Trail to lose itself, so far as he knew, somewhere in the open country beyond.

Riding the blue roan and leading the dun, he started for the camp on the Vermejo. He told himself he was ready for anything, and he was still telling himself that when he spotted the camp under some cottonwoods.

There was already a good gathering of cattle, and he could see various riders bringing in more. He passed near one rider, a tall, lean man with red hair, but the rider seemed not to notice him, although Chantry spoke.

He rode up to the chuck wagon and swung down. French Williams was leaning back against his bedroll, smiling. And it was not a pleasant smile. It was taunting, challenging, showing, something that might be contempt, and might be curiosity. As Tom Chantry walked forward and started to speak, a man came from behind the chuck wagon. He stepped out and stopped, waiting.

The man was Dutch Akin.

CHAPTER 4

FOR A MOMENT all action was suspended. Tom Chantry could feel the heavy pounding of his heart, and his mouth was dry, but when he spoke his voice was clear and steady. "Hello, Dutch. Want some coffee?"

This was what Chantry had not expected, yet it was what he might have expected from French Williams. And it was an indication of the extent to which Williams was prepared to go.

"Don't mind if I do," Dutch said.

Chantry picked up the pot and filled Dutch's cup, then his own. "Sorry about the other night, Dutch," he said, "but I had no reason to kill you, and I had no wish to die."

Dutch shrugged uncomfortably. Sober, he was not a belligerent man, nor was he given to talk. If you had a job to do, you did it. If you had a man to shoot, you shot him. But talking about it made him uneasy, wanting to be away and finished with it. " 'S all right," he said, gulping the coffee. "I got no argument with you."

French Williams sat up. If he was disappointed it did not show, and Tom Chantry doubted that he was. It had been in the nature of an experiment, and had they killed each other he would have been no more disturbed.

Chantry indicated the cattle. "They're in good shape. Some of your stuff?"

"Uh-huh," French said. "They've been held in the high meadows where there's lots of good grama." He glanced toward the horses. "I see you got yourself some horses. Two won't be enough, you know."

Chantry's expression was bland. "I had an idea you'd already selected some mounts for me, French, so I only bought two."

"You'd ride a horse I'd pick for you?"

"Why not? Well, let's just say I'd try."

The other hands who had been loafing about, obviously to see what would happen when he met Dutch Akin, now drifted off about their work. Tom Chantry drank his coffee slowly, studying the various men, watching the work, and enjoying the brief respite from what was to come.

He was no cowhand and would not attempt to compete with them on their own ground. He could round up cattle, he could read brands, and so could make himself generally useful. He would not be an idler. It would be wise to move slowly at first, to see who could do what, and generally become acquainted.

He had gained no ground by facing Dutch. He had simply done what had to be done, and he knew the hands would be waiting to see what kind of a man he was—and most of them, he felt sure, had made up their minds about that.

As he watched the cattle the enormity of what he had undertaken slowly came over him. His own capital he was free to do with as he saw fit, but he had gambled a large sum that belonged to Earnshaw and

Company. Therefore there was no choice. The herd must go through, and it must arrive in good shape and be sold to advantage . . . no matter what the cost to him.

Riders were bringing in small bunches of cattle from draws and breaks. Saddling the dun, he rode out and helped here and there, at the same time noting the brands. All of those being held had come from French Williams' own outfit. Some of the brands were fresh, but he saw no evidence of reworking.

At daybreak he was on the range with the others, and was there when Lee Dauber's cattle began to arrive. They came divided into three herds for easy handling, and Dauber moved them along at a good clip. These were big, rangy steers, older than most of Williams' stuff, and in not as good shape.

During the following days while the cattle were being brought together for the drive to the railhead, he worked hard, harder than he had ever worked before. He was up before the first streak of light in the morning sky, and tumbled into his bedroll when supper was over. With the others he stood night guard, and in many ways that came to be the best time.

Only three men rode night guard at a time, and they were scattered, meeting only at intervals as they rode around the sleeping herd. It was a time for thinking, a time for remembering. Yet, oddly, he rarely thought of Doris, and rarely of his home in the East. His thoughts kept reaching back into his boyhood, before his father was killed.

He remembered the hot, still hours in the town, walking barefooted up the dusty street, seeing the tall, still-faced men in boots and spurs sitting along the boardwalk in front of the hotel, or seeing them leaning on the corral bars, watching the horses.

The parched brown prairie, long without rain, the tumbleweeds rolling before the wind under dark, rain-filled clouds, the blue streaks of a distant rainstorm viewed from far off . . . the call of quail at sundown . . . his father washing his face and hands in the tin basin outside the kitchen door, sleeves rolled up, showing the white of his arms where the sun never reached.

He remembered the Indians who came to the ranch, squatting around near the corral, and his father feeding them, carrying the food to them himself . . . and the night the wounded brave had ridden up to the house, clinging one-handed to his horse's mane. That was on the old ranch, before Pa lost it in the big freeze . . . where had that ranch been, anyway? His memories were mostly from the later period when Pa was marshal.

They had gone back to the ranch once, all of them, driving in a buckboard. "There it is, Helen," Pa had said, "fifteen years of brutal hard work and a lot of dreams, all gone in one freeze."

Tom Chantry remembered the tall old cottonwoods around the house, the log cabin his father had built, then added to . . . the cold water from the hand-dug well. "I planned all this for you, Tom," his father had said, "but I reckoned without the snow and the cold."

The old ranch had been somewhere east of here, he believed. A boy doesn't have much sense of location when he is six.

Suddenly, he remembered The Hole. At least, that was what he called it.

There had been a small spring about a mile from the ranch, and he had ridden over there once when he was about six. The spring came down from under an overhang of rock, about two feet off the ground, and the water fell into a rock basin, trickled over its lip and down into the meadow below, where it was again swallowed up.

Some dirt had fallen into the spring from one of the overhanging banks, and he was scooping it out with his hands when, at the back of the spring where the water ran down from the darkness under the rock, he saw The Hole.

Actually, it was where the water came from, but the opening was much bigger than the space taken up by the trickle of water. Peering back into the deepest shadow, he could see the hole was about three feet across and almost that in height. He stood barefooted in the cold water, and could look back into the hole, but could make out nothing. Looking down at his feet, he could just see the light across the water.

Evidently spring rains had shot out of the hole with some force and had gradually worn the rock back until there was space enough for a boy to stand. With a long stick he poked into the darkness. There was a pool of water where it trickled over the edge, but his stick could not reach either wall or roof. Later, with a longer stick he probed the darkness and succeeded in touching rock on the right side of the stream. Overhead he could find nothing, but there was a rock floor on the left of the stream.

From outside there was no indication of anything

like the cave. There was only a dip in the prairie, a natural runoff for water, and a slab of rock was exposed from under which the water ran. Anyone stopping by for a drink would suspect nothing. Although a man might enter the opening once he knew of it, only a child or a small animal would be likely to find it.

He named the place The Hole, and told his father about it.

All that was long ago . . . he had not thought of The Hole for twenty years that he could recall.

TOM CHANTRY GAVE no orders. If he saw anything that needed doing he did it himself, or reported it to French. He had no friends in the outfit, although French talked to him occasionally. Chantry was puzzled by him. Of French's background he knew nothing, but somehow the man gave him the impression that he had education, and a better background than most of the men in the outfit, but French volunteered nothing, and Tom Chantry knew better than to ask.

In general, the men ignored him. Oddly enough, when he did begin to make a friend it was Dutch Akin, of all people.

It began casually enough. He was riding back to the chuck wagon when he saw another rider following a route that would bring them together. Not until they were too close to turn aside did either recognize the other. It was Dutch.

"Beautiful country, Dutch," Chantry said.

Dutch merely grunted, then after a few minutes of silence he said, "You better not rest too easy. French is a holy terror. He's a good man to work for, gen'rally speakin', but he'd rather stir up trouble than eat. You let down one minute an' he'll be all over you."

"Thanks. He's not an easy man to understand."

"That he ain't," Dutch agreed dryly, "but he knows cows and no man alive is better on a trail than him." Then he said, "Mr. Chantry, I ain't one to stick my nose in, but if we all come up to trouble, you'd best run it. French will shoot you right into a range war . . . he's quick and he goes hog-wild an' mean. I've seen it."

"Thanks again." The horses walked a dozen yards before Chantry spoke again. "Dutch, do you think I'm yellow? I'm asking a question, not trying to invite a fight."

Dutch grinned, and then he said soberly, "No, I don't think nothin' of the kind. I might have. But not after the way you come up to me back there. I'd say you used better judgment than me back in Las Vegas.

"The only thing is," he added, "you not carryin' a gun makes a lot of them think you're scared . . . and believe me, it won't keep you out of trouble."

"But we're both alive, Dutch."

"Uh-huh, and if it wasn't for you one of us would be dead, but that cuts no ice. You just plain lucked out with the Talrim boys . . . they'd shoot you soon as look at you."

When they rode into camp together several heads turned, but there was no comment. French noticed it, without smiling. He gave the impression of being coiled, ready to lash out.

He was eating when suddenly he put his plate

down. "We got twenty-two hundred head, Chantry. You want more?"

"No . . . let's move 'em out."

"Daybreak?"

"Yes."

"For Dodge?"

"No."

They all looked up then, surprised. French was the most surprised of all, Chantry thought, for until that time Chantry had left all the handling of the cattle to him.

"We'll take the longer route," Chantry said, "by way of Clifton House."

He realized he could not hope to compare his information about the area with that of French Williams, but they would not know how much or how little he knew, and must proceed accordingly.

"Have it your way," French said mildly. "There's more water, easier drives." He grinned at him. "And it will take longer."

Tom Chantry lay that night, looking up at the stars, and, tired as he was, there was little sleep in him. The way they would follow had been traveled by cattle herds occasionally, more often by pack trains, army commands, and mountain men, but every foot of it was alive with danger and trouble.

The men with whom he rode were silent toward him. They did not trust his courage, and were not prepared to respect his leadership. Most important, perhaps, he had a partner in whom he must trust to some extent, but who had everything to gain by not getting the cattle through on time, or at all.

Lying there in the darkness, he felt suddenly very

much alone, but he remembered something his father had said. "Don't ever be afraid of being alone, boy. The strongest man is he who stands alone."

And then Pa had added, "To just that extent that you lean on somebody, or rely on them, to that extent you are a weaker man."

CHAPTER 5

WHEN THE HERD moved out in the morning Tom Chantry rode on ahead.

The stars were still in the sky, and the cattle were a bobbing mass of black without shape or substance. Then as the gray sky grew paler, here and there a horn glistened in reflected light, or a balky steer moved out from the herd and had to be shoved back.

Slowly a few of the cattle moved out ahead and the herd strung out along the trail, not an impressive sight to anyone who had seen buffalo in their great masses on this same grass, but this slim north-pointing finger was a symbol of change in the West.

The cattle could not exist here until the buffalo were gone, but in their time many of the cattle would go, too. Even as they displaced the buffalo, the forerunners of their own replacements were building shacks and stringing fences west of the Mississippi. Lone cabins appeared, with occasionally a barn, and a field plowed up.

Better than the others, Chantry knew what that meant, for he had lived in the East. The buffalo had to give way to cattle to feed the growing population of eastern cities; in their turn the cattle would go because farmers wanted to grow crops, they wanted to plant corn, wheat, and rye on the ground where the grazing grass grew.

Nor could the Indian, free-roving as he was, compete in his hunting and food-gathering existence with the farmer, for the Indians needed thousands of acres for even a small group to exist, and on much less ground the farmer could grow crops for himself and for shipment east.

Tom Chantry thought of the disappearing buffalo with regret, but he could not deny the inevitable.

French moved up beside him. "They're stringing out well, Chantry. We're off to an easy start." After a momentary pause he said, "Why'd you choose the long way? The Cut-Off is much the fastest. It's drier, but we could make it. Were you scared, or just cautious?"

"Maybe a little of both. Why take the chance?"

French glanced at him. "It doesn't seem to bother you much that the boys think you're yellow."

Chantry felt a quick surge of anger, but fought it down. His voice was calm when he replied. "It does bother me. There's still enough of the kid in me for it to bother a lot, but I've got enough man in me not to be a damn fool about it."

"You can't duck a showdown. You can only postpone it."

"Maybe. But when the showdown comes you'll be the first to know."

French looked at him sharply. "Are you saying that when you have a showdown it'll be with me?"

"That's hardly likely. I need you to get to Dodge. Anyway, I'm not a gunfighting man. Remember that."

"I'll be damned if I can figure you out, Chantry.

You talk like a man with sand, but you sure don't act up to it."

"French, this will be a long drive. You know that better than I do. If I'm to get these cattle through I'd better stay alive, and I want you alive, too."

"What if it comes to gun trouble?"

"They tell me you're the fastest man in the country. I'll leave the gunfighting to you."

French Williams couldn't leave it alone. "But you can shoot? I mean, you're packing a Winchester... why?"

"Meat... we've men to feed, and I don't want to butcher my own cattle if I can help it."

"Can you hit anything?"

"Well," Chantry said seriously, "the man who sold me the rifle said that if I'd point it in the right direction I'd have a pretty good chance. Of course, he said, I'd have to hold steady. I'll give it a try sometime."

French was silent, uncertain whether Chantry was serious or not. "What else did they tell you about me?" he asked finally.

"You know what they'd be likely to say. That your cows were the best in the country, giving you four or five calves a year... that sort of thing."

French grinned. "Maybe I'm just lucky," he said. He stood in his stirrups to scan the country ahead. "Why'd you pick me, then?"

"Because they said you might steal a man's cows, but you'd never cheat at cards. They said whatever else you were, you were a man of your word. Also, they said you had guts and knew cattle. I decided you were the man I wanted."

French swung his horse and rode back along the line of the drive.

Chantry, after a moment of hesitation, rode on ahead at a fast trot. He wanted to see the country, and if anybody was coming down the trail he wanted to see them first. He needed to know, needed desperately to know about that railroad.

He topped out on the low ridge that crossed the trail. Far off to the east he could see a moving black patch, some scattered black spots that must be buffalo. Nearer, there was nothing.

The sky was fantastically clear . . . no clouds, and a view that carried the eye away to a vast distance. The roan tugged at the bit, eager to be moving, but Chantry waited, studying the land. This was what he must do . . . he must learn to *see,* not merely to look. He must learn to recognize the things at which he looked, and to draw conclusions from them. Out here a man's life might depend upon it.

Despite his feelings about carrying a gun, he found himself occasionally wishing he had one. It was a kind of insurance.

Now, feeling alone upon the plains, facing the situation in which he had placed himself, he had time to be afraid. He could not help but think of what he was risking for himself and for Earnshaw, gambling that he could stay with the herd to its shipping point. The presence of Dutch Akin was a hint as to the lengths to which French Williams would go to drive him off.

Had French expected him to turn tail and run? It was more than likely. But he had not run, and now the next move was up to French.

Turning in his saddle, he looked back at the long

line of cattle. He was more than a mile in advance of the drive and from where he sat he could see it to advantage. The men riding drag appeared only occasionally through the dust, but the flankers on either side he could see easily, and the two men riding point. Off to the east was the chuck wagon, and not far behind it the wranglers with the horse herd.

Twenty-two hundred head, give or take a few, and fifteen men to ride herd on them—sixteen, including himself. And ahead of them twenty to thirty days' drive, depending on conditions, and on how far west the railroad had progressed.

Aside from choosing the destination, he could do little in the way of planning. Their final destination was in his hands; the management of the herd and the men was up to French.

The season was well along. Here and there water holes would be drying up, but for most of the early part of the drive they would be near the Canadian or some of its branches.

To the east was buffalo country, and Indian country as well, and before very long they must turn east; at no time would they be safe either from Indians or from rustlers.

Chantry did not believe French would try to steal the herd . . . too many people knew the circumstances of their bargain, and French would deem it a personal failure to win by any means other than driving Chantry from the herd . . . or so Chantry believed.

For that reason, he must be wary of tricks. Searching back into his childhood, he tried to remember the tricks played by cowboys on trail drives or roundups.

The bucking horse was the first and most obvious, and Chantry was sure that would come his way again. The rattlesnake in the blankets was another... or something that might appear to be a snake.

Worst of all, he had no friends in the crew, and Akin was the only one who even took the time to talk to him; but that might change. Slowly, he studied them in his mind, trying to pick out the ones who might at least stand for fair play.

McKay...a short, stocky man with a shock of rusty brown curls and a hard-boned face. He was twenty-four or -five, a first-class bronc stomper and a good hand with cattle. A steady man, asking no favors of anyone, doing his share of the work and a little more. He packed a gun, and by all accounts could use it.

Helvic...a quiet-mannered man, somewhat reserved, and four or five years older than McKay. A good hand from Illinois, four years a soldier in the frontier cavalry, a year as a freighter, and four years a cowhand.

Hayden Gentry...called Hay Gent, from Uvalde, down in Texas, his family among the first settlers west of the Neuces. Long, lean, and tough as mule hide. Easy-going, full of humor, and fast with a gun, so it was said. Nobody wanted to be known as good with a gun around French, not unless he was a trouble-hunter.

Rugger, Kincaid, and Koch were good hands, but they were cronies of French, and probably not one of them had been born with the name he was using. A bad lot, as were most of the others.

Chantry rode on. The grass was dry, but there was plenty of it. Twice he saw buffalo, but only a few, and those were scattered out. Evidently they were on the outer edges of the great herd, or were forerunners of the herd.

The country was open, slightly rolling. Ahead loomed Eagle Rock, near where they expected to bed down for the night. Twice, Chantry drew up. He had the eerie, uncomfortable feeling of being watched, but he could see nothing, hear nothing. Nor was there any movement within sight, only the brown grass on an occasional slope being bent by the wind.

There were no fresh tracks.

Suddenly wary, he swung his horse and rode off to the west, scouting for sign. He found nothing. Tracks of buffalo, occasionally old horse tracks. He stood in his stirrups and looked off toward the breaks of the Canadian, not far to the east.

The creeks that flowed into the river had cut deep at places, and the sides were lined with heavy growth of trees and brush. In those breaks, Chantry reflected, an army could be hidden . . . it was something to consider.

He was high on a grassy hill with nothing in sight for a far distance when he heard the cry—a faint, choking cry, like nothing human, and it came from not far off. The roan, head up, ears pricked, looked off toward the right, toward the breaks of the Canadian.

Chantry waited, listening. Had it been human or animal? And if an animal, what kind could make such a sound? Suddenly he was sure the cry was human.

Turning his horse, he started in the direction the roan had looked, and peered ahead for the first glimpse of whatever it was.

He looked around slowly, studying the surroundings with infinite care. It might be a trap. He did not believe all he had heard of Indians, but he was cautious by nature. His horse walked forward, taking each step gingerly, as if ready to bolt. Obviously the roan did not like what it sensed was near.

Chantry's inclination was to turn and ride away, swiftly, for what lay before him was terror . . . perhaps horror. Instinctively he knew he should escape while it was still possible, but something urged him on . . . to see, *what?*

For a moment Chantry thought he could ride back, warn them of something ahead, and then approach this place with a dozen riders . . . yet what if there was nothing? He would have shown himself to be both a coward and a fool.

No, he knew he could not go back, and he rode on, walking his horse. He could feel its reluctance in the tenseness of its muscles, its urge to turn away.

Suddenly they topped the low rise and he was looking into a shallow place that sloped away with increasing steepness toward the river, but Chantry did not see that. All he saw was the man staked out before him. He dismounted and took a step nearer.

The man was stripped naked, hands and legs outspread, each ankle and each wrist tied to a stake. Already the sun had turned the white flesh a deep red in ugly burns, but burns could be as nothing to him, for he had been horribly mutilated.

In each thigh there was a deep gash along the top of the muscle from the hip to the knee. His stomach had been cut open and piled full of rock. The sides of his face were cut, and the muscles of his biceps. For a frozen moment Tom Chantry stared, shocked motionless, and then, of a sudden, his horse shied violently.

Turning sharply, he saw himself facing half a dozen Indians. He saw them, saw their hands still bloody from the deed before them, and realized his rifle was in its scabbard on the saddle. It was no more than six feet away, but it might have been as many miles. If he made a move toward it, they could kill him. Would they?

Before him was the evidence. They had killed this man. No doubt he had fought them, no doubt he was an enemy taken in battle. As for himself, if he was to survive he must face them down. He spoke suddenly, keeping his tone moderate.

"This was not a good thing to do," he said, speaking carefully. "One man could do you no harm."

One of the Indians spoke, surprisingly, in English. "He do nothing to us. We find track. We follow. We kill."

"Why?"

The Indian appeared to think the question foolish. He replied simply, "Why not?"

"Go. I will bury him."

"All right." The Indian said something to the others and they chuckled. "All right. You bury. Only him not dead yet." Then admiringly, "He strong man. He no cry, no beg. He laugh, he swear. Strong man."

What was he saying? The tortured man was not dead.

"I will bury him," he repeated. "You go."

"We watch," the Indian replied. Then he said, "You strong like him?"

"Go," he said, fighting down the horror and the fear that crept up within him. "Go." And surprisingly, they went.

He stood for a moment, staring after them, not willing to accept what his eyes told him. Then from behind him there was a shuddering groan. Chantry turned sharply.

The tortured man said, "If you got any water, I'd like it."

The tone was calm, controlled.

"You—you're *alive?*"

"It ain't for long. You git me that water and I'll be obliged."

Chantry turned swiftly to his horse and the canteen on the saddle horn. Kneeling beside the man, he held it to his lips. Feverishly, the man drank. For a moment he lay quiet and then he said, "I reckon that's the best thing I ever tasted."

"I'll untie you. I'll—"

"No! Don't you pay it no mind." The eyes opened and looked at him calmly. "I'm dead, man, can't you *see?*" And then he added, "I beat 'em! I beat those red devils at their own game! I never whimpered!

"You tell 'em that at the fort!" His voice was suddenly hoarse. "You tell 'em McGuinness never whimpered! Tell 'em that!"

"The chuck wagon is coming," Chantry said. "We have medicinc, we—"

"Don't be a damn fool," the man said. "You tell 'em at the fort. You tell 'em—"

His voice faded away and his eyes suddenly were still. Chantry straightened to his feet. The man was dead....

CHAPTER 6

"IS HE GONE?"

Chantry faced sharply around. French Williams, Dutch Akin, Gent, Helvie, and Koch were on the rise behind him. All carried rifles.

"How could he be alive?"

"There wasn't much give in him," Hay Gent commented. "A man like that might live through anything."

"Ride to the wagon, Dutch," Williams said, "and bring up a shovel. We'll do the honors."

He glanced at Helvie. "You want to say the words? Or shall we let Chantry?"

"No!" Koch shouted. "I'll be damned if he will! Not over a man who died like that!"

Chantry felt himself go sick with shame, then fury. Suddenly he was in a killing rage. "Koch," he said, "I'll—"

"Shut up!" French laid his voice across them like a lash. "Helvie will read. Chantry, you'd better get back to the wagon while you're all together."

Chantry stood stiff, his anger vanished in the cold awareness that only Williams' intervention had saved him from another shooting situation.

"All right, but I hope you will notice that I was unarmed, yet the Indians did not attack me. If this man had done the same, perhaps—"

Helvie interrupted impatiently. "He was unarmed too. Can't you see? It didn't save him. If you'll look at the tracks . . . we followed them here. They raced beside him, striking, bedeviling him. Then they began the torture.

"This man was a soldier—a deserter perhaps. He had no gun. They killed his horse. Didn't you hear what the Indian said? The man had done nothing to them. He was a stranger, therefore an enemy. They were Kiowas. It did not matter that this man was a white man. Had he been a Ute he would have fared no better."

"You *heard* them? You were *here?*"

"Why do you think they rode away? Because you were nice and peaceful. They left because they saw our guns on them from right over that ridge. We weren't begging a fight, and under the conditions neither were they."

French turned his back on him and walked away as Akin appeared with a shovel.

Tom Chantry hesitated, then swung into the saddle. He had made a fool of himself. Had not the others come when they did he might now be lying dead beside that dead man. Still, how could he *know?*

Nonetheless, he was displeased with himself. In their eyes he had come off badly. At best, he had been inadequate, and he did not like the feeling that he was despised. They were competent men who knew their jobs, men of proven courage and stamina, accepted by each other. He had proved nothing to anyone. Not even to himself. In their eyes he was a man who failed to measure up. They did not think him worthy to read the final words over a dead man.

It was hard to take, and he rode back to camp, ate, and turned in. Clifton House lay ahead, and there might be news. With luck the drive might be a short one.

Clifton House was a stage stop and a gathering place for cattle. Suddenly, before falling asleep, he made up his mind. He would ride on ahead, reach Clifton House well before the herd, and gather what information was available. Undoubtedly the herd would stop for the night not far from there, but he might learn whatever was known in time to change their route.

At daybreak he told Williams, "I'm riding to Clifton House. I'm expecting mail there."

"Better take somebody along to wipe your nose," Koch remarked. "There's some mighty mean men hang out at Clifton."

From one of the others he might have ignored it, but Koch was a sour, mean man with no breath of goodness in him, and after his remark of the day before Tom Chantry was in no mood for any more of it. He put down his cup.

"Koch," he said, "I don't believe in killing men. I've no such feelings about giving one a whipping when he asks for it."

For a moment the camp was slack-jawed with amazement. Koch stared at him. "You gone crazy? Are you talkin' to *me?*"

"To you," Chantry got to his feet. "Just take off your gun belt."

Koch had the reputation of being a fist-fighter, and he liked to be known for it. He put down his plate and unbuckled his belt. "This here," he said, "is goin' to give me pleasure."

He got up, placing his gun belt on the ground, and he swung from that position. The blow was totally unexpected, and caught Chantry on the chin. His heels flew up and he hit the dust on the back of his shoulders, Koch rushing up to stamp on him. The cowpuncher's first kick was launched too soon and caught Chantry on the shoulder. It was the first time he had ever been kicked, and suddenly he realized that all he knew of fighting would do him no good unless he got into action fast.

Rolling over, he lunged to a crouching position and dived at Koch. The cowboy had been expecting Chantry to try to stand erect, and the sudden lunge made him step back quickly. On his high-heeled boots he staggered, and Chantry smashed into him.

Tom Chantry was lean and strong, and in good shape. He had boxed and wrestled a lot, but simply for fun. He had had only two fights since he was a man, both of them in the stockyards where he bought cattle, but the men with whom he had boxed and wrestled had been above average, and he knew how to handle himself.

Ugly with anger at being knocked into the dust, Koch was up quickly. He swung a looping right. Chantry saw it coming and stepped inside, smashing a right to the ribs that made the larger man gasp.

Koch grabbed him, tried to butt, then stamped on Chantry's instep with his boot heel. A stabbing pain went through Chantry's foot, and jerking back he threw the cowhand over his hip with a rolling hiplock.

Koch sprang to his feet and came in fast. He hit Chantry high on the cheekbone, splitting the skin. Another blow caught Chantry on the chin. Tom staggered, blocked a blow with his elbow, and countered with a stiff right to the body.

He was warmed up now, and suddenly he felt good. This was something he could do, and he liked to do it. Koch, at about one-ninety, was twenty pounds the heavier man, but he was slower. A skilled rough-and-tumble fighter, he knew nothing of boxing, and less of defense.

Tom Chantry had caught three brutally hard punches and was still on his feet. He had been down, but he had gotten up. He was sure Koch had hit him as hard as he was likely to, and he had taken the punches and was still coming.

He sidestepped as Koch swung, and hit the bigger man in the belly, but made no effort to follow it up. Koch wheeled, and came in slowly, looking for an opening. Tom feinted at the ribs, and when Koch dropped his hand, he hit him on the ear, splitting it and showering him with blood. When Koch's hands came up, Tom whipped an uppercut to the wind.

His timing was right now. Koch might be a good man with a gun and a brawler with some success, but Tom was realizing now that boxing was not in Koch's experience. He struck a stiff left to the face, and repeated it. He feinted another, then struck to the wind.

Koch moved in, and suddenly kicked for the groin. Chantry saw it just in time and, stepping back, tripped over an extended leg, whose leg he did not know. He staggered and fell, and Koch stamped at his head. Rolling away from Koch's boot heel, Chantry caught a vicious backward kick from Koch's Mexican spur, driven into the face.

Chantry lunged up from the ground. The viciousness of the attack appalled and infuriated him. He brushed a punch aside and smashed both hands to Koch's face in short, wicked hooks, and then as the man staggered back, Chantry broke his nose with an overhand right.

Blood was running down the side of his face, but Tom Chantry had no thought now but to destroy. He feinted, smashed another right to the already broken nose, then hooked both hands to the wind in short, lifting punches, and an overhand right to the side of the neck.

Koch staggered, and Chantry moved in, left and right to the face. Koch fell back against the chuck wagon and Tom uppercut to the wind, then smashed another right to the face. Koch started to fall, but Chantry caught him by the shirt and held him while he hit him in the face. Then he dropped him into the dust.

Chantry turned, looking at the men crowded around. "I don't believe in killing," he said, "but that doesn't mean I am yellow, or afraid to fight. If anybody has any argument they can step out now."

French had been sitting back, one leg crossed over the other. He uncrossed them now and stood up. "You'll leave us shorthanded, Chantry, so you better leave it as it is."

He looked at the holes in Chantry's face made by the spur. "He drove it deep. You better have that looked at."

Chantry went to his horse and leaned his head into

the saddle, his breath coming in great, tearing gasps. Slowly his breathing came back to normal and he began to feel the cuts and bruises. He took water from the barrel on the chuck wagon and bathed his face and his raw knuckles.

He had nothing with which to treat the deep cuts in his cheek, so he bathed it with whiskey. Then he returned to his horse, swung into the saddle, and rode away.

His knuckles were raw and bleeding. When out of sight of the herd he turned toward the Canadian, and at a small branch that flowed down to the river he dismounted to wash the blood from his hands. Suddenly he looked up and saw an Indian in a black hat standing on the other bank, watching him. His rifle was still in its scabbard, a dozen yards away. In his confusion after the fight and in his desire to bathe his knuckles, he had not remembered to keep the rifle with him. The Indian, had he wanted to, could have killed him by now.

Tom got slowly to his feet, and the Indian said, "Me Pawnee. Friend."

Chantry jerked his head to indicate the cattle, out of sight and some distance away. "I ride with the cattle."

"You have fight?"

"Yes," and with satisfaction he added, "I won."

The Pawnee sat down on a rock and took out the makings. When Chantry refused them, he began to build a cigarette. He gestured with the cigarette. "That is French Williams?"

"Yes."

"His herd?"

"Mine . . . if I get to the railroad on time. If I don't stay with him all the way, it becomes his."

The Pawnee looked at him. "He do this?"

"No. A man named Koch. I brought it on myself."

"Maybe." The Indian lit his cigarette. "Koch a bad man. I know."

Tom Chantry was trying to remember what he knew of the Pawnees. Great fighting men, among the best trackers, and they worked with white men as allies. He studied the Indian but his decision was already formed, and he liked what he saw.

"You gamble big," the Pawnee said, and added, "You do not go to Dodge?"

"Williams wanted to, but I've heard the railroad was coming on west. I did not tell him that and I do not believe he knows they have started building again. I think if we drive north, then east, we will meet it."

The Pawnee considered. "But they are his men? I think he will leave you. He will take his men. What you do with cattle then?"

"I'll drive the herd alone." He was talking nonsense, and knew it. "Or find some other riders." He got to his feet. "Are you riding toward Clifton's?"

"Yes."

"Ride with me. Tell me about the country." And he added, "My father used to tell me the Pawnees were the bravest of warriors. He told me of the fight at Pawnee Rock."

"It was a fight."

"I am Tom Chantry."

"Sun Chief."

They rode for over an hour in silence, and when Clifton's was in sight Chantry said, "You want to work for me?"

"To herd cattle with French Williams? No."

"To scout for me." He drew up. "Find the railroad and tell me where it is. Check the water holes and tell me where there is water. I would not want you to come into camp at all. Report to me when you can, but where no one will see." He smiled. "Sun Chief, I want you to be my ace in the hole."

"All right. I do."

Tom Chantry reached in his pocket and withdrew a gold piece. "You ride for me and you will get another like this."

"I do. You keep. You pay all when finish." He pulled off. "I ride now."

Clifton House loomed ahead, and Tom Chantry trotted his horse toward it. The stage had just stopped and some people were getting down. One of them was a girl.

CHAPTER 7

TOM CHANTRY RODE up to Clifton House and left his roan at the hitching rail. He glanced at the other horses . . . six saddled horses, and a buckboard. He had not yet acquired the westerners' habit of noting brands.

He went up the steps to the first-floor porch, and entered the door. Several men standing at the bar turned to glance at him, but none offered a greeting or comment. What his business was remained his business, no matter how curious they might be.

Chantry ordered a beer, then turned to the man beside him. "Join me?"

"Thanks."

He was a long-geared man in shotgun chaps and denim jacket, a faded blue shirt, and a tied-down gun. "It's a dry country," the man added.

"I'm heading north. Do you know the country along the Picketwire?"

"Some. I just come over it."

"Water up there?"

"Enough. But no more than enough. The range is dryin' up." He lifted the beer. "*Salud.*"

"Cheers." Chantry drank, then said, "I'm Tom Chantry. Driving north with a trail herd."

"Bone McCarthy. I'm driftin'."

They talked in a desultory fashion, but with half

his attention Chantry was listening for mention of the railroad.

"Seems a shame," McCarthy was saying.

"What?"

"Them Injuns. Takin' the country off 'em. In good times it must've been a fine life they had, huntin' and fishin', or driftin' down the country on the trail of the buffalo. I ain't sure what we'll do to the country will be any better."

"Have you lived among them?"

"Brought up around 'em. I've fought 'em off an' on since I was a kid, and they're good fighters. Maybe the best."

"But we've whipped them. The army has, I mean."

"Lucked out, I'd say. Mighty few Injuns have rifles, and never enough ammunition to last out a fight, but you never seen their like for creepin', crawlin', bein' where they ain't expected.

"It won't be at war that the white man whips 'em. He'll beat them with his store-bought things. When the Injun made all he needed he had no troubles to speak of, but the white man showed him all sorts of things he was greedy for, and now he wants 'em. He has to get 'em by war or by trade."

"Whiskey?"

"That's the least of it, believe me. Knives, guns, pots, pans, and such. The Indian was whipped the first time a white trader came amongst them to trade with things the Injun couldn't make with his own hands."

"I hadn't looked at it that way."

Bone McCarthy took a swallow of his beer. "You're ridin' with a herd? Whose?"

"Mine . . . if I can stay with it to the railhead. French Williams is trail boss."

"Williams? You got you a live one, *amigo*. He's hell on wheels with a gun."

"Do you know him?"

"Can't say I do, but there's talk goes up the trail. What did you mean when you said it was your herd if you stayed with it?"

Chantry explained, and to leave nothing out he coolly told why he was forced to make such a deal, and also spoke of his feelings about guns.

McCarthy listened in silence. It was obvious that the others at the bar, or some of them, heard what Chantry was saying. He did not care. He had acted as he saw fit.

"You're carryin' some bruises. Did you get throwed?"

"No. Because I wasn't anxious to shoot, a man named Koch questioned my courage. We had a bit of a go-around. I whipped him."

He drank his beer. The conversation along the bar began again, and Chantry asked McCarthy, "Did you ever run across a Pawnee named Sun Chief?"

"Uh-huh. Good man. He was one of Major North's Pawnee scouts. Got wounded and had to drop out. Heard he was up and around again."

"I hired him to scout the trail for me, the trail to the railhead."

"You takin' on anybody else? I'm rustlin' work."

Tom Chantry drained his glass. "McCarthy, you heard my story. I'm not a man who believes in guns, and there are some who think I'm yellow. You still want to join me?"

McCarthy shrugged. "Every man's entitled to think the way he chooses, the way I see it. I think you're wrong, and I think the time'll come when you'll pay for it. What you're sayin' is that I got to take my own chances that you'd back me up in a tight spot, ain't that it?"

Chantry felt anger stir within him, and with it a feeling of resentment. Why could things never be simple? Yet, what would he do if it came to that? Supposing he was caught in a situation where he must fight or die? Or worse still, where he must fight or one of his men would die?

"You'd have to gamble on it, McCarthy," he said. "I believe a lot more can be done by reason than by guns."

"All right. You trust to reason," McCarthy said, "but you won't mind if I wear my guns, will you?"

"As you like. I'm not a reformer."

McCarthy lifted his beer. "Luck," he said. "You're sure a-goin' to need it."

He ordered another beer. "This'll have to be the last," he said. "I ain't carryin' any more money." When the beer arrived he said, "Now that I'm workin' for you, what do I do?"

"Bring your beer along," Chantry suggested, "and we'll sit over there at the table. I'm going to order us a couple of dinners and you're going to tell me every way you can think of that Williams might use to drive me off the herd."

For an hour they talked. Bone McCarthy was a cool, knowledgeable man with much experience on cattle drives and roundups. He ran through the possible ruses, one by one. Bad horses, Indian scares, maybe a rattlesnake in the bed. "He may even have put Koch up to jumpin' you. It's the sort of thing he might do."

After a while McCarthy was silent, but he seemed to have something on his mind that he hesitated to say.

"What is it?" Chantry asked.

Bone looked up at him, then filled both their coffee cups. "You know damn well what he'll do, Chantry. He'll have somebody brace you with a gun. He'll catch you when you're armed, and you'll have no excuse."

"I simply won't shoot."

Bone stared at him. "You don't seem to read the sign," he said. "If you don't shoot, he'll kill you... whoever French Williams gets to bully you into a fight. It won't matter one damn what you do, whether you drop your gun or whatever, he'll shoot, and shoot to kill."

"He'd kill me for that herd?"

"You must be dreamin', man. Of course he will. He'd kill his whole outfit for that herd. Right now I'd say the odds are a hundred to one against you makin' the next fifty miles."

They stopped talking then, but Tom Chantry considered the matter. French Williams was a known thief. He had killed men. He might offer an appearance of fair play for the look of the thing, but Bone was sure to be right. Somebody who rode with them would challenge him, and at his first move, would shoot and shoot to kill... any move Chantry made would be construed as a move for a gun—a move to shoot.

The only thing he could do was avoid carrying any weapon at all. He said as much.

McCarthy shrugged. "Worse comes to worst, they'll get you out on the grass somewheres, shoot you, and plant a gun on you. It's been done."

He looked hard at Chantry. "Can you shoot? I mean, did you ever use a gun?"

"I can shoot. I've hunted a lot."

"How about with a handgun?"

"Yes. I've used one."

"Can you draw? I mean, can you get a gun out of your holster without dropping it?"

"Yes. My father showed me when I was a youngster. He had me practice. But I never liked it."

"Just get it out, and no matter what he does, even if you get hit, you level that gun and shoot. Take your time, but make that first shot count. You may never get another one."

"There's no use to talk of it. I won't be carrying a gun."

"Well, in case you change your mind, you make that first one do the job. I've seen many a fast-draw artist who got his gun out quicker'n scat, an' then put his first bullet right out in the dust betwixt 'em, an' never got another shot."

Chantry pushed back from the table. "Here's what I want you to do." He put a twenty-dollar gold piece on the table. "Get yourself some grub, and then you keep an eye on the herd. You see whatever goes on, but you keep out of sight. If anything happens that you think I ought to know, you get in touch with me. I'll be riding out from the herd every day."

"All right." Bone McCarthy stood up.

"You watch yourself, do you hear?"

THE TAWNY PLAINS swept away in all directions, a gently rolling stretch of grama and buffalo grass with patches of greasewood; over some of the higher levels the plain was dotted with Spanish bayonet, or yucca. Far off, the moving black mass of a small herd of buffalo showed against a brown slope, and in a gully the stark white of scattered bones.

The herd was behind him again and he rode warily, without his rifle, carrying only the bowie knife he carried for work around the camp, or casual use. His eyes swept the horizon, hesitating here and there... but nothing moved.

The dust held no tracks, and when he came up to the riverbed he saw that it was dry and cracked into plate-sized slabs of gray mud, baked and crisp.

No water.

Chantry mopped the sweat from his face and squinted his eyes against the sun. It was midafternoon, and the herd had been without water since daybreak... there had been an expectation of water at this place.

French Williams had mentioned casually, in an offhand manner that they would water here. Had he known the creek was dry? Chantry suspected it, but had no way of knowing.

It was twenty miles to the next water, which meant a dry camp tonight, with a parched and restless herd, hard to hold. He glanced at the sun. Had they swung farther west? Williams was pointing the herd now. This morning it had been Koch.

Williams knew far more about the ways of cattle on a drive than Chantry would ever know, and he had driven over this country before . . . whether by this route or not, Chantry did not know. Undoubtedly the man had a plan of operation, and was not proceeding in a haphazard manner. He was a cool head, seemingly reckless and careless, but Chantry had quickly divined that the gunman was basically cautious.

He scanned the horizon again. Here at the river bank there was a little brush, and farther away there were trees. Turning his horse down the dry watercourse, he walked it slowly toward the trees. There might be water down there, some isolated pool where he could at least water his horse.

Even while his senses were alert to the surroundings, he was considering his problem. He now had two assets in Sun Chief and Bone McCarthy, neither of them known to French Williams. But his greatest asset was the fact that French Williams underrated him, considered him a tenderfoot. He on his part was aware that Williams was a dangerous and treacherous adversary. That is, he knew from his own guesses and from what McCarthy had said, and it was enough to make him cautious.

Tall cottonwoods suddenly loomed ahead and the watercourse was so narrow that he could no longer proceed. Ahead of him it narrowed into a rocky channel, impassable for a horse, and fell off sharply into a canyon.

He rode up the bank and into the trees. There, in their dappling shade, he paused to listen.

The cottonwoods rustled, somewhere a crow cawed into the hot afternoon, and then he heard a low murmur, followed by a faint clink, as of metal on metal.

Dismounting, he tied his horse with a slipknot, and walked cautiously forward, moving from tree to tree. Back in the East he had often stalked game in the woods, and he knew how to move quietly.

Suddenly the ground dropped away before him and he was looking into a small, grassy park scattered with cottonwoods, with willows growing along the streambed. Near the edge of the willows two men sprawled lazily near a dying fire. They were too far off to identify them, but he had no need, for their horses were grazing nearby, and one of them was the horse he had ridden out of Las Vegas.

The Talrim boys! Hank and Bud Talrim, who had taken his horse at gunpoint.

He drew back, and carefully made his way to his horse. Mounting, he rode back the way he had come.

What were the Talrim boys doing *here?*

Of course, they might have gone anywhere. But they were escaping from the law, and one would imagine they would keep on running. Instead, they had for some reason circled back and were now here, close by his herd.

Curious, he rode back to the herd, switched his saddle to his other horse, and rode out again. Glancing back, he saw Williams staring after him, but he rode ahead directly east from the herd, cutting for sign. He had gone only three miles when he found it—the tracks of two riders, tracks not many hours old, and one set was the tracks of his own horse.

All right. So they had come up from the south, but that was necessary, for when he had met them they were heading south. He backtracked them for several miles on a route parallel to the herd. On at least one occasion they had ridden high enough on a low hill to look over and watch the herd.

In itself, that meant nothing. They could have heard the lowing of the cattle and simply come to take a look. On the other hand, it was worth thinking about. Was it simply coincidence?

He had to remember that French Williams had gone to the trouble of locating and hiring Dutch Akin. Had he somehow gotten in touch with the Talrim boys? Were they to be his ace in the hole?

They were known murderers... wanted men. Would they kill for hire? They would. They would even kill simply to kill.

He swung his horse from their trail and started back to the drive.

For the first time he found himself wanting a gun. He was a fool, he told himself. With such men as the Talrims one did not reason. One did not sit down and discuss their mutual problems, because there were none. These men were killers.

This was a different land from the East, ruled by a different set of principles. The circumstances and conditions were different; it was a land to which law had not yet come, nor the restraints that society can exercise upon its members.

Heretofore he had been protected, one man of many who were protected by law, by the pressures of society, by fear of retribution. He had not had to fear, for other men stood between him and danger, but here there were no such men. A man was expected to stand on his own feet, to protect himself.

He was realizing how cheap are the principles for which we do not have to fight, how easy it is to establish codes when all the while our freedom to talk had been fought for and bled for by others.

Tom Chantry was no fool. He had won his battle with Dutch Akin by restraint and reason, but he was wise enough to know that neither of these would prevail against such men as the Talrim boys. Reason or restraint would seem weakness to them, and they were the kind to strike quickly when they discovered weakness. They had been quick to take his horse when they discovered he did not carry a gun, and they had shot at him, almost casually, as an afterthought, not caring greatly whether they killed or not.

He looked off in the direction in which his cattle had gone, then touched his spur lightly to his horse's ribs. He would go back. It was time. There were decisions to be made.

CHAPTER 8

THE CATTLE MOVED north with the rising of the sun, stirring the dust across the short-grass prairies, blue grama with occasional patches of little bluestem and curly-leaved sedge, and on some slopes a scattering of prickly pear. The cattle moved slowly, grazing as they walked, and Tom Chantry rode the drag, considering his problem.

Dutch Akin switched horses and rode back to join him, lifting a hand as he passed, hitching his bandana over his nose to keep out the dust.

It was very hot. McKay went by, circling to bring a bunch-quitter back to the drive. When he had driven the steer where he belonged he dropped back, riding beside Chantry.

They had fallen back to be clear of some of the dust and to keep an eye on any laggards that might cut out for the flanks.

"Quite a whippin' you gave Koch," McKay commented, "an' he had it comin'."

"There's a difference," Chantry said, "between a man who doesn't want to kill anybody and a man who's afraid. He just wasn't reading the sign right."

"You be careful," McKay said. "He's been talkin' that it ain't over."

At the nooning Chantry rode in to switch horses, and got his saddle on the little buckskin that was one of the horses allotted for him to ride. He planned to scout wide of the herd that day, as he went to the wagon for his rifle.

As he stepped up to the wagon he heard Koch grumbling about something nearby, then heard his voice suddenly grow quiet. He read nothing into it, but had just drawn his rifle clear of the wagon when Koch said, "All right, you blasted tenderfoot! Now you got a gun, turn an' start shootin'."

The rifle barrel was in Tom's left hand, which gripped it close to the fore-sight. Koch was not more than a dozen feet from him, and Tom wheeled sharply, swinging the rifle. As he came around he let it go, sending it flying toward the big man's face.

Koch ducked and Tom Chantry lunged at him. The big man staggered, caught his balance and swung the gun around, but it went off of itself before he brought it into line. With the smashing report the cattle suddenly lunged and were running.

Chantry hit Koch with his shoulder, knocked him sprawling, then fell on him, knees in the big man's belly. Without moving a knee, Chantry swung two hard punches at his face. Then he leaped back and, as Koch started to rise, smashed him in the face with his knee.

Men had leaped to the saddle and were plunging after the stampeding cattle, which were frightened by the sudden shot.

Chantry waited a moment for Koch to get up, but thoroughly angry now, he walked up to him and struck him twice in the face before Koch could lift his hands, hit him in the belly, and then when he started to fall forward, brought a hammer blow down on his kidneys.

"You're fired, Koch," he said. "Get your outfit and get out. I don't ever want to see you around again . . . anywhere." Chantry picked up his rifle and walked to his horse.

He rode out, swept wide, and began gathering cattle, pushing them toward the center. He gathered about twenty head, and then came upon a bunch that had slowed to a walk, and started them all back. Hay Gent joined him with a dozen head.

"What happened back there?" Gent asked.

"With Koch? I whipped him again, and then I fired him."

"What if he won't stay fired?"

"He will."

"But if he don't?"

"Then I'll whip him again, and again, until he stays fired."

Gent made no comment, and they drove the cattle in, meeting McKay, Helvie, and Rugger also bringing in cattle. It was the work of hours, but slowly the cattle were all gathered.

"We'll move on," French said. "Maybe there's water up ahead." He looked around. "Where's Koch?"

They were all listening. "I fired him," Chantry replied. "That shot started the stampede. This is no place to be settling personal grudges."

Williams looked at him thoughtfully. "We'll be shorthanded," he said. And he added, "He'll carry a grudge. Likely he'll lay for you."

"He'll have company then," Chantry said.

"What's that mean?" Williams asked quickly.

"Men leave tracks, French. I'm not so much a tenderfoot that I can't read sign."

They were all looking at him, but he left it at that, and the cattle started to move.

Riding out from the herd, he found a promontory and rode cautiously up the side to look over the ridge and survey the country. A few miles ahead and off to the right of the trail there was a hollow with a touch of deeper green.

Half an hour later he came up to it, a wide slough boggy along the sides, but with water a-plenty. Skirting it, he found it had a gravelly shore, and turned back to guide the herd.

"Water?" French was skeptical. "I don't know of any water around here."

"You do now," Chantry said. "Hay, turn the herd."

Hay Gent glanced at Williams, who merely shrugged, so the herd swung. By the time the cattle had watered and a few head had been snaked out of the mud it was coming on to sundown, and over by the chuck wagon there was a fire going.

There was little talk around the fire. The men were dog-tired, and when they had eaten they hunted their bedrolls. French alone loitered at the fire, smoking. From time to time he glanced across at Tom Chantry.

"You are a difficult man, my friend," he said at last. "Whatever else you may be, you are not a coward."

"Thanks."

"I will win, however. It's a long way to Dodge."

"It is that." Chantry looked up from his coffee. "And when you get there, I'll be with you."

French's gaze hardened, then he laughed. "You

might be at that," he replied cheerfully, "and if you are, I'll give you credit for it."

"You'll need the credit," Chantry replied. "I'll have the cash."

He got a plate and his food, and sat down a bit away from the fire. If they didn't accept him, the hell with them he could go his own way. But there was something in him that was different now; he had grown harder, tougher. The wide plains and the long winds of morning were having their effect; but French Williams, the Talrim boys, and Koch had contributed... yes, and Sparrow back there at Las Vegas, and Bone McCarthy at Clifton's. These men had experienced far more living in the West than he had. Perhaps, he thought reluctantly, perhaps his thinking needed a bit of revision.

How much of what he believed about not using guns was left over from that bitter day when they brought his father home on a shutter? Or was it what his mother had taught him? Deep in grief over the death of his father, she had shrunk from the possibility of such an end for her son.

Killing was wrong—on that score he could not change. However, there was no law here except the law enforced by men with guns, and did such men as the Talrims, and even such men as Williams himself, understand any other law?

If a man would not put restrictions upon himself, if he would not conform to the necessary limits that allow people to live together in peace, then he must not be allowed to infringe on the liberties of those who wanted to live in peace. And that might lead to violence, even to killing.

The trouble was that back east men had lived so long in a society that demanded order and conformity that they failed to understand that there were societies where violence was the rule, and where there were men to whom only the fear of retribution placed a bridle on their license.

But Tom Chantry knew there was more than his father behind him, for the fighting tradition of the Chantrys did not begin with him, nor with his grandfather, who had stood with LaFitte and Jackson at the battle of New Orleans. There were generations before that, who had crossed over from Ireland.

The principal thing he had learned was that simply because he himself did not believe in violence was no reason that others would feel the same. In the future he must be more wary. But what if the Talrim boys' presence was not coincidence? What if French *had* arranged for them to be near? What if French intended the Talrim boys to eliminate him?

At daybreak he was out riding the drag, and when he broke off he caught up another horse from the remuda. This was a *grulla* mustang, small but wiry.

"Watch him, *amigo,*" Dutch Akin whispered. "That one is mean."

The little mouse-colored horse stood quiet until saddled, but just as Chantry put his foot in the stirrup and rested his weight on it to swing to the saddle, the little horse folded up like a closing knife and then snapped open viciously. Tom Chantry slapped into the saddle as the horse came down, was almost thrown as it sun-fished wickedly, then crow-hopped for half a dozen jumps, and switched ends suddenly. More by luck than anything else, Tom stayed in the saddle. He had ridden spirited horses, but nothing that bucked like this. Just as he was sure he was going to have to grab for the pommel with both hands, the *grulla* stopped bucking, ran a few steps, and settled down.

Chantry rode over to the chuck wagon and, taking his rifle, shoved it into the saddle scabbard. Then he turned and rode out on the plains.

He had not ridden more than half a mile when he saw a rider emerge from a draw just ahead and stand waiting. It was Bone McCarthy.

"Howdy, boss. You huntin' comp'ny?"

"Why not?"

"I ain't been up to you sooner because I figured you knew about them. I mean I saw your tracks back yonder."

"The Talrims? Yes, I saw them."

"I can't decide what they're after. They're traveling too slow unless they've got somethin' on their minds. Whatever it is concerns you or that herd. Every now and then they crest a ridge to study you."

Chantry had his own ideas about the reason for their presence. Somehow, he felt, French Williams had gotten word to them, and they were lying in wait for their chance to kill him. He might be mistaken, but there was the presence of Dutch Akin as an indication that Williams thought along such lines.

"They've dogged your trail a couple of times. I'd ride careful, if I was you."

"Any sign of Sun Chief?"

"Not hide nor hair." McCarthy dug into his saddlebag for a strip of jerky and began chewing on it. "Chantry, you're ahead of your time in this country—

I mean, you not wantin' to carry a gun. This ain't the kind of world you came from, and it won't be for a few years. Whenever a man enters a new country like this his way of livin' drops back hundreds of years. You ain't livin' in the nineteenth century here, Chantry."

"You don't talk much like a cowhand."

"That's nonsense. Whoever said a cowhand was any special breed? Cowhands, like freighters, bankers, and newspaper editors, are apt to come from anywhere. They just like the life . . . as I do."

Chantry glanced at him. "Where did you come from, McCarthy?"

"Ireland . . . where else? Twelve years ago I left there, but at the end of the War Between the States I went back for a few weeks, and got into trouble again."

"Again?"

"The first time I was visiting a friend in Glenveagh and there was trouble over an eviction . . . I had to leave the country. I joined up with the French, as many a good Irish lad has done over the years, and after a bit I migrated to this country. I had two years in the war, then back there, and straightaway I got into the Fenian troubles and was lucky to get out with a whole skin. Back here again, and two years fightin' Indians with the Fifth Cavalry."

"The McCarthys are an old family, I've heard."

"Yes, some say we're the oldest family in Ireland. We owned Blarney Castle at one time."

"How does it happen that sometimes you talk as if you'd been born in the West."

McCarthy shrugged. "Saves questions. A good

many men do it, you'll find. They just fall into the habit as I have, of talkin' the Western way. You put on a way of talkin' when you change your clothes. It's as simple as that."

They rode on, scouting the country. "By the way," Bone McCarthy said, "back there at Clifton's the day I met you there was a girl there."

"I saw her."

"Well, she saw you. And she's been askin' questions. Aside from the fact that you're a handsome, upstanding man, why would she be so all-fired curious?"

"I don't know. She was a pretty girl, I remember that."

"I remember it too, but I've got an idea neither of us should. I've got a nose for trouble."

"She was asking questions?"

"She was. She was askin' the wrong questions, too. I mean, not questions a girl would ask who was interested in a man . . . but questions of somebody who wanted to know where you was goin', what route you'd be likely to take, and how many hands you had workin' for you."

"It doesn't make sense," Chantry commented.

"It did to her," McCarthy said dryly.

CHAPTER 9

THE GIRL DID not concern him. She would not be the first curious person he had encountered, and women had a way of asking questions about strange young men who are, or seem to be, unattached . . . and vice versa. Tom Chantry was more concerned with the Talrims and with worrying over when Sun Chief would reappear.

The cattle had moved slowly. Water holes were scarce, and it seemed they came to them early in the afternoon when French Williams invariably suggested it would be risky to drive on and make a dry camp. Twice at least his claims had undoubtedly been correct, for they were followed by long, dry drives.

On the drive itself all went well. The cattle were well broken to the trail, there was no friction among the riders, and nobody was troubling Chantry. His two victories over Koch seemed to have settled the matter of how much nerve he had, and the stampede caused by Koch had meant much additional work for them; they wanted no repeat performance.

Hard though the work might be, it had settled into routine, and this, Tom Chantry knew, increased his danger. Routine had a lulling effect upon the senses, and he knew his security demanded that he be alert at any moment for whatever might come.

Despite his impatience, he had to recognize that

the short drives were having their effect on the cattle. Settled down after their stampede, the short days offered more time for grazing and they had gained weight. If nothing happened to change their present rate of progress and if the grazing continued to be good, the herd would arrive at market in excellent condition.

Was this what Williams was thinking of? Or was it something else? Why was he moving so slowly? Was he, too, waiting for word from the railroad?

There was no sign of Sun Chief.

Bone McCarthy was close by, and several times, riding out from the herd, Chantry came upon his tracks, as well as those of the Talrims, who seemed to have been joined by a third person. The new set of tracks were those of a smaller, shod horse.

Trinidad was not far ahead, and although it was only a small settlement it had already acquired a reputation as a tough place. In 1859 Gabriel Gutierrez and his nephew had come up from New Mexico with a herd of sheep. The men built a cabin on the south bank of the river and settled down there, grazing their sheep, hunting and farming a few acres of land. Others moved in, and the settlement was named for the daughter of Trinidad Baca, one of the first-comers.

Was French Williams waiting for something to happen at Trinidad? Chantry told himself he was imagining things.

"I got to hand it to you," Williams said one night as they sat by the fire. "You've done your share. You've stood up to the work better than I figured you would. You've changed, too. These last days you've honed down and sharpened up considerably."

"Thanks. You've done your job, too."

Williams chuckled. "But we still haven't reached Dodge and the railroad."

"Call it off if you want to," Chantry replied carelessly. "I'll pay you the going price for your herd on delivery at Dodge."

"You quitting on me? Trying to welch on your deal?"

"You know better than that. Just trying to let you make a dollar. Don't worry, French. When we deliver these cattle, I'll be there to collect."

"You got any idea what's ahead?" Williams studied him, his amusement apparent. "The Kiowas are out, and believe me, nobody is worse. They'll give us bloody hell."

"And there's been no rain, so we'll have water trouble. And there are rustlers. You've told me all that." Chantry leveled his eyes at Williams. "And don't pull another Dutch Akin on me. I won't stand for it."

"What will you do?"

Chantry knew the hands around the fire were listening, but he did not care. "If anybody shows up hunting me, French, I'll figure he was sent by you."

"And then?" Williams' voice was low.

"I'll take your gun away and break your neck."

Williams laughed. "I'd kill you, Chantry. Nobody will ever put hands on me the way you did with Koch. Gun or no gun, I'd kill you."

"Better have your gun out when you see me coming, then. You'll never get a chance to draw it." He got to his feet and walked over to the chuck wagon for the coffeepot. Coolly, he filled Williams' cup and then his own, putting the pot down by the fire. "And while you're at it, French, you'd better tell those Talrim boys to light a shuck. They might lead to some misunderstanding."

He looked at French, and suddenly he smiled. "I wouldn't want to break your back and then find it was all a mistake. You tell them to light out, will you?"

French Williams shook his head. "Chantry, if I wasn't so set on beating you out of that herd, I could like you."

THE NEXT DAY broke cold and raw, with a long wind in their faces, and the cattle had to be forced into it. And the wind did not let up as the sun rose behind the low gray clouds.

There would be water in the Picketwire where they would camp, and some shelter in the river bottom, if they were lucky. Tom Chantry rode the drag for a while, spelling a rider there, then he moved up into a swing position. After the noon break he took the *grulla* from the remuda and went scouting.

It was still cold, and he wore a buckskin jacket over his blue wool shirt. He went directly east, riding warily. Twice he came upon pony tracks; each time they were several days old. He held to low ground, climbing the ridges only to peer over the crest, showing himself as little as possible. He was uneasy, and after a bit he took his rifle from its scabbard and held it in his hand.

The wind was raw. He turned up the collar of his jacket, tucked his chin into it, and pulled his hat low. He was studying the ground, then suddenly looked up to see he had ridden right into the bend of an elbow of hills. He must either skyline himself by crossing the ridge or follow along the side until he could reach the cattle trail. It was the country ahead he wanted to see, but caution told him the longer way was best.

He had turned to ride along the side of the hill when he glimpsed a notch, almost at the bend of the elbow, a small gap by which he could get to the other side of the ridge without showing himself on top of it. He swung his horse toward the notch.

His horse scrambled up the last few feet. At the opening of the notch he could see only that it was a sort of cleft in the ridge that seemed to lead all the way through. Old tracks told him the buffalo used this route, so it must go all the way through.

He walked his horse into the gap, traveled about a hundred yards, then suddenly rounded a low shoulder of the hill and emerged on the other side.

He never heard the shot, but he felt the blow. It was as if somebody had struck him suddenly across the side of the head with a whipstock.

He knew he was hit, he felt himself falling, he remembered the necessity of clinging to his rifle. He hit the dirt, smelled the dust that rose, and then he neither felt nor heard anything but the vague sound of his horse.

Cold . . . icy, teeth-chattering cold. It was cold that brought him to consciousness, it was cold that opened his eyes.

It was night . . . cold and black, and there was a smell of rain in the air, and a distant rumble of thunder. He was lying sprawled on the earth, the smell of dust and parched grass in his nostrils. He started to move, a spasm of pain went through him. He lay still, wanting no more of that.

He had been shot. He had fallen from his horse. He had been shot sometime in the middle of the afternoon, but if anybody was looking for him they could scarcely find him here.

A spatter of rain struck his shoulders. Shelter . . . he must find shelter. He risked the pain, and tried to sit up. On the third attempt he made it.

He was still at the cleft of the hills where he had been shot. He felt around him for his rifle . . . it was gone.

His knife? Gone. He felt then for his money, but it was gone, too. It was only then that he realized how cold his feet were.

His boots were gone.

Gingerly, he touched his head, which throbbed with a dull, heavy beat. His hair was matted with blood. He got to his knees, then shakily to his feet. He looked around slowly, blinking against the pain.

His horse was gone, too. He remembered then that he had heard it running off. It might not have gone far, and he called out. There was no sound in answer, no sound and no movement but the falling rain.

He staggered to the lip of the cut and looked around, but it was too dark to see anything.

The herd would be ahead and to his left. Taking a careful step at a time, he moved slantingly down the hill, toward the northwest. He stumbled over a rock and fell. When he got heavily to his feet, he realized that the butts of his palms were bloody, skinned in the fall.

Whoever had shot him, had left him for dead—or if not dead, sure to be dead soon.

He fell three times before he reached the bottom of the slope, and by then his socks were worn through and his feet were hurting. He peered about, trying in the distant flashes of lightning to see something he might use for shelter, but there was nothing.

First of all, rain or no rain, he needed some protection for his feet. Fumbling in the debris at the foot of the rocky slope, he found a jagged piece of rock, and removing his buckskin jacket he sawed off the sleeves a little above the elbows. He slipped these over his feet and used thongs made from the long fringes, knotted together, to tie the sleeves around his ankles.

Putting on his coat again, he moved out, walking carefully, trying to avoid the rocks and the patches of prickly pear.

A dark line ahead warned him of trees, and he went even more slowly, wary of Indians who might be camped there. Under the cottonwoods he stood close to a tree trunk and listened to the falling rain and the rustle of water in the creek bed, but he could hear no other sounds.

His eyes searched for a fire, or some evidence of human life, but there was nothing. He worked his way among the trees until he found a place where several bigger ones were grouped together in such a way that their entwined branches made a sort of shelter.

Here he leaned against a tree trunk and closed his eyes with weariness. After a moment he opened them, and his eyes, now accustomed to the darkness, saw a fallen limb from one of the cottonwoods. He went to it and, huddling there in its partial shelter, he leaned back against the tree, and slept.

Around him the rain fell softly, steadily. Overhead the cottonwoods rustled. In the hollow of a tree not twenty yards away a squirrel peered out at the rain for a moment, listening, then tucked its bushy tail around it once more and went back to sleep....

In a saloon in Trinidad a cowhand on the drift lighted a cigar and glanced at his cards. "I'll take two cards," he said.

More than a thousand miles to the east a girl in a white dress with lace at the throat looked down the table at her father and said, "Pa, I haven't heard from Tom. It isn't like him."

Earnshaw looked up, and said quietly, "I hope everything is all right with him. I have written to him, telling him what has happened here. Everything depends on him now."

She was a gentle-appearing and lovely girl, but in the coolness of her eyes now and the set of her chin there was something that reminded her father that she came of pioneer stock. "Pa, I want to go west," she said. "I want to go to him."

"That's impossible. He's out on the range. From what I hear it's very wild country."

"He may need help."

"What help do you think you could give? You are

a single girl, and we have no friends there, no one to whom you could go. It would be unseemly."

"Nevertheless, I want to go."

"Wait. We will hear from him."

CHANTRY AWOKE, SHAKING with a chill. He was wet through to the skin, without shelter, without food, without fire. He had lost blood, and he was very weak. He had no shoes, only the crude moccasins made from his sleeves.

He struggled to his feet and clung for a moment to the trunk of the cottonwood. He was shaky and uncertain, but he knew he must move, he must get on. A faint light under the trees indicated that daylight was not far off. He picked up a broken branch from the ground. It was almost straight, and was about seven feet long and almost two inches in diameter. Using it for a staff, he started to walk. For the first time he realized how sore his feet had become, but step by step he went through the cottonwoods to the far side.

By now the herd would be moving, or about to move. To overtake it in his present condition would be impossible. He had left the herd by riding east, and at a rough guess he must be about fifteen miles from Trinidad.

The clouds were low, the light still dim, and there were no landmarks visible. Fisher's Peak or the Spanish Peaks would have given him direction, but they were out of sight behind the clouds. Yet there was something he could go by.

Leaning on his staff in the partial shelter of a tree,

he furrowed his brow against the throbbing in his skull, and thought of the Purgatoire, called by cattlemen the Picketwire. It lay ahead of him, crossing his line of travel had he been with the herd. The creeks in this area flowed north into the Picketwire, so the nearby creek would be flowing north, or in that general direction. To reach Trinidad he must turn at right angles to the flow of the creek and keep it at his back, and so go west.

Nobody would be looking for him. Williams had everything to gain and nothing to lose if Chantry never turned up again, or if he failed to be riding with the herd when it reached the railhead.

His body was chilled through, but he started on weaving a slow way among the trees. He managed a dozen steps before he stopped, then another ten. Ahead of him he could see the bank that marked the edge of the river bottom; once he climbed that bank he would be in the open, without any shelter at all.

Yet he could be no wetter than he now was, and not much colder. His only hope lay in keeping moving. Ten steps . . . then five. The buckskin on his feet would not last long. There was one thing to be thankful for: no Indian was fool enough to be out in the rain.

He came to the small bluff that marked the river bottom, and blinking his eyes in the rain, he looked for a path, and found it. Slowly, slipping and tugging at his staff, he climbed the bank.

Now for the first time he felt the wind. It went through him with icy fingers, probing at his strength. Clinging to the staff, he plodded on, turning occasionally to be sure the line of trees was at his back.

He thought of what had happened. Who had shot him? An Indian? French Williams? One of the Talrims? Or perhaps some stranger who needed a horse? No matter. There would be time to think about that when he was warm again, and when he had eaten.

Warm? Would he ever be warm again?

He hobbled westward, depending on his staff, and pausing every few steps to ease the pain in his feet. The ground was muddy from the rain, and he had to stop often to shake the mud from his foot coverings.

When he had gone scarcely a mile he found another creek bed and descended into it, pushing through the brush. He scooped up water and drank, then crossed on scattered stones and climbed the far bank.

Every step now was agony, but he plodded on simply because he knew he must not stop. He had thought at moments of giving up, he had thought of surrendering to whatever ill fate awaited him, but it had never really been in him to do so. Somewhere beyond the muddy plain across which he was slogging lay Destination, a place where there was food and warmth, a solution to his immediate problem.

When he fell down again it was at the edge of some trees. He had come to another creek, and the water still ran north, so he was on the right track. He got up and stumbled to the flat ground under the trees, and here he found the remains of an old campfire.

He searched the ground for something useful, perhaps a broken knife blade, something for a weapon. But what he finally found was a shelter, a lean-to, tightly made and with dry leaves and grass on the ground inside. He fell to his knees, rolled over, and slept.

Words awoke him. He did not open his eyes, for he heard the first words spoken.

"Leave him be, Sarah. He's as good as dead, can't you see?"

"And if he doesn't die?"

"But he will!"

"I'm going to make sure that he does, Paul. I did not come this far to have anything else happen. I want him dead. I want French to have those cattle... then there'll be just one man."

"Is it worth it? There are only about two thousand head, Sarah."

"And in Dodge they are worth ten thousand dollars with the outfit."

"Ten thousand? You will have to pay the hands."

"You talk like a fool, Paul. Let me have your gun."

"*My* gun? Why?"

"Because I am going to kill him with it. Then I am going to put the gun in his hand and when he is found they will think he shot himself because of the hopeless situation he was in."

The words of this creature called Sarah came to him clearly and plainly. He was to be murdered, for some reason he did not know. He was not sure whether he could move or not, but he was about to try when Paul spoke again.

"Let's make a fire and have some coffee. I'm cold, Sarah. We can take care of him anytime. He isn't going anywhere."

They moved off under a tree and the man built a fire. When they had coffee on and both were sitting down, Tom Chantry lifted his head. The sleep and the emergency had brought clearness to his mind. He looked around cautiously.

Their horses were over there, sixty or seventy yards off.

He eased slowly to his elbows and began to crawl. Moving with infinite care, he made no noise on the sodden ground. Out of the lean-to . . . behind a tree . . . then angling off to come at the horses from the other side.

There was talk between the two at the fire, the smell of coffee . . . He reached the horses, pulled himself up. He got to the brush where they were tied, pulled the loose end of the slipknot, and holding the reins, he grabbed for the pommel. The horse side-stepped away from the smell of him and he fell against the saddle.

He heard an exclamation and made a wild grab for the pommel and caught it. The horse jumped and started to run as his foot reached the stirrup. He fell into the saddle, and then the horse was running and somebody was shooting.

CHAPTER 10

THE HORSE WAS a good one, a fast starter, probably somebody's cutting horse. Now it was frightened, and it lunged into a dead run at the first jump. It went through the trees like a jackrabbit, hit the slope, and was up it and topped out on the bank beyond before Chantry could get settled in the saddle.

He took one quick look around and headed the horse westward, where it seemed inclined to go anyway. For half a mile he simply let it run, then eased it down to a trot, held for another half-mile, then a walk and a trot again.

There was no trail that he could make out in the darkness, but he was heading for Trinidad and, weak as he was, he knew nothing under heaven was going to get him off that horse until he reached the town.

It was nothing much when he got there. A few cabins, a scattering of houses and corrals, a few haystacks, and then a saloon or two, a two-story building with a sign that said HOTEL, and a restaurant beyond. A few other places of business were all closed and dark. The street itself was empty.

Still short of the lights he pulled up and swung down, hit the borrowed horse a slap across the rump, and went up the steps and into the hotel.

There were three men in the room. A man wearing

a green eyeshade and sleeve garters shuffled and dealt cards at a table alone; another man was behind a desk, and a third sat behind a newspaper at one side of the room.

They all looked up and stared at him. He was sodden with rain. His feet squished as he walked across the floor, leaving mud and water behind him. His hair streaked down over his head, and his cheeks were haggard. The wound on his scalp had reopened and bled.

"I want a room," he said hoarsely, "a room and some food."

"Mister," the clerk protested, "you comin' here like this! You got money to pay for it?"

"I am owner of the herd French Williams just drove through. I was dry-gulched and left for dead. I need that room, mister, and I can pay for it. What I don't need is an argument."

"Now, see here—"

Anger gave him strength, anger and a desperate impatience, for he felt that at any moment he might fall on his face. He reached across the desk and took a handful of the clerk's shirt. "Give me that room—and no more argument!"

"Give it to him." The cool voice was familiar. "I'll stand good for it."

Chantry released his hold and turned half around. Sparrow was walking toward him, folding a newspaper.

"All right," the clerk said grudgingly. "If you say so, Mr. Sparrow."

The cattleman held Chantry by the arm, and took

the key the clerk held out. "Come on, young man," he said, "we've got some talking to do."

As they entered the hall to the ground-floor rooms he turned and called back to the gambler, "Mobile, do me a favor and get hold of Sam Baker for me."

The man got to his feet and took his coat off the back of the chair.

Sparrow walked Chantry back to the room, went in, and closed the door behind them. "Get out of those wet clothes," he said. "You need a stiff rub-down and a drink. You get undressed. . . . I'll get the drink."

He went out and Chantry dropped to the wooden chair and stooped to pull off the rags of buckskin that hung from his feet. He got one off, and then he pitched over on the floor.

But only for a moment. Slowly, he pushed himself up . . . there was so much to do. He needed a horse. He had to catch up with the herd. He pulled off his buckskin coat and his shirt, both heavy with water. He took the rough towel and began to dry his head and his face and chest. He sat down again, unbuckled his belt and got out of the soaked pants, torn and ragged from his struggles against the brush and the rocks.

Sparrow came back bringing a bottle and a glass, "Get a jolt of this into you. I'm not much of a man for whiskey, but in your condition it's what you need."

Chantry took a gulp of the whiskey and felt the heat of it go all through him. He waited a moment, then took another.

"You get some sleep now," Sparrow said. "We can talk in the morning."

"We'll talk now," Chantry said. "Morning may be too late." He took another gulp of the whiskey, a small one this time. "Somebody tried to kill me." Briefly he told of Sarah and Paul, and the horse he had let loose.

"Do you know them?" Sparrow asked. "I don't."

"Strangers . . . but they knew me. They wanted me—I don't know why." He added, "They didn't look or act like western people . . . from the border states, perhaps."

Sparrow reached into his waistband. He took out a short-barreled .44. "Do you still have a prejudice against using one of these? They'll trace that horse, and they'll find you."

"I just lost my prejudice," Chantry replied shortly. "Give me the gun."

"Keep it close by," Sparrow said.

There was a rap on the door. The gambler named Mobile and another man, somewhat older, stood there.

"Come in," Sparrow said. "Baker, this young man is a friend of mine. He's going to need an outfit, from the skin out, and he'll need it tonight. He'll also need a pistol and a Winchester. Can you open up and get them for him?"

"For you? You're damned right." Baker turned away. Then he glanced over his shoulder. "From the look of him, what he needs is some hot soup . . . a lot of it."

"I'll get it," Mobile said. "It'll have some rain water in it by the time I get back, but it'll be soup and it'll be hot."

Chantry pulled a blanket around him. The liquor

and the warmth of the room were taking effect, but he was feeling very tired.

"Sparrow, why are you doing this for me?" he asked. "I thought you had no use for me."

Sparrow smiled, and took a cigar from his pocket. "I didn't," he said, "but you've been moving and you've been making friends. I ran into Koch down in Las Vegas. He hates your guts, but he carries the marks to show why. That was part of it, and then everybody is talking about your deal with French."

"You know about that?"

"Everybody does. That's why I knew you'd need an outfit. I'll have a horse for you, too, the best one I can find."

"Do you think French had me shot?"

"No, that doesn't sound like him. He'd have it done right out in the open where anybody could see it. He's got his own sense of honor about things. He'll steal everything you own, and he'll get you killed in a gunfight if he can, or by a bad horse or a steer, but I doubt he'd ever have a man dry-gulched. Of course, that's just one man's opinion."

Mobile came in with the soup, and he stayed behind after Sparrow left. "You get some sleep," he advised. "I'll kind of set around and keep an eye on things."

"You don't even know me."

Mobile shrugged. "I don't have to. I used to punch cows for Sparrow. I came up the trail with him from Texas, decided that was too rugged a life for a man, and settled down here to deal cards. Contrary to what you might figure, I don't make much more than I would punchin' cows, but I sleep in a bed at night and I don't have to ride drag."

Slowly, carefully, Tom Chantry stretched out on the bed and drew the covers over him. His muscles, stiffened by cold and weariness, slowly relaxed.

"Mobile?" His eyes opened. "Do you know a couple of people named Sarah and Paul?" He went on to describe them, and added, "They'll be hunting that horse, but I've got an idea that horse came from town here, sold to them or rented. He sure wanted to come this way. He was a big bay, about sixteen hands, with three white stockings. It looked like a Pitchfork brand. . . . I caught a glimpse as he ran off."

"That's Henry Hazelton's. He's got a ranch outside of town—deals in horses and mules. I've used that horse myself." He took a step toward the door. "Now you get some sleep. I'll ask around."

The door closed, and there was silencc in the room. For several minutes Chantry lay quiet; then he got out of bed and limped across the room and propped the chair under the knob. It was an inside room with no window. He closed his eyes. Nothing had ever felt so good as this bed, nothing ever would.

He slept . . . and outside, rain fell upon the town—a rain that drowned the sound of a horse's hoofs splashing through the mud. It smothered the sound of footsteps of a man walking along the alley and trying the back door of the hotel, then entering.

It did not wipe out entirely the sight of a young woman walking across the street and mounting the outside steps of the building across the way.

Mobile, shuffling cards at his table, saw the girl dimly through the rain, saw her put a key in the lock and enter the door. Mobile Callahan trusted neither people nor the appearances of things. Of Tom Chantry he knew nothing beyond the fact that he was respected by Sparrow.

Two people had apparently tried to kill Chantry, one of them a girl, one a man. A girl had just mounted the stairs to the rooms and offices across the way, and it was unlikely that there would be two young women out in the rain on such a night. And where was the man?

This was the only hotel in town, and anyone looking for a homeless man would be likely to come to it. Anyone wishing to kill such a man would not be likely to come by the front door, for he would be seen and remembered.

Mobile made a neat stack of his cards and got to his feet. A glance told him the light in the back hallway was out, and he could smell the faint fumes left by a coal-oil lamp that has recently been blown out. Somebody wanted it dark, and Mobile Callahan was not going to walk along a dark hallway looking for a killer. His mother had raised no foolish children.

His own room was the first on the right side of the hall, Chantry's next to the last on the left side. Mobile stretched and yawned noisily. "Looks like a chance to catch up on some sleep," he said to the clerk. "I think I'll turn in."

He walked back to his room, ignoring the bit of dark hall that lay beyond the light from the lobby, and opened his door. He went in, closing the door, then promptly eased it open a fraction of an inch.

Standing in the darkness with a drawn gun, Mobile listened and heard a faint creak from down the hall, then another. Gently, he eased his door open a little more. By standing tight against the wall he could look along the door and down the passage. At first he could see nothing, and then he made out a darker shadow, and from it a hand that took hold of the knob on Chantry's door and tried it, ever so carefully. Turned it, and pushed . . . nothing happened.

Mobile heard a muffled curse, then the man put a shoulder to the door and lunged against it, but it did not give. Chantry had put a chair under the knob and braced the door.

What happened next was completely unexpected, and ready as Mobile was for almost anything, he was not ready for this.

The man stepped back, drew his gun, and suddenly opened fire.

He held his gun low and Mobile saw the stab of flame in the darkness even as he heard the thunder of the gun in the narrow hall.

Caught flat-footed, it was an instant before he could react, an instant in which the unknown gunman got off at least two shots.

Leaping into the hall, Mobile fired. The gunman wheeled, fired one quick shot at him, and fled. Mobile fired again as the man went through the door.

Doors burst open, the clerk came running. Sparrow, gun in hand, appeared in a door in his longjohns. Mobile ran to him. "He tried to kill him," he said to Sparrow. "I'll light up."

He scarcely noticed the warmth of the lamp chimney as he removed it and applied a match to the wick of the hall lamp.

A dozen men were gathered outside Chantry's

door, while Sparrow hammered on it. "Chantry? Are you all right?" he called.

The wall near the door was of one-inch pine boards, and it held three bullet holes. A .44 could penetrate several inches of pine, and the bullets had been fired to strike a man lying on the bed.

For a moment there was no sound inside the room; then a chair scraped on the floor and the door opened. Tom Chantry looked out.

"Are you all right?" Sparrow asked again. As Chantry stepped back, Sparrow entered, followed by Mobile.

"I'm all right. I was lying on my back. If I'd been on my side he'd have gotten me."

Mobile glanced at the bullet holes, then at the wall opposite. In the light from the bedroom lamp he pointed out a bullet buried in a washstand, another that had gone through the wall on the opposite side of the room.

When the others had left, Mobile told about the girl he had seen climbing the steps across the street.

"That's Webb Taylor's office," Sparrow said. "He's an attorney, but so far as I know he's out of town."

After the two men had gone Chantry stretched out once more on the bed. They would not try again—not right away. Hands clasped behind his head, he tried to put things together to make sense.

Out there in the woods the girl had said, "I want French to have those cattle. Then there'll be just one man."

One man? For what? And why did she want French to have the cattle?

He thought and thought, but found no answers, and presently he fell asleep.

Across the street, in the upstairs office, Sarah looked at Paul with disgust. "You fool! Now everybody will know somebody is trying to kill him."

"They'll believe it was French, or that other man we heard about . . . Koch."

She was silent for a few minutes, and then she said, "We've got to stay out of sight, Paul. So you leave town. Now."

"In this rain?"

"They've seen you, Paul. They caught a glimpse of you, anyway. Go up the trail of the cattle. You can be sure Chantry will be coming along, and you can kill him then. But this time don't make a mess of it. Take your time and be sure you get him. Ten thousand dollars may not be all the money in the world, but it is all we're likely to have."

Paul went to the door and peered out. The night was veiled with rain.

"All right," he agreed reluctantly, "I know where there's a shack up the line. I'll stop there." He paused for a moment. "What about you?"

"They know nothing about me. I am just here visiting Webb Taylor and getting some legal advice. You go ahead—and be careful that nobody sees you."

Paul opened the door quickly and went down the stairs, turning at the foot of the steps to walk back to the barn where he had left his horse.

At the back of the building next door and some thirty yards away there were several old boxes and barrels. Crouching among them, and sheltered from the rain, Mobile Callahan, gambler, cowhand, and drifter, watched him go, and looking through the open door of the barn, he saw him lead his horse to the door.

Paul was a slender man about five feet ten, weighing perhaps a hundred and fifty pounds, give or take a few. He wore two belt guns and there was a rifle in the scabbard on his saddle. This horse, too, was from Hazelton's place.

Mobile watched him go, and when he heard the hoofbeats die out, he studied the rooms in the building opposite. There was a lamp lighted now, and occasionally somebody moved back and forth between the light and the window.

After a few minutes he got up and walked back to the hotel. Sparrow was waiting in the lobby.

Mobile told him what he had seen, and Sparrow considered it. Taking two cigars from his pocket, he offered Mobile one of them, then bit the end from the other.

"Mobile," he said slowly, "I've heard it said around the cow camps that you're a good man with a gun."

"That's a reputation I never hunted, Mr. Sparrow, and it's one I don't want."

"I understand that. I don't want just a gun. I want a man with judgment, and you always had that. I want you to ride up the trail and see that Chantry stays alive."

"He's already got one man. He's got Bone McCarthy working for him."

"How do you know that?"

"I saw Bone a while back. He was askin' questions around. I just put two and two together."

"Just the same, I want you to help Chantry get through. I'll pay you two hundred and fifty dollars to stay with him to the railhead."

Mobile drew on his cigar, and looked at Sparrow. He had known Sparrow for going on eight years, and had never known the man to make a foolish or an unnecessary move. "What's your stake in this?" he asked. "Two hundred and fifty dollars—that's seven, eight months' wages for a top hand."

"I have my reasons." Sparrow got to his feet. "You do that, Mobile. I don't want you to get yourself killed, just be around a little while. I think Tom Chantry is riding into more trouble than he can handle. He's a good man. Maybe as good a man as his father was. I want to see him have his chance."

After Sparrow had gone to his room Mobile sat alone in the lobby, drawing on his cigar. Presently he crossed to his table, picked up the deck, and began to deal the cards. He always thought better when he was handling cards.

He shuffled the deck and dealt a hand, then turned them over and looked at them.

Aces and eights . . . *black* aces and eights. *The dead man's hand.*

Who was to die? Was it him? Was it Chantry?

Who?

CHAPTER 11

TOM CHANTRY OPENED his eyes and lay still. Slowly it came back to him. The shot out of nowhere, the missing horse, knife, and boots, his struggle to make it through the rain, and then the discovery by the two who intended to kill him... why, he didn't know.

He turned his head toward the door. The chair was propped under the knob.

Throwing back the covers, he swung his feet to the floor, but when he tried to stand the pain brought cold sweat to his forehead. Dropping to his knees, he crawled to the door and removed the chair.

When he eased the door open he found several packages wrapped in brown paper. He brought them into the room, and opened them on the bed. A dark red wool shirt, a black handkerchief for his neck, a pair of black jeans, and a wide belt. A couple of suits of underwear, another shirt, socks, and boots. There was also a gun belt and a holster containing a .44 Smith & Wesson, as well as several boxes of cartridges. There was a black, flat-brimmed hat and a fringed buckskin jacket, obviously Indian-made.

The man named Mobile had brought him some salve and bandages the night before and Chantry treated his feet now with the salve, bandaged them, and slipped on the socks.

The day clerk came down the hallway and rapped on the door. Chantry opened it, his right hand holding the pistol.

"No need for that," the clerk said. "I brought you this Winchester. Mr. Sparrow's up and havin' breakfast if you'd care to join him."

"Is Mobile around?"

"Him? He's around somewheres. He's the kind you only see if he's a good mind to have you see him."

Taking the rifle in his hand, Chantry went along the hall to the lobby, and across to the dining room. It was small, with just six oilcloth-covered tables, one of them long enough to seat a dozen, family style.

Hobbling, Chantry crossed the room and sat down opposite Sparrow. "Thanks," he said to the cattleman, "thanks for everything. I don't know why you've done all this, but I appreciate it."

"Better eat while you've got the chance. You're two, maybe three days behind your herd."

"One good day's ride if I have a good horse."

"You'll have one. But don't forget you have enemies." He glanced at the gun on Chantry's hip. "You're wearing a pistol?"

Tom Chantry shrugged. "My sense of what's right and just tells me I shouldn't, but my sense of survival warns me I'd better."

He studied the cattleman. "Aren't you off your beat? I mean, I didn't think you operated this far north."

"Let's just say I was curious. Stories get around, you know, and I heard about your run-in with the Talrims. After our conversation I was wondering how your convictions were matching up with the situation."

"And now you've seen. They've failed."

"Nothing of the kind. You have merely learned that a situation observed from a distance—a safe distance, I might add—is never the same as when met face to face. It is easy to say you do not believe in using guns when you have never faced a gun in the hands of another man, and you unarmed.

"Understand one thing, Mr. Chantry. You can make laws against weapons but they will be observed only by those who don't intend to use them anyway. The lawless can always smuggle or steal, or even make a gun. By refusing to wear a gun you allow the criminal to operate with impunity."

"We have the law."

"But even the law cannot be in your bedroom at night. But there are other things to consider. If you are not to lose your herd you must overtake it, and quickly. Believe me, French Williams will lose no time. He'll drive that herd as he never has before."

"The worst of it is, he may not have far to go."

Sparrow looked at him sharply. "What's that mean?"

"The railroad is building west, and they'll be moving fast."

"You're sure of that?"

"Yes. The only thing I am not sure of is where they are now." He glanced up from his pancakes. "That was my ace in the hole."

After that they ate in silence, but when Chantry finished his coffee and pushed back from the table,

Sparrow said, "Understand me, Mr. Chantry. I approve of your stand on guns. Many a man has shot too hastily or been roped into a killing he wishes had never happened. You are wise to restrain your hand, so continue to be wise . . . but not foolish."

"What do I owe you? I mean for the clothes, the outfit?"

"Nothing, if you lose your race. Put it down to the fact that I like a good contest. If you win, I'll give you the bill. Now you'd better be riding."

The horse was a line-back dun, and a good one by the look of it. Mobile Callahan was idling nearby when Chantry came to pick up the horse. A slim, attractive-looking man with cool gray eyes and black hair, he wore a black suit, a fresh white shirt with a black tie, and a black hat. He was wearing a pistol, Chantry noted.

"I've been through the town, Chantry," he said, "and that Paul, whatever-his-name-is, has flown the coop. The girl's still here, but I've a hunch if they tried twice they will try again, so watch your step."

Tom Chantry mounted and turned his horse toward the old Santa Fe Trail. The trail went north by east, but French Williams knew this country well and he might drive further to shorten the trail to Dodge.

When he had gone scarcely more than a mile from town he swung from the trail, but when he had again gone no more than a mile he swung back toward it, scouting for sign as he rode. But he saw no tracks made since the rain.

He was remembering things his father had taught him. At the time he had not thought of it as being taught. But on many occasions his father had often pointed out things along the trail, or told him stories of Indians and Indian fighting and trailing.

"If you're in risky country," he used to say, "don't let 'em set you up. Swing off your trail, change directions, keep 'em worried so they can't lay for you. And study the sign. Watch wild animals and birds, they'll tell you plenty. Most of all, trust to your horse, particularly if he's from wild stock. If there's anybody around, a horse will know it."

His father had never seemed to be teaching, and yet when he thought of it now he realized that Borden Chantry had said things that counted. "If you want to live easy in your mind, son," he used to say, "be sure folks respect you. Saves a lot of trouble."

He was riding warily, alive to every shadow, every suspicion of movement. He avoided places where a man might easily lie in wait, and several times he changed direction.

So it was that he glimpsed the pony tracks. They were off his line of travel, but his eyes caught a certain roughness in the grass and he swung his horse over to have a better look.

Unshod ponies... at least six, perhaps more. He knew he was no match for six warriors of the Kiowa or Comanche tribes. Deliberately he turned his mount away, backtracking them.

He had gone no more than a quarter of a mile when he saw where the riders had drawn up their horses and stayed for several minutes, partly screened by a thick patch of willows and young cottonwoods. They had all been facing toward the wall of brush, obviously looking over it. At what? Not at him, for he had not come that way.

Sitting his horse where they had sat theirs, he looked over the brush and could see nothing but a barren slope, empty of life.

He found an opening in the wall of brush, worked his way through, and scouted the slope. Sure enough, he came upon the tracks of a lone horseman who had ambled along the slope unaware of the Indians watching him from cover.

Tom Chantry backtracked the rider, and saw that the tracks showed frequent hesitations, as though the rider had somebody under observation or was scouting a trail. Suddenly Tom realized the rider had been watching *him!* And now that rider was being stalked by Indians.

Who could it be? Was this the man called Paul? Whoever it was, he now had problems of his own and Tom Chantry decided to let him deal with them as best he could.

Keeping to open country, avoiding possible ambush spots, he rode hard, occasionally veering to confuse any watcher, his one idea being to catch up with the drive.

The herd's tracks were there, but they were a day or two old...it was difficult to tell for sure. Obviously, French was taking advantage of Chantry's disappearance and was making time.

Tom Chantry was becoming aware of something else. There was movement among the Indians. He came upon their sign several times, parties riding unshod ponies crossed the cattle trail, riding east, small parties riding to become one big party, gathering in the direction to which the cattle must be driven.

Was it the cattle they were after? Or a drive upon

the buffalo hunters in the Panhandle area? Or an effort, a last effort perhaps, to stop the rails?

He slowed his pace. He must not encounter such a party, for if they were bound for an attack for any of those reasons they would not hesitate to kill him en route.

By sundown the tracks of the cattle were fresher, and the cattle drive had veered toward the east, perhaps only to reach a water hole.

Chantry circled a low hill, studying carefully for tracks, and when he saw none that went up the hill he made his way to the crest. There were boulders and low brush as well as half a dozen trees there, the only cover he had found in some distance. From the summit he could study the country all about in the last light.

To the west there was nothing; it was broken, empty country with mountains rimming the skyline. All around him the horizon was empty, except that off to the northeast there was the faint glow of what must be a fire . . . the cattle herd?

He was about to leave the hill when he heard, off in the distance, a burst of firing. Stare as he might, he could make out nothing, and he had swung into the saddle preparatory to riding off the hill when he heard a pound of hoofs.

For several minutes he saw nothing, and then it was a lone rider, coming fast, low over his saddle. He swept by, turning toward the direction of the herd, and was scarcely past when a band of Indians, riding hard, followed.

There were at least six in the bunch—in the now vague light he could not be sure of their number. He waited a moment longer, listening, and then rode down the hill and headed north.

As he rode he made his decision. The thing to do was not to join the herd but to let the herd join him. He would ride ahead, make a dark camp somewhere along the line of travel the drive must follow, and when they came up to him, he would join them... in daylight, when there would be no mistakes.

To the north there had seemed to be a low rim of darkness... a line of trees? The river? He knew the Purgatoire took a bend somewhere ahead of him, and it was probably the trees along that stream, partly hidden by the depth of the riverbed.

How far had he come? His route had seesawed back and forth so often that he had lost track of distance in his effort to avoid an ambush. Probably he was no more than sixteen or seventeen miles from Trinidad.

In the gathering dark he continued his way north, growing more and more wary as he neared the river. Several times he drew up to listen into the night, but he heard no sound except the faint rustle of wind.

The first stars appeared. The ground fell away slightly and he saw the dark wall of the trees. Descending into the river bottom, he could feel the coolness rising from the water. He walked his horse along in the darkness, every sense keyed for trouble.

He had drawn his pistol as he went under the trees, and he allowed the horse to go forward to find his own way, which it seemed to be doing without hesitation, ears pricked and alert.

He was apparently on some sort of trail, for the

horse's hoofs fell evenly, and the dun held to a good, fast walk. Suddenly water gleamed gray before him.

The dun stopped and its head came up. It seemed about to whinny when Chantry spoke sharply but softly. "*No!* Steady, boy! Steady!"

Although the dun jerked its head impatiently, it made no sound.

Then he caught the smell . . . *wood smoke.* Somebody, somewhere quite near, had a fire going.

The smell was faint, but with it there was something more. Coffee . . . !

Chantry, gun in hand, walked the dun forward toward the gray water, toward the fire he could not see.

CHAPTER 12

THERE IS A subtle awareness in the night. The darkness around you does not sleep; it is awake, alert, sensing. It is alive to movement, and feels the changes in the air, the smell, the temperature.

The trees are aware, and the bushes. The birds and small animals are aware, and they listen, hesitant, suspecting. Awareness of danger is an element of their being. It is like their breathing, like the blood in their veins, and one who lives much with the wilderness becomes so aware, too. Living with stillness, he detects sounds unheard by the casual passersby, sees things they do not see, catches odors too faint for their nostrils. Half of woodcraft is attention, and all of survival.

Tom Chantry had been bred in the West, and in the East he had spent much time in the woods, but what was happening to him now was different, strange and exciting. For the first time he was not *in* the night, but was a *part* of the night. He had come in recent days of scouting, riding, suffering, and struggle to a point where he belonged to all this.

Only a short time ago he had ridden, unseeing, past things that seemed of no importance to him, but now he sensed them. His ear was learning the difference between a movement of the wind and that of a small animal or bird. His eye was quick to catch the difference between a bird that flew up from fear and one going about its usual business. He could detect, by the changes in temperature, hollows or creek beds before he came up to them, for they were cooler in this weather, more humid.

Chantry walked his horse a few steps, then drew up, waiting.

He felt a faint stir from the wind, lost the scent of coffee for a moment, found it again. He heard no sound, and he felt that the man who had the fire was moving silently or was listening. The scent of the coffee was enough to tell him the man was awake.

A slight dampness, a coolness, coming to his right cheek indicated a hollow or a spring close by. He turned his mount ever so slightly and edged it through the trees. His gun was still in his hand, and he was ready.

It might, of course, be the Talrims, but he did not think so. They would be closer to the herd, watching for him, or carrying out whatever they meant to do. Whoever it was, he was prepared.

The gleam of the fire caught his eye, and there it was, not twenty feet off, in a hollow below some brush. He drew up again and waited. When he at last heard a sound, it was a voice.

"Welcome to my fire. I am Sun Chief."

The Indian materialized from the shadows and Tom Chantry dismounted, holding out his hand, and the Pawnee took it.

"There is coffee. In the light I would look for you, but you find me first."

He took Chantry's dun and stripped the saddle

from it, picketing the horse in a small glade close by. Then he came back to the fire, where Chantry had already filled his cup.

"How did you know I was around?" Tom asked.

The Pawnee shrugged. "I know you come. And on the road I met the man from Trinidad—the one called Moby."

Moby? Mobile? But what would the gambler be doing out here?

"He told me you were coming."

There were other things to consider, and Chantry put aside the question of Mobile Callahan's movements. "What about the railroad?" he asked.

"Three days maybe, for the cows. The Pawnee filled his cup and Chantry shared the food from his saddlebags. "If there is no trouble."

"Where is the herd?"

Sun Chief pointed. "Where the creek begins. The creek called Caddoa."

Knowing nothing of that creek, Chantry inquired, "How far from here?"

The Pawnee gestured toward the north. "Not far. I show you."

The campsite the Indian had chosen was a good one. It was under the edge of a cut that dropped off to a creek bed, but was some twenty feet back from the river and at least ten feet above it. There would have been room for one more man and his horse.

When the Indian had smoked he crawled into his blankets, and only then did he tell Chantry one last thing. "There are Kiowas at Big Timbers. The Cheyennes and Arapahoes have gone."

Kiowas at Big Timbers? And Big Timbers lay between his herd and the railroad. If the Cheyennes and Arapahoes had left such a favorable camping ground there must be a reason. Were the Kiowas planning an attack in which the others did not want to be involved?

Big Timbers... why did the name sound a bell? Perhaps because of a story his father had told him long ago, or some chance phrase remembered from a conversation in his home when men had talked of the far plains and the shining mountains, the forests where no man had walked. The name had a special sound to it. *Big Timbers...?*

At breakfast they ate jerky and drank coffee, Chantry inquired about Big Timbers, and listened to Sun Chief tell in a few phrases what he knew.

"Big trees... what you call *alamo*... cottonwood. Fourteen miles long it was, but many cut for logs or fires... no brush around... only grass. Springs and streams... a place the Indian likes. Big powwows held there... fights, too. It is a good place.

So it undoubtedly was, but the trouble-hunting Kiowas had taken away its charm for Tom Chantry.

They had ridden no more than a mile in the morning sunlight when Sun Chief pointed across the tawny slopes at black dots circling against the pale sky. "Buzzards. Something dead."

"Or dying," Chantry said. "We will see."

They rode on, their horses' hoofs beating on the drying turf. When they topped out on the rise below the buzzards they saw a man's body, stripped and bloody lying in the hollow beyond.

Riding down swiftly, they drew up close to it.

Streaked with bloody gashes, it lay there, an ugly thing under the flat sky.

Tom Chantry passed the reins to Sun Chief and stepped down, fighting his repugnance. He turned the body over. It was Paul, and he was not dead. His body twitched and his fluttering eyes opened wide.

"I did not even see them," he said distinctly. "It was sundown, and I was looking for you."

"We'll take you to the herd," Chantry said. "They're pretty handy with wounds."

Paul's eyes stared blankly. "I shouldn't have listened to her. I should never have come. I never wanted money that much, but she did. She wanted money, or she wanted blood . . . I was never sure."

Chantry knelt and started to slip an arm under him.

"No!"

He stopped, waiting, but whatever Paul had been about to say was smothered in the blood that came from his mouth. He rolled over on his side, choking and gasping. "No," he managed again . . . and died.

Chantry pulled a handful of dry grass and wiped the blood from his fingers. He looked at the body, and then walked to his horse.

He started to speak. "If we had a shovel . . ."

"No time," Sun Chief said. "We ride."

He pointed. Two hills away were Indians, a dozen of them, coming toward them.

Chantry turned his mount, and riding beside each other, they moved away, trotting their horses, not running them.

The Indians came on riding faster now. Chantry

drew his rifle from the scabbard, letting them see the shine of it.

"No shoot," Sun Chief said, but he was showing his own rifle.

The Indians came up to the body and drew up, looking after them.

They saw the fire before they reached the cattle. The herd was bunched for the night, and the men were around the chuck wagon, except for those on night herd and one man on a high knoll as lookout.

The herd was bunched in the open, the remuda held near a small patch of trees and brush.

Helvie was first to see Chantry. He looked from Chantry to Sun Chief, and back again. "Figured we'd seen the last of you," he said dryly. "What happened?"

"I got dry-gulched," Chantry answered.

"It wasn't him," Helvie said quickly. "He ain't left the herd."

"Didn't think it was. That doesn't seem to be his style."

"You're smarter'n I thought."

French Williams was standing near the fire, watching as they rode in. "Howdy!" he said. "Better eat up. We're making a night drive."

"Where to?"

"South and west. There's a bunch of Kiowas north of here."

"Heard of them." Chantry poured coffee. "They got you buffaloed?"

Williams turned his head quickly. "No. It's the wisest thing to do, that's all."

Chantry sipped his coffee. "They know you're here," he said, "so you aren't fooling anybody. They can catch up anytime they've a mind to. And," he added, "there's bunches of Indians south of here, too."

"What's on your mind?"

"Go north," Chantry said, "right past Big Timbers. No sense in letting them think we're afraid of them."

"All right," Williams replied carelessly. "It might just work. If they ride out to talk, you going to make palaver with them?"

"I might," Chantry replied.

"You do it," Williams said. "I'd like to see how an Eastern gent gets along with Indians." He glanced at Sun Chief. "Where'd you find him?"

"He's been working for me right along," Chantry answered calmly. "He was one of Frank North's Pawnee scouts."

"I know him," French Williams said. "He's a damn good man."

Suddenly a thought came to Chantry. "French," he asked, "does anybody want you dead?"

"Me? Maybe fifty people. Why?"

"Somebody tried to kill me, somebody I don't know. I don't have any enemies that I can think of and nobody stands to gain if I die."

"Why tie it to me?"

"There was a mention that if I was dead there'd only be one more. Now, I don't share anything with anybody but you."

"The herd?"

Chantry shrugged. "I can't think of anything else."

"What about your pa? Somebody killed him. With you back west again they might think you've come out here to wind that up."

"It isn't likely. That was a long time ago."

Both of them were silent for a minute, and Tom listened abstractedly to the mutter of conversation around the fire.

"Anyway," he added, "the girl wanted money. That's what Paul said."

"Paul?"

"The girl called him that." Then, concisely, Chantry told his experiences of the past few days: the dry gulching, his escape, the attempted killing in Trinidad . . . and Sparrow.

"What's he doing in this?" French Williams asked. "I don't figure Sparrow."

"He said he wanted to see how I'd manage without using a gun."

"That don't make sense. I know Sparrow. He's a no-time-for-fooling-around man. I never knew him to do anything like this before." French looked at him quickly. "Is he any relation of yours?"

"No."

"Then it certainly don't make sense. Unless," he added, "he figures to pick up the herd himself."

Chantry got up and threw the dregs of his coffee into the buffalo-chip fire. "I think it concerns you and me," he said, "and nobody else."

As he walked to the wagon for his bedroll, he glanced at the men, somber over their coffee, speaking little, their rough-hewn, unshaven faces thrown into relief by the firelight. They were a solid, capable lot. Even the bad ones were good men with the cattle, hard workers to a man. . . . Suddenly, for the first time he felt a kinship with these men who shared with him what would in the East be considered as nothing less than an adventure. Here it was the day's work, and little different from any other day's.

All of them knew the Kiowas were out there, and every man among them knew the Kiowas for fearless, dreaded fighters, yet they were prepared to ride on, right past their encampment—or through it if necessary.

Some of these men were of a sort he might never have encountered had he not come west, and they were, in some cases, men whom he would not have chosen for friends, but when trouble showed they would be men who would stand by until death, if need be. For the first time he clearly understood what Sparrow had told him, what Lambert meant, and the others who had tried to tell him what the West was like.

These were hard, lonely men, driven by no man knew what impulses, what secret dreams or thoughts, and they came from all walks of life, all kinds of backgrounds. There was no pattern beyond the one of hardihood and courage.

"You know, French," he said, when he went back to the fire, "no matter how it turns out, I'll have learned a lot on this trip. I wouldn't have missed it for anything."

French looked up, a sudden smile on his face. "Maybe we'll ride another trail, my friend, another trail besides this. You've come a long way since that night in Cimarron."

Yes . . . yes, he had. But how much further was he to go? It might be no farther than the camp of the Kiowas, nor as far as the railhead.

There was not much time left, not many days, not many miles, and then he would know.

CHAPTER 13

DAWN BROKE COLD and gray. Tom Chantry rolled out of his blankets, scrambled into his clothes, and tugged on his boots.

Helvie and McKay were at the wagon, plates held out for the cook. Chantry stood up, stamped his feet into his boots, and slung his gun belt around his waist. Helvie looked at it, but made no comment.

Rugger strolled up to the wagon, throwing a sour glance at the gun. "You strap that on an' you may have to use it."

"If I have to, I will," Chantry said, and he added, "When this drive's over, Rugger, if you have any money to bet, I'll outshoot you for whatever you've got."

Rugger stared at him. "Huh! You must think you're good. I'll take that bet."

French Williams rolled out and sat up. "You'd better not, Rugger. I think Chantry can shoot. I think he'll surprise the hell out of you."

Rugger snorted, but he was less confident. If French thought Chantry could shoot, it was a good bet that he could. For French Williams made few mistakes in such matters.

"French, do you know Clay Spring?" Chantry asked.

"I been there a time or two. I guess everybody in this country knows it."

"How about stopping there tonight?"

"I'd sort of figured on it."

Williams was a neat, natty man who looked well in whatever he wore. This morning he wore a blue army shirt, black jeans, and a flat-brimmed hat. His boots were almost new, and were decorated with large-roweled Mexican spurs. He wore his gun tied down. Chantry suspected that Williams had a better background than was implied by his conversation or by his way of life.

"That man the Indians killed?" Williams asked now. "You say his name was Paul?"

"Yes."

Williams walked away without comment.

Within minutes the herd was on the move, pointed east now. The dust beneath the hoofs of the cattle rose in clouds. The sky remained dull, leaden.

Clay Spring, if Chantry remembered rightly what he had been told, lay at the foot of a mesa where several runoff springs combined to form Clay Creek. He had never been there, but Bone McCarthy had mentioned it.

From there they would drive to the vicinity of Two Buttes, and this would be what the Kiowas would expect. But their next move would, he believed, surprise the Indians. It might also confuse them. For instead of driving away to avoid the Indians, they would drive right toward them. And he had his own ideas about what to do next.

Oddly enough, he had come to like French. The arrogant gunman, with his amused, taunting eyes, puzzled him, but Chantry wasted no time in trying to figure out his personality. His liking stemmed from the fact that Williams was good at his job, and Tom Chantry always admired a man who knew what he was doing and did it well.

The thought came to him that he might have to kill Williams, but if so he would do it with regret. That thought gave him pause. He . . . kill? Such an idea had been foreign to him, but now he was considering the possibility, if there was no other way out.

His readiness to accept the possible necessity of it worried him. He must guard his emotions and his actions all the more now. He must not only be wary of others, but of himself.

In spite of the dust, there was a feeling in the air that he liked, a smell from the land. Eastward the rising sun shone in the faces of the cattle. They walked stolidly on, sometimes trotted a little, then walked again.

Today he stayed with the herd, interested to see how easily his horse responded to the work, and how accustomed to it he himself had become. His hand was sure, his movements easy . . . he had changed.

But he must not permit the ready smile of French Williams to put him off. Why had Williams so easily accepted the idea of going north into the face of the Kiowas? Did he think Chantry would fail when he faced them and lose the herd there? Or had Williams already approached the Kiowas, perhaps on a share-and-share-alike basis? It would not be the first time Indians had raided a herd or a wagon train at the instigation of a white man.

As he rode, his thoughts returned to the girl called

Sarah. Of the two, the girl had been the stronger, the more dangerous. And she was an attractive woman with a good figure, enough to take the eye of any man, east or west, but this was the West, where women were scarce.

He had been thinking there must be some connection between them and Williams, but Williams had seemed to know nothing about them.

The cattle went ahead steadily, heads swinging to the rhythm of their walk. The cowhands lounged in their saddles, thinking of the campfire ahead, the strong black coffee, and the warm food.

Tom Chantry swung out from the flank where he had been riding, and loped his horse along the slope of the low hill. Clay Creek Spring was not far ahead, hidden in a notch of hills. Below it was a holding ground, somewhat higher than the ground around it, a pleasant place for the cattle.

A bird flew up, from almost under his horse's hoofs. The saddle creaked, his spurs jingled, and he topped out on the rise.

The three Indians came out on the ground around him without warning. They had been lying down, horses concealed beyond the rise, and their dusky bodies blended with the brown earth and the growing shadows. He heard the explosion of a gun, felt the jolt of it in his fist, then the hammer fell again and he saw an Indian spin and fall, the knife dropping from his hand.

An arm came around Chantry's throat from behind, and he knew, instinctively, a knife would be in the other hand. He kicked his boots free of the stirrups and threw himself from his horse.

Hitting the ground with a thump, he rolled over, and jolted free of the Indian. He came to his feet quickly, just as the warrior, knife held low, sprang at him. He was a big man, tall as Chantry, and equally broad in the shoulders.

The Indian crouched, then came in. Chantry moved swiftly, and with the ease of long practice, a practice he had never used until now except in friendly wrestling matches. His left palm slapped the Indian's knife-wrist to his right and out of line with his body, his right hand grabbed the wrist, and he stepped across in front of the Kiowa and threw him over, hard.

The Indian hit the ground, but he retained his grip on his knife, and came up fast. The man was like a big cat; his black eyes gleamed as he circled to come in again.

Chantry's gun lay where it had fallen, several feet away. His horse, the blue roan, had trotted off to one side and stopped, the red sunset on his saddle.

The Indian's hand was lower now . . . he was a wily fighter, not to be taken by the trick again.

"You are a brave man," Tom Chantry heard himself say. "I shall hate to kill you."

Did the man understand? Chantry heard him suck breath and then he came in swiftly, slashing right and left with the knife. Chantry sidestepped to his left to put the Indian out of position, but the warrior turned abruptly and lunged again.

Chantry sprang back, but in his boots he was not agile enough, and as he went back he tripped over the body of one of the other Indians. His opponent lunged forward, but off balance, and tripped over Chantry.

Tom sprang to his feet, more quickly this time, and kicked savagely at the Indian's head. The boot heel glanced off the Indian's temple and sent him rolling.

Leaping on him, Chantry slipped an arm under him and across the warrior's throat, clapping the palm of his right hand against the Indian's skull, his left hand grasping his own right arm in a stranglehold. He knew he could kill the Indian now, and he put on pressure, fighting for his life.

Suddenly horses were all around them, and Williams was saying, "Step back, Chantry. I've got a gun on him."

Slowly Tom Chantry released his hold and stepped away from the Indian, who lay gagging and choking, and then slowly the brave got to his feet.

Rugger was there, and Helvie and McKay; there were four guns on the Indian, and Rugger eared back his hammer. "I'll kill him!" he yelled. "I'll—"

"No!" Chantry snapped the word. "You kill him, and you'll have to kill me."

He turned to face the Indian. "I am Tom Chantry," he said. "You fought well. Go in peace."

The Indian looked at him, then at the others.

"You going to let him go?" Helvie asked in astonishment.

Suddenly Sun Chief was there beside them. He held out Chantry's pistol and Tom took it, dropping it into his holster.

"He goes free," he said. "He's too good a man to shoot down."

Rugger swore. "He's nothin' but a damn redskin. He'll kill you the first chance he gets."

"Maybe. But in the meantime he goes free." He spoke to Sun Chief. "Tell him he can go. Tell him I shall come to the village under the Big Timbers to see him . . . soon."

"No need to tell. He knows what you say." The Pawnee's rifle was in his hands. "That's He-Who-Walks-With-Wolves, but often he is called Wolf Walker. He is a big warrior."

"Let him go."

Wolf Walker looked at him a moment, then deliberately he turned on his heel and walked away.

French Williams looked at the two dead Indians and commented dryly to Rugger: "You'd better copper your bets, Rug. That's as good shooting as I've ever seen, left and right, both dead center."

"It was luck," Chantry said. "They surprised me. Came right up off the ground."

"So you just killed two of them with two shots, and then whipped Wolf Walker bare-handed—and him with a knife. Mister, you call it what you want to, only don't call it luck."

Sun Chief caught up the blue roan and Chantry swung into the saddle. As they started back toward the herd, Helvie rode alongside Chantry and held out his hand. "Whatever I may have thought about you back at the start, I take it back. Next time you need a hand, you just call my name and I'll come a-runnin' . . . no matter where you want to go."

"Because I was able to handle those Indians?"

"No, sir. I don't regard that. It was the way you let Wolf Walker go. That shines, mister!"

The cattle passed over the end of the mesa in the last moments of light, all shades of hide lost in a uniform darkness. The hands circled them to a stop on the flat below Clay Creek Spring, and the chuck wagon lumbered over the rocks and swung into place. While Dutch unhitched for him, the cook lowered the back of the wagon to make his table, and began setting out the grub.

Tom Chantry gathered sticks from the remains of old campfires and, using dry grass and leaves for tinder, got a small fire started. He added buffalo chips and hunted out some dried brush.

It was a good camp—the best camp so far, Tom thought. Rugger was surly, and Kincaid still avoided him, but Dutch, Helvie, and McKay were friendly and easy. The fire burned brightly, and the food tasted good. For the first time in days, Tom was not hurting anywhere, and now he had a good feeling about the fight with Wolf Walker. He did not think about the two Indians he had killed. They had attacked him without warning, and his reaction had been immediate and instinctive.

French Williams was curious. "Now, that shootin'," he commented, "surely didn't look like the work of a man who never used a gun."

"I never said I had never used a gun," Chantry replied simply. "Pa was a good hand, as you know, and he started teaching me early. I've always had a knack... good coordination, I guess. I've hunted a good bit, and shot up a lot of ammunition at targets. Up there"—he jerked his head back toward the scene of the fight—"was the first time I'd tried to get a gun out fast in a long time."

"We heard the shots," McKay commented, "just *boom-boom,* almost like one sound."

Chantry glanced over at Williams. "How far is it to Two Buttes?"

"Fourteen, fifteen miles, I'd guess. I never did ride directly from here to there. We'll make a proper day of it."

All the men were tired, but the last events of the day had excited them and stirred them to conversation. Chantry leaned back against his bedroll and listened to Helvie, who was telling of a famous fight back in 1867, a running battle between Indians and the riders of a stage headed for the Big Timbers station.

From that the talk continued—talk of cattle and buffalo, of the stage lines and the Santa Fe Trail. Finally Tom carried his bedroll into the shadows near the wagon, and pulling off his boots and his gun belt, he rolled in and slept.

His last memories were of the occasional crackle of the fire and the low murmur of conversation.

When he opened his eyes the fire was down to the last red coals. All the men were asleep except those with the cattle. He was about to turn over and go back to sleep when he saw Rugger slip from his bed and move off into the darkness. Something about his manner moved Chantry to watch him go—not toward the horses, but off into the darkness, obviously anxious not to be seen.

Where was he going? And for what reason?

CHAPTER 14

FOR A MOMENT Chantry thought of following him, then decided the man was probably just going into the woods on some business of his own, and Chantry turned over and went to sleep again.

But in the morning he remembered this small incident, and when he had belted on his gun and stepped into his boots he glanced around.

Rugger was saddling a horse, as were Helvie, McKay, and Kincaid, getting ready to ride out and relieve the night guards. He saddled his own horse, and waited until they had gone. Then, leaving the dun at camp, he went into the woods where he had seen Rugger go.

He had no trouble in picking up a track. A heel print here, a kicked stone there . . . for a hundred yards he trailed him back into the brush and scattered juniper, and then across the slope of a hill. There the faint trail went down into the hollow beyond.

Here the trail ended. Near a flat rock there were two cigarette butts.

For several minutes Tom Chantry stood there, trying to puzzle it out. Rugger was not exactly a contemplative man, not the sort who would walk all this way to be alone with his thoughts. He had come for a reason.

Chantry looked around. Due east lay the trail to Two Buttes, an open stretch of valley two or three miles wide, and easy going, bordered on the south by Two Buttes Creek. About five or six miles away lay the Santa Fe Trail, or one branch of it. Two Buttes, the highest of which lifted about three hundred feet above the surrounding country, were dimly visible on the horizon.

Nothing else . . .

He had turned away when he saw, in the shelter of another rock, a place where a small fire had been built. Not for warmth, for the man had not sat near it, and it was built so that it would be visible only from the valley below.

A signal then. But to whom?

There were no other tracks, so if he had expected anyone to meet him, that person had not arrived.

Had he left any word there?

Carefully, searching with this fresh idea in mind, Chantry looked around, and suddenly he saw it, near where the fire had been . . . a tobacco sack. Picking it up, he felt something inside and opened it . . . there was a page torn from a tally book, and on it, written in a clumsy hand, these words

2 Butes

Big Timbers

Kiwas at Big Timbers

He returned the note to the sack and replaced it. Then he walked back to get his horse.

The others had eaten, and the chuck wagon was packed and ready. The cook turned to glance at him, then gestured toward the seat. "I put some grub an' coffee out for you. Figured you'd be hungry."

"Thanks."

The cook waited while he ate, and presently he said, "I like your style, Chantry. Can't say I cottoned to you right off, but you've shaped up."

"Thanks," Tom said again.

"What's goin' on? I don't like it a-tall, the way things are. French ain't like himself, an' there's hard feelin' among the boys . . . like they were up to something they didn't care for."

Chantry finished eating, cleaned the plate with sand, and passed it to the cook. "You can't lose, Cookie," he said. "Either French or I will pay you boys off if we get through with the herd."

"They tell me you're figurin' to drive right through Big Timbers."

"Why not? Look, if the Kiowas want us they can ride up on us anytime. By driving in any other direction we still couldn't get away—cattle move too slow. If they mean to attack, we can't avoid it. So why not take the quickest way, where there's the best water and grass? Why not drive right at them so they know we're not afraid? We know where they are, and they know we know, so they'll be wary of a trap. They'll be sure we've got reason for being confident. Anyway, I never found that a man could avoid trouble by running away from it."

He waited while the wagon pulled out and started over the ridge. When it was lined out on the trail, he rode south to the banks of a creek that flowed into the Two Buttes almost due south of Clay Spring.

The banks were cloaked with shrub willows, many of them growing ten to fifteen feet high. He went in among them, drew up there, and stepped down from the saddle searching for a vantage point from which he could watch the rock on the hillside where the message had been left.

From time to time he looked toward the herd, now only a dust cloud down the long valley. He drank at the stream, and let his horse browse on the rich green grass along the bank.

An hour passed. Just as he was about to step into the saddle again, he heard the beat of hoofs. From over the ridge behind him came two riders, who cantered down the slope, splashed through the shallow stream, and went up the opposite slope to where the message had been left.

They were some distance off, but he needed no closer view to know who they were. The Talrims!

The Talrims and Rugger in this . . . and who else?

But the message? What did it mean? Two Buttes was obvious enough, and it was their next stop. After that they were going to Big Timbers, though not in one long drive. And at Big Timbers there were Kiowas.

Rugger was apparently telling the Talrims their direction of travel, and warning them about the Kiowas at Big Timbers. But what else? Despite himself, Chantry was worried. There might be some other meaning which he did not grasp, some other reason for the message.

When the two riders had disappeared over the ridge in the direction of Clay Spring, he rode out of the willows and followed the herd.

The drive to Two Buttes was an easy one, and Chantry rode the drag all the last half. They bunched the cattle on the plain north of the Buttes, avoiding the breaks along the canyon that lay just to the south.

Twice during the last part of the drive they saw Indians. Two of them sat on a ridge watching, apparently unworried about being seen. That night the camp was quiet.

"What do you think, French?" Akin said at last. "Will they tackle us?"

Williams shrugged. "Maybe yes, maybe no. From what I hear, that passel of Kiowas shapes up like a war party, and if they want beef there isn't any closer than we are. The same goes for scalps. They know they've tackled my drives a couple of times with no luck, so that may steer 'em off, but I doubt it."

"I think we're in for a fight," McKay agreed.

Chantry sipped his coffee, listened to the talk, and watched Rugger. When he had finished eating, Rugger strolled over to where Kincaid was repairing a broken bridle. For several minutes they talked in low tones, and nobody seemed to be paying any attention. Williams was lying on his back, his hat over his eyes.

Rugger and Kincaid were two of Williams' boys... did Williams know what was going on? Was this a part of a plan? The Talrims had kept pace with them for days, and Chantry was sure they were Williams' ace in the hole. A shoot-out at the last minute; and with Chantry dead the cattle belonged to Williams.

Suddenly he remembered the girl Sarah... where did she figure in all of this? Did she know that Paul was dead? Had she given up whatever she was trying to do?

She had wanted Tom Chantry dead because then

only one man would stand between her and what she wanted, and that one man had to be French Williams. Yet French professed to know nothing about her... or was it Paul? Had he ever mentioned Sarah's name to French?

He suddenly said to French, "We've never talked about your background."

Williams' eyes were level and cold. "And we are not planning to," he said.

"I was thinking about Paul," Chantry went on. "We need not talk about it, but you had better do some thinking about it."

"I do not know anyone named Paul."

"And there was the girl named Sarah," Chantry continued.

Williams stared at him. "Sarah? Sarah and Paul? It can't be."

"Those were the names. They spoke of killing me, and then added that there would be only one man left. Williams, the only thing you and I have in common are those cattle. If both of us die before we get to the railhead, who gets the cattle?"

The cynical amusement was gone from Williams' eyes. His face looked drawn.

"You wouldn't have gotten to Dodge," he said, "so the cattle would belong to me. And if I died... no, it is absurd! I can't believe it."

"Sarah would be nineteen or twenty," Chantry said; "Paul a few years older."

"And Paul is dead? The Kiowas killed him?"

"Yes."

"Then it is over," he muttered, half to himself. "That will be an end to it."

"I don't think so," Chantry insisted quietly. "The girl was the stronger one. She was the one who was pushing hardest. Without her I don't believe Paul would have done anything; nor do I believe she will quit."

Williams stared at Tom. "I thought they had forgotten me," he said. "Now they find me again, and it is for this!"

They were alone—the others had gone out on night guard, or were asleep. "I wanted to go back some day," Williams said gloomily. "It is not a place to forget. My boyhood was there, and where a man has lived as a boy . . . he has feelings for it."

"My first home was out here somewhere," Chantry said. "I never knew exactly where . . . I think it was over east of here. You know how it is . . . plains are plains; and afterward my mother never would talk about it. Pa was well-off until that norther wiped him out and we had to move into town."

"I always wanted to go back," Williams said. "I had a good time as a boy."

"You can always go back."

"You have much to learn, my friend. No one ever really goes back, for when you return you are not the same as when you left, and everything is different, and strange. You look about where everything ought to be familiar, but nothing is right. I know, my friend. But still I did want to go back."

"What have Sarah and Paul to do with it?"

Williams shrugged. "Perhaps nothing. But I do not think there is much to go back to if they have come so far to kill me. . . . Yes, I know them. They are the children of my cousin. With me, they are the last of our line. My father always told me I should avoid them.... They were no good, he said, and he should know, for he came of the same family."

"What about your mother and father?"

"Dead. My mother died when I was very small—my father only a few years ago. My mother was lovely...she came of an old, old line. My father was a common soldier who rose from the ranks to become an officer. That is not an easy thing to do in the French Army. As a boy he dreamed of going off to India, of becoming a general.

"Actually he served in Africa, and lost an arm there. He came home then, married my mother, and bought a farm...call it an estate if you will. His own family he did not like, and he avoided my mother's family as well.

"They had refused to sanction the marriage until it became obvious that my mother would refuse to obey, and then they sanctioned it, but unwillingly. Later, after my father was visited by some of France's foremost military men, their attitude changed, but he was a proud man and would have none of it.

"He had the devil's own temper, and my own was like it. When I was not yet sixteen the arrogant nephew of an important man demanded that I hold his horse, and I refused. He attempted to horsewhip me, and although he was three years older and larger, I pulled him from his horse and gave him a beating. I thought I'd killed him, so I went home and put a few things together to run away.

"My father came to stand in the door. He asked me about it, and I told him. He said that if I wished to stay he would face them beside me, but I refused.

Then he offered me a dozen gold coins, but I knew they were all he had, and I refused that too. Finally we split them, and I shook his hand and left. I never saw him again."

"That was in France?"

"Yes."

"But the name Williams? It doesn't fit."

"It was a name I took when I needed a name in a hurry, that's all."

"What do you think our chances are now with the Kiowas?"

"You can never tell about Indians. They might attack, and they might not. They might try to stampede the herd, and then get us one by one as we try to round them up. This is a war party, hunting trouble. The other tribes who pulled out knew that, and did not want to be involved. If we put on a bold face we might ride right through them."

"I'm going into their camp," Chantry said.

French stared at him. "You're crazy."

"I've heard that an Indian would never kill a man who came willingly into his camp. Maybe before or after, but never in camp unless he is brought in as a prisoner."

"Yes, but you just might find an Indian who didn't think that way."

"In the meantime, you boys can drive the cattle right on . . . by going east."

"I know where Dodge is." Williams threw his cigar into the flames. "If you've got nerve enough you might bring it off, but I wouldn't want to bet on it."

Chantry got to his feet. "I'm turning in." He

paused for a moment, and then asked casually, "How much do you trust Rugger?"

"Rugger? He works for me, but I don't trust anybody. Including you."

"You don't have to trust me. You know what I'm doing, and what I'm after."

"What about Rugger? Why do you ask about him?"

"You figure it out. He's your man."

When Tom Chantry stretched out in his bed he looked up at the sky and started to think about what he would do next, but somehow he fell asleep.

The fire crackled, then hissed as a few drops fell. It began to rain quietly and, without waking up, Chantry burrowed deeper into his bedroll.

CHAPTER 15

THE CAMP WAS quiet as the men climbed out of their bedrolls in the morning, packed them up, and stowed them in the chuck wagon. The rain had stopped, but the sky was gray and thunder rumbled in the distant hills.

French Williams, Chantry noted, avoided him, as if he regretted having talked so much the previous evening. Chantry took only coffee for breakfast, saddled up, and the herd was moving before the night guard had finished breakfast.

Undoubtedly the Kiowas knew of every move they made, and would be discussing the sudden shift from driving east to pushing the cattle north to the Big Timbers. Sun Chief had told him a good deal about the Indian ways, and it was this that had decided Chantry on riding into the Kiowa camp.

He would wait until almost the last minute so that his ride to the camp would take him only a little time. During that time he would be in danger . . . every yard he gained would be a yard won.

Nobody talked, and the cattle did not seem interested in grazing. They seemed to want to move on, and by now they were well broken to the day's travel, except for a couple of well-known bunch-quitters, and they could be watched.

McKay dropped back beside Chantry. "We're goin'

on past the bend of the Clay," he said. "Frenchy says we'll be drivin' sixteen to eighteen miles today."

"The Clay? Does it swing this far east?"

"Uh-huh, an' then it points right north for the Republican."

McKay rode on and the herd moved ahead steadily, occasionally trotting. Obviously Williams was hoping to drive far enough so that he could hit the Big Timbers early in the day. By mid-morning they crossed the Santa Fe Trail, cut deep with the marks of freighters' wagons and the countless pack trains that had come this way.

Once, far ahead on a knoll, they saw two mounted Indians watching them, but it was not the Kiowas Chantry was considering today. He drew up, mopping the sweat from his forehead and watching the cattle go by. He was thinking of the note left by Rugger and picked up by the Talrims.

Two Buttes... Big Timbers... Kiowas at Big Timbers... What did it mean? Merely that their next stop was to be Two Buttes?, and that they were headed for Big Timbers from there? Or did the message mean something else? Apparently the Talrims were watching the herd and would know where it was going. Perhaps the last phrase was the important one *Kiowas at Big Timbers.*

Was it a warning? Or was it a suggestion that if anything was to be done it must be done before the Kiowas could beat them to it?

Did they plan to kill him? Or to steal the herd?

If it was killing they wanted, it would certainly be best for them to wait and see if the Kiowas would not do it for them, and if nothing happened at Big

Timbers there was still a chance to do what they wanted, and even blame the Indians for it.

If it was the herd they wanted, they had best steal it at once, before the Kiowas could act. But three men could not take a herd from this crowd unless they had some others working with them.

Was this a move planned by French Williams himself? Still, he had seemed genuinely puzzled over Chantry's comment on Rugger.

Chantry let the herd move on ahead. He was riding the blue roan, and if trouble developed its speed would put him into the action without delay; and by riding well back he was able to survey the entire herd as well as the hills around.

Chantry decided he must watch Rugger. If anything was to happen the man's actions would betray him. He let his eyes range the hills, and sweep the draws on either side, as much at least as he could see of them.

The country was deceptively open-looking, but there were draws on either side, the beds of intermittent streams, that would make good places of concealment for an ambush.

He suddenly thought of Bone McCarthy. Where was *he*? Had he simply pulled off on his own? Had he been ambushed perhaps to meet the same fate as Paul?

Several times during the morning Chantry saw Rugger and Kincaid meet, confer briefly, and return to their jobs. It was nothing to be remarked . . . it happened a dozen times a day during such long drives, but now his mind was alert with suspicion.

Sun Chief fell back beside him for a short time.

The Pawnee had proved a good hand on the drive, working along with the herd in between brief scouting forays into the hills.

Alone on an isolated knob, Chantry stood in his stirrups and let his eyes range the country. The feel of it was coming back—this was the land where he had been a boy, and certainly the place could not have been far from here.

This was a land where a man could grow, where he could build. He found himself wishing he could have known it as the Indians had. He glanced again toward the herd. Rugger and Kincaid were together again.

He was turning his mount to ride back to the drag when he saw the black, muddy trail where a party of riders had gone down the draw to his right. Swinging his horse, he rode down to read sign. There had been perhaps five or six riders, and they must have gone by only minutes before he had reached the crest of the knoll.

Honest men did not avoid a trail drive. They would ride down to pass the time of day, at least. He tried to single out tracks, but he saw no evidence of the Talrims. But all were shod horses, and by the length of their strides they were good stock, running stock.

Tom Chantry skirted the knoll and cut down along the slope, not heading for the drag, but for French Williams, who was riding point. Williams turned as he approached, no welcome in his eyes.

"Keep your eyes open," Tom said. "We're riding into trouble."

"What's that mean?" French asked.

"I cut sign on half a dozen riders, maybe more. They passed us only a few minutes back and didn't come in to talk."

French Williams rode a few minutes in silence. "So you figure something's building up?"

"You bet I do. I think somebody hopes to grab this herd before we get to Big Timbers."

"That means tonight."

"Or today. Or on the drive tomorrow."

Williams said no more, and rode on. Tom Chantry dropped back, and as he passed Helvie he said again, "Keep your eyes open. We're riding into trouble."

"Kiowas?"

"Maybe somebody closer to home."

Helvie shot him a quick look. "If you mean French, I ride for the brand."

"But who is the brand here? Is it French? Is it me? Or the herd?"

Helvie was silent a moment, considering that. Then he said, "The herd. I'm a cattleman."

"I'll ask nothing more. We both signed on to take this herd all the way."

"McKay will stand."

"I think so too. And I think Dutch will."

Helvie glanced at him. "Dutch? Yes, I think he will. You're not mentioning Rugger or Kincaid."

"No, I'm not. I don't know about them, but they've been doing a lot of getting together this morning." And he told Helvie about the note Rugger had left, and the Talrims picking it up. He also told him about the fresh trail, just over the ridge from the herd. "Maybe I'm chasing wild geese," he said, finally, "but I'm going to ride loose and listen."

Sun Chief hung well back from the drag, urging those steers that lingered behind, but never closing in tight on the drag. Seeing him there gave Chantry reassurance, for he had great respect for the Pawnee and his awareness of what went on.

But where was McCarthy?

Twice they saw Indians, but they were only watching. If they planned an attack they were content to wait until the cattle were driven to them.

Were they aware of those other watchers? Chantry asked Sun Chief. "They know," he answered.

Chantry pulled his horse around the herd and rode toward the point. He drew up alongside Rugger. "How're they going?"

"All right." Rugger spoke sullenly, not inviting conversation.

"Keep your eyes open," Chantry said. "We're in Kiowa country."

"I know that."

"There's some outlaws around, too," Chantry added casually, "but we needn't worry about them. We can handle them."

Rugger stared at him, narrow-eyed. "Outlaws? There ain't no outlaws around here."

"What about Bill Coe's outfit from Robbers' Roost? Or the Talrim brothers?"

"They ain't likely to be around," Rugger said.

"No?"

As he turned his horse he smiled at Rugger. What he had hoped to accomplish was little enough, but he might have sowed seeds of doubt in Rugger's mind. At least, he felt that he had worried him, and Rugger might attempt to call off the impending raid, if that was what was planned.

But the day passed quietly, and the herd had kept moving north. It was sundown when they were circled and bedded down in a small bend of Clay Creek. The creek was no longer running bank full, but had dropped to a small stream at the bottom of the creek bed, enough to water the cattle.

While the others watched over the cattle, Hay Gent and Chantry rode out to scout the country around. Sun Chief had already vanished into the gathering dusk. From the crest of the ridge, a mile back from the camping ground and some two hundred feet higher, they scanned the surrounding territory. There was nothing to be seen.

"Could be an army out there," Gent commented. "There's lots of dips and hollows."

"Sleep light," Chantry advised. "Tonight and tomorrow will be the danger time."

While Rugger and McKay watched the cattle, grazing on the easy slope along the stream, the others ate hurriedly; then Helvie, Hay Gent, and Akin went out while the others came in to eat.

Tom Chantry wasted no time. He ate, drank an extra cup of coffee, and then rolled in his blankets.

The cook had promised to wake him at midnight, but he awoke shortly before that. For a moment he lay perfectly still, listening. He heard no sound . . . not a snore, not the crackle of burning wood . . . nothing.

Suddenly alert, he strained his ears . . . nothing. Very carefully he sat up. The fire was there, burned down to coals now. The wagon was there, the red light from the fire throwing black shadows of its spokes. The bedrolls were there, but all were empty.

He put his hand to his gun . . . but there was no gun.

Slowly, he got to his feet and moved one quick step into the deeper shadow of the brush.

His mouth was dry, his head throbbed dully.

He had been doped . . . *the coffee.*

He stepped back to his bedroll and slid his Winchester from the blankets. That they had been unable to get, for he had been almost lying on it. Holding it in one hand, he picked up his boots with the other, and stepped back into the shadows. Putting down the rifle, he pulled on his boots, shrugged into a coat, and then took up his hat and rifle.

He edged around the fire and started toward the remuda. It was gone . . . all the horses gone.

He stood for a minute trying to clear his dulled mind . . . he had suspected an attempt to stampede the herd, and he had tied the line-back dun out in the brush, saddled and ready.

Now he slipped back there like a ghost . . . the dun was there, a good fifty yards back in the brush along the route by which they had come.

He tightened the cinch and stepped into the saddle, coiling the picket rope as he sat there, thinking.

Then he rode out to the cattle. And they were there, bedded down and quiet; but no riders rode around them, no voices sang.

Oddly, at that moment he remembered his own curiosity about why cowpunchers sang to cattle. The answer was simple enough. The longhorn steer is a wild animal, quick to stampede, and the men riding herd at night sang so that the cattle would not be surprised at the sound of their approach. Hearing the familiar voices reassured the animals, and they continued to doze or sleep. Trail drivers sang during the night watch more for the sake of the cattle than for their own amusement.

Riding up to them now, he began to sing softly, just loud enough so they could hear him. Slowly he swung around the herd, then made a second circle, farther out. He was looking for anybody or anything he might find. But he found nothing.

What had happened? Had they abandoned him, and the cattle? Had they all been spirited away by Indians? If so, why had he been left? Was this part of Williams' game to win the herd? And what could he do now? What could he do alone?

As dawn began to break he rode back to the camp. He found no signs of struggle. The bedrolls lay as they had been left. Evidently the men had got up, pulled on their boots, and walked quietly away, whether of their own volition or under the threat of a gun he had no way of knowing.

Going to the chuck wagon he dug out a side of bacon, filled a small sack with coffee, a couple of loaves of bread, and some odds and ends. He took a spare coffeepot, his cup, and whatever else he might need. Then he rode back to the herd.

The cattle were already up and stretching, grazing a little. The brindle steer that had been the leader since the third day had moved out and, head up, was waiting.

"All right, boy, let's go!" Chantry said, and he started off, riding point. The brindle steer followed.

Slowly, the others fell in behind, broken to the trail by long days of driving.

How long he could keep them together he did not know. The brindle steer pointed north toward the Big Timbers, and Tom Chantry circled back, driving in the laggards. The herd was moving.

Warily, he rode back to the point, watching the country around, which was relatively open.

What had he been expected to do? Cut and run? Start scouting for them and leave the cattle? Left to themselves, the herd would soon scatter, and no doubt they would soon realize he was alone and begin to fall out of the drive anyway. All he had going for him was that brindle steer and the ingrained habit of the days on the trail. But for the time the cattle moved off willingly enough.

The cattle had been moving steadily for nearly an hour when the Indians appeared.

First there was one, then another, then a dozen. They lined the crest of the low rise half a mile on his left and watched him.

They could see he was alone, one man and a great herd of cattle, held together only by the habit of the trail.

Suddenly from out of a draw, Sun Chief appeared. He rode to the drag, bunching those cattle that were beginning to lag and scatter.

A moment later, Bone McCarthy came from the shadow of a juniper on a low ridge, and rode down to the flank, and the cattle moved on toward Big Timbers and the Arkansas River.

At noon the Indians were still with them, watching. Bone circled around and turned the point inward, and between them they bunched the cattle. With Sun Chief and Chantry standing guard, Bone McCarthy fried some bacon and made coffee.

"I found your railhead," Bone told him. "It's this side of the Colorado line, coming on about a mile a day, more or less. I found something else, too. I found a telegram for you."

He handed the handwritten message to Chantry. It was brief and to the point.

Reverses here. Without the herd I have nothing. All depends on you. Doris sends love.

Earnshaw.

"Did you read this?"

"Couldn't help it, open like that. Besides, I figured if I lost it I'd still know what it had to say. . . . Tough."

"He's a good man, Bone. I can't let him down."

"Three men? More than two thousand head of stock, no remuda, and those Kiowas lookin' down our necks? Man, you've bought yourself a big job."

Chantry glanced toward the ridge. The Kiowas were there, watching, and somewhere nearby he could be sure the outlaws who wanted his cattle were watching too.

But most of all, he thought of French Williams. No matter what the man had been, Chantry had always, deep down within himself, believed that French would play his hand out, fair and square.

They rode out to the cattle and Sun Chief came to the fire.

The Kiowas were still out there, more of them

now, and the Big Timbers were not far ahead, where he had promised to visit the Wolf Walker.

"Boss?" McCarthy said.

"What?"

"We got company."

Chantry turned in the direction McCarthy indicated.

A rider was coming toward them, walking his horse, and singing *Tenting Tonight on the Old Camp Ground.*

It was Mobile Callahan.

CHAPTER 16

"LOOKS TO ME, Chantry, like you could use a good hand," Callahan said. "I've been round and about, and up the trail a time or two, and I'm a fair hand with a rope or a gun."

"You've got a job."

"Don't want you should worry about that. Mr. Sparrow is payin' me plenty to help you get to the railhead."

"Sparrow? *Paying* you?"

"Uh-huh. He some kin o' yours?"

"No."

Mobile glanced toward the Indians. "You've got to figure on them, of course, but what you really need are horses. What happened?"

Chantry explained in as few words as possible, his eyes straying from the cattle to the Indians.

"You think it was French Williams?"

Chantry shrugged. "The Talrims are around, and I think Rugger was planning something with somebody else. All I know is that everything I've got is riding with this herd; and worse yet, everything my boss has got is, too. If we can bring it in we can make something; and if not, a good man and his daughter have gone down with us."

They rode on in silence, keeping moving constantly, but trying to save their horses as much as possible.

At intervals all four men got off and walked. They could see the trees along the Arkansas, the looming tops of the Big Timbers. They circled the herd, and while the cattle were resting they built a fire.

"I'm going on into the Indian camp," Chantry told them. "I said I was going, and I must. I don't know what they are planning, but my chances are as good there as here. Stay with the herd, but if you're attacked, scatter and run for it. We can always get together and fight again. I don't want to lose any of you."

"If you go into that camp," McCarthy warned, "you'll lose your hair."

"Maybe." He hesitated, finishing his coffee. "On the other hand, I might make a deal for some horses. You can help me cut out about six head of good beef. I'll drive them in for a gift to Wolf Walker."

From the knolls the Indians watched as the men cut out the beef, and they followed Chantry when he started for the Big Timbers with them.

Suddenly, four Indians came riding down to him. They drew up.

"I am going to your camp," Chantry said, speaking slowly. "I take a present to Wolf Walker. To He-Who-Walks-With-Wolves."

One older buck with a strong profile demanded, "Why you do this?"

"I am Tom Chantry. The Wolf Walker and I fought. It was a good fight. He fought with great strength. It is good that we be friends."

Nothing more was said, but the Kiowas closed in around him and around the cattle. Soon they dipped down, forded the river as far as an island, then went on to the further bank and were among the cottonwoods.

The huge trees were scattered, and the grass was thick beneath them. There was much shade, and the small fallen branches and twigs provided kindling for fires. Here and there were dead trees, and he could see where some had been felled in the past.

Suddenly the lodges were before him. This was the sort of camp the Kiowas or Comanches preferred, among open timber. The Sioux liked their camps near water, but away from timber because of their dread of ambush. The Osage, Omahas, and Shawnees preferred dense thickets.

As they rode in, women and children came from the lodges, from among the trees, and from the banks of the streams. Several warriors strode up to Chantry and one grasped his bridle with a strong hand.

"I come to make talk with the Wolf Walker," he said.

An Indian pushed back the flap of his tipi and stood up. It was the Wolf Walker.

"I bring you a gift," Tom Chantry said, and he gestured toward the cattle. "We fought well, you and I." He held out his hand. "I am Tom Chantry."

An older Indian who stood nearby grunted and said something to those who stood about him.

Wolf Walker said, "Red Buffalo speaks your name. But he speak Bor-den."

"Borden Chantry was my father." Suddenly Tom remembered the Indians who had come often to the ranch when the weather was cold and hunting was bad. His father had fed them, had traded horses with them.

"The Kiowas were our good friends," he said. "They came often to my father's lodge. I was papoose."

The old Indian grunted. "Come! Eat!"

Chantry dismounted and followed the older Indian to his lodge. Others followed them, and they sat cross-legged on the floor.

"Where you go?" the old Indian presently demanded.

"To the Wagon-That-Smokes," Chantry said, "to ship the cattle to my people who are hungry."

"You men . . . where they go?"

He shrugged. "Some friends, some no friends to me. They steal my horses. They wish to steal cattle . . . the wo-haws," he added, remembering the Indian name for oxen.

As he ate with them, they asked of his father. "He is dead," he said. "Three men killed him—long ago."

"You kill them now?"

"I have lost their sign. Many years I was far away." He gestured toward the east. "They are gone. Maybe dead."

"No dead," the old Indian said quietly. "Me know them. Two men are where iron trail ends."

"What!" he exclaimed. He was not sure they had understood, or that he had. "You say the men who killed my father are at the railhead?"

"I say. Five men now. Three big men"—he indicated the rusty stain on a pot—"hair like so." He tapped the rusty spot. "One who has no scalp, one the Little Bird."

It made no sense, but he was not interested now in the men who had killed his father; that was all water under the bridge. Nor did he believe he would find them at the railhead. All he wanted now was freedom from attack, and he believed he had won that.

Any man who entered an Indian village of his own volition was safe as long as he remained there. Though anyone outside the tribe was a potential enemy, peacc within the village was of first importance. As there had been no chance of outrunning the Kiowas with a trail herd, his best chance had been to come among them. Without a doubt they believed he had returned to avenge his father; had he denied it they would have lost respect for him, and any friendship they might have had would be gone.

Until now he had almost forgotten that his father had been a friend of the Kiowas, onc of the fiercest of all the Plains tribes. He had traded with them, fed them when they were hungry, sheltered them often, and interceded for them with the Army. He had done it out of respect and admiration, not in fear, and this the Indians knew. It followed that they would have known who killed him.

He got to his feet. "I will come again to your village," he said. "My father was your friend, and so shall I be."

He turned to Wolf Walker and thrust out his hand. "Someday we will hunt together."

The Indian took his hand, and the black eyes gleamed.

Turning his back, Chantry went out, and an Indian boy held his horse. He stepped into the saddle, raised his right hand, and rode away.

When he got back to the herd the cattle were moving. The riders came back and gathered around him—Callahan, Sun Chief, and McCarthy. "What happened?" Mobile asked.

He explained, and then added, "They told me the men who killed my father are at the railhead."

"Waitin' for you?" Mobile asked.

"After all these years? Why?"

"When you've lived a few years longer you'll no longer wonder at the motives of men. They're mixed, Mr. Chantry. And sometimes they don't know the why of them, themselves." After a moment, he went on. "Sometimes a man regrets. You ever know regret, Mr. Chantry? I have. It is a powerful motive, a mighty powerful one with some folks."

"And maybe they think you've come back to hunt them down," McCarthy commented ironically. "Maybe they just figure to get you before you get them."

After a moment Mobile Callahan said, "Did you see them? Would you know them now?"

He considered that a moment. "I don't know. One of them was slight, and young. The other two—well, one of them was very big, and red-headed. But I doubt if I would know them now. It has been a long time."

"Being gun-handy is a risky thing, Mr. Chantry," Callahan said. "If a gun comes easy to your hand you're apt to let it happen when it shouldn't. I've used a gun a time or two, and most times whoever was on the other end had it a-comin', but there was a time—"

He swung wide and brought a laggard steer back to the herd.

"There was a time when I killed a man that didn't need killin'. It was in a poker game. Nobody blamed me for the shootin', but it didn't do me a damn bit o' good to tell myself that I gave him ever' chance—I knew I hadn't. The gun came too easy to my hand.

"He had a wife and three kids, and he said her name when he was dyin'. . . .

"I did what I could for 'em."

Mobile Callahan was silent for a few minutes. "I regret that shootin', Mr. Chantry, I surely do. I always have."

Tom Chantry rode out to the point, thinking about what had happened. Where were French Williams and the others? Had they deserted him, or had they been taken away at gunpoint? Had he been doped that night, in the coffee?

By sundown they were nine miles west. Whoever had told him there were only three days of driving to go had been mistaken. Of course, there had been delays. There had been frequent stops, some of them overlong, and their route had not always been the most direct.

How far now? He wanted to ask Bone McCarthy or Sun Chief, but they were scattered out and there was no chance. The herd had handled easily so far, but it seemed as if they were becoming aware that the riders were fewer. However, the old brindle steer stayed right on the line where his nose was pointed, heading toward the railroad as if he could smell the steam and the cinders.

The sun was low and it was time to circle for the night when the riders came upon them. A moment before they had been moving placidly enough, and then, almost out of nowhere, or out of the sinking sun, the charging horsemen, the thunder of guns, and the longhorns broke into a run.

Mobile Callahan was riding drag, Sun Chief was working the north side of the herd, and Bone McCarthy was on the south. Chantry himself was riding point, and when the herd broke he was swept along, riding at breakneck speed to keep from being trampled by the frightened, maddened cattle.

Somebody yelled, "Kill him! Kill Chantry!"

As the dust and the cattle closed around him he saw one person, sitting a horse alone on a small knoll, watching him. It was Sarah.

And then his world was filled with the thunder of hoofs, the shouts of men, the shots—and somewhere a scream of pain drowned by the roar of the stampede.

CHAPTER 17

THERE WAS NO fighting the maddened rush of more than two thousand head of cattle. The sudden charge from out of the sun, the burst of firing, and the cattle were gone. His only hope was to run, to keep ahead of them, and to pray that his horse would keep its feet. If the horse fell . . .

He was surrounded by tossing horns, and there seemed no chance to break out of the herd. There was nothing to do but run with them until the impetus of the charge was broken and the cattle stopped of their own volition.

Suddenly the sun was gone, but the red glow remained in the sky. He had his six-shooter out, ready to kill a steer to pile them up if he could, but so far the dun was keeping its feet and was running freely. He had no idea how far they had run, but he knew that his horse could not hold such a pace for long.

A gap showed between the steer ahead and the steer to the right, and Chantry put the dun over, hoping he might work his way free of the herd. Even in this moment of danger the thought came to him: who had screamed back there? The stampede must have caught somebody and trampled him down.

Then he found another gap, eased into it, and suddenly he was at the edge of the herd and was fighting his way free of it. He had run another half-mile before he was out of the press of cattle and running the flank.

He slowed the dun, watching the herd stream by. The time was not right for turning it, and anyway he did not have the manpower. His best bet was to let them run, then as they slowed down, begin gradually turning them to point them north once more.

The stars were out; the sky was black above, the earth was black below. The cattle were slowing now, the fever run out of them, and the fear gone.

He listened, and above the steady pound of hoofs he heard only the occasional clack of horns bashing together. No voices, no other sound.

He moved in close to the herd now, and began to sing to them, trying to calm them, and pushing a little toward the east as he did so. Slowly, the cattle turned before him. He saw a few scattered ones, and swung wide to intercept them, turning them back into the herd.

As he had them streaming out toward the east, suddenly three riders topped out on a knoll. Instantly he recognized one of them—it was Sarah!

And the Talrims!

At the same instant a shot rang out from behind him, he felt a solid blow on the cantle of his saddle, and heard a bullet whine off into the distance. He managed one quick glance over his shoulder and saw four riders closing in from behind. Sarah and the Talrims all threw up their rifles at once, and he slapped spurs to his horse.

The dun was running its heart out now. It went over the hill and down a ridge, and Chantry saw ahead of him several tall cottonwoods. He almost pulled up.

Though the trees were a good mile off, he saw in the scene something more, something familiar.

It was home! The home ranch!

A bullet kicked dust just head of him, and he threw one wild glance over his shoulder. Fanned out behind him were seven or eight riders. Another was closing in from the flank.

A volley came from behind, and he felt the dun stumble. He raced into the trees, swung around and pulled up, staring at his old home.

Only the shell remained. The roof had partly fallen in, some of the logs had been pulled from the end wall to build a fire. The old barn where he had once played was gone; there were only the charred remains.

He heard the pound of hoofs and swung his horse around. There was no place here to make a stand. He could only run until—

The Hole . . . it rushed into his mind.

He had not thought of The Hole in years. Was it still there? Was it large enough to take a man? He shucked his rifle from the scabbard and rode the staggering dun down the draw, then kicked free of the saddle, and dropped. As he did so, he grabbed at the saddlebags and had barely got them when the dun slid to a stand, half falling.

"Sorry, old boy, I can't help you now!" He ducked and ran.

He saw the brush where he had played at Indian as a child; the ditch cut by runoff water was larger now. He ran along it, safely hidden now, as he had been then. He went over the slight rise and into a buffalo wallow. The wind had scoured it deeper; he crawled, slid, and worked his way ahead.

He could hear them yelling and swearing as they searched around the ruins of the old house. He went over the narrow ridge and saw the spot before him.

The sound of hoofs was not far off, and he heard an angry shout. "His horse is down! We got him!"

He ran up to the place. No water. No spring any longer . . . only a sandy basin about a dozen feet across and a slab of rock where the hole should have been.

He grabbed the rock with both hands and stood it on edge. There was a hole there, scarcely large enough for a man—but it was a hole.

Was it deep enough? His only chance was to try. He turned around and backed into it, kicking obstructions away. When he got in all the way he pulled his Winchester in after him.

He found a ledge on which to place the rifle, then reaching out he grasped the slab. At first it refused to budge. He dug at its base and it slid forward, falling over the opening, closing him in. . . .

He was buried alive.

Literally, he was buried. Could he push the stone outward again? Could he dig around it? As he remembered, there had been a solid ledge there.

Crouching in the hole, he waited. Had he left any marks they could see? The sand of the basin had been churned by the feet of buffalo or cattle. But if the stone had left any fresh earth exposed—what then?

What was most in his favor was the sheer unlikelihood of a cave or opening anywhere around. There was simply no probability of such a thing.

As he crouched there he heard horses' hoofs again,

and muffled talk, then a woman's voice. It was shrill, and he could make out the words faintly. "Nobody can vanish into nothing like that! He's got to be here!"

For a little while the muttered talk continued, then there was silence. He put a hand on his rifle and moved it about. Behind the ledge where it had been lying was a solid wall, but behind him and on the other side of him, he touched nothing.

He listened, but there was now no sound outside. The air around him seemed fresh enough. He felt in his pocket and found a match, and struck it on the hammer of his rifle. The match flared, burned up brightly, and he peered around.

The cave sloped down toward the back. Where he had crawled in, it was a narrow tunnel, no more than three feet across, and where he now stood it was a little more than six feet. Behind him, he had the impression of vastness, and from somewhere he heard the drip of water.

When he had found this cave as a child he had shown it to his father, but there had never been time to explore it. How large it was or where it led he had no idea.

From a few sticks, perhaps pulled in by some animal long ago, he selected a couple and lighted them. They were dry, and they burned well enough. He made his way down the slope and found himself in a fairly large room from which a passage led. At the bottom there was a pool of clear water. A small stream trickled into it, and this at one time must have been the spring he had drunk from as a boy, but the floor of the cave seemed to have fallen and the trickle of water no longer reached the surface at this point.

He tasted the water and found that it was cold and fresh. He drank, then drank again. Then he returned to the spot near the opening and sat in the dark and chewed on a piece of jerky. When it was finished, he crawled up in the hole and pushed against the slab of stone. It would not budge.

He pushed again, but it did not move. Desperately, he lunged against it, but in the narrow passage it was difficult to exert any great force. Finally he drew back, struggling for breath.

He sat down and fought against the panic that was welling up within him. He forced himself to think, remembering something his father had said. "Use your head, boy. That head of yours is the one thing that makes you different from an animal of any other kind. When you feel yourself getting scared, sit down, relax, and let yourself be calm. Then study it out. You will find an answer."

He sat quietly, and slowly the panic left him. That stone weighed no more than fifty or sixty pounds. It was several inches thick and it had slid down from above the hole. The old runoff water from the spring had fallen into the sandy basin, several inches lower than the hole. So if he put the pressure on the very top of the slab, it might be tipped forward and over.

But what if those outside had found what he had done? Suppose they knew there was a hole here and that he had crawled in? And knowing that, suppose they had heaped earth over the rock, packed it in, to let him stay there and die?

There was no use in supposing. He was not going to escape his dilemma by sitting and worrying about it. What he had to do was try for a way out.

He crawled up in the narrow hole once more, but this time he did not fight the rock. He felt with his fingers for the very top of the slab, and then he pushed.

Nothing happened.

He waited a moment, gathered strength, and pushed harder; the slab moved and a trickle of sand fell into the cave from above.

A moment longer he waited, and then he pushed again. The slab moved outward a little more and fell, and the hole gaped at the top, letting in both light and air.

Again he pushed . . . and a bullet clipped the top of the slab and spat sand into his face.

"Stay there!" The unfamiliar voice was harsh. "You're dead, so stay dead!"

He backed away. He might chance a shot, but he would have to get far enough into the hole to be able to see a target outside before he could fire. On the other hand, they would have a target they could not easily miss.

He put his rifle down carefully, felt for the sticks, and held a match to the frayed end of one. It caught, went out, but caught with the next match. Taking up his rifle and several other sticks, he went down the slope toward the back. The flame bent slightly back toward the way he had come. There was a draft here, a slight movement of air from somewhere ahead.

He went on, moving as swiftly as he could. He found occasional small pieces of wood, changed sticks, lighting from his previous torch. He crossed the room-like area and glimpsed several dark openings, but went on in the direction of the draft.

There was a trickle of water on the cave floor, and he bent over and dampened his face. It cooled quickly from the movement of air. He had walked perhaps a hundred steps when he saw a faint gleam of light. He lighted another dry stick and hurried on.

The gleam of light came from a small opening only a few yards ahead, but suddenly he came to an abrupt halt. For the light he saw was coming from an opening at the edge of a heavy canvas curtain, weighted at the bottom with a wooden pole. He went up to it and pulled it slightly aside.

He looked around in amazement, then swore softly. He was standing at the back of the root cellar on the ranch where he had grown up. Before him was a wall of shelves. He started to move it, and found the wall turned on a pivot.

The place was empty, dusty, long-undisturbed by anything other than pack rats. Here his family had stored vegetables they had raised in their small kitchen garden, and here, his father had always warned them, they were to take shelter in case of Indian attack.

He remembered the day he had shown his father his cave that he called The Hole. His father had been properly astonished, properly admiring; and his father, he now knew, had known of it all the time.

Now he knew where he was, and he knew where the ones outside must be. He checked his rifle and went to the door. It was half hidden behind the bole of a huge old cottonwood, and there was a little light coming through the crack where the boards of the door had shrunk. He peered out and could see nothing, but he did hear horses cropping grass.

Rifle in his right hand, ready to fire, he moved the door with his left. Dust and sand fell, but it moved easily.

Nothing out there but the trees and grass, the ruins of the barn, some scattered gray boards, and the brush beyond. Then to the right he glimpsed the horses, cropping the grass.

He went up the last step, and moved out. He stood listening, but heard nothing.

From behind the cottonwood he scouted the area carefully with eyes and ears. Nothing.

He walked toward the horses, and took the bridle of the first one. He stepped into the saddle, and catching the bridle of the other, walked the horse carefully away. The men who watched the hole for him could continue to watch, but they would have a long wait.

He rode to where he had left the dun. The horse was down, and dead. He swore bitterly. The dun had been a good horse, a noble horse, and he wanted to see no horse die. He stepped down, stripped his gear from the dead animal, and exchanged it for that on the horse he was riding. Then he mounted up.

Leading the spare horse, he started north. The first thing to do was to find the herd.

CHAPTER 18

FROM THE HILL above Butte Springs he glimpsed some scattered cattle and rode toward them. He gathered them, taking it easy to save his horses; he led the extra mount so he could switch if need be. There were eighteen head, and he bunched them, then pushed on, gathering more.

Beyond Plum Creek he could see still others scattered out and grazing. The day was warm and clear and his eyes ranged the country around, alert to sight any movement of men or animals. If he could gather enough of the herd he would start them toward the railroad, which must be north of him now, and near the river. He would drive what cattle he could gather, pick up some hands, and return to make a sweep of the plains.

Beyond Granada Creek he could see the dusty trace that marked the Sante Fe Trail. By the time he was midway between Plum and Granada he had gathered more than a hundred head. Leaving them to graze, he trailed the reins of the horse he was riding and switched to the other. He left his first mount with the cattle, rode west, and began to gather more.

Alternating horses he had by nightfall added another two hundred head to his herd, finding them often in bunches of a dozen or more. He pushed them north a couple of miles to fresh grass, and when they had begun to lie down, he made his own camp near a pool of water left from the recent rains in an arroyo that emptied into Plum Creek. He did not build a fire.

With his horses picketed close by, he went to sleep, trusting to them to alert him to any danger. The night passed quietly, and before dawn he was up, saddled his horses, and rode out to continue his gather.

A few cattle had drifted into the basin and he added them to what he had, then crossed the Sante Fe Trail into the breaks around the head of Wolf Creek. On the slope below him he saw some five hundred head of cattle bunched together, and two picketed horses. Keeping out of sight, he worked around on foot until he could see their camp.

Two men were sleeping under a bank near some junipers. A thin tendril of smoke lifted from the remains of their fire. Recovering his horse, he rode in a small circle to a place among the junipers near them, and then crept down the slope until he was on the bank just above them.

A dim path, evidently made by buffalo or antelope, went around the junipers and down into their camp. It was all he needed. Moving quietly, he made his way closer until he stood in their camp. Actually, his movements were practically silent.

He picked up their rifles and put them behind him, then went to the sleeping men, each of whom had a six-shooter near him. As he bent over, holding his rifle in his right hand, and just about to reach with his left and pick up the nearest man's gun belt, the man lunged up from his bed and grabbed at the rifle. As he lunged, Tom Chantry swung a short butt-stroke to the temple and the man dropped as though hit with an axe.

Coolly, Chantry picked up the other gun belt, then booted the sleeping man in the ribs.

He raised his head and said, "What the hell?" And then he saw Chantry standing over him.

"Get up," Chantry said. "And get your boots on. We've got some cattle to drive."

"Go to hell!"

Chantry stooped suddenly, grabbed the man's bed and jerked. As he tumbled from the blankets, Chantry stepped in and kicked him in the stomach.

The man rolled over, retching.

"Now get up and get your boots on," Chantry repeated. "You're going to find out what it means to steal another man's cattle."

The rustler gasped for a few minutes. He looked at his companion. "What happened to *him?*"

"He got a little ambitious. Maybe his skull is busted."

"An' you don't give a damn?"

"No, I don't. What happens to a thief is his own tough luck. When you start out to steal, you're anybody's game, remember that.... Now you get your horse saddled. We're driving these cattle."

"What about him?"

"If he revives, he can help you. If he doesn't, the buzzards will take care of him. Get moving."

Chantry backed to the fire and picked up the coffeepot. Some coffee sloshed in it, and he drank from the edge. Keeping a good distance, he let his eyes range the area, seeking out any possible cover.

A groan from the other man alerted him, and he

saw him stirring. He walked over and booted him. "Get up! Get into your boots."

"I'll kill you for this!" the man growled.

"Get into the saddle," Chantry said. "If you drive those cattle and don't get funny, I may let you live. Make a wrong move and I'll shoot you. I'm out of patience."

With the two rustlers working under his rifle, Chantry gathered the bunch they had and drove them over to his own small herd, which had scattered a bit as they grazed.

When the cattle were bunched with his own, he faced the two rustlers, staying fifty yards off from them. His rifle on them, he said, "What became of my riders?"

"Wouldn't you like to know?" said the heavier of the two with a sneer.

"Yes, I would." Tom Chantry smiled pleasantly at them. "You boys can tell me or not, as you choose. I've got this rifle, and I can drop a running rabbit with it, and you boys make a good deal bigger target. You're cow thieves—maybe murderers. Whether you get out of this alive depends on how you cooperate, and on my whim. I've a good notion to shoot you both where you stand. If you're found dead out here nobody is going to ask questions. Of course, it would make it easier to handle the cattle if you boys work along and help."

They looked at him, and they did not like what they saw. The rifle was ready, and they judged him as they would themselves. After all, why should he keep them alive?

"All right," the bigger man agreed. "We'll ride

along and he'p with the cattle. An' we'll stay right with you up to the rails. But what then?"

Chantry shrugged. "I don't want either of you. You help me get my cattle to the railhead, and then you can get out of the country as fast as you can ride. Start any sooner than within sight of the rails, and I'll shoot you, wherever it is."

Would he? At that moment Chantry had no idea. He knew that, come what might, he must get these cattle to the railroad.

He strapped their rifles to his own saddle, and their gun belts as well. They started the cattle, pointing them north. It could not be more than twenty miles to the railroad now, and probably was less.

For an hour they moved steadily. Chantry worked well back, out of the dust, his rifle ready to use at any sign of betrayal.

But they had no need for betrayal. For suddenly, without warning, a dozen riders appeared. They swept down upon him, four of them rushing at the herd, the others forming up near him, a few yards off. And they came at a time when his rifle was in his scabbard, the first time all morning when that had been the case.

Rugger was there, and Kincaid. Koch was there, grinning at him, a triumphant grin. The others were strangers. To his relief, not one of the men with whom he had worked so well, McKay, Hay Gent, or Helvie, was among them.

"Looks like you he'ped us round 'em up," Rugger said, "an' we thank you for that. Now we're takin' them over."

They were going to kill him. Koch would never have it otherwise, nor Rugger either, for that matter.

"Let me make you an offer, boys," Chantry said pleasantly, and drew his gun.

They were off guard, his speed was greater than they expected, and their reaction time was against them. He drew, and shot Rugger out of the saddle, then switched the gun to Koch.

Koch's rifle was coming up and Chantry's bullet, aimed for his mid-section, hit the hammer and glanced upward, catching Koch under the chin. He toppled from his horse, blood streaming from his throat, and the horse went galloping away over the prairie.

Rugger was on the ground; Koch was gone. The others found themselves staring at a six-shooter that seemed to have come from nowhere.

"Shuck those guns!" Tom Chantry said. "Or I'll empty some saddles! Quick!"

Kincaid hesitated, and a bullet broke his arm at the elbow.

Reaching over to one of the captured holsters, Chantry took another six-shooter with his left hand.

There was no need for it. The others were loosening their gun belts. The shooting had happened so fast that not one of them had even had time to register the need for a draw.

"Now get out of here!"

With a thunder of hoofs, the riders were streaking away. The men near him swung their horses and started to ride away, and he let them go.

Once more he was alone with the cattle . . . and then he saw why the others had fled. Riding toward him in a long array, was a line of at least fifty Kiowa braves.

Ahead of them they were driving several hundred head of cattle.

Wolf Walker rode toward him, a dozen braves close behind. He stopped in a swirl of dust.

"We come. We help. We drive wo-haws for friend."

"I thank you," Chantry said.

Slowly the herd bunched again. From somewhere came Old Brindle and stepped into the lead, and the cattle moved off slowly. From out of the draws other bunches of cattle came, driven by Kiowas. By nightfall the cattle all seemed to have been gathered.

But Tom Chantry was worried. Where were French Williams and the others? Williams himself was an uncertain quantity, a man he had never trusted completely. Helvie, McKay, Gent, and Akin had all seemed good men, and dependable.

Behind it all, he was sure, were the operations of Sarah. She must have found and employed the Talrim brothers, and she must have recruited the others to help her... she would know what arguments to use. If what she wanted was ownership of the cattle, she would have clear title once he and Williams were out of the way.

But now there seemed no way she could win. The railroad was only a few miles away, and the Kiowas who guarded the cattle were fighting men, not to be trifled with. Chantry recalled what she had told Paul about not paying the men who helped her, and he was sure she had something of the sort in mind now.

She was not the sort to give up easily, but what could she do?

She must believe that the cards were all in her hands. She probably had French Williams a prisoner, or had killed him. And perhaps she still thought that Tom Chantry was trapped in The Hole.

Some of the outlaws who had been driving the cattle might have gotten in touch with her, but that he doubted.

What would she do now?

The cattle would be delivered at the railhead, placed aboard cars there, and shipped east. It began to look as if Sarah was whipped, and French Williams, too.

And then he remembered that at the railhead were the men who had killed his father. What was he going to do about that? And what did they plan to do?

CHAPTER 19

THE RIVER WAS not far off now, and the railroad followed it. He pointed the way, occasionally glancing back to see if any enemies were in sight, but he trusted the Indians to alert him to any danger. This was the short-grass country, blue grama, buffalo grass, and some needle grasses. Patches of prickly pear appeared now and again, and yucca, often called soap weed from the Indians' use of it, dotted the plains.

The cattle, seeming to sense the river with its abundance of water, moved steadily onward, and the Kiowas proved efficient herdsmen, working with the cattle as if born to it. They were magnificent horsemen and managed their quick ponies without effort.

Twice Chantry glimpsed antelope, and once a small bunch of buffalo, moving southward, away from the river. Suddenly, from far off, he heard a train whistle.

The Kiowas drew up to listen, and even the steers lifted their heads, staring wild-eyed, at the unfamiliar sound. A thin trail of smoke showed in the sky.

They topped out on a low rise and the river lay before them, and somewhat to the east of north, they saw a cluster of buildings and a train, its locomotive giving off the smoke he had seen.

There was a sudden flurry of action near the town,

men running, and mounted men beginning to assemble.

Wolf Walker came up to Chantry. "They see us," he said grimly. "Think we come for fight."

"Hold them. I'll ride ahead."

He started down the slight slope at a canter to meet the horsemen. He was nearly at the town when he came up to them, two dozen men armed and ready to fight.

"Take it easy, gentlemen!" he said. "Those Kiowas are driving my cattle for me."

"Like hell!" blustered a huge bearded man. "This here's a squaw man—he's one of them!"

"I'm not one of them, and I am driving these cattle from Cimarron to load on the steam cars. Rustlers scattered my herd and the Kiowas helped me gather them and drive them on. They have been very helpful."

"I don't believe that!" the big man exclaimed. "I—"

Chantry swung his horse to face him. "My friend," he said, "I am losing patience with you. If you say that again you'd better have a gun in your hand."

The man started to speak, then stopped, but his eyes were ugly.

"Hold your horses, Butler," another man said. "Sparrow told me about this man. He's the one that stock buyer is waitin' for. This here's Tom Chantry."

"Chantry!" Suddenly Butler was all confidence. "You're the one that took water from Dutch Akin! Well, by—!"

"Mr. Butler," Chantry interrupted, "you are right. I am the man who refused to fight a stranger against whom I had no animosity. Under the same circumstances I would do the same thing again.

"However, a few miles back along the trail you will find two men who attempted to take my cattle, Rugger and Koch. You will find them dead. I'm afraid their intentions caused me to develop some animosity very quickly, and you are now creating the same situation. If I were you I'd throttle down while you are still in a condition to do so."

He turned to the other man. "Thank you, sir, for speaking up. I need a few good hands to take my herd and bring it in. The Kiowas would prefer not to come into town."

"I'll help." The man turned in his saddle. "Joe? How about you, Bob and Sam? Want to help this man?"

Chantry rode back with them and cut out a dozen steers. "Take them," he told the Kiowas, "but wait until I return." And he rode on to the town.

There was little enough there—a dozen flimsy shacks, two dozen sprawling tents. Saloons, dance halls, general stores, a barber shop, horse dealers, stock buyers, and two hotel tents, as well as the private cars on sidings.

Chantry swung down in front of the big tent with a General Store sign and went inside. He said, "I want twenty blankets, twenty new hunting knives, and twenty packets of tobacco."

"You a trader?"

"No," he replied, "just a man paying off a debt."

A voice spoke behind him. "There are other kinds of debts. They all have to be paid." It was Sparrow.

"I have met your Mr. Earnshaw. A fine gentleman,

and a lovely daughter." Sparrow studied him thoughtfully. "Mr. Chantry, I understand you and Miss Earnshaw are to be married?"

"We have discussed it."

"Fine . . . fine. I am glad to hear it. And then you will be going back east?"

Chantry hesitated. *Was* he? "I don't know," he said. "Temporarily, perhaps."

"If you stay here there will be problems."

"Why not? There are problems everywhere."

"These are different. I understand you killed two men on the trail?"

"It was necessary. I did not wish to do it."

Sparrow was quiet for a moment, and then he said, "Have you heard that the men who killed your father are here, in this town?"

"I heard it."

"You intend to do nothing about it?"

"That was long ago, Mr. Sparrow. I believe that circumstances will make them pay far better than I could. If they leave me alone, I'll not disturb them."

"You are right, I think," Sparrow said, "in saying that circumstances can make them pay. For one reason or another, all of them have suffered."

"You know them?"

"Yes."

Chantry turned abruptly. "I must ride back to the Indians. These are presents to pay them in some measure for what they have done. These things will be useful to them."

"You amaze me, Mr. Chantry. Only a few weeks in this country, and the Kiowas, one of the bloodiest tribes on the plains, come to your assistance."

"It was because of my father. Long ago when I was only a boy we lived out here. The Kiowas were always welcome on our ranch, and during bad times we fed them, although I suspect we could little afford it. We never had much, you know. And just when my father had built a herd that could make him wealthy, he was wiped out by a norther."

Sparrow was silent. After a moment he said, "Your father was a good man. Those men who killed him little knew what kind of man he was, and they must not kill you."

Chantry smiled. "They won't. I'm quite good with a gun, you know."

Sparrow's eyes were bleak. "Yes, I was afraid of that. You have your father's hands and his eyes." He put a hand on Chantry's sleeve. It was a sudden, uncharacteristic gesture, and it startled Chantry.

"Please. Don't carry it any further, Tom. Don't kill anyone else. A man can go too far with it."

"Thanks," was Tom Chantry's only reply.

ON A HIGH rise, with the sun growing lower in the sky, he presented his gifts to the Kiowas.

"You have helped me," he said. "That I cannot repay. I give you these small things to show you that I value your friendship. I hope nothing ever comes between your people and mine."

"We go," Wolf Walker said.

"Go. One day I shall come to see you again. I shall come to your lodge."

"You will be welcome. My fire is yours."

He watched them ride away, straight backs dark against the sunset.

He swung his horse and rode back to town. Back to the haunts of men, the bargaining places, and the risks that attend living among rough and violent men. But he was at home now. This was his country.

And now he must see Doris. He must tell her of his plans.

The lights were on in the town. The great tents glowed with the lights inside, and black shadows moved across their canvas walls. Music came from within, and the click of poker chips and a roulette wheel.

Men leaned against the lamp posts topped off with lanterns, or thronged the muddy streets, churned by hoofs and boots. Horsemen rode by; other horses stood three-legged and sleepy at the hitching rails. He led his horse to a place near where he had bunched his cattle, and picketed it on good grass.

A man came out of the darkness and stood near him. It was Mobile Callahan.

"I figured you were dead," Chantry said.

"No. I've been about my business."

"Which is?"

"Keepin' folks off your back."

Ignoring the remark, Chantry asked, "Where's Bone? Did he make it?"

"Yeah. The cattle carried us west. We figured we'd better sit tight, after roundin' up a few. There was trouble brewin' here, and we knew you'd want Earnshaw and his girl looked after."

"You were right. What danger are they in?"

"They're close to you? That makes it enough.

There's some folks don't give up easy, and one of them is that she-cat Sarah."

"She's here?"

"She's here all right, and the Talrims are with her. And they ain't all. She's teamed up with two other galoots. Seems they are the ones who killed your pa."

"There were three."

"Two now. Only one of them's got some boys as mean as he is."

He listened to the music, heard a loud laugh and the jingle of spurs, hard heels on a boardwalk . . . the only stretch of walk in town, in front of the general store, the biggest hotel tent, and a gambling place.

"Where is Earnshaw?" he asked.

Callahan nodded toward the siding. "Private car, yonder. He came west with a friend of his, a railroad man."

Chantry turned to go. "Watch your step," Callahan warned. "They know you're in town. They know they've got to kill you."

"Where's French?"

"Nobody has seen him. The word is that he pulled his men away from you, figured you'd never get the herd in without him, and then he would have the herd if the Kiowas didn't get it. I heard that some of his boys didn't want to leave you, but he took them anyhow."

"I hope that's right. I liked those boys."

Chantry walked back to the street. He stood for a moment against the side of one of the frame buildings, looking up and down the street. It was crowded, any of those men might be the ones who sought him. He stepped out from the shadows and made his way between the scattered tents toward the siding where the private cars waited. Lights showed from their windows.

He studied the layout with care, but no one seemed to be about. Fifty yards or so away were a dozen empty boxcars and some flatcars, and beyond them the stockpens and a loading chute.

After a moment he crossed the open space to the nearest of the private cars and, grasping the handrail, swung up the steps to the platform at the rear. The door was of frosted glass, and he rapped gently.

The door opened and a white-coated Negro showed him into a comfortable lounge of plush-covered furniture, crystal chandeliers, Venetian mirrors, looped and fringed draperies, and antimacassars.

Doris Earnshaw was seated on a sofa, a book in her hand. At the sound of his voice she rose hurriedly and came to meet him.

For a moment she looked at him in astonishment. "Tom! How you've changed!"

He grinned. "I need a bath," he said. "I just got in off the range."

"But . . . but you've *changed!* You're bigger, older, browner . . . everything!"

"Part of it will wash off. Out where I've been, having a bath isn't a simple thing."

Earnshaw came in. "Tom! Am I glad to see you! How are the cattle!"

"We brought most of them in. Around two thousand head, give or take a few."

"What did you pay for them?"

He explained as briefly as possible. "Then the herd is ours?" Earnshaw said. "It all seems unbelievable."

"Out here," Chantry said, "almost everything is."

Earnshaw listened as he told of the beef situation and the conditions in the area. "I can get twenty-two dollars a head for your stock right now, if they are in good shape," he said. "What would you say to a quick sale right here, then buy another herd to ship east to our own plant?"

"Fine."

He was thinking of the street out there, and what remained for him to do. "I'd prefer that you two stay in the car," he said, when Earnshaw had finished outlining his plans. "Let me handle the outside business. This is a pretty rough place."

"I gathered as much," Earnshaw said dryly. He gave Chantry a quick, searching glance. "What is this I hear about you?"

"Things are very different out here, sir." He indicated the street. "Every man out there carries a gun. I expect you've heard some shooting." He hesitated. "There are several men out there, and at least one woman, who want to kill me."

He could see they did not believe him. "That's silly!" Doris said. "Why would—" She broke off. "Tom, you're serious. You mean it."

"Yes, I do."

"A Mr. Sparrow told me something of the sort," Earnshaw said, "but it all seemed rather melodramatic."

"Mr. Sparrow," Chantry replied, "is a businessman. He is a cattleman and a rancher, and from all I gather, a very successful one."

"He is certainly interested in you," Earnshaw commented. "He assured me you were quite a remarkable young man."

"But we knew that, didn't we, Papa?"

Earnshaw studied him. "You've changed, Chantry. I don't know what it is about you."

"I've survived, that's what it is. I think periods of change are rather drastic out here, as compared with what happens in the East."

When Earnshaw had retired to the sleeping compartments Doris came closer. "Tom, you mentioned a woman. What is she like?"

He shrugged. "I don't know," he said honestly. "I actually met her only once, and we weren't exactly introduced. I don't even know her last name; her first name is Sarah. She is here in town, I hear, and she seems to believe that my death would be advantageous. My advice to you is to keep your door locked at all times. Don't let anyone in unless you know them well."

He paused a moment. "Doris, your father mentioned a quick sale. Whom did he have in mind?"

"Colonel Enright. His car is right behind ours. He is here to buy beef, and he will pay cash . . . in gold."

Chantry sat on the edge of the plush sofa, his hat in his hand. He was restless and uneasy. Was it the sudden change of surroundings? Was it only that he needed a bath, a change of clothes? Or was it the knowledge that out there in the dark trouble awaited him, trouble he could not avoid.

Slowly, almost thinking out loud, he reviewed for Doris all that had happened. When he had finished, she said, "What will she do now? You have the cattle here. You are alive, and possibly Mr. Williams is alive too. So what can she do?"

"If you were she, what would you do?"

She answered quickly. "I'd go for the money. When you sell the cattle, I'd steal the money."

He considered that. Until now Sarah had been working to inherit the cattle and sell the herd herself, and she had balked at nothing . . . nothing at all.

Yes, he agreed reluctantly, she would steal the money. She would do just what Doris had suggested.

He knew what the trouble was, for he had a touch of it himself. There was a feeling here that this was somehow out of the world, that what one did in the West belonged only to the West, and when one left, it could be left behind. Of course, that was not true. But . . . hadn't it been true for some people?

So many of them had that idea. They came to get rich and get out.

CHAPTER 20

WHEN HE LEFT the private car, Tom Chantry moved quickly to the shadow of a pile of lumber. There, crouching in the darkness, he waited and watched.

He had been in the West only a short time, but it was true that circumstances had changed him. He had grown more watchful, less trusting of people or appearances. He had enemies of whom he knew little except that they seemed prepared to stop at nothing. He had some friends, but he could not feel entirely sure who were friends and who were enemies. He would do well to play out his hand as if he were alone, and without help.

Undoubtedly Earnshaw wanted to make a quick deal, a quick profit that would put him on his feet once more. Then there could be the purchase and shipment of a second herd that would launch him into business again. That made sense, and this was the place to do it.

But Sarah was in town, and she had with her the Talrims, who killed without qualm or hesitation. Apparently she had also established a working arrangement with the killers of his father. These were his enemies, persons to whom his death seemed a necessity.

The area covered by the town, even with the scattered piles of building materials, corrals, and freight cars, was small, and his enemies would be moving in and around that area; there was small chance of avoiding them. He must locate their headquarters, for there had to be a focal point.

He thought of Mobile Callahan, who had helped him, paid to do so by Sparrow . . . why? For the time being he would dismiss that, while keeping it in the back of his mind. No matter what the motive, this did not present any immediate danger.

Bone McCarthy was, he believed, still working for him. Of Sun Chief there had been no sign, and it seemed likely that he had been killed in the stampede. And where was French Williams? Knowing the man, Chantry was sure he would not give up without a fight.

Crouching and waiting to see if he had been followed, or if anyone was watching the car, he considered his situation.

Sparrow's warning had been a good one. He must avoid further shooting if possible. What he had to do was simple enough. He must bring the sale of the cattle to Colonel Enright to a conclusion, get the money into Earnshaw's hands, effect the purchase and shipment of a second bunch of cattle, and then get out.

Though a move now against the herd was possible, it was unlikely. Doris' conclusion, he felt sure, was the right one. Sarah would be apt to make an attempt to get the purchase price into her hands. So . . . the car must be guarded against any such attempt.

He must get Enright and Earnshaw together at once, and effect the sale and the transfer of money.

And then he had to find a herd of cattle available for purchase within a reasonable distance of the railroad.

All this he had to do while avoiding trouble with any of his enemies. He was going to need eyes in the back of his head.

Sarah would wait until she found out the payment had been made for the cattle, and she would keep the Talrims in check until then . . . at least, that was the way he saw it. With him out of the way, the whole affair might be moved along quickly.

He straightened up and went around a tent and between two piles of lumber to the street. He stopped there, scanning the street carefully.

It was likely that this town was only temporary. This was for a brief time the end of the tracks, and when they built them on west, the town itself would move too. Everything here was set up to be torn down. The camp of the construction workers was a mile further west even now; but the whiskey, the women, and the gambling were still here.

The street was scarcely two hundred yards long, with frequent gaps. There were occasional piles of lumber, stacks of goods covered with tarpaulins, wagons drawn up, back end to the street. At least fifty men were walking or standing along the street, most of them only dark figures, and any one of them might be an enemy. The tents and shacks were jammed to the doors with men.

Chantry waited a moment, then crossed the street and made his way back to the herd.

Bone McCarthy was squatting by the fire. "Gettin' worried about you, boss. I nigh come a-huntin' you."

"Who's out there?"

"Four cowhands from town. All of 'em busted and glad for the work. Good men, too. I punched cows with two of 'em down on the Brazos one time."

"Bone, I want you to guard that private car where Earnshaw and his daughter are." He explained the situation, and added, "There's just the two of them and a man named Whitman. He's out here for the railroad, and the private car is his. I don't expect any trouble until the gold is transferred from Enright to Earnshaw. I understand that Enright has a couple of tough railroad detectives guarding his car on the inside."

"Have you seen French?"

"No."

Bone filled his cup. "Worries me, that does. It ain't like him to give up."

With the cattle guarded and Bone McCarthy taking over the job of watching over Earnshaw and Doris, Chantry had made his first move in the events that were shaping up.

He left McCarthy and went to the general store, where he bought a new outfit, with several extra shirts and pairs of pants. He selected a new pistol, oiled it well, and tried the balance. He loaded his belt with cartridges, filling all the empty loops, and then, carrying his purchases, he went to the barber shop, where he got a shave and a haircut. He went back to the private car and asked for the use of the bath. He scrubbed and soaked, and came out wearing fresh clothes and feeling clean for the first time in days.

When he glanced outside the car window there was no one in sight. A minute later Colonel Enright appeared with Earnshaw.

"I've been looking at your cattle, young man. They're in good shape. I'd buy another herd of the same size at the same price."

"We'll see what we can do," Chantry said.

Then they discussed the price, and it was finally settled at twenty-two dollars per head—more than he had expected, much more than Sarah had hoped for. In round numbers it came to forty-five thousand dollars in gold.

"You'll have to come and get it," Enright said, and added, "Once that gold is out of my hands it is your responsibility—and if I were you I'd have myself ready for trouble."

"We'll be all right," Earnshaw said. "I don't expect any trouble."

Chantry walked out on the brass-railed observation platform. Bone McCarthy was loitering nearby and he strolled over.

"You stay where you are, Bone," Chantry said. "Keep an eye on things and don't let anybody get behind you."

"All right."

Chantry went back inside. "Doris, keep the door of the car locked while we're gone, but be prepared to open it quickly to get your father inside."

"Do you think they will try to steal the gold?"

"You figured it out last night—remember? I think you were right."

They talked quietly, and of many things, but always his ears were alert for other sounds. Earnshaw came from the inner room and stood waiting.

Chantry looked up. "Now?"

"Yes."

"It might be safer to wait until daylight."

"They wouldn't attempt a robbery right here in the middle of everything. I think we're safe enough, Tom. Let's go."

Reluctantly, Chantry got to his feet. He opened the door. "Excuse me," he said, and stepped out first.

All was quiet. On the street, perhaps sixty yards away, there were the usual sounds. Occasionally a wild cowboy yell would leap from the jumble of sound and hang in air for an instant.

A dozen yards away was a pile of lumber, and beyond it, much further off, were several boxcars and tents. Tom went down the steps facing forward, and stepped off. There was no sign of Bone McCarthy, but he had expected none. Earnshaw came down the steps after him and together they walked back beside the track to Enright's car.

Inside it was just as ornate as the other. Two tough-looking eastern men loafed in the drawing room with a pair of shotguns across the table before them. They had been playing checkers.

At a call from one of them, Enright came from the sleeping room, bringing a sack of gold. He returned for another, then made more trips until there were eight sacks in all.

"That's a fair load," he said. "You'll have to make more than one trip."

Chantry liked none of it. One trip, loaded down with gold, was bad enough, but several? With each step the odds piled up against them, and no matter what they carried each man must keep one hand free to use a gun.

He glanced at the two guards. "You two want to help? We'll pay you."

One man shook his head. "Mister, I've got a family back in St. Louis. I wouldn't stick my head out of that door with a sack of gold for anything on earth."

"Nor me," said the other. "Guarding inside of this car is one thing. The Colonel here, he's got steel plates in the sides of this car. He's ready for anything that happens. From in here we could stand off an army, but outside there in the dark? Mister, maybe I'm not very bright, but I'm not crazy, either."

"Besides," he added, "we've heard all the talk. I'd like to help you, but I just can't see my way clear to committing suicide."

Earnshaw stared at them, then he looked at Tom. For the first time he appeared to realize the gravity of the situation. "Is it that bad?" he asked.

"Mr. Earnshaw," Chantry said, "out there tonight in that cluster of shacks and tents are perhaps a hundred men who have committed every crime in the books. They come here to prey on the track-workers, but they'll grab anything that's loose. Aside from them, there are at least two groups who feel they should have this money. One of them has already killed men in the process of trying to steal the cattle. They are not in town just to have a little recreation."

"It's only a few yards," Earnshaw said. "We'll move it now."

Chantry bent over and looked out of the car windows. All was dark and silent. There was a faint glow of light from the windows of the car they were in, and he could see light from the other private car further along the track. There might be any number of men hidden out there, and they could remain invisible until they opened fire.

"We'll cover you from the door," one of the guards volunteered, "but that will help for only a few yards."

Chantry picked up two of the sacks and slung them over his left shoulder. In his right hand he carried his gun. Earnshaw took two sacks and they stepped out of the door.

Chantry went down the car's steps and dropped off to the dirt. This was, he felt, the crucial moment. Nothing happened.

He moved out, gun ready, and waited until Earnshaw reached the ground. With Earnshaw close behind him, he started for the other car.

THREE HOURS EARLIER, and a few hundred yards from town on the bank of the Arkansas, three big men got down from their horses, tied them to brush, and descended a steep path to the door of a dugout in the river's bank.

The door of the dugout was above the water level and some distance back from the river's edge, but the dugout had been the work of some optimist who was ignorant of western rivers. The Arkansas in flood was far from being the placid stream that now flowed along not far from the door. In flood it was another story; at the first high water the dugout would be flooded, washed out and away. At the moment, four people sat inside awaiting the arrival of the three big men.

A table, two benches, and four bunks were in the small room. Hank Talrim was sprawled on one of the bunks, chewing on a straw. Bud was at the end of the table, watching Sarah, who was playing solitaire.

The fourth person was a tall, slim man with an oddly twisted look to his face. He was sallow and unshaven, and his mustache was stained with tobacco. There was an expression about him of ingrown bitterness and distaste.

The door opened and all of them looked up. The man who entered first was huge, with broad shoulders and big hands; his once red hair was freely sprinkled with gray.

"Howdy." He glanced once at Sarah, then at the sallow-faced man. "Hello, Harvey. You seen Sparrow?"

"Sparrow? Is he here?"

"Uh-huh. What you reckon that means?"

Harvey shrugged. Ruff always irritated him. It was the man's size. They had worked together a dozen times over the years, but Harvey never failed to be angered by Ruff's very presence. And now to make things worse, there were the two boys as well, huge men too.

"Maybe he's here same as us. If Chantry's boy is huntin' us he surely ain't goin' to have to look far."

"Stay away from him!" Sarah said curtly. "He'll get his when we get the gold. Leave it at that, and stay out of sight."

"I still say the best time is when they are transferring the gold from one car to the other," Harvey said.

"And that's why you've got nothing," Sarah replied sharply. "They will be keyed up, ready for trouble. Chantry will have some men around, some we don't expect to be there. Let them move the gold. We'll take it when they're off guard and think they can relax."

"What d'you think?" Frank Ruff looked at Bud Talrim.

"I like her thinkin'. What she says, goes."

Ruff sat down, and the two boys, Mort and Charlie, squatted on their heels. "I don't like it, Sparrow bein' here. He's always been sore over that shootin'."

"Forget him!" Harvey said. "He never amounted to nothin'."

"Have you seen him lately?" Charlie Ruff spoke mildly. "He's mighty high-toned now, got him a big ranch down Texas way, and another in New Mexico. He runs fifteen, twenty thousand head of cattle."

"I don't believe it," Harvey said.

"Believe whatever you're of a mind to," Charlie said. "That's a fact, what I said."

"Some of those cattle Williams and Chantry were drivin' were his," Mort Ruff commented. "Sparrow's in this somehow."

"Maybe if we wait," Frank Ruff said, "he'll do our killin' for us."

For a few moments there was only the sound of the shuffling of the cards.

Then Sarah spoke. "Those cattle," she said, "will bring nearly fifty thousand dollars."

"I never seen that much money," Hank Talrim said. "Somehow it don't make no picture."

Bud gave him a disgusted glance. "You can make a picture out of a dollar, can't you? Well, anything you can buy with a dollar, you can buy fifty thousand times as much."

"Whoo-ee!" Hank exclaimed. "I don't know what I'd do with it all."

Sarah's face was still. Only her eyes seemed to move, and they missed nothing. Secretly she felt only contempt for these men, but they were useful to her. And she did not underrate them. The Talrims seemed willing to do what she said, but they would turn on her and kill her as quickly as a cat. The others, she was sure, would not kill a woman.

As she played she studied them, considering which one she would need the most. Once the money was in their possession, she must get rid of the Talrims. Harvey was as treacherous as the Talrims, and Frank Ruff was too suspicious. Charlie was the smartest of the lot, the best-natured, the only one around whom she felt safe, but at the same time she believed he would be less easy to fool.

Mort was the one. Somehow she would have to work on Mort... she had caught him stealing glances at her. And somehow she must trigger trouble between Harvey and the Talrims... after they had the gold.

Once Paul was gone, she had moved at once to use the Talrims. She had crossed their trail a few times, knew where they were likely to be, and she had approached them, demanding their help. She was still not sure why they had gone along, nor did she dare approach either one separately. Each one seemed aware of what the other was thinking, and she was intelligent enough to perceive that there was no separating them.

They had told her about Rugger. He was a cow thief, and worse. So she had waited for him one night on night guard around the herd. She kept out of sight until he appeared, led him off to one side, and suggested stealing the herd. The others had come in as a matter of course.

When the theft failed she saw at once that the death of French Williams was no longer important. They were too close to the railhead, and the thing to do was get the money after the herd had been sold. She intended to have that money and to go to England or France with it and live her years out in style.

She was sure that at least one and probably two of the men helping her would be killed. And a fight between Harvey and the Talrims would not be difficult to start . . . eliminating one or two.

She had no clear plan, but she had a driving desire and the ability to move quickly when the moment came. She was ready.

CHAPTER 21

TOM CHANTRY SAT on the car steps, staring into the night. The gold—all of it—had been carried from one car to the other without trouble.

Earnshaw was pleased, and mildly triumphant. "See? I knew nothing would happen. We're perfectly safe."

Chantry glanced at him, then looked away. Doris had been silent, but presently she said, "Well, I was wrong, too. I was sure that girl would get them to try to steal the gold when it was being moved."

"Maybe they're not so bad as we think," Earnshaw said mildly. "Tom, I'm afraid you frightened us all needlessly."

"I don't think so," Chantry said stubbornly. "They've just made other plans."

After that he had gone outside and sat down. Doris was going to bed, Earnshaw was shaving. Suddenly Bone McCarthy came out of the darkness, and a moment later, Mobile Callahan.

"What happened?" Bone wondered.

"They're not around town," Callahan said. "I've been keeping my eyes and ears open. None of them's around, and none of them's been seen. By morning, if they're still here I'll know where they are. I've got the kids looking for them."

"Kids? Here?"

"Sure. There's a couple dozen of them in camp. I got some of them together and promised I'd buy them some rock candy if they locate that crowd, and if they're here those kids will find them."

They talked for a while, discussing possibilities. Neither McCarthy nor Callahan believed that Sarah and the Talrims would give up. Finally Tom went inside and went to sleep on the sofa in the car's drawing room, with the door locked and a chair under the knob, his pistol beside him.

FOR THREE DAYS events moved without a hitch. Colonel Enright had the herd loaded and shipped. McCarthy and Chantry, riding wide over the country, located a small herd bound east for Dodge and arranged for purchase at the railhead. On the fourth day they found another herd after learning it was being held on a range north of the river for fattening.

Mobile remained in town. He gambled a little, talked a little, listened a lot. Twice he glimpsed Harvey on the street, and Sarah moved into the frame hotel and began making herself known around the area.

She was polite, reserved, well-behaved. To Mobile, who had learned much during his lifetime, it was obvious what she was doing. She was establishing a reputation for being a lady, a well-behaved lady interested in finding a brother who had disappeared somewhere in Colorado.

Under the circumstances she was free to talk to anyone, in search of information, and if she was seen in conversation with the Talrims she could simply explain that she had heard they had information about her brother.

Tom Chantry was puzzled. Over dinner in the private car with Earnshaw, Whitman, and Doris he confessed: "I'm worried. I know they haven't given up."

"Tom, you're obsessed with this woman, whatever her name is, and with those men. If they had intended to do anything they would have done it when we moved the gold. We were vulnerable then."

"Yes, I know. And the fact that we're in a settlement wouldn't stop the Talrims. I am sure they have some other plan."

"I've seen the young lady about town," Whitman said, "and certainly I'd never suspect her of wrongdoing. From what I hear, she is searching for news of her brother."

"Her brother was killed by the Kiowas. She knows that, and knows when it happened."

"Does that seem likely? What would she be doing here, then? A young woman like her would have no reason to spend her time in a place like this."

"Unless she planned on picking up a good bit of gold."

Whitman shook his head doubtfully and changed the subject. Tom could see that even Doris was becoming somewhat impatient with him, and he said no more, but he did a lot of thinking.

When they bought the two herds, amounting to fifteen hundred head, the amount of gold they had aboard the train would be seriously depleted. Did Sarah know of their plans, he wondered.

Mobile Callahan strolled up to him as he stood on

the street. "Mr. Chantry," he said "the kids got 'em spotted."

"Where?"

"In a dugout down on the river. The whole crowd is there, and give 'em a few more days and they'll probably be mean enough to kill off each other."

"No sign of French?"

"Not a sign."

"I haven't seen Mr. Sparrow."

Mobile Callahan made no reply for a moment, and then he said, "He's around." He added, "I don't quite see what he's up to. My job was to keep trouble off your back... why? What's his interest in you?"

"I don't know." Suddenly Tom was not thinking of Sparrow. "Mobile, I'm going to see Sarah."

"You're *what?*" Mobile stared at him. And without waiting for a reply, he said, "Take a tip from me and stay away from her. That woman's trouble."

"Nevertheless—There she is now."

She was looking every inch the lady, her skirts gathered daintily in one hand as she crossed the street. Men stepped aside for her and tipped their hats.

"Tom"—it was the first time Mobile had ever used his first name—"these folks would hang you to the highest tree if you so much as said a word against her. And don't think she hasn't planned it that way."

They could hear her heels on the boardwalk, and then she stopped behind them. "Mr. Chantry? It *is* Mr. Chantry, isn't it?"

"It is."

"I understand you sold your cattle, you and Mr. Williams?"

"I sold them. French Williams no longer has any share in them, Miss—?"

"Millier. Are you going back east now?"

"No." Suddenly he realized there could be only one reason why she would want to stop and speak to him. She wanted information. Coolly, he gave it to her. "We're buying more cattle. Prices have gone down somewhat, so we're going to reinvest."

For just an instant he saw the stunned apprehension in her eyes, an expression quickly gone. "Do you think that is wise? You seem to have done very well with the first cattle you bought, but why buy cattle when the price is down?"

"That's the time to buy. Back east the market is good. The problem is getting cars right here. Buying cattle means holding them for some time. However, we are in a position to get the necessary cars."

He shifted ground quickly. "I understand you are looking for your lost brother. He was killed by the Kiowas, as you know."

Several people were within listening distance, and at least one man turned sharply around to hear better.

"I know nothing of the kind!" she replied, and walked away.

Mobile looked after her, and said softly, "What are you trying to do, Chantry? Start something?"

What *was* he trying to do? But he knew... he wanted to force them to move. He wanted it over with, ended once and for all. He was tired of watching, tired of waiting. Now they knew the gold they wanted would soon be gone, spent on cattle. If anything would bring matters to a head, this was it.

"I'd like to be listening in when she gets that word to them," he told Callahan grimly.

He walked back to the private car. Enright had pulled out on the morning train and the track was clear. Thoughtfully, he considered the possibilities.

The cattle were being brought down for delivery. Whitman, owner of the car and Earnshaw's very good friend on the railroad, had arranged for cars. Once delivery was made, gold would be paid to the cattlemen who brought in the herds, and Earnshaw and Doris would be free to return east . . . and so would he.

He glanced at his reflection in one of the panel mirrors in the car. He saw there a tall, bronzed young man with wide shoulders, narrow hips, and a quietly commanding way about him. Above all, there was no softness. The hard riding on the plains had taken off the extra flesh, hardened what remained, and toughened his nature. He was a different man now.

Why go back east? There was money to be made in the cattle business, there was land to be had, and several times lately he had heard men speaking of western Colorado. They had built a railroad out there, too, in that land of mountains and meadows, of running streams and forests.

Doris was standing behind him. "Tom, what are you thinking of?"

He turned around. "Doris, how would you like to live out here? Further west, in the mountains?"

"Is that what you want?"

"I don't know. I think it is. This country has changed me. Maybe it has only brought me back to myself, back to what I should be. Yes, I do know. I want to stay."

"All right," she said, "we'll stay." She hesitated a moment. "Can I bring my things out from the East?"

"Whatever you like."

Suddenly he heard steps on the platform behind him, and he turned swiftly, looking toward the frosted glass door. There was a light tap.

"Who is it?"

"Callahan. Can you open up?"

Gun in hand, he opened the door. Mobile was alone. "All right," he said, "you did it. All hell's breakin' loose. Harvey was on the street tonight with Mort Ruff. Sarah Millier has been talking about buying cattle, maybe starting a brand of her own. I don't know what that means, but you can be sure she's got some bee in her bonnet."

"Any sign of the Talrims?"

"No . . . but I'd swear I caught a glimpse of French Williams. It was near the store, and I walked down that way, but there was nobody around."

Whitman and Earnshaw had come from the dining room. Chantry turned to the railroad man. "Any chance of getting a locomotive? We may want to move this car, and fast."

"The cars are on the siding a mile east of town," Whitman said. "As I understand it, the cattle are to be there for loading by daylight." He paused. "I can have an engine ready to move your car at any hour you wish."

"At four o'clock in the morning then. Move this car to the loading area. Maybe we can put through the whole deal before they realize what is happening."

Earnshaw smiled. "Tom, you worry too much. There won't be any trouble. Porter and Wills will be there with their cattle, we'll load them, pay them, and start east. Doris tells me you two want to be married. Well you can come east and be married there, even if you want to return here. Just don't worry. I think you're being overconcerned."

"You may be right. Anyway, humor me enough to say nothing about the move."

Outside he talked briefly to McCarthy and Callahan, and then headed for the street.

Would he know his father's killers? It had been so long ago, and he had only a glimpse of them then. But the big man he would surely know, for there weren't many like him. He walked down to the store, looking carefully around.

This was where Mobile Callahan thought he had seen French. What would Williams' role be in this? Would he try to get the gold for himself? He was a strange sort of man who did many things on impulse. He was ruled by whim, by impulsive likes and dislikes that seemed to follow no rule.

The street was crowded as usual. Chantry went into one of the huge gambling tents for the first time. It was filled with pushing, bearded, sweating humanity. His eyes roamed the room . . . not a familiar face in sight.

Suddenly, across the room there was one. Familiar, yet unfamiliar. A huge, red-haired young man loomed head and shoulders above the crowd. It was not the man who had helped to kill his father; he was too young. From the description this had to be Charlie Ruff.

Their eyes met. For an instant the smile left Ruff's eyes and he stared, hard-eyed, at Tom Chantry. Then the smile appeared again, and the big man came shouldering through the crowd, ignoring those he brushed against. Angry looks changed quickly when they saw the size of the man who had shoved them out of the way.

He stopped, wide-legged, in front of Chantry. "Howdy! You'll be Chantry. I've heard a lot about you."

Several heads had turned, watching.

"You've come a long way for what you're going to get," Charlie said, grinning. "You better tuck your tail an' run while you got a chance."

"And what am I going to get, as you phrase it?"

A big young man, secure in his huge size and strength, Charlie Ruff had walked through life with little trouble. There was no fear in him, and there never had been. Men stepped aside for him, or backed away. He liked it that way, and he was used to it.

But he guarded his words now. "You're going to get what you've got comin'," he said, "and I'm goin' to give it to you."

"Then why not now?" Chantry asked.

Charlie's grin stiffened a little. He had never been challenged before, never called to back up a threat. The games had come to a halt, people were backing away. Tom Chantry unbuckled his belt and handed it to a croupier. "Why not now, Charlie?" he said again.

Charlie Ruff was in a quandary. When he had started for town the last thing his father said was for him to stay out of trouble. "Watch a little, play a little, see if any of that crowd are around town, *but stay out of trouble!*"

It was too late to think of that now. He had wanted

to throw a scare into this man. He had wanted to push a little just to see the man back off, as others had done.

"Sure," he said, "why not now?" And he swung.

Charlie Ruff had thrown his huge fist with intent to demolish. Not a man in the room, with the exception of the croupier, who had seen many men and had learned how to judge them, and a couple of old-timers, expected anything but a quick, brutal beating. But what happened then Charlie Ruff was unprepared for.

Tom Chantry slipped inside of the ponderous right and smashed a right to the ribs. It was a beautifully timed punch and it landed solidly. Instantly he rolled and hooked a left to the same spot, then came back just enough and brought up a short, wicked uppercut to the chin.

Charlie Ruff went down, his breath knocked from him, his nose streaming blood.

He hit the dirt floor of the tent with a thud that shocked him through and through. Never before had he been hurt, never had he been knocked down.

He stared, then with a grunt he came off the ground and ran into two hard fists. The first split the skin under his eye, the second pulped his lips. But he was big and tough, and he kept coming. He reached out his huge arms and Chantry stepped back to get distance, but the crowd shoved him back. The huge arms caught him and enveloped him in a bear hug.

Charlie Ruff was a powerful man, and now he was wild with anger. He wanted to kill this man, to break him in two. With all his power he began to squeeze.

For one brief, agonizing moment Chantry thought he was gone. He felt a hard fist crushed against his spine, felt himself bent backward. Charlie Ruff was at least fifty pounds heavier, and much stronger.

There was one thing to do and he did it. He kicked up both feet and fell backward.

The sudden yielding fooled Charlie Ruff and he fell forward, stumbling in trying to catch his balance, losing his grip on Chantry as he did so.

Chantry was up and around in an instant. Charlie got his balance and turned, and caught a sweeping right to the jaw that knocked him against a tent pole. The whole tent trembled, and then the big man turned and came in, trying for his hold again.

Chantry stabbed a left to the mouth, and as Ruff lunged he side-stepped away from him.

For a moment they faced each other. For the first time Charlie Ruff knew fear.

He blinked through the sweat and blood at Chantry, standing there ready, lean, hard, and dangerous, waiting for him. Charlie Ruff had strutted and pushed and shoved all his life, smaller men had stepped away from him, appalled not only by the sheer size of him, but by the knowledge that where he was his father and brother were not far behind. But now they were not here, and he was alone.

The crowd was packed tightly around him. There was no place to run. He had felt those iron-hard fists, and he did not want to feel them again. The only way out was to kill Chantry. He was bigger, he told himself, and Chantry had been lucky so far. Slowly he began to circle, and Chantry turned coolly to face him as he moved.

Suddenly he charged, head down, arms flailing. A

sweeping right smashed Chantry on the shoulder, staggering him and numbing his arm. The big man lunged into him, grabbing and pounding. Charlie knew nothing of fighting, but he had size and power.

His fists thudded and banged. Chantry staggered, shuddering under the power of Charlie's blows, and Charlie tried to smother him with sheer weight and size. Chantry went down, narrowly avoided a ponderous kick, then lunged up and caught Charlie with an overhand right. He slipped inside of a swing and smashed with both hands at the big body.

Pulling Charlie Ruff back, Chantry leaned into him and battered his body with short, wicked blows to the wind. Suddenly stepping back, he whipped up an uppercut that caught the bigger man under the chin. His head flew back and his knees buckled. Charlie hit the floor on his knees, but in the instant before he hit, Chantry swung a hard right to the jaw. Charlie fell forward on his face.

For a moment, Chantry stood looking down, and then he stepped back. The croupier held out his guns. "You'll be needing those." And he added, "I know that outfit. Watch yourself."

"Thanks."

Bloody, his shirt torn, Tom Chantry pushed toward the exit. He had wanted none of this. He had not liked Charlie Ruff, but he had not wanted to fight him; now it was done, and he had won.

Outside the cool wind chilled his sweaty body. He started up the street, wanting to get under cover, to bathe, and get into a clean, fresh shirt.

CHAPTER 22

HE WENT TO the frame hotel. The lobby was empty except for the clerk, an older man with a round, moonlike face.

"Hello, Mr. Chantry. Looks as if you've had trouble. Want a place to wash up?"

"Yes... and a shirt if you can rustle one up."

"I'll try. Come along." He led the way down a passage and into the back room on the ground floor. "There's a well out back. I'll get you a bucket of water. You'll want some hot water for those hands."

When he returned with the bucket and began kindling a fire in the stove, he asked, "What happened?"

"I had a fight. With Charlie Ruff."

The clerk whistled. "Ruff? You must have whipped him. You're not badly beat up."

"I did what I had to do."

"A lot of people will be pleased—not only here, but down in Texas too."

The clerk sat down. "My name's Finlayson. We haven't met but I've seen you around, and you're a friend of Mr. Sparrow's. Is there anything else I can do for you?"

Chantry was about to say there was not, but changed it. "One thing. What do you know about Sarah Millier?"

"Enough not to be so gullible as most of the local

citizens. She had visitors, Mr. Chantry. Mostly they used the back stairs, but I saw them once or twice—the Talrims or Frank Ruff. She saw me noticing them once, and commented that they had some information on her brother."

Chantry explained about the brother, and gave some background on Sarah and Paul. "There's some connection with French Williams, but I don't believe it's friendly."

"I always liked French," Finlayson commented. "Well, I don't know what to think about her, but I'm glad she's gone."

"Gone?" Chantry straightened up, water dripping from his hair and hands.

"Checked out about an hour after sundown. There was a rig waiting out front. I didn't see who was driving."

Tom dried his face and hands, working gently over his bruised and battered knuckles. He worked his fingers to keep stiffness from settling in the muscles.

He was terribly tired, but there was no time to rest. After thanking the clerk, who refused payment, he went out and made his way to the corral. His horse was there, and he roped it and saddled up.

He swung into the saddle and turned his horse toward the siding where the private car was waiting.... Only it was gone.

He rode to the main track, and looked around, but there was no car... it had pulled out.

He swung his mount and raced across town, weaving in and out among the buildings, the tents and stacks of lumber, to the other sidings. A small shack was over there where relief engineers and other trainmen bunked.

Dropping from his saddle, he went in the door. A man turned sleepily in a bunk. "Who's that?" he muttered.

Chantry struck a match and lighted the lamp. "Whitman's private care is gone. Where is it?"

The man swung his feet to the floor. He was wearing red woollen long-johns, now faded to a vague pink. "Whitman's car? I'm supposed to take that out m'self. It's gone, you say? That can't be."

"Where's your engine?"

"On the siding. Right back yonder."

Both men rushed to the door. There was no engine. The siding was empty.

"Stole! Somebody stole the engine!"

He turned back into the room and yelled at the other trainmen, now half awake. "The engine's gone! Somebody stole it!"

"It's Harvey!" A tall, skinny man started up. "I seen that outlaw Harvey aroun'! He used to be a trainman back Missouri way!"

Tom Chantry went to his horse. They had Doris! They had Whitman and Earnshaw too, and the gold, and they had a start of an hour or longer; but one thing about a locomotive... it had to keep to the tracks. Somewhere, not very far off, they would have horses waiting.

He started along the tracks at a canter. Where were McCarthy and Callahan?

A mile out of town the loading pens showed their skeleton frames against the sky, but there was no train. He pushed on, riding beside the tracks, watching the skyline ahead.

He had no idea what lay before him. That they would be stopping soon, he was sure. The outlaws would not dare risk going into the next station. He rode on into the night, his eyes probing at the darkness ahead.

Suddenly the shapes loomed up. The locomotive stood silent, except for a faint hiss of steam. The private car was lighted, but no sound came from it.

Slowing his pace, gun in hand, he circled the car at a distance. The hoofs of his horse made little noise as they moved through the grass.

He rode closer, then dismounted and ground-hitched his horse. Close to the car, he stopped to listen. No sound. He stepped up on the road bed, caught the rail, and swung up to the platform.

His left hand closed on the knob, turned it. The door opened easily and swung inward. The drawing room was empty, the door to the bedroom stood open. He went past it . . . empty.

There were signs here of hasty dressing; clothing was thrown about. The safe stood open, papers were scattered on the floor. They had the money, and they had Whitman, Earnshaw, and Doris.

He found a red lantern, lighted it, and hung it out on the east end of the locomotive. There were no trains west of this; the next to come would be from the east.

He searched the car, found two boxes of .44 cartridges, which he took, as well as an extra pistol, hidden under the pillow of Whitman's bed. He thrust that into his waistband. He gathered some food, found a canteen and filled it. He found a good deal of hunting gear in a closet under Whitman's bed, but nothing he could use. Outside, he stuffed the food into the saddlebags, hung the canteen around the pommel, and then scouted for tracks, using a lantern.

He found a place where horses had stood, several of them. And there was a faint trail leading off to the south.

For a moment, after he was in the saddle, he sat thinking. They must have taken the three prisoners so there would be nobody to tell who had taken the gold, or where they had gone. It was unlikely they would keep them for long. Sarah would be for killing them. She had intended to kill him back there under the trees in the rain, even though her brother had not wanted it. She would want no witnesses, and the Talrims would agree.

The Ruffs? No telling about them, they might agree, and they might just ride off and leave it to Sarah and the Talrims.

Just then he heard the pound of hoofs, and, turning, saw a rider approaching along his own trail. The man pulled up when he saw him.

"Chantry?" It was Sparrow.

"Here." Chantry held his gun, waiting. There were a lot of things about Sparrow that were unexplained.

"Are they gone?"

"Yes . . . and the money too."

"They'll ride south," Sparrow said. "I'm sure of it. They'll head for Coe's old hideout."

"Do you know where it is ?"

"No . . . only approximately. Nobody but outlaws knew where it was, but we can look."

"Maybe," said another voice, "you'd let me help."

They turned sharply, and faced a horseman who had come up quietly through the drift sand on the side of the track. It was French Williams.

"Howdy, Tom," he said, and Tom could almost see the taunting, appraising look in his eyes. "I see you got the herd through."

"No thanks to you," Chantry replied shortly.

"I wasn't supposed to help . . . remember? I will say that some of the boys set up a fuss when I pulled them off the herd. You make friends, d'you know that? Helvie, Gentry, and them, they swear by you."

"We've got a job to do," Chantry said. "Come along if you like."

"I'd better. No use lettin' you boys handle all that money. Nor the trouble, either." Williams turned his horse to ride along. "Surprised to see you here, Sparrow. I'd heard you were a man who avoided trouble."

"That has been my policy."

"Uh-huh. I recall. A changed policy now, is that it?" Williams chuckled. "You're the unlucky one, Chantry. You're ridin' alone, so to speak. Sparrow and me, we know where you stand, but you got no idea where we're placed in this setup. We can count on you; you don't know whether you can count on us or not."

"I'll fight my own battles. You stay out of it."

"Fire-eater, aren't you?" Williams said. "You sound a whole lot different from the fellow who backed off from Dutch Akin a while back. You got any idea what you're ridin' into?"

Williams, whether for his benefit or Sparrow's,

had dropped into the casual, easy talk of many western men. He could speak well enough when he wanted to.

"I know. The Talrims, Harvey, and the Ruffs, six men, and a woman who's worse than all of them."

"You got any idea what kind of men they are? The Talrims, you know them. A couple of dirty-mean rattlesnakes. But Frank Ruff? Now there's something else. Frank Ruff could file twenty-seven notches on his guns if he was tinhorn enough to do it.

"You hear of men who've killed a few, but when you get to pinnin' it down to names and places you lose most of them. Not so with Frank Ruff. Him you can list for twenty-seven and you can find the names, dates, and places to match them, and ever' one of them standin' up and facin' him, one way or another. Mort, he's tallied about six, near as a body can figure, and Charlie about four, maybe five."

"Five," Sparrow said.

"So look at it any way you like, you're takin' on something more than a handful of pilgrims."

"You don't have to come."

"Wouldn't miss it. I got to see the boy who wouldn't draw against a drunken man face up to a pat hand like that, with Sarah for a joker in the deck."

They rode on then in silence. The sand dunes loomed, and Chantry swung his horse, riding up into them. Around a dune, and then he saw the buildings . . . two of them. Some scattered, weathered boards, a fallen-in roof . . . many tracks, but none that could be defined, because of the loose sand.

Chantry swung down and looked into the buildings. Nothing. Why had they stopped here, then?

"Chantry?" It was Williams. "Look here."

He emerged from the building and went toward Williams, who was around the corner, standing on the edge of a small pit.

In the bottom lay two bodies. Jumping down, he bent over, and saw that both the men there were bound and gagged, but very much alive. He untied the gags.

"They've got Doris," Earnshaw said. "If anybody follows they'll kill her."

"They will anyway," Williams said shortly. "Or leave her to the Talrims, which would be worse."

Hastily, they cut the men loose. Earnshaw stood up. "Go get them, Tom. For God's sake, find them in time! They left us here, said the sand would bury us in a few hours. Talrim said there was a storm coming up."

"The stars are going. Maybe he was right," Sparrow said. "Head back for the train. It's only a little way."

South again.

The air grew cooler. Clouds covered the sky.

"How far to Robbers' Roost?" Chantry asked.

"Too far. They'll see this coming and head for shelter. It's going to be a gully-washer."

Tom Chantry was silent. In the last few moments an eerie feeling had been creeping over him. He knew where they were going, knew exactly.

"Do you believe in fate?" he asked Williams.

"I believe in a gun and a horse," French said, "and not much more."

Sparrow edged his horse over. "Why? What about it?"

"Two of the men who killed my father are in that bunch," he said. "And do you know where they're going for shelter? They're going to my old home—to Borden Chantry's ranch!"

Sparrow pulled up and came back. His voice was odd. "You mean the place up ahead belonged to your father? It was his land?"

"Yes, and he built the house."

They started on. He was coming right back to where he had barely escaped from the outlaws. Only now he was not driving cattle, or riding with anything on his mind but the men ahead . . . and Doris.

"How far behind them are we?" Sparrow wondered.

"We've gained—they stopped to leave Earnshaw and Whitman. They probably lost thirty minutes. And I don't think they are expecting pursuit . . . not yet, I mean."

A few spattering drops of rain fell. They drew up, got into their slickers, and rode on again. Occasionally there was a flash of lightning.

"They're walking their horses," French said. "We'll be gaining on them."

An hour passed . . . suddenly a light gleamed ahead, then vanished. Chantry thought of the house—the logs that had been pulled from the walls, the roof partly fallen in. They would be in the house, and might not even know about the root cellar.

He led the way to the cottonwoods. Huge branches ran out from each tree and merged with others from nearby trees. Under them there was fair shelter from the rain, and when he was under them he stepped down from the saddle. The horses of the outlaws were outside the house.

"We'll have to wait until morning," Sparrow said.

"With the girl in there?" French said. "You're forgetting her, Sparrow."

"All right," Sparrow agreed. "When you're ready."

"We'll have to get them outside," Chantry said. "In close quarters she might be killed."

"They've started a fire," Sparrow commented. "I don't think they've been here long."

"Speaking of morning," Chantry said, "it's almost that now."

"You won't have to worry about your girl yet," French said cynically. "They'll split the money first."

"Look out! Somebody's coming!" Chantry warned.

They waited, their bodies merged with the trunks of the trees. Light showed as the door opened, and a girl stepped out. That would be Sarah.

She moved toward them, and stopped. A light showed again and a man appeared, a big man. He walked toward Sarah, stopping not much more than twenty feet away from them. "You wanted to see me?" He sounded puzzled. "It's Charlie the girls always want to talk to."

"I wanted to talk to you, Mort." Sarah's tone was soft, friendly. "I'm afraid, Mort. I'm afraid of the Talrims."

"Of them? They won't hurt you none. Besides, they got that other girl."

"I don't mean that. I'm afraid for all of us. You don't know them as I do. I'm sure they don't intend to divide that money with any of us. I was sure you would understand, Mort. Charlie is too . . . well, he doesn't seem as serious as you do."

"He laughs a lot, but Charlie's all right." Mort was obviously turning the idea over in his mind. "I don't take to them Talrims myself. I thought they were friends of yours."

"Oh, no. They sort of . . . well, they just joined up with me, and what's a girl to do? I couldn't drive them off, and I hadn't anybody to help me."

"I'll help you," Mort said earnestly.

"Be careful, then. Watch them. If they start for their guns . . ."

"Don't you worry none. I'm faster'n them. I'm faster'n anybody, except maybe Pa."

"You go back in. If they say anything, you tell them you like me—that you thought you might talk to me a little."

"All right. Only don't you worry none."

When he had gone, Sarah stood alone for a moment, and then, just as she turned to go back, French stepped out and said, "Sarah, it won't work."

She was calm. "Why not?"

"You'll be in there with them, Sarah, and if shooting starts, you're as likely to be shot as anyone."

French Williams started toward her, talking quietly. "Looking at the size of the place. There will be six guns going in there."

"Seven," she said. "I'll do some shooting myself."

"Do you know who I am?"

"Of course. You've lost most of your accent, but it's there . . . I haven't seen you since I was a little girl."

He was close to her now. "You favor your father."

"You never liked him, did you? I can remember that."

"We didn't share the same ideas."

"I wonder if *we* do?"

"About that gold in there? I think so. You'd like to have it all, and so would I. You spoke of shooting. Who were you going to shoot?"

"Frank Ruff—who else? But not at first, not until he'd helped kill the Talrims." Her voice was matter-of-fact. "Mort will start it, and Charlie and their pa will have to back him. If anybody is left, I'll do the shooting."

She paused. "Or you can. After all, Uncle Henri, blood is thicker than water."

"Whose blood, Sarah? Surely not yours."

"Don't do it for blood then. Do it for the money. It is better that we have it than that they should."

"I'll agree to that," he said cheerfully. "But I will have no part of any shooting with that girl in there. She is the daughter of a friend. Get her out first, then we will see."

She hesitated, and French Williams glanced toward the house. Soon they would be wondering what had become of her, and if they came out now...

"Wait. I'll see what I can do," and she turned and went back inside.

"Do you trust her?" Sparrow asked.

"Only to do what she thinks is best for her."

The sky was gray in the east. The rain, which had ceased, stood in pools like sheets of steel, and the leaves dripped. The clouds were breaking.

"They'll be moving soon," Sparrow warned. "They

know that by this time the car has been missed, and the search will begin."

Sarah emerged from the house again, Doris beside her. Right behind them was Hank Talrim. As they walked toward the trees, Talrim watched them, then he went back inside.

Sarah stopped suddenly and Doris continued to walk ahead, moving toward a point just to the right of the trees and out of the line of fire.

Harvey stepped out the door, followed by Hank Talrim. "Hey!" Harvey yelled. "Come back here!"

As he shouted, Doris threw herself to the ground and rolled over into the shallow cut that led toward the spring.

Harvey started to run toward them when Talrim called out, "Harv! Wait!"

As Harvey turned, Hank Talrim shot him. He fell, and rolled over, and men burst from the house, guns in hand.

Hank laughed, and tilted his gun. He was ready to fire when Frank Ruff's big voice cut across the morning air with a shout. "No!" He pointed. "Look!"

All of them turned.

The morning sun had come from behind a cloud, and its light was reflected from a pool of rain water near the trees. It was enough to draw the eye.

French Williams stood there, and Tom Chantry and Sparrow.

For an instant no one spoke. Then it was Chantry, hoping, but not believing, that a shoot-out might be avoided. "Leave the money," he said clearly, "mount your horses, and ride out. We'll call it quits."

Frank Ruff ignored him. "Aren't you on the wrong

side, Sparrow?" he said. "Seems to me you should be over here with us."

"I am where I always should have been, Frank. You lied to me, you know."

Chantry was cool. He had an empty feeling inside, but his mind was clear, his eyes appraising. These were men of violence, and they would shoot. Even if Frank Ruff, older and perhaps wiser, might see the sense in just riding off, the Talrims would not.

Hank and Bud were the ones nearest the house. The three Ruffs were at the other side, scattered out, watching.

On his own side, Williams was a known gunfighter, a man of tested ability. He himself . . . well, he could shoot. As for Sparrow, he knew nothing about him except that the man was calm, controlled, and ready.

"You'd better do like the man says," Williams said, almost pleasantly. "You boys were never going to make it anyway. I've got four men between you and the hideout. They're coming up the country right now, scouting for sign."

They had forgotten Sarah.

Standing alone, she watched, her face cold and still, here eyes measuring. All she had come west for, all she had bargained for, all she wanted was in that house. The first part of her plan had begun to work when Hank Talrim had shot Harvey . . . that was one less. She had talked to the Talrims in confidence, and she had talked to Mort. No matter how it turned out, there would be fewer among whom to divide the loot.

According to her thinking, when the Ruffs burst into the open and saw Harvey down, they should have turned their guns on Hank; and in turn Bud would have started shooting. With her own gun to account for Frank Ruff, if need be—or whoever survived . . .

It could still work. Williams and Chantry and Sparrow . . . the Talrims and the Ruffs . . . when it was all over she might still be alone.

She stood for an instant, knowing that the slightest move might start the shooting. She was hesitating, trying to decide what could be done that would be best for her, when Chantry spoke again.

"There need be no shooting here," he said quietly. "As you gentlemen know, I am against violence. Leave the gold, Ruff—just take your horses and ride out of here."

"What about your pa?"

"My father faced his problems in his time. I shall face mine in my time. What you did to my father was murder, Ruff. I have a feeling you will hang—if not for that, for some other crime. I see no reason for me to kill you, when your end is inevitable."

"You talk mighty fancy," Frank Ruff said. "All I hear is that you want to back out."

"I did not come hunting you. That was your own idea. I came west to buy cattle, as these men can testify. I have bought my cattle.

"You now have two sons. No matter who wins, the odds are that when the shooting is over you will have one less, maybe two less. Is that what you want?"

"He's right, Frank. It's a Mexican standoff," Sparrow said.

Sarah saw only one thing. Frank Ruff was hesitating. The last argument had reached him. In a moment he might decide to quit, then there would be no shooting, and the gold would go to Chantry.

She knew the Talrims. Their first instinct, always, was to kill. If she moved at this tense moment, her move would draw the eyes of the others, and she knew what the Talrims would do then.

"Hank?" she said softly, and moved suddenly.

Eyes swung toward her, and the Talrims grabbed for their guns.

All eyes had turned but Tom Chantry's. Even as the Talrims drew, his gun was coming up. His first shot caught Hank Talrim in the stomach and knocked him to the ground; the second hit Bud in the shoulder.

And then a thunder of guns, stabbing flame. A man running, a man falling . . . a grunt, a scream, and then silence.

How long had it been? Only a few seconds. Tom Chantry still held his gun up, ready. But it was all over. So many lives, so short a time.

He could hardly realize yet what had happened. From the corner of his eye he had seen French Williams . . . his gun had come out so fast it seemed almost to materialize out of thin air into his hand, spouting flame. Now Williams was down, hunched against a tree, his eyes still bright, his gun still ready, but his shirt was slowly turning crimson.

Sparrow was leaning against another tree, a trickle of blood on his cheek, more blood on his shirt.

Hank Talrim was dead. Bud was crawling toward his horse, but anybody could see he wasn't going far. Frank Ruff was dead, literally shot to pieces by

French Williams. Mort Ruff was seemingly unhurt, and was bending over Charlie, who was down.

Doris came from the ditch where she had been lying. "Tom, are you all right?" she asked.

"I think so. Take care of French."

He went over to Sparrow. "Better get your coat off, Mr. Sparrow. I'll want to look at your side."

"It's just a crease. Tom, did you hear what Frank said? About me being on the wrong side?"

"So? I think you were on the right side."

"You don't understand, Tom. I want you to understand. I was a youngster . . . only sixteen. I'd been working with Frank Ruff and Harvey. They told me there was a man needed killing, that he'd killed a friend of theirs, and they wanted me to join them. I believed them, and I went along, and I didn't know what I was shaped up for until it happened. I didn't figure on an ambush, Tom. I didn't even know your father, but I helped shoot him down, and it wasn't until I read it in the papers and heard folks talking that I realized what I'd done.

"They lied to me, Tom, but I went along—maybe because I wanted them to think me a big man. I wanted to show them I had as much nerve as anyone. I didn't know until afterwards that the man I had helped to kill was a good man, a better man than any one of us."

"We'll consider your part past and done with now." And Chantry uncovered Sparrow's wound.

It was a crease, but a deep one. He tore the shirt and made a pad, then bound it over the wound. There was nothing much else to be done here.

"I tried to make it up to you, Tom. I tried to help."

"You did."

Then Mobile Callahan and Bone McCarthy came riding hard down the slope. And from the south, came Hay Gent, McKay, and Helvie.

Chantry went over to French. "How is he?" he asked Doris.

"He's been shot three times—low on the left side, through the thigh, and the chest muscle on the left side where it joins the shoulder."

"They were shooting for his heart."

French looked up at him. "I've got no heart, Tom. That's why they couldn't hit it."

Callahan dropped from his horse and brought his saddlebags with him. "Let me at him. I've had something to do with this sort of thing."

McCarthy and Helvie were looking at the outlaws. Mort Ruff got slowly to his feet. "Charlie's hurt bad," he said. "Can you help him?"

"I'll try," Helvie said.

Bud Talrim was dead.

"We'd better report this," Chantry said.

Sparrow looked at him. "To whom? There isn't any law within a hundred and fifty miles that I know of. You report it if you like. I'm going to forget it."

McKay and Gent were pulling poles from the roof of the house. "We'll make some travois, like the Indians use," McKay said. "Carry the wounded back."

"I can ride," Sparrow said. "We'll need just two, for Williams and Charlie Ruff."

Suddenly Doris looked up. "Where's Sarah?"

Chantry looked blank. Nobody had thought of Sarah.

She was gone. Two horses were gone, and the money was gone.

Mobile started for his horse. "We'll find her. Come on, Bone."

"All right if I come?" Helvie asked.

They rode out, and Chantry watched them go. Somehow the money did not seem so important now, although he knew it was. It was Earnshaw's future, Doris' future, and his.

But was it? They could start over. Out here that was possible. A setback was only that. Nothing to put a man down. You took such things, accepted them, and went on from there. It was a matter of the mind, that was all. If you weren't whipped in your mind, nothing could whip you.

"Let's get on with it," Tom Chantry said. "Back to the railroad."

Had there ever been a time when he was not riding toward the railroad?

CHAPTER 23

SARAH MILLIER WAS vastly content. She was safely away with two horses and all the gold. She had a good rifle, a pistol, and a map.

The map showed the location of the Arkansas River, it showed Trinidad to the west, Tascosa to the southeast. It was drawn on a piece of tablet paper, and Tascosa looked reassuringly close.

There was a stage from there to Fort Griffin and points east, and her horses were fresh. She would ride to Tascosa, catch the stage, go east to the railroad, then to New York; and within a matter of a few weeks she would be in Paris with nearly fifty thousand dollars in gold.

Nothing on the map said anything about the Llano Estacado . . . the Staked Plain.

Nor did it mention distance, nor the factor of time. She had just asked a man in Trinidad to show her how the places lay in respect to each other. She had said nothing to him about the fact that she might want to ride over that country.

She had the gold and she was safely away, and if anyone had survived that shooting back there they would be having trouble enough without following her. She rode blithely south, and a little east.

The day was warm and pleasant, and she made

good time. By nightfall, when she camped on Wild Horse Creek, she had put twenty-five miles behind her.

There was a good bit of water in Wild Horse Creek, and she drank and her horses drank. There was food in the saddlebags, so she ate. Another hard day's ride, she thought, and she would be in Tascosa. That was the way it looked on her map.

Sarah had no canteen, nor did she realize the need for one. She had no idea that Wild Horse Creek was more often dry than otherwise. The next day she started out at daybreak, alternately walking or cantering.

At noon she was far out on a wide plain of sparse grass, with nothing in sight anywhere. Her horse no longer cantered, but was content to walk. A light wind began to blow, the sky was clear, the sun warm. She was thirsty, but unworried. When she saw brush ahead she knew it was a creek. Half an hour later she sat her horse in the dry bed of that creek. There was no water, no sign of any. She pushed on.

The pack horse carrying the gold lagged, and impatiently she tugged on the lead rope.

She rode on, into the sunlit afternoon. Tascosa could not be far away now. The distance on the map the man had drawn had seemed so small, and she had no idea that she would never see Tascosa, that it was far away beyond the horizon, beyond many horizons, and that in all the land between water was scarce, even for those who knew where to look. Shortly before sundown she came upon the bones of cattle, and after that she saw them frequently.

Finally, unable to go on, she got down, tied her horse to several skulls pulled together, and slept. Before morning she awoke. Her throat was dry, and she was scarcely able to swallow.

She walked until the sun came up, then got into the saddle. She could see that her horses were suffering, the pack horse most, for the gold was heavy and a dead weight.

When the sun was high she looked all around her, and saw nothing but an endless plain, level as a floor, it seemed. She found water holes where the earth was cracked from the heat, but no water.

She came at last to a riverbed. Instantly, her heart leaped with excitement. Tascosa was on the Canadian. This must be it! She was going to make it, after all!

The bed was dry.

The Cimarron, still far to the north of the Canadian, was often dry. She turned upstream, and after plodding for some distance she found a small pool behind a natural dam formed of rocks and brush. She drank. The water was bad, but she drank. And the horses drank, and the water was gone. In the shade of some brush she lay down to rest, after tying the horses to the brush.

She slept like something dead, then was awakened by the sun on her face.

The pack horse was gone. The branch to which it had been tied was broken. Her horse, tied more securely, had not gotten free.

There was a myriad of tracks of buffalo or cattle or something. Among them all she could not make out which were those of the horse, for the sand was soft and left no well-defined print.

She rode on upstream, found another miniature pool, drank and let the horse drink, them scrambled him up the bank. Seeing a low knoll, she rode to the top.

She stared, and a dreadful emptiness crept into her, for wherever she looked there was nothing, only the vast plain that swept away to the horizon. Never in all her life had she seen or imagined anything like this. It was a vast brown sea, rolling endlessly away.

There was no movement anywhere, no sign of life.

Something seemed to shrink inside her. She no longer even thought of the gold, only of life. Nothing in all her years had prepared her for this.

Yet she must keep on. It could not be far. Surely, surely, it must be close.

She turned the horse down the slope and headed south.

ON THE FIFTH day, Mobile Callahan sighted the pack horse. It was standing alone, head hanging. When they rode up they could see the pack had slipped around until it was under the horse's belly.

They cut the pack away, gave the horse a drink from water poured into the crown of a hat, then dividing the gold between their horses, and leading the pack horse, they turned back.

Bone McCarthy, standing in his stirrups, looked all around. "Beats all," he muttered. "Where do you figure she thought she was goin'? Ain't nothing off that way for miles!"

"Lost, maybe. Only she surely held to her course."

"What d'you think?"

"Figure it out for yourself. She had no water with her, and besides, water's too far apart in this country. I'd say she was dead."

"Come on. Packin' all this gold we'll be lucky to make it back ourselves."

THIRTEEN YEARS LATER, two cowboys hunting strays in the lonely lands where the Panhandle of Oklahoma gives way to the Panhandle of Texas, came on some bones.

"Hey, Sam. Looka here!"

Sam rode over, looked into the shallow place behind the clump of bear grass. "What d'ya know? Woman, too."

"White woman." The first cowhand indicated the twisted leather of a boot sole and heel. He held up a finger bone. On it was a gold ring with a diamond—or what looked like one.

"What would a white woman be doin' away off here?"

He looked around. Some of the bones had been pulled away by coyotes. There was no sign of a grave. Somehow she had come to this point, died here, and remained lying there until now.

"Ought to bury her," Sam said.

"With what? We got no shovel. Come on. We got miles to go an' we'll be late for chuck. If we're late the cook will throw it out."

"What about the ring?"

"Leave it with her. Maybe she set store by it. And anyway, she's got nothing else."

They rode away. The sound of their hoofbeats died away. The wind stirred, and a little dust drifted over the whitened bones, and then lay still.

About Louis L'Amour

"I think of myself in the oral tradition—
as a troubadour, a village tale-teller, the man
in the shadows of the campfire. That's the way
I'd like to be remembered—as a storyteller.
A good storyteller."

IT IS DOUBTFUL that any author could be as at home in the world re-created in his novels as Louis Dearborn L'Amour. Not only could he physically fill the boots of the rugged characters he wrote about, but he literally "walked the land my characters walk." His personal experiences as well as his lifelong devotion to historical research combined to give Mr. L'Amour the unique knowledge and understanding of people, events, and the challenge of the American frontier that became the hallmarks of his popularity.

Of French-Irish descent, Mr. L'Amour could trace his own family in North America back to the early 1600s and follow their steady progression westward, "always on the frontier." As a boy growing up in Jamestown, North Dakota, he absorbed all he could about his family's frontier heritage, including the story of his great-grandfather who was scalped by Sioux warriors.

Spurred by an eager curiosity and desire to

broaden his horizons, Mr. L'Amour left home at the age of fifteen and enjoyed a wide variety of jobs including seaman, lumberjack, elephant handler, skinner of dead cattle, assessment miner, and officer on tank destroyers during World War II. During his "yondering" days he also circled the world on a freighter, sailed a dhow on the Red Sea, was shipwrecked in the West Indies and stranded in the Mojave Desert. He won fifty-one of fifty-nine fights as a professional boxer and worked as a journalist and lecturer. He was a voracious reader and collector of rare books. His personal library contained 17,000 volumes.

Mr. L'Amour "wanted to write almost from the time I could talk." After developing a widespread following for his many frontier and adventure stories written for fiction magazines, Mr. L'Amour published his first full-length novel, *Hondo,* in the United States in 1953. Every one of his more than 120 books is in print; there are nearly 300 million copies of his books in print worldwide, making him one of the bestselling authors in modern literary history. His books have been translated into twenty languages, and more than forty-five of his novels and stories have been made into feature films and television movies.

His hardcover bestsellers include *The Lonesome Gods, The Walking Drum* (his twelfth-century historical novel), *Jubal Sackett, Last of the Breed,* and *The Haunted Mesa.* His memoir, *Education of a Wandering Man,* was a leading bestseller in 1989. Audio dramatizations and adaptations of many L'Amour stories are available on cassette tapes from Random House Audio Publishing.

The recipient of many great honors and awards, in 1983 Mr. L'Amour became the first novelist ever to be awarded the Congressional Gold Medal by the United States Congress in honor of his life's work. In 1984 he was also awarded the Medal of Freedom by President Reagan.

Louis L'Amour died on June 10, 1988. His wife, Kathy, and their two children, Beau and Angelique, carry the L'Amour tradition forward with new books written by the author during his lifetime to be published by Bantam.